SHADOW MAGIC

SHADOW MAGIC

Jaida Jones
❦ and ❦
Danielle Bennett

BALLANTINE SPECTRA BOOKS

Here and there the blue stone sparkled, but it was no more than feeble protest in the bleaching sunlight.

The destruction of the dome had been a particularly crushing blow to our people, though perhaps not the one the Volstovics intended. We were not a society based heavily on magic; war had forced our hand in advancing the skill of our magicians. And though in later years the dome became a perfect gathering place for the magicians, it had first been built as a temple of worship for our gods. Its demolition had been a huge blow to the morale of the people, as a symbol more than a practical structure.

Iseul pushed his fingers through his hair, each heavy braid a commendation of his prowess as our father's general. He was on the verge of pacing, but practice kept him fearsomely still.

"The delegation arrives tomorrow," he said. "We shall meet them as planned."

The entire city must have known by then—or would soon know—of my father the emperor's death. From somewhere deep in the green garden just below my window, I heard the sudden throaty wail of a songbird, trembling upon the air. The sound echoed the faint trembling of my brother's fists, and I averted my eyes.

The dew had barely left the leaves.

"We'll meet them as though nothing has changed," I said, with the hint of a question.

Iseul's eyes flashed in anger. "Nothing has changed," he insisted.

I sank to my knees before him at once when the look in his eyes betrayed the lie. Everything *had* changed. Our father was dead and my brother the emperor in his stead, and I had shown grave disrespect to my new lord by neglecting to bow to him; shock had overwhelmed all memory of protocol. I struggled with my shame and could not lift my eyes.

"Mamoru," Iseul said, in place of how he had once addressed me. *Brother.* "Do not do this. Rise."

"I swear to serve you," I said, instead of obeying him. This old custom was more important even than brotherhood. We were no longer two princes, and I had wasted too much time already without acknowledging his new place as emperor of the Ke-Han. "In seven ways I shall serve you. In seven ways I shall offer my life to you. In seven ways, if it is in my power, I shall die beneath your blade, as your blade, for your

Here and there the blue stone sparkled, but it was no more than feeble protest in the bleaching sunlight.

The destruction of the dome had been a particularly crushing blow to our people, though perhaps not the one the Volstovics intended. We were not a society based heavily on magic; war had forced our hand in advancing the skill of our magicians. And though in later years the dome became a perfect gathering place for the magicians, it had first been built as a temple of worship for our gods. Its demolition had been a huge blow to the morale of the people, as a symbol more than a practical structure.

Iseul pushed his fingers through his hair, each heavy braid a commendation of his prowess as our father's general. He was on the verge of pacing, but practice kept him fearsomely still.

"The delegation arrives tomorrow," he said. "We shall meet them as planned."

The entire city must have known by then—or would soon know—of my father the emperor's death. From somewhere deep in the green garden just below my window, I heard the sudden throaty wail of a songbird, trembling upon the air. The sound echoed the faint trembling of my brother's fists, and I averted my eyes.

The dew had barely left the leaves.

"We'll meet them as though nothing has changed," I said, with the hint of a question.

Iseul's eyes flashed in anger. "Nothing has changed," he insisted.

I sank to my knees before him at once when the look in his eyes betrayed the lie. Everything *had* changed. Our father was dead and my brother the emperor in his stead, and I had shown grave disrespect to my new lord by neglecting to bow to him; shock had overwhelmed all memory of protocol. I struggled with my shame and could not lift my eyes.

"Mamoru," Iseul said, in place of how he had once addressed me. *Brother.* "Do not do this. Rise."

"I swear to serve you," I said, instead of obeying him. This old custom was more important even than brotherhood. We were no longer two princes, and I had wasted too much time already without acknowledging his new place as emperor of the Ke-Han. "In seven ways I shall serve you. In seven ways I shall offer my life to you. In seven ways, if it is in my power, I shall die beneath your blade, as your blade, for your

CHAPTER ONE

MAMORU

On the seventh and final day of mourning for the loss of the war, my brother Iseul came to my chambers to tell me that our father was dead.

I had been expecting the news for some time. There was ritual ensconced in the hour of his death—this, on the seventh hour of the seventh day—which made it all the more unsurprising to see the truth in my brother's eyes, lining his mouth and hardening his jaw. The news was no shock to us. Our father had taken his life in apology for our defeat at the hands of the Volstovics, as we always knew he would; all we could do now was join him or suffer his legacy. For either of these, we were equally prepared.

My brother came with black robes and no kohl to line his eyes, rather than with knives of ceremony. I saw then that his decision had been made. In this as in all things, I would follow the path my brother had chosen for us.

Outside the window, just past the quiet gardens of raked sand and contemplation, loomed the broken roof of the magicians' dome, like the rounded edge of a broken sky as seen from above, where the gods once sat and watched over us in dominion. It was far enough away that it looked almost like a shattered bowl overset, or a forsaken cup of tea dropped by clumsy hands. What remained of the dome was charred.

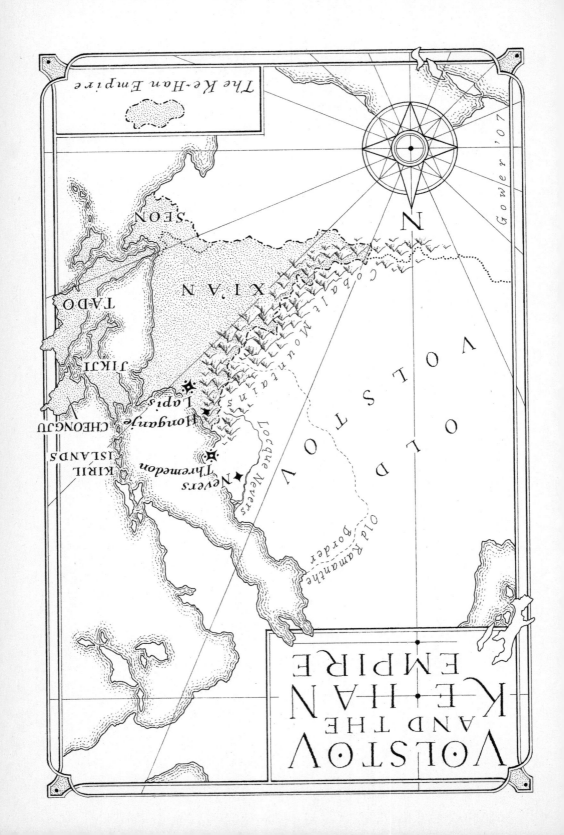

This book could not have been written without the incredible, loving shape given to it by our editor at Bantam Spectra, Anne Groell, and our agent, Tamar Rydzinski. Thanks also must be given to our assistant editor, David Pomerico, and copy editor, Sara Schwager, for tirelessly working on this book in all its many stages. Another person without whom this book would never be is our ruthless mom: thank you, ruthless mom, for always saying something didn't make sense when it didn't make sense, and for not giving up when we insisted it did. (Because usually? It didn't.) Thanks also to Uncle David, for driving to Costco; to Grandma Fay and Grandpa Terry, for watching movies on silent with the subtitles while we were writing; to Nick, for always giving us a West Coast home; to Bob, for the mosquito netting and what that represents; to Tide, for never forgetting to ask us why we're not Hemingway; to Liz and Caitlin, whose hard work on the LJ community Thremedon made our hard work on *Shadow Magic* seem a little less mighty; and to all the artists, writers, icon makers, and thoughtful conversationalists who hung out there during the week it was spotlighted, being just plain awesome. We couldn't have done it without you guys and your support. Thank you from the bottom of our hearts.

To my mom and dad, who always knew this would happen,
even when I didn't.
Danielle

To Jonah, with whom I first imagined different worlds.
Jaida

Copyright © 2009 by Jaida Jones and Danielle Bennett

Published in the United States by Spectra,
an imprint of The Random House Publishing Group,
a division of Random House, Inc., New York.

SPECTRA and the portrayal of a boxed "s" are trademarks of Random House, Inc.

Library of Congress Cataloging-in-Publication Data
Jones, Jaida.
Shadow magic / Jaida Jones and Danielle Bennett.
p. cm.
ISBN 978-0-553-80697-7
eBook ISBN 978-0-553-90675-2
I. Bennett, Danielle. II. Title.
PS3610.O6256S53 2009
813'.6—dc22
2009013270

Printed in the United States of America on acid-free paper

www.ballantinebooks.com
BVG 9 8 7 6 5 4 3 2 1

First Edition

Book design by Lynn Newmark
Map by Neil Gower

SHADOW MAGIC

Jaida Jones

 And

Danielle Bennett

BALLANTINE BOOKS

blade. May your reign be prosperous and long." Then, closing my eyes, I strayed from the words I'd known since before I could form them with my own mouth, the prayer with which I was born. "May the people love you as I do," I whispered. "Iseul—"

My brother held up his hand, fingers spread wide. As always, it was a small sign, but the shame I felt was assuaged by the openness of the gesture. If my brother's fingers had been all together, I would have sensed his anger at my actions, but I had never given my brother cause to close his hand and his heart against me.

"Enough," he said, his voice cold. He must have already been preparing, mentally, for the arrival of the delegates. "Rise."

I did as he'd bidden me. It was as things would be between us from then on, and it was as things had always been, for I respected my brother's elder position just as I loved him, and it stilled the quaking in my chest a little to know that not *everything* had changed.

"What—" I held my tongue, breathing the way I'd been taught to hide the uncertainty in my voice, my movements. "What happens now, Iseul?"

He shook his head, looking out over the gardens as though expecting to find some answer within their soothing patterns. Of course, my brother was a man who needed no such reassurance. I myself felt an unbidden longing. The sand had no need to worry as to what direction to take, what shape, what form. There was a plan in mind for the sand, and it had only to follow. My brother and I had no such luck.

I fiddled with the smooth, soft fabric of my overlong sleeves, trying not to seem as though I was waiting on my brother's response. Surely the new responsibility was weighing heavily on his mind, and he would have a great many things to discuss with the warlords, our own diplomats, before the delegation from Volstov arrived tomorrow. The proper thing, I knew, was to beg my leave, expecting to be informed of what my new role within the negotiations would be at a later hour, when my brother had taken his time to sort it out. Knowing this, however, did not preclude my stubborn desire to stay nearby. After all, with our father dead, Iseul was all I had of family, and I the same to him— for even as the elder prince, my father had not yet seen fit to find my brother a wife. Now he was emperor, but still my brother, and I would not leave until I'd found some sign that I'd not lost him to dark thoughts of what was to come. But he would not look at me.

"Iseul," I began, and felt reassurance opening like a blossom within me. It seemed then that I knew, from some unseen source of certainty, that everything would be healed in time for my brother and for me. For our people, for all the Ke-Han. We would put our heads together, Iseul and I, along with my father's old advisors; and we would manage the task set to us as best we could. I hadn't yet grown past the childish notion that there was nothing we couldn't accomplish together. And indeed, even our father had been proud to claim that Iseul's strengths balanced against mine so fittingly that together we made a nearly invincible pair. Today was going to be onerous for him, and I could not expect reassurances—rather it was my place now to reassure him, in his new station, for if I did not support our new emperor with all my being, then what man could be expected to do so?

We would find ourselves within this new rhythm once we'd settled into this new way of being. It was only a matter of time.

My brother's face turned toward mine, and then to the door as Kouje cleared his throat just beyond, filling the silence my brother had left in the wake of my appeals.

"Your pardon," Iseul said to me, sounding distant somehow, but how could I blame him? He moved with a steadiness of purpose that I longed to imitate, and slid open the door on the kneeling figure before us.

"My lord Emperor," Kouje began, proving that news traveled faster among the servants than I'd have believed possible, and that my brother's decision was known now throughout the great-house, if not the palace proper. "Word has been sent that the delegation from Volstov is set to arrive rather—earlier—than we anticipated."

"Earlier," my brother repeated.

He did not need to phrase it as a question; it was Kouje's duty to anticipate and respond in kind.

"We believe they may be here in a matter of hours, your Supreme Grace."

It was then that I envied Kouje's propriety in keeping his face averted. This way, he did not have to see my brother's expression at that moment, terrible as the gods' fire.

"Gather the warlords," said my brother, in a voice I didn't recognize. It was a voice that had commanded our warriors in the mountains. "We will hold counsel in the green room."

Kouje rose, clad all in mourning black. The sight of it seemed to remind my brother of something, for he lifted his hand—an emperor making his decision. I scarcely had time to marvel at the completeness of my brother's transformation, as though he'd been living all his life on its cusp.

"Take the prince to be dressed," Iseul commanded. "The seven days have passed, and the delegation must find us prepared to receive them with all due hospitality."

Kouje bowed, though not so low as to find himself on the floor once more, and turned to me with a waiting expectation I'd come to know well.

"Iseul," I said. I was quiet enough, but I found myself unable to keep my silence entirely. It would have been different, in the company of servants, or the other warlords; but before his death Kouje's father had served ours as Kouje did me. While he was not of distinguished blood, he was certainly trustworthy—too trustworthy, in fact, for he had forgiven me many an error in decorum over the years. I didn't have my brother's facility in assuming the responsibilities of a prince, nor could I possibly imagine the weight on his shoulders now that he was emperor. Still, we were brothers. I could offer him comfort, if nothing else. "We shall persevere."

We had no other choice beyond that, save to perish in the attempt. But I left unsaid the second half of the old warrior's idiom, knowing it would only make my brother frown and Kouje regret teaching me such things in the first place.

"Go with Kouje," said my brother. His voice betrayed nothing but an iron calm that so reminded me of our father that for a moment I was overcome with a sharp awareness of how things were to change between us. "Then . . . return to your chambers. I will send for you."

I bowed low to my brother, the emperor. Despite his remonstrations to the contrary, it never occurred to me to act in any other way.

We parted ways without further talk, and I found myself relieved for the silence. My brother never had such troubles as I with keeping his silence or maintaining the peace of his spirit; I was always at war with myself, my father had once said, and it seemed a quality I might never entirely lose.

Kouje, too, said nothing. There were no lamps lit, nor were there servants moving swiftly and surely in preparation. The halls seemed like the winding passageways of a warrior's tomb.

Luckily, there were tasks immediately to hand that would serve as ample distraction from this unfortunate comparison. While Kouje waited just outside the door, I slipped into the silent, hot bath that had been drawn for me, holding my breath as I sank deep inside. The water was hot enough that I felt it might scald all my skin from my bones—a clean, new birth.

I knew with certainty that my brother had been strong enough not to shed a single tear for the father we had both lost—and not only our father but our lord emperor as well. He had died the only noble death left for him, and though I mourned the victory for which we had all hoped, I could do nothing more than be a loyal son to him.

The bath was swift, and the incense already burning when I stepped out. Servants came to dry me, twisting dry the braids of honor in my hair. This, for the victory at Dragon Bone Pass. This, for the victory of the tunnels. This, for the victory of the forsaken men. This, for the victory of the auspicious moon.

I bore no scars from those battles. I was a general, a second son. I rode no horse, but did the best I could to keep the men serving me from dying. In the later months of the war, when the fighting had grown too fierce for an unexpected general such as me, the council of warlords had recommended my return to the palace. In place of earning more braids, I had attempted to set up facilities of care for those displaced by the war. It was a necessary task, and I took great pleasure in helping those who'd been caught living too closely to the Cobalts, but I was no warrior.

I imagined that I would always bear the shame of my own shortcomings held against my brother's fiercer nature were it not for something my father said to me, less than a week before the dragons' final assault on the capital.

"The people's needs are never so simple as they seem," he said, taking his favorite seat in the pavilion, built overlooking the koi pond. "Even I, with two such hands as these, could never hope to meet them all at once. My sons will not suffer with such difficulties. Your brother protects what land we have, while you provide for our subjects. Just as we cannot provide if the land is taken from us, so the protection becomes meaningless if you squander what gifts may be gleaned from it."

My father had never been one to waste words on meaningless praise. He had never spoken to me thus before, and I sought to memorize his words even as I watched the multicolored fish swarming over and past one another like brightly colored veils, orange and white, blue and gold.

I had not returned to the pavilion since the assault on our city, but it bolstered my spirit somewhat to know that the fish would remember our conversation. That though I could no longer ask my father for confirmation of his words, there was some creature left who had been witness to them.

The women combed back what was left loose of my hair, leaving the warrior's braids to hang tight and wet over the left shoulder. That configuration meant I was still little more than a child. There was jade in my hair, jade pierced through my ears, jade hung round my neck and clasped around my wrists. Yet it was white jade, for only the emperor could wear the green. I wondered at the sight my brother would present to the retainers of our house, and to the seven closest houses beneath us, when he stepped out into the sunlight to greet the diplomats from Volstov. I wouldn't see him until they did.

I hoped they would tremble at the sight, proud as our father would have been. I hoped they would feel shame, or at least the barest whisper of terror.

Pride welled up in my heart, bitter and fiercely strong. Now that we were at peace, I no longer wore the robes of a warrior; nevertheless, the crest of my father's house was woven into the fabric of my robes, the same as it was woven into the robes my brother wore.

I could almost hear my father say: *This, too, is a warrior's duty.*

The servants fell away from me, all but one, who dropped to his knees and slid the door open. Kouje was waiting for me in the hall, bowing low, so that I couldn't see his face.

I didn't have to.

"My lord," he said, "all is ready."

It was then that we heard the sudden commotion from without. From where we were on the eastern side of the palace, just above the courtyard, the sound of the carriages arriving was harsh and jarring. Kouje did not even lift his head, and though the servants scattered, I held myself in place and checked my desire to run to the window and see them as they were, invaders from a distant land arriving under the colors of peace.

My hands trembled.

"My lord," Kouje said again.

I straightened myself as my brother would have done. The trick, I knew, was to rein yourself in as you would a wild horse. A man had two hearts, one public and one private. The latter held all his truths while the former was more easily steered and more easily broken.

"The emperor is waiting," I said. "Come."

CAIUS

We had already reached the Ke-Han gardens, but still I had no idea who had decided that General Alcibiades should be among the delegation of peace to the capital. Presumably it must have been the Esar who made that choice, as he was the supreme ruler of all Volstov's subjects, but I had never known the Esar to exhibit even the slightest sense of humor. Such peculiar capriciousness simply wasn't his style, and while I was personally amused, I was also bewildered. This suggested that there must have been some other element in his decision-making process, which meant that Alcibiades had some hidden quality that did not become apparent even when one shared a carriage with him from one capital city to another.

So as yet, I could see no reason beyond accident or my own good luck for such an unexpected anomaly to have occurred right here, and in *my* carriage of all places.

In short, I was delighted, although I suspected the other members of our party did not see eye to eye with me on the matter. There were nine of us altogether, seemingly gathered from all corners of Volstov. Representing the magicians were myself, of course, alongside the charming Wildgrave Ozanne, and Marcelline, whom I'd met during our tiresome sojourn in the Basquiat. The two of us would have so much catching up to do, since the last time we'd spoken we'd both been somewhat under the weather.

Alcibiades, I supposed, was part of some sort of misguided military representation that included two lieutenants whose names I hadn't bothered learning. They seemed like dreadfully boring sorts, in any case. We had a scholar by the name of Marius—another survivor from our little study group at the Basquiat—and bringing up the rear were

Margrave Josette and our leader Fiacre, who I could only assume were both here to represent good common sense.

In order to somewhat soften the blow that the Ke-Han were the conquered nation—and, I presumed, in order to avoid causing an international incident wherever possible, since most of us were quite sick of war—we had retired our more garish colors. None of us wore red, the Esar's royal color and favored for generations among the court, except as subtle reminders—hints of satin lining, perhaps, or the stripes on one general's regulation jacket. We did this to show respect, if not deference, for we had conquered the people across the Cobalts despite how nearly they had come to conquering *us*.

The Ke-Han much preferred the color blue. Again, I was delighted, for blue suited my complexion much better than Volstov's overly assertive red. During my exile, I wore blue at every possible occasion, but one couldn't be so rash before the Esar himself. This diplomatic mission was my opportunity, therefore, to dress as I pleased, and I was one of many such peacocks trussed up in conciliatory colors—though thankfully I wasn't one of the awkward soldiers adjusting their tight collars or the red-faced magicians frowning out the windows of their carriage.

Rather, I was dressed all in splendid midnight blue, though it was accented with the aforementioned discreet red lining, and I was thrilled to have the chance to dress so. Also, it appeared to be causing Alcibiades great displeasure, firstly because he was my lone carriage companion, and secondly, because he himself was dressed entirely in his red uniform.

When first we'd met—weeks ago during that unpleasant period of quarantine in our own Basquiat—I admit I found him somewhat akin in coloring and in shagginess to the long-haired golden dogs that were favored by the Esarina a hundred years ago, and could thus be found in every single portraiture of that period, slobbering all over everything and looking wildly pleased with themselves.

Alcibiades, however, never looked wildly pleased with himself, or indeed with anything. In the carriage, he simply looked wildly red. When I broached the subject with him—quite tactfully I thought—I was met with something resembling a horse's snort and a brusque, "I'm Volstovic, not a bastion-bloody Ke-Han."

I liked the man already. It was at some point between Thremedon and Ke-Han land that I decided we would be friends, although I was yet uncertain how to make this equally obvious to Alcibiades himself.

By the time we reached the Ke-Han gardens, which were both opulent and refined at once—nothing at all like the wildly overgrown greenhouses with their vibrant colors and abuse of perfectly good tulips that one is subject to in Thremedon—the strict formality of the place made me realize that there would hardly be any time for such diversions as friendship. The gardens flanked us on either side, deceptively tranquil. The palace itself rose before us, tiered roofs dark blue and black. And, standing still as little statues, there were at least fifty retainers in the bleached white courtyard, stark and square and rather like a box.

Their faces betrayed nothing. They might just as well have been statues for all their eyes revealed.

Our carriages erupted into their world with the stomping and whinnying of horses, the commotion of wheels on the sand, and the immediate chaos that began as nine delegates from Volstov stepped out of their carriages all at once.

Fiacre kept his composure best, stepping neatly from his conveyance only to turn right around and offer a hand to *his* carriage companion, Margrave Josette. She declined the gesture, stepping down and stirring up a delicate cloud of white dust with the prim swish of her skirts. Next, and nearest to us, was Wildgrave Ozanne, who was busily adjusting the length of his sleeves as Marcelline pursed her lips next to him, looking relatively unimpressed with the whole affair.

"Hello, my dear," I murmured as an aside.

"Greylace," she said, looking wary but nonetheless unsurprised.

On our other side were Lieutenants Casimiro and Valery, their names coming to me in a fortuitous coincidence with Alcibiades' grunted greetings. They looked very uncomfortable in their new uniforms, especially Casimiro, the larger of the two. He kept glancing to one side at Alcibiades, as though to somehow divine the mystery of how he'd managed to wear his own reds across the border unscathed.

Lastly, and quite alone, that fortunate creature, came Marius, a scholar at the 'Versity as well as a magician associated with the Basquiat. In fact, now that I counted our party, the numbers were overwhelmingly in the favor of magicians, myself included. This meant that the only men *without* Talent were Casimiro and Valery, though Alcibiades' Talent was as good as nonexistent for all he used it.

What a curious group. We seemed more like a circus than Volstov's best—the soldiers looking like clowns, and the magicians from the Basquiat even more so. For a man as uncomfortable around magicians as the Esar was, he'd certainly chosen a great number of them to represent his interests. Or perhaps he merely considered us expendable, should any trouble arise.

And amidst the chaos, there was Alcibiades, a bright red thumb in the noonday heat.

I drew up close to him, the silk of my blue jacket—cut especially after the Ke-Han style—rustling about me.

"One of these men is rather unlike the rest," I murmured, taking his arm.

He stiffened, as if I had just produced a dead mouse from his pocket. His eyes were alert, and I decided then that he must be far more intelligent than the fashionably long-haired, golden dog that I too had once owned as a pet, to see what all the fuss was about; though her eyes had been very kind, they had never once been what any man might label "alert."

"All the same to me," he muttered in an undertone, which was more of a reply than I'd got to many of my observations during the long carriage ride. I felt especially heartened.

He was alert, but not particularly perceptive, then, for there were certainly differences in the men ranged before us, close together as though in defensive battle formation. Surely it wouldn't be prudent to spend all my time among the Ke-Han thinking in terms of our warring past, though, and I dismissed the thought as swiftly as it had come. Our men and women of Volstov began to arrange themselves close as well, as though they'd been prodded into a showing of proper etiquette by the Ke-Han delegation arrayed before us.

We didn't manage to stand nearly as straight or as still as they did, though.

We'd been counseled before coming over, by three *separate* professors from the 'Versity no less, that the culture of the Ke-Han was one deeply fixed in ceremony and that our most royal presence the Esar would be vastly disappointed if any of our number derailed the course of diplomacy simply by erring in decorum. Subsequently, our preparation for the journey had included an intensive course in ceremony, which I had thoroughly enjoyed. There was a certain grace and purpose of reason about all their cold and calm rules that I found quite fascinating. It was a shame I'd found no one to share my enthusiasm with, but that would soon change once I'd brought Alcibiades around. It would be more difficult, perhaps, than training a dog, but then I was accustomed to such challenges.

One of the Ke-Han diplomats stepped forward—not the one I'd singled out, but the one standing just over his shoulder. He wore his hair tied back in the thick-braided style of their generals, though I hadn't had the proper time to study the significance of each plait. Indeed, it was a shame my own hair was not quite long enough yet to adopt a similar style, for I thought myself rather in need of such a change, and surely it would be a most flattering display of solidarity. The diplomat clasped his hands and bowed low to our arrival party. Unlike our own clothing in varying patterns of the same shade, the men of the Ke-Han were dressed in many different colors, with seemingly no rhyme or reason. Each, however, wore a sash of midnight blue that denoted their patriot status in what I felt was a very tasteful and stylish display. Perhaps I could speak with Alcibiades about doing the same, though perhaps that conversation would be better saved for later, once I had discerned the best possible way of phrasing it. I could be quite convincing when I put my mind to it.

"Welcome," said the diplomat, speaking as though he could not quite wrap his tongue around our thick Volstovic vowels. The Ke-Han language was quick and darting, quite musical and lovely in its own way; but it was on conqueror's terms that we had come, and even on foreign soil it was to be *our* men who dictated the terms of the treaty.

I was a *velikaia,* and even though my Talent lay in creating visions and not reading minds, I could still sense the animosity behind each impassive face.

"We have prepared rooms for your arrival," the diplomat continued, slow but certain of his wording. "Shortly we will dine, then begin our talks."

Some of the men seemed surprised at this, though I myself was only too grateful not to be leaping headfirst from carriage to conference without even so much as a hot bath in between. Whatever could be said of the Ke-Han—and I was certain I'd heard the bulk of it in recent years—their hospitality was a marvelous thing. At my side, Alcibiades snorted—though whether it was out of some specific affront or the burden of having to bear any length of time among the Ke-Han, I couldn't say. Knowing him only as well as I did, though, I could imagine that he'd been eager to dive into the talks straightaway. Perhaps his ideal would be for us to have been finished by nightfall, though among our number there were a great many men who enjoyed the sound of their own voices a little too much for that to be a possibility.

The diplomat clapped his hands, and into the courtyard filed a line of men and women in robes the color of ripe persimmon. They bore lanterns and kept their eyes averted to the floor. Like the diplomats, they maintained a stony silence of expression that I would have admired were it not for the creeping loneliness of the thing. Surely, outside the confines of diplomacy, it would not be amiss upon occasion to express a human emotion, and I would have said as much to Alcibiades if for a moment I thought he might appreciate the irony in my words.

We were going to have *such* high times, he and I.

ALCIBIADES

There were seventeen ways to bow to a Ke-Han statesman, and I didn't know a single one of them. Which, by my way of thinking, was just fine, because I wasn't bowing to any Ke-Han, statesman or no.

The Esar had his reasons for sending me along with the rest of the diplomats, no doubt because I knew Ke-Han ground pretty well, and I suppose I was there as backup in case a sticky situation got stickier and there wasn't anything to do about it besides reach for the sword. I guessed it was also to do with my Talent, more like a *disease* to my thinking, but there wasn't really much I could do about it now. The Esar'd said that it was more likely to be useful than not, having a magician no one knew about in along with the rest of the diplomats, and I couldn't exactly argue with him on that—much as I hated thinking of myself as a magician. There were enough of *those* already, and I didn't exactly see how sending me was a big secret when more than half the people along with us had been stuck in the Basquiat right alongside me during the magician's plague. Caius Greylace, Marcy, and Marius had even been in on the little group we'd put together to try and figure it all out—before Margrave Royston's child-bride farm boy had gone and done it for us, that was.

Anyway, point was, it was no big secret that I had a Talent, except to the Ke-Han, and I guessed that was probably the point.

There were other military men there besides me, at least— Lieutenants Casimiro and Valery—who'd somehow got roped into this sorry state of affairs the same as I had. Casimiro was a big fellow who talked too much, and Valery was a little man who didn't talk *ever,* but we respected each other well enough to stay out of each other's hair, and that was good enough for me.

That didn't mean I had to like this arrangement, though. It was uncomfortable days of riding in a carriage to come to a place I didn't want to set foot in, to put on a smile I didn't want to wear on my face, and to bow to men who'd just as soon have cut me down if everything had worked out a little differently.

It was too short a period of time to go forgiving an entire country for fighting so underhanded that they almost won. There were some tactics you never forgave.

I didn't like their blank expressions, or the way their women hopped-to quick as soldiers might've, just to serve the enemy. That was the sort of behavior that made a man wonder what the women he knew back home would've done if the coin had fallen to the other side. Everyone in the Ke-Han palace was too fucking polite.

At least I hadn't slapped on enemy colors just to keep them happy. I could feel every last one of them staring at me, but I wasn't playing any games or crawling into bed with an enemy I'd only just got the better of. This was Volstov's victory. It was bad enough being sent there to hammer out the terms of a more lasting treaty; I didn't have to make it worse by dressing like them and pretending I didn't hate it just as much as they did.

Their whole palace was a tricky affair designed to be treacherous, its narrow hallways winding around each other like the individual threads of a spider's web and its walls made of paper so thin you could see shadows passing before them, in the rooms hidden just on the other side. Whispers chased us when we got too close, and now and then the sound of a woman's ghostly laughter followed close behind. On top of that, with all of us feeling like exhibits at the zoo, there were mirrors slanted against the ceiling, fitted into every corner where simple lamps should have been. Any sort of light you wanted came from your own personal tight-mouthed Ke-Han groveling bastard, who followed you around like he'd stab you in the back as soon as light the way for you.

We were esteemed guests, all right—so esteemed we wouldn't be able to go anywhere or do anything without having someone watching us. Well, I told myself, if they wanted to assign some poor fool the job of listening to me snore and being privy to when and where and how much I shat, that was fine by me. Chances were it'd be worse for him than it would be for me. It was a waste of everyone's time, and I wasn't bothering myself any by thinking about it.

"Do you know," said Caius Greylace, coming up on me unannounced like some kind of winter ailment, "that the mirrors show you everything happening all along the halls? How clever!"

I wasn't in the mood to praise Ke-Han ingenuity like some fat country noble might praise his favorite spaniel. Chances were, this Caius creature would get bored soon enough and find someone else to bother; it didn't matter who, so long as it wasn't me. I didn't like spaniels.

"Looks like," I said.

"I suppose they must have an awful lot of trouble with assassination," Caius went on. He was dressed half like a woman and half like a lunatic, breezing through the halls behind our lamp-bearer, the fabric of whatever it was he *was* wearing swishing all the way. "Or perhaps they're simply inbred. I hear it causes paranoia in noble bloodlines as old and as carefully guarded as theirs."

I didn't say anything to *that* at all.

We were all split up by where we slept—a fact I didn't enjoy for a second. And I would have made it clear at the time I realized it, too, if Caius hadn't exclaimed over a peacock wandering across the courtyard, effectively ending all conversation on the matter of lodgings.

What really set all the warning bells off in my head was the way we were put here and there, and most of us halfway across the palace from one another, with real careful regard paid to status and nothing else. Josette, Fiacre, and Wildgrave Ozanne were all quartered together in the West Wing of the palace, for example, whereas Casi and Val were somewhere in the south nearer to the stables and the menagerie. I hadn't even *seen* Marcy and Marius since we'd arrived, which tickled me the wrong way. I didn't like a second of it. I didn't like it especially because the whole East Wing of the palace, which was where I'd be spending bastion-only-knew how much time, stank of some particular incense that burned my throat and my eyes. It was real distracting, and I didn't doubt that they were doing it on purpose. Ke-Han was made up of tricky bastards.

"In any case," Caius continued, moving neatly around a corner, then pausing to wait for me to join him, "I believe we're staying above the . . . eastern gardens? Is it the eastern gardens? The peacock certainly was a distraction. I wonder if we can have one brought in especially for entertainment. They're very rare, but I would so like a closer look."

"Heard the Ke-Han eat them," I ground out.

The servant leading us paused for a moment, but it was only because we'd fallen behind and it was his duty to wait for us. I picked up my pace, and this time it was Caius who hurried to keep alongside me, rustling all the way.

"Eat peacocks?" he asked. One of his eyes was queerly discolored, and being looked at by him felt like you were having a conversation with two different people, and both of them equally insane.

"Right," I said. "Eat peacocks."

I'd heard the rumors about Caius Greylace, the same as any. Kept as the Esar's pet lapdog practically since birth, for his Talent in visions and his lack of qualms about using them to get information. He tortured anyone who possessed information and quite a few people who didn't, if the rumors were anything to go by. Then, because he was young and wild, he went after some other poor bastard at court—the reason changed depending on who you asked, but the result was always the same—and drove him mad without blinking an eye. Well, not even the Esar could overlook that sort of thing, so he was banished quicker than a flash, exiled at fourteen and not brought back until three years later, when everyone'd been recalled for the final push. Just before we'd all gone and got slammed by that blasted plague.

He didn't look so mad as they made him out to be, though—in fact, he just looked small and very pale, with an odd habit of pursing his lips between sentences—but I set no store by appearances. They didn't mean as much as the deeds a man did.

His were a little queerer than most, but then we'd all done worse than we might've wanted, during the war.

"I doubt that's true," Caius rallied swiftly, adjusting one of his sleeves. "I believe you're being truculent."

The servant stopped a second time, saving me from having to make any kind of reply, and hooked the lamp in a sconce by another of the Ke-Han's many useless paper-square doors. They didn't have any locks, and for the servant to let us in, he had to go through a complicated dance of kneeling, sliding the door open, and finishing off, for no reason I could see, by bowing so low his forehead was pressed to the ground.

The whole thing made me uncomfortable.

Caius, on the other hand, seemed right at home. I guessed it had something to do with how he was used to being exiled—and maybe being sent to nanny a conquered nation was a step up from where he'd been last time. It wasn't my place to judge.

The servant didn't budge.

"Well," Caius said, "either they have grossly underestimated our number, or we're in the same room."

"Maybe he's waiting for us to do something," I replied.

There was no telling if the servant spoke our language or not, and I was pretty sure neither of us spoke his. Chances were we could stand there all night doing nothing while he got intimate with the floor or maybe started kissing our boots for good measure, and I'd never get my chance to sit alone for even a fucking minute, just piecing things together inside my own head and figuring out how it was I'd landed here, when all I'd *wanted* was to go home.

The war was over, but I was still surrounded by Ke-Han. The world was too funny like that sometimes, only I couldn't see my way toward laughing along with it.

"Ridiculous," I snapped, and reached for the lamp myself.

The servant looked up as if to protest, but then scrambled quickly away, bowing his head like his life depended on it. Maybe it did; I didn't know. The lamp, even though it looked light enough for something made out of rice paper, was surprisingly heavy, but not half so heavy as a Volstov blade. I thrust it inside the room, which lit up bright as day.

Everything—the strange flat bed, the canopy hung above it from the ceiling, the short tables, the pillows, the screen standing in the far corner—was some shade or another of blue.

Next to me, Caius began to laugh—a gentle, curious sound that reminded me of the whispers that'd followed us all the way there.

"Yours must be the next room over," he said. "And what is that lovely scent?"

Nothing was going to get done if we kept at it, bandying words around like we were already in talks with the statesmen themselves. From the direction the servant was bowing and scraping in, it seemed as though Caius had guessed right about where my rooms were. Without saying anything about the incense—which was like as not going to turn my eyes as red as my coat by morning and do worse to my throat—I got inside my own quarters, slid the door shut hard, and wished to bastion I was anywhere but where I *was.*

At least my room wasn't so much blue as it was turquoise green, but I got the picture clear enough.

I was alone finally, so I could unbutton my collar, and there were lamps in the room at least, thank bastion, which were tricky dangling oil-and-wick affairs that took some coaxing to get themselves lit. But they weren't going to get the best of me, not when I'd lit fires out of less and trickier besides. I got a couple of them going, shadows dancing across the walls whenever I moved this way or that. Mostly, it was just dark, because apparently the Ke-Han, with all their inventing, hadn't seen fit to invent windows.

Maybe they just didn't like looking out at their ruined city. For that, I didn't blame them.

In the next room over, I could hear the sound of water being run. There were some men who couldn't stand even a little grit on their skin, and I guessed that Caius Greylace was one of those. I didn't think there was much time for a bath, and I didn't much want to wrestle with the tub, either, which was round and half-set into the floor and hidden by a standing screen.

No, as far as I could see, there was nothing for it but to wait.

Unfortunately, there wasn't anywhere to *sit,* just a few large, seating pillows grouped together in the corners, and the bed, which wasn't more than a pallet as far as I could see, complete with the most bastion-awful-looking pillow I'd ever seen. At least, I thought it was a pillow. It might've been some weird Ke-Han torture device. Whatever it was, I wasn't sleeping on it—it was no more than a glorified slab of wood. No doubt royalty got a proper bed and pillow, but this was good enough

for us Volstovics. I was sure it was just their way of thumbing their
noses at us, a good little dig at the victors. Sneaky all over, that was the
Ke-Han for you. Well, I was going to ask for some proper chairs.

Aside from that, there were the bath and the screen, and a low, long
table and desk, and then something I guessed had to be a chair for lack
of anything else it could be. It looked like a crescent moon, made all of
black wood, polished so bright I thought for a minute it might've been
metal.

It didn't look like a room to live in. It looked more like a room for
getting bowed to in, and if there was one feeling I'd learned to hate in
the past few minutes, it was being bowed to.

On top of all that, there was only the one door, which didn't settle
my nerves any. Part of the wood on the wall that joined my room to
Caius Greylace's looked different, so there might have been a sliding
panel.

And that was it.

My things were coming up later, but I hadn't brought with me half
as much as some of the others. To my way of thinking, this wasn't some
holiday. It was business, the Esar's business, and I was there to serve
him, not take in the sights or dress myself up like a game bird on the
table.

So maybe I was predisposed not to enjoy myself, but this was enemy
territory. And would continue to be until we signed more than a few
provisionary treaties about islands hundreds of miles from here and
dragon parts that were barely more than scrap metal now.

I was just about to break my chair down into something more comfortable when the strange panel of wood I'd noticed before slid open,
nice and smooth. The Ke-Han kept their doors well oiled, which was
something to note, in the service of a silence that got under my skin
and stayed there.

"What in bastion are you doing?" I demanded, ready to use my
chair as a weapon. It was better suited for that, just the right amount of
heavy, and fitted with sharp corners at the ends.

"Are you going to hit me with that?" Caius Greylace, fresh out of a
bath and smelling like *roses,* was standing in the open space; light from
behind him poured through into my dimly lit room, and steam, too. "I
don't know whether to be flattered or terrified."

I put the chair down. "Is something the matter?"

"Yes," Caius said. "Something *dire*. Something dreadful."

"Well?"

"I've no idea what you're going to be wearing tonight," he went on smoothly, brushing damp, pale hair out of his eyes.

"Red," I snapped, eyeing him warily. "Why in bastion d'you want to know that?"

"No, no," he said, waving his hand about. "Of course you'll be wearing red; I ascertained that earlier, in the carriage. I meant what *style* of garment."

"Style?" I repeated.

He gave me a look like he thought *I* was the insane idiot of us two, which made me wonder if I hadn't been right in the first place when I was still thinking he was a Ke-Han assassin. I should have hit him with the chair. "Style," he said. "Of garment. That you will be wearing. Tonight. During the festivities. In our honor. Are you suffering from some sort of postwar mental deficiency? I hear it plagues old soldiers something dreadful."

"I'm going to be wearing red," I repeated.

"Are you going to be wearing *that*?" he asked.

I figured he meant my jacket, which was fine as far as I could see, and I bristled. "Served me well enough during the war," I ground out.

"Yes, I'm sure it did, by the look of it," he said. "Well, if you insist. I'm not entirely sure I have anything that will match even remotely, but I suppose I shall have to do the best I can under the circumstances."

"Best you can," I said.

"Under the circumstances," he concluded.

"Right," I said. "Except—we're *matching*?"

I was starting to realize that all the stories about Caius Greylace I'd heard from disreputable and reputable sources alike—about how he was seventeen different kinds of cracked, about how his parents had just as good as let wolves raise him, about how you couldn't be near him without getting the queer feeling that you were riding the center of some wild fucking storm—had been truths, all of them. Mostly I got that from the way he was looking at me, all uneven, because of the unevenness of his eyes.

As if he could read my thoughts—and maybe he could; I didn't know much about that kind of thorny Talent—he pushed some hair over the bad eye, the left one, and set to examining his nails.

"Of course we're matching," he said. "If we're to arrive together."

"This isn't dolls and houses," I muttered.

"Oh, *no*," he said, offering me a sharp-toothed smile. "It's so much better."

KOUJE

I was a boy when my own father died, younger than either of the princes, but better prepared, since his had been a long-fought battle with illness.

Before his condition worsened, he often took me to the river while my mother slept, her face grown thin and weary with caring for him. He towered over me, then and forever, since I never had the years in which to grow and surpass him.

"Look, Kouje," he said to me, one large hand placed against my shoulder, his voice ragged with the cough that had taken root in his chest. "See how the river flows ever onward, pouring all it has into the distant great ocean?"

I was still young, and more interested in the sunburnt autumn leaves or the toy boats bobbing cheerfully in the current. Nevertheless, I loved my father. What was more, it was my duty to listen when he spoke.

"Our family has served the Emperor for countless proud years," he continued. There was more gray than black in his beard, though his hair remained dark as ever, his jaw cut sharp and proud. "When I am gone, you will be sworn to his youngest son."

My father always looked out at the river. Never at me.

I had not understood then—as I came to in later years—that my father's message to me was a gift. In his own way, he tried to tell me that the best servant is as the river, patiently giving over everything in its body to the greater ocean. After some time, I came to understand that it was not a simple man's will that governed this balance but nature itself. It was thus my duty and my nature to watch over Mamoru, the youngest prince, and serve our great Emperor in this fashion. I did this, to the best of my abilities, since the day my lord Mamoru was born, twenty-five years ago. At the time, I was no more than seven.

Then, sudden and violent as all things in war, matters changed.

It was not a cataclysmic change, though many would have argued the fact. When the Emperor took his own life for honor, it was a subtler change, like a shifting of weight that came over the palace where before everything had been well balanced. Our lord Iseul was of course the rightful heir to his father's legacy, and any man with an eye for strategy could see that it was perhaps not the *worst* time for him to ascend to the throne. For despite our losses at the hands of the Volstov, the eldest prince had gained much respect among the people for his cunning as a general of war. If anyone could lift us from the depths of our shame and defeat, it would surely be the Emperor's firstborn son, who was now Emperor himself. Iseul was young enough yet to begin his own era but old enough to have been tested as a warlord and found capable.

It was a better chance at rebuilding than any one man among the Ke-Han could have hoped for.

It had shattered my prince to lose his father in ways that it had not shattered Iseul. But then, that was only to be expected. Of the two, Mamoru was the more tender.

"Ready enough," Mamoru said, from the depths of his room, "if not prepared."

"My lord," I said, bowing low. It was a game we often played before parties or banquets—though it was habit this time, and not youthful nervousness, which compelled the exchange.

The jade ornaments in my lord Mamoru's hair clacked softly against one another as he stepped past me, the sound of them almost hidden in the hustle and bustle of servants rushing up and down the hall, gossiping with one another over the distant, uncultured thud of foreign boots. It seemed strange to imagine that, not so long ago, the sound would have signaled the approach of enemy troops. Perhaps the lords in charge of talks would remember that, and tactfully request that the diplomats remove their shoes.

Their doing so wasn't entirely likely. The lords charged with governing the talks had been chosen specifically for their absence from the war itself. As I understood it, they were for the most part courtiers, men who hadn't seen enough to personalize the conflict and so could approach peace with a clear head.

I envied them their clear heads, just as I envied them their untroubled sleep. They would not reach for their weapons at night when they heard the tremor of heavy leather boots against the floor.

The prince paused at a junction in the hall. Perhaps he, too, was ill at ease among the new flurries of activity everywhere one turned. A servant was not meant to make noise where he or she walked, but with the early arrival of the diplomats from Volstov, many of them had succumbed to near panic, and allowed their footfalls to sound heavily against the floor without care for who heard their comings and goings.

There was to be an audience that night between the diplomats and our esteemed Emperor Iseul, as well as the seven houses that held a place of honor beneath his crest. Preceding that, there would be a dinner in the Emperor's own dining hall.

If things had been different, the death of an emperor—so fierce a warrior, so proud a man—would have disallowed feasting in all forms, and only plain rice would have been eaten so as not to offend the gods with excess while mourning.

Things, however, were as they were. No small river could change them.

I had my own interest, carefully concealed, in whether or not the men from Volstov would be able to stomach an exchange of hospitalities with our men or whether our generals would be the first to break. Certainly, there were men of the seven houses who did not have so much to lose as I had by speaking out against this occupation, however prettily clothed it came.

We came to the back entrance of the dining hall, placed specifically for those others sitting at the high table, so that no man but the Emperor himself would draw attention by crossing the room to the dais at the back. That was where Mamoru settled himself, between Lord Temur of the western prefecture, and the throne once reserved for his father. Mamoru's place was at the Emperor's right hand, just as it had been Iseul's place before him.

The men and women from Volstov sat at the lower tables in groups, as moths huddled around the reassurance of a flame. Some were dressed in the Volstovic style, but wore the Ke-Han shade of blue—some show of deference, I supposed. We had a history between us of talks for peace thwarted by things so simple and yet so fundamental as the color of our clothes.

Others wore a style of clothing more similar to our own, but the similarity was undone by their broad, expressive faces and the nervous way they glanced about, as though expecting an ambush at any moment.

A man with hair the color of dried wheat laughed too loudly.

"Kouje." Mamoru lowered his voice, beckoning me to bend my head.

"My lord?"

The doors at the front of the room opened, and Mamoru tightened his posture with the precision of a musician tuning a lute. Three of Iseul's retainers preceded him into the dining hall, their clothing the plain dark brown robes that denoted their status as distinguished servants. The four men behind him clad in green were the Emperor's own vassals, trained as warriors to protect their lord at any cost. Their faces, clean-shaven and hard, betrayed nothing. They were the men that the former Emperor had trusted most in all the land. It would be for Iseul to decide whether or not to retain them or to replace them with men he trusted more.

They should not have been dressed so colorfully, but the honorable dead had been forgotten in favor of the honorable future.

The newly anointed Emperor himself wore ornaments of green jade threaded through his many warrior braids. There were rings, perfect smooth circles for victories past and sharply curved pieces that resembled a fierce predator's teeth; pins that formed the shape of a dragon, a catfish, a maple leaf. On his wrists he wore dozens of deep green bracelets, and heavy strands of stone beads around his neck. His robes were embroidered in green and gold with the symbols for strength and for power—signs the emissaries from Volstov would not be able to interpret explicitly, but which they would sense by his comportment, his posture, the very tilt of his chin. Over his heart was his father's crest, which was now his own. The fabric beneath the needlework burned a deep, rich red—not the vulgar, glaring red of our Volstovic guests, but the color of a good wine, or the blood that flowed from a too-deep cut.

Everyone at the high table bowed as one, their foreheads scraping their plates. The diplomats from Volstov moved to stand—as was, no doubt, their poor way of recognizing a king of kings—before they too hung their heads in ungraceful bows. They numbered nine, men of all sizes—and two women, an unorthodox practice among our own people. Some were clearly soldiers, brawling men built for a good fight, while others were clearly scholars, men who had no doubt been recruited for their knowledge. There was even one who could not have been long past his boyhood, pale as the koi my lord favored so highly and dressed up like a peacock.

Iseul's face was blank as he took his seat, his eyes as cold and as dark as flint-rock. His poison taster sat down at his side, just behind the lord Maidar from the southernmost prefecture.

Our new Emperor looked every bit the part, and I could feel my lord Mamoru's pride in him. It was as evident as if he'd spoken it aloud.

There was no reason for the shade that rose like a mist over my heart. There was no reason why I should not have felt the same pride in my new ruler, and even a kind of gladness for this day, when we could still perform our customs with pride in the face of our enemies' occupation. The shade was there, though, and I could do nothing but push it aside with the experience born of long practice.

Things were not as they should be. My father, even weakened by illness as he was, would still have summoned the will to refuse to dine under such an inauspicious roof.

I sat at Mamoru's right, just behind him, that I might better taste the food as it came and before it reached my lord's own lips. I had only been poisoned this way once before, by enemies of the Emperor's house. It had caused a dreadful fever in my blood, rendering me unfit for duty over a long and torturous period of weeks. In the end, it was nearly a month. Such an experience, however, was made worthwhile when I considered how I had done my duty for my lord and how Mamoru had been spared the suffering.

The rice came first, and there was no taste of any malevolence to mar its clean flavor. I passed it up to the table.

Mamoru nodded his thanks, the gesture curt and mannered.

The men from Volstov were staring up at the high table still, their mouths open in awe, as though, in all their years since birth, they'd never learned to close them. If they were waiting for the Emperor to make a speech, they would be waiting a long time. Custom dictated that discussions of politics were to be had only after a proper dinner. Fire could be lit in an empty belly. In a full one, there was no room for it.

Iseul seated himself with a rustling of fabric, his taster at his left, so that no man would come between him and his brother. It was important, now more than ever, to make a show of unshakable unity.

If pressed to the point of a sword, I might have admitted that my unease did not subside throughout the course of the meal. Rather, it remained fixed firmly in my mind, impossible to ignore, like the weight in the air before a lightning storm.

I had grown up alongside Iseul. I had never been assigned to his service, but we were nearly peers in age, and as such I had been privy to his growth into a man simply because I had been doing the same thing at the same time. As such, I could recall an incident with Volstovic prisoners of war, taken captive when my lord Mamoru had been just shy of four, and I myself had been eleven. I was allowed into the great reception hall for the first time that year while my lord took his afternoon nap—his condition being particularly delicate in his earlier years—and it was there that I first saw the elder prince in full regalia, dressed every inch like the heir to the empire, and seated beside the Emperor himself with the gravest of expressions on his face.

"It is for my son to decide their fates," the Emperor had said. "For soon enough, every decision for the well-being of this country will be his, and how else might he learn than through practice?"

The seven warlords had nodded their assent, any mistrust carefully hidden beneath their courtly masks. How could a child be trusted, after all, to understand the gravity of their situation?

The young prince had raised his head, eyes sharp and lined with kohl.

"Have them killed," he said. "The chance for escape is too great. We fight Volstov from outside our borders, and we cannot afford to fight them from within as well."

I could not have read any of the expressions in the room, even if I'd tried. The experienced members of court had all been trained since birth to keep everything to themselves, and as someone relatively new to palace life, I could not hope to breach those barriers. Yet I was still experienced enough to perceive that his decision had been an unexpected one.

No one, of course, expected a child to have such capacity for ruthlessness. Iseul proved himself to be a man filled with surprises from a very young age.

It was an impression I have never forgotten since—the first indication of his capabilities, but certainly not the last.

Soup came after the rice, then the fish course. All were untampered with. In my time at the palace, and with the war's end it was my charge to look after the prince Mamoru, to taste his food for poison and to guard his person from those who would wish him ill. If I could only perform my duty well enough to take in the poison before it reached my lord, in whatever form it came, I could consider my life well spent.

CHAPTER TWO

ALCIBIADES

According to Caius Greylace, it wasn't a show of solidarity or support for Volstov that the new Emperor had this big red spot on his robes, but that didn't stop me from feeling better about how eager everyone was to turn colors. I was the only man wearing red at the dinner, save for the Emperor and Caius, who was wearing what looked like some kind of red bow in his hair.

"It's a local hair ornament," Caius said.

To my way of thinking, though, he looked too much like one of those stuffed bears you win for your childhood sweetheart at a fair. But, I had to admit, out of everyone who was trying to affect the Ke-Han style of dress and failing, Caius Greylace was the only one who didn't look like a giant, ass-backwards fool. So that might have been one reason why the crazy little snake had been added to this mission in the first place.

Other than that, the new Emperor's way of dealing with us was not to talk at all for the first half hour of the meal—as though he thought he could make us crack just by sitting up straight as a rod, with all eyes on him, taking his food from his poison taster and eating it like he was king of the world and not, in fact, the Emperor of a conquered country.

"Isn't the young prince nice-looking, though?" Caius murmured at my left, putting a hand on my elbow and almost making me drop my bowl of half-cooked food. It wouldn't have made much difference. *I* didn't have a poison taster, and *I* wasn't eating it.

I gave Greylace a look that put across all my disgust. He cooed happily, like a pigeon.

"It's remarkable they're brothers, that's all I mean," Caius murmured demurely. It was a whisper so quiet, I didn't even know how I heard it.

I hadn't even noticed another prince. I knew there *was* one, of course, since before we'd left the country some 'Versity experts had tried their best to teach us which end was up by drawing us all a helpful little chart of the hierarchy in the Ke-Han. The Emperor was at the top, of course, and his two sons below him; beneath them were seven lords that, for whatever reason, he favored more than the rest. I didn't have to know the *whys* of it, just who I was supposed to bow lowest to.

Of course, the Emperor had seen fit to off himself—which put us in quite the situation, arriving so awkwardly on the very day of his death. The Ke-Han didn't seem to hold that against us. At least, not yet.

The man Greylace was indicating sat just as straight as his brother, with white stone jewelry in his hair and around his throat. Maybe if the Ke-Han had spent a little less time dressing themselves in the morning and a little more time planning out their strategies, we wouldn't have won the war. Never mind the fact, of course, that they'd been tricky enough to see that we nearly lost.

Anyway, next to the Emperor, the younger prince looked like a pale ghost. Since I wasn't eating, and since Caius didn't seem at all inclined toward leaving me in peace until I answered his question, I thought about what he'd said. The younger prince's face seemed more expressive than the Emperor's did, that was for certain. He looked more like a person, and less like the stern-eyed statues we'd seen standing in the outer gardens.

"He's smaller," I said, since I couldn't say half of what I wanted: that he looked less full of himself, too. Such things went against the spirit of diplomacy, and who knew who was listening and for what purpose?

"Aren't you eating that?" Caius wanted to know, gesturing toward my plate. "It has the most divine flavor!"

"It looks like—" I stopped myself partway, poking at the bowl with one of the little sticks they'd given us to eat with. They were dainty and delicate and slippery, and I'd managed to snap the other one in half earlier. I was half-expecting my meal to poke back, but it just sat there, soggy, like it didn't care one way or another whether I ate it, which was pretty much in line with what I'd learned about the Ke-Han so far. "Well, I'm full anyway."

"Then you won't mind if I help myself," Caius reasoned, merrily plucking away whatever pale, uncooked thing had landed in my bowl to begin with.

The unofficial leader of our merry band, a man by the name of Fiacre, had told us all beforehand that anything we didn't recognize was most likely fish, but I wasn't taking any chances. I guessed he was of a more diplomatic nature than I was though, since at the table just next to ours he was eating everything off his plate and chatting to Wildgrave Ozanne about something that had happened on the way over. Next to him, Josette and Marcy were having some kind of tête-à-tête over something that had eight wriggly legs.

There was some luck in the world after all. That creature hadn't landed on *my* plate.

It seemed to me that any man among the Ke-Han wouldn't be too broken up over the loss of a diplomat, however mysterious the cause of death.

Dinner—endless, uncomfortable, and quiet, since no man dared to say anything so long as the Emperor wasn't talking—ended with a funny, moss-colored dessert that Caius Greylace insisted was melon-flavored gelatin. My stomach, meanwhile, was growling like one of our long-lost dragons. After the plates were cleared, the man who'd stood out to greet us held up his hand for attention. I guessed he'd been assigned the unhappy position of herding us diplomats until further notice. I wondered what he'd done to piss off the Emperor, getting stuck with a job like that.

"There will be a short recess after dinner for our most esteemed Emperor to prepare himself for the talks," the shepherd said.

Greylace leaned away from me to murmur something to Marcelline about hiding silverware in their napkins to prepare for an ambush. It wasn't my type of humor, but at least it made me feel a little better about being so suspicious of the Ke-Han Emperor's good intentions. If there had *been* silverware, I might've even gone for that sort of thing myself, even though I didn't have the Talent Marcy did. She could command metal like a breeder gave orders to his pups. It was a beautiful thing to behold in wartime, but that was neither here nor there.

I didn't know what we needed with magicians at all, now that the war was over, but I wasn't the sort of man chosen to make decisions. It was the soldier in me, bred in too early and nothing to be done about it now but to follow orders. Maybe I'd be able to scare up some food during this recess.

My growling stomach bode ill for any peacocks I might run across in the courtyards.

Caius Greylace slipped his arm through mine as we stood up, and I nearly flipped him over the table.

"You've got to stop doing that," I told him.

He laughed, the infuriating little snake. It was a high and tinkling laugh that reminded me that he'd been a member of th'Esar's court back at home and I hadn't. Of course, all that nobility amounted to a hill of beans when we'd both been sent packing to Xi'an, and at least common blood like mine didn't stoop to marrying first cousins or closer.

"Do you think we'll have time to change before the talks? Although I'd hate to exhaust my wardrobe on the first night, only to be caught wanting later on." Caius touched the bow in his hair fondly, chattering on without much care as to whether or not I was listening.

"I don't know," I said. "Depends on how long it takes the Emperor to ready himself, whatever that shit means. Do you think he'll be changing?"

"Oh, *no,*" Caius said, and he looked so certain that I believed him immediately. "That's traditional dress for the evening; he won't be changing out of it. Do you know, I heard that, according to custom, the Ke-Han should still be in mourning for their Emperor? Only we've arrived early and forced them to speed along their proceedings. They're a *marvelously* adaptable people, don't you think?"

I could think of a few words I had for the ritual-obsessed Ke-Han, and "adaptable" wasn't one of them. I grunted, just to show I'd heard him.

"No, you're right, I don't think I'll change," Caius said. "At least, not until I've spoken to their tailors. I'm assuming most of the men are wearing green and not blue because they don't want to offend anyone."

He finished this with a pointed look at my army jacket. Fuck him, I thought. Little rat didn't know what it meant to be a soldier, and I wasn't about to sweep all that I knew the Ke-Han were capable of under the carpet just yet.

I adjusted my collar, which wasn't too tight, and took stock of my surroundings. There weren't any windows in the place, since it was right in the middle of the palace and surrounded on all sides by the narrow halls—no good for making a quick exit, should the talks turn sour. It felt like being boxed in, like the tunnels in the Cobalts had been modeled after the palace itself.

As far as the Ke-Han were concerned, there wasn't a friendly face to be found in the crowd. In fact, there wasn't a face at all in the crowd that didn't wear a mask of stony indifference, save for one, and that was what surprised me. It was the younger prince himself.

Things were pretty awkward, I'll give them that, but that was to be expected. Except that Fiacre and another member of the Basquiat, Josette, seemed to be drawn to the younger prince like a horse to the feed, and when I looked over in their direction, they were actually talking to him. Josette was laughing. I shot a glance at Lieutenant Valery, who himself was looking pretty annoyed and pained by Casimiro, who'd somehow snagged himself a conversation with one of the bowing, scraping servants. He'd caught this one midscrape, and she had her head down like she wanted to plan an escape but couldn't decide whether or not she'd be breaching etiquette. Damn, talking to Casimiro was bad enough when you *understood* the language. I couldn't help but think it'd be worse if you were a foreigner.

Marius stood leaning up against the wall and speaking in low tones with Wildgrave Ozanne. They were both observing Fiacre's discussion with the prince with interest, but also like they were too smart to go over there and get in the line of fire themselves.

The younger prince was flanked by a man who looked as put out by this whole situation as I was. I couldn't tell how unhappy he was from his face but from the set of his shoulders. He was a soldier, and there was something resigned and tense in the way he held himself—like he thought he was going to be attacked, too.

"Now, that's hardly fair," Caius said, almost like he was getting ready to sulk. "I thought it was the height of rudeness to go up and *talk* to a member of the royal family."

"Just the older prince," I replied, distractedly.

It was obvious, at least to me, that while the Emperor was maintaining his mystique or whatever it was he thought he was going to accomplish with this recess, he'd left things up to his more personable younger brother, who was probably making polite conversation about the weather and the price of silk with two of our most esteemed diplomats.

From the looks of the Emperor—from what kind of man he obviously was—it was likely a good thing, I thought, that he wasn't in the room to see how nicely his younger brother got on with the men and women from Volstov.

"Come," Caius said, without any warning, giving my arm a fierce tug. I almost flipped him again. That time, it was harder to squash the instinct. It wouldn't do to make a scene, and the last thing I wanted was to give th'Esar any more reason than he already had to exile me. Not that a diplomatic mission was exile, but it might as well have been, and after it was over I was looking forward to a good long rest back home. I didn't need to give anyone any reason to be pissed off with me. After all, I'd only just got back from the front lines, to find myself in the thick of it once more. Somehow or another, I'd managed to piss somebody off. Killing a member of the Basquiat in front of all the Ke-Han warriors in the middle of treaty talks, no matter how much I wanted to or how easy it would have been, wouldn't look nice on my résumé.

So I managed not to kill Caius Greylace. But barely.

"We simply *have* to talk to him, don't you agree?" Caius asked. And, for an incredibly small creature, I had to admit, he was also incredibly strong. He made good use of his size, too, squeezing up next to Josette as though he'd been there all along.

The man flanking the prince narrowed his eyes, like maybe *he* was thinking about flipping Caius Greylace over, if he got any closer. He was a bodyguard then, or whatever the Ke-Han equivalent of that was. His hair was all thick black braids, pulled back into a complicated twist that left them to spill neat as you please down his back—though unlike the Emperor, he didn't have any fancy jade dangles to make noise when he moved. Didn't matter though, since from what I'd learned, it was the braids that were important. Something like our version of medals of honor. The man, whoever he was, had been a soldier. I thought it would have been pretty fucking hilarious if we'd recognized one another, but the truth was that all the Ke-Han looked the same to me, and this poor bastard was probably thinking the exact same thing about us.

"I am very pleased to hear you enjoyed the dinner," the smiling prince said, his words softened and masked by a heavy accent. Still, there was something about the way he looked *so* delighted to be speaking our language that you couldn't help feeling a little of it too.

"Oh, the dessert was especially wonderful," Josette told him. "And so light! I expect I'll have to be refitted for all my dresses by the time we leave."

The prince laughed politely, like he'd understood maybe half of what Josette had said, or at least enough to know that it was a pleasantry.

"Who intends to leave?" Caius asked. "You put us *so* to shame with your hospitality, I've half a mind to stay here indefinitely once the talks are over."

The prince trained his eyes on us, uncertain for a moment while he tried to sort out the words. I thought about that glimpse we'd got of the Emperor, his brother, as compared to the lamb in front of us, lips moving silently like he was reading a book. He looked more like a foreign 'Versity student than a prince. His brother, on the other hand, had looked every inch like haughty royalty. Maybe it skipped the second-born.

"Thank you," the prince said carefully. "It is my—it is *our* hope—that you feel comfortable here."

Caius ducked in a deep and graceful bow. "I'm Caius Greylace." He elbowed me in the stomach, just above the hip, which I guessed meant I was supposed to bow too.

Didn't mean I wasn't going to get him for it later, though.

"This is my companion," he went on, like we were there together or something.

"Alcibiades," I said gruffly, because it was too late in the day to be getting into titles, and besides, I didn't have one.

The prince nodded, taking in the latest display of prostration on my part with clever dark eyes. I didn't trust him, not for a minute, but then he had fewer braids in his hair than the man who stood beside him. He was more a prince than a warrior, yet.

"This is Prince Mamoru," Fiacre said, looking pleased to have *something* to say. "Haven't managed to catch the name of his stalwart companion yet, but ah, he seems very . . . tall."

Prince Mamoru's eyes lit up with happiness, probably at recognizing his name in among all our messy foreign words.

"Mamoru," he said, resting a hand against his chest.

He was delicate enough that he reminded me a little of Greylace, though he was certainly quieter, and heaps more reserved—so a Greylace I would have better liked to have around.

"Prince Mamoru," Caius repeated, replicating the accent and the strange round R like he'd been practicing the language for years. "Might I say quite candidly that I am simply in awe of your jewelry? It's incomparable to anything in Volstov!"

He reached out a solicitous hand, likely to admire one of those bracelets, or maybe just to make another sweeping bow—I wouldn't ever be sure, since the man standing next to the prince seized Caius's wrist with the speed of a practiced soldier.

I found myself reaching for my sword, before I remembered two things: that the war was over, and that it was forbidden for us to carry a weapon within the Emperor's palace.

Josette's smile slid off her face like a piece of creamed eel. Prince Mamoru's eyes went wide. Caius Greylace looked as though he'd never had as much fun in his entire life, even when the man released him, and bowed lower than I would have thought he'd been capable of. He murmured something in a low voice, rough and alien. I could only presume it was an apology.

Fiacre caught my eye and nodded toward the door. The Emperor had arrived, standing with his seven separate bodyguards, or poison tasters, or whatever the hell they were.

"I suppose we'd best take our seats," Josette said. Her smile was back in place, but it was a diplomat's mask of a smile, and there was no authenticity to be found in it at all.

The man muttered his foreign apology again before standing and ushering the prince to his seat.

Caius turned to me with the air of a fisherman who'd caught lobsters in his trap.

"That was *thrilling*," he whispered, as we moved away to take our seats. "Didn't you think so? I wonder who that man is. He moved so quickly! Perhaps he was a general, or some other manner of warrior servant. He was so *strong*."

" 'Thrilling'? He almost killed you," I pointed out, just in case Caius hadn't noticed that part.

"I know *that*," Caius said. "Why else do you think it was so delightful?"

He was the only person it was my misfortune to know who would have said almost being killed by a Ke-Han bodyguard was "delightful" or "thrilling." I was beginning to despair for all of Volstov, if this was what was happening to our nobility. And I was beginning to despair for myself, if *this* was any example of how the rest of the talks were going to go.

The younger prince had taken his seat once more. I could see him from where I was quite clearly, and his bodyguard, too, in case he wanted to try anything again. I may not have had my sword with me, but then again, he didn't either. The way I saw it, we could still manage to figure out how to kill each other properly with just our hands.

Prince Mamoru murmured something to his brother, then bowed deeply to him. It made me feel all kinds of uncomfortable to know that we were transacting our business with a people who made their brothers bow to them on a point of formality.

Then the Emperor Iseul lifted his hand.

Even though his father had just died—even though he was new to it, and he had a hell of a lot to prove—he held himself like he'd been doing this all his life, or at least like he'd been *waiting* for it that long.

"Now," he said, in a voice made all the more formal by its stilted Volstovic accent. "Lords and Ladies of Volstov, our esteemed guests: the Ke-Han welcome you."

And the way he said that, I thought, folding my arms over my chest and getting ready for a long night, made it obvious that he was the Ke-Han. Even though he'd been a prince this morning, he was an emperor now. But those were just the times we lived in.

KOUJE

My lord Mamoru was kind. It was always almost impossible to apologize to him.

My forehead scraped the floor of his personal chambers nonetheless. When we'd been younger, and my lord more outspoken, he'd commanded me once to stop my bowing—which, after a long week that made no sense to either of us, I'd explained to him was like asking a fish to live out of water, or a songbird to keep silent. If I'd done my duty as his servant poorly, then it was my job to appease the natural order of things by begging his forgiveness.

"It was a misstep," I said, my hands in fists at either side. "It was clear he did not intend to harm you. I should not have acted so rashly."

"Kouje," my lord said, "surely you've apologized enough."

That was the trouble with my lord: He was too kind. The Emperor had known it, and had done what he could accordingly. My lord Iseul, too, had tried to stamp it out. Some men, however, were made to be like Iseul, and some men like Mamoru. You could no more have taught my lord imperiousness than you could have taught me to stop bowing.

"Indeed, nothing came of it," Mamoru went on, unplaiting the jade from his hair and setting it upon a low, dark table. It was worn with the polish of true craftsmanship, the fine patina of age. He'd had it since he was a child, and dressed—as was sometimes the custom with second sons—in the swaddling clothes of a little girl, to see him alive and unharmed through his first five years.

Assassins targeted sons but left daughters in their cradles.

I bowed my head again. "My lord," I protested, "if there is some fitting punishment for the offense..."

"Shall I make you scrub the floors all night?" my lord asked. There was a warmth in his voice I knew well; it meant there was a fond twinkle in his dark eyes. That he was, in some ways, laughing at me. If I would stop my obsequies and lift my head, then we might laugh together.

But things were different now, more serious. I could not laugh off what I had done as simply as I laughed off other, smaller transgressions. My lord Mamoru was lenient with me, but I had no cause to be lenient with myself.

"My lord knows that they have already been scrubbed twice over for the arrival of our guests," I said, with as little humor as I could manage. It was still more of a jest than I should have allowed. Having known my lord since his birth, however, had instilled in me some traitorous familiarity that, try as I might, I found incredibly difficult to stamp out.

Mamoru laughed outright this time, the sound of it soft and welcoming. It filled the silence in this part of the palace, where all the servants were either asleep or busying themselves with their last duties before bed. The wing of the palace that had once housed the princes—and was now for Mamoru alone—was kept separate from the newly disruptive intrusion of the delegation from Volstov.

"I suppose there is no fitting punishment at all for what you've done then," Mamoru mused. When I lifted my head, there was a faint smile upon his lips, his braids undone around his face.

When my lord had been much younger, that face had resembled a pale, round moon, or perhaps a mountain peach.

"My lord," I said, bowing my head again, this time in thanks.

"You might call my servants in to ready me for bed," Mamoru said. He did not often acknowledge my thanks for his actions, as though he felt that were the only way to behave and not something to be thanked for in the first place. "I'm certainly not going to be able to get out of all this by myself."

I kept my smile hidden in the left corner of my mouth. My lord had never done very well with formal dress.

"I'll alert them at once," I said. "Do try not to create a situation, in my absence."

It was an old joke between us, in the days when Mamoru had been much more my charge and mine alone, and the weight of the responsibility had made me reluctant to leave him for even a moment.

"I won't become tangled in my sleeves," he assured me, with the same faint hint of a smile.

The palace halls were empty and darkened, since the prince had already retired, and there was no one else in that wing who would have need of the servants to bear lanterns. I knew my way by memory, turning at first to the left, summoning Mamoru's servants, then back up to the prince's room, where my own quarters were stationed two doors away. It was close enough to hear any approaching dangers, but the distance still bothered me some nights.

On that night, with the taint of unease still shadowing my heart, I did not like the two doors' distance between my lord and me. Yet, I grudgingly admitted to myself, he was a man grown now, and I could no longer sleep at the foot of his bed.

There was a soft, scuffling noise in the hall up ahead, the source of which I could not make out. I felt instinctively for my sword before privately cursing the laws of diplomacy that had disarmed us, along with the party from Volstov. There was no sword, only a short, ornamental fan stuck into the sash at my waist: a gesture of goodwill to our guests from the conquering nation.

I heard the noise again, closer then, like an unwelcome footfall. But all the servants here were trained explicitly well to serve the prince in a ready manner, swift and silent. Whoever it was approaching was no servant. I pressed myself back against the wall and waited for a shape to appear.

When it did, it became apparent that the approaching noise had been a man, and that it was a man who had drunk too much of our wine.

He said something unfamiliar, coarse and sharp; no doubt it was a curse. And then, upon seeing me, he reached out to grab my arm with unfathomable familiarity. I recoiled before remembering myself, my duty, and what I had done earlier to shame my lord.

The man's face was foreign, which meant that he too was a member of the diplomatic envoy. I couldn't afford to offend anyone else so soon. Perhaps he only needed to be led back to his part of the palace. I wasn't among the servants assigned to herd the Volstovics hither and yon as though they were stray peacocks and not people at all.

"You're lost," I said, though it was plain that at least half the men and women from Volstov did not understand our tongue. Interesting, then, that we should have worked so hard and so diligently at learning theirs.

This one seemed to, however, or at least he straightened up and began looking about back and forth, as if confused as to which direction he'd come from.

"Your quarters are this way," I added.

A firm hand could sometimes bridge what language could not.

Since the man demonstrated no desire to let go of my arm, I curbed my temper and began the task of leading him down the hall, past the servants' quarters, and out of the prince's wing entirely. He said something in Volstovic, and he stumbled once when I rounded a corner too swiftly, but the drink had made him amenable. No doubt he was not used to the strength of Ke-Han wine.

We passed the very same room in which the Emperor had conducted his talks, as well as the great hall that led up to the Emperor's private quarters. There had been some furor over housing the delegation from Volstov so close to the Emperor, but Iseul himself had declared it be so, stating that he was not afraid and nor should any of us be, since the Volstovics were there on a mission of peace and diplomacy, and hospitality alone could rebuild what centuries of warfare had undone.

To house them elsewhere would have betrayed a lack of conviction on our part.

We had only just rounded the corner, my charge and I, when I caught the first glimpse of soft lanternlight. The servants had doubtless been instructed to stay about later in this part of the palace, perhaps to see to it no diplomat from Volstov lost his way as the man by my side had done.

I took the man's hand from my arm. He seemed to calm once he'd noticed the lantern up ahead. He made a sluggish gesture, starting down the hall before pausing—an inelegant lurch in his motion—to turn around.

"Thank you," he said, halting and crude in our language.

I bowed as low as was proper and watched to make sure the servant up ahead had taken notice of him.

We were in an important stage in our country's rebuilding, perhaps the most important. I knew it as well as any other man in the palace. Still, as I turned to make my way back to the other end of the palace, I couldn't help thinking how I would welcome the day when the delegation from Volstov left us forever. As things stood, their presence was too much like the threat of a headache lingering at the back of my mind.

When I reached the center point of the palace there was a gentle light spilling down the corridor that led to the Emperor's suites. I felt the same curiousness that had overtaken my heart at the dinner—a nameless dread, all the more powerful because it *was* nameless as of yet.

I couldn't see any lantern-bearing servants, which meant the light must have been coming from the Emperor's rooms somewhere up ahead. I wondered if perhaps another man or woman from Volstov had become turned around. If that was the case, then it was my duty to ask the Emperor what service I might do him. It was possible, too, that my apprehension came solely from the drunkard's invasion, from knowing that a foreign diplomat could easily stumble into the Emperor's chambers. Whether he meant to do ill or had merely swallowed too much wine at dinner did not seem to matter much.

I had no wish to spend my night ferrying diplomats from one end of the palace to another, but my duty had nothing at all to do with what I wished.

There were no servants lining the hall to the Emperor's private audience chamber, which adjoined his private quarters, but I could see the outline of the lantern-bearers through the rice-paper walls, just as I could see the kneeling outline of three men set before the Emperor, and the four kneeling behind them. It was an audience of the seven lords, I conjectured—though of course, I couldn't be certain.

What did seem certain was that the Emperor would not be needing my services for such an audience.

"It grieves my heart deeply, even deeper still to make such a decree so soon after the death of our father." That was Iseul. His voice was unmistakable. My heart began to contract in my chest.

"You are quite sure, my lord?" The question came from one of the seven, his voice less certain in the matter than Iseul's, but I could recognize the timbre of loyalty.

"Quite," Iseul said, the word like the sharp edge of a sword.

"*You* saw the way the young prince was speaking with the delegation from Volstov. Forgive me, my lord, but it's the truth. And if the Emperor himself doesn't think he can be trusted, then it isn't for us to question."

"Too true," murmured another lord.

"It's settled," Iseul spoke, and his voice held no room for doubt. "As of this evening, Prince Mamoru is deemed a traitor to the realm, to be routed at any cost."

I knew then why I had felt the heaviness in the air as an approaching thunderstorm, for now I was surely a man trapped in the very heat of it, lightning tearing the familiar shape of the sky I knew so well into jagged strips.

"Be discreet," Iseul went on, "and be cautious. We wish for this matter to be dealt with swiftly, but we are loath to think of how our negotiations might be disrupted if the diplomats from Volstov were to learn of such a traitor in our midst."

"Or how they might turn such knowledge to their advantage," another lord cautioned.

"That was what most troubled my mind about the matter," Iseul said. I could hear the shifting of silks; he had not yet disrobed for the night and was still dressed in his father's finest. He was an emperor now, and my lord Mamoru only a prince. "It would seem that Mamoru is too well suited to be used by these men, rather than capable of using them. You know as well as I how weak he is. I would cut out my own tongue before I betrayed my own brother, but I would cut out the contents of my belly before I betrayed the Ke-Han."

"It is for the Ke-Han," the first lord said.

A murmur of assent passed among them. An answering echo of dread sounded in my chest.

It was more than I should have heard—more than I should have stayed to hear. My allegiance was to my Emperor; he owned my loyalty, my services, my soul and heart. Though I served my lord Mamoru, it was merely to serve my Emperor before him, and to serve my Emperor was to serve the Ke-Han.

It is for the Ke-Han, I thought, grateful as I always was that my father had trained me so well. No sound could be heard when I moved through the halls; my feet were silent even on the most ancient of floorboards.

I thought of my many years of service, of Mamoru as a baby, of the first fever he suffered, which had by no means been the last. It was true that he was not as strong as his brother—the gods had been unusually kind when they made Iseul the heir and Mamoru the second son—but he was not a traitor. If he had been, I would already have known it.

In his room, two doors from mine, my lord Mamoru was no doubt already asleep for the night. He had been proud of himself today; I'd watched him as he sat, learning the Volstovic vowels that so confounded me, in the long days and weeks that followed our defeat. I'd guided him in battle, taught him archery and the sword, and, when he was much smaller, held his hand through fevers or changed the final words of the saddest stories to keep him from weeping.

As my father had wished it, I'd endeavored to be a servant not only worthy of his name but worthy of the Emperor.

To know that my lord was in danger was to feel the point of the sword against my own throat. If the threat had come from any other source, I would have taken up all my weapons, in spite of the terms of the diplomats' treaty, and hunted the men behind it down like criminals and dogs. As with all prior attempts, my lord Mamoru would never have known the precariousness of his own life in these dark hours.

But Iseul's words were spoken for the good of the empire, and I was merely a servant. What was my will worth, against that of an emperor?

CAIUS

It was my first evening with the Ke-Han, and already the second prince's bodyguard had tried to kill me. Things would have been much more intriguing if it had been the second prince himself, but when one was in the midst of exotic, curiously refined savages, one took what one could get.

Alcibiades, however, was still having a fit of pique over it.

As he made it very plain that he actively disliked me—he hadn't come around just yet, and he was stubborn as a mule and smelled like one, too—I had no idea why he was making such a fuss over it.

"In fact," I was in the middle of explaining, "everything's gone rather better than I thought it would have by now."

As a response, Alcibiades managed an indelicate grunt. I'd learned, however, the sound was his particular and special form of communication. One had to adapt if one wanted to find any sort of conversation at all. I had already garnered a reputation among some of the other diplomats, so Alcibiades—grunting, mulish aroma and all—would have to suffice for the moment.

I did what I always did: I continued talking. "Why, didn't you expect the sparks to fly?" I asked, knowing full well I would get no more than a grunt in return. From what I gathered, not only was Alcibiades in a poor mood, he was also hungry. He'd barely touched his food at dinner. No doubt he'd expected bread and cheese and bleeding meat, and was disappointed to discover the subtle flavors of Ke-Han cuisine. Either that, or all the half-raw fish. "If it wasn't someone else who gave the first offense, I thought for certain it would be you."

That seemed to surprise him. "Me?" Alcibiades demanded. Although it sounded distinctly gruntlike, it was almost certainly a word; I counted that as a triumph, and made a mental note of the time and place. Late evening, my quarters in the palace. When we'd returned after the lovely meal, I'd immediately opened the adjoining door between our rooms so that we might chat better.

"You were wearing red," I pointed out.

"Good color," he replied.

I sighed, though I wasn't really exasperated. He was more than just a character, the recently promoted General Alcibiades; he had an interesting sense of what was allowed (offending all the Ke-Han by wearing Volstov's colors in the midst of a diplomatic mission) and what wasn't (admiring the second prince's very fine jade necklace).

"One almost thinks you want to be recalled," I said slyly.

Alcibiades looked at me sharply, and I wondered if I hadn't hit the mark, after all. Something about his expression reminded me of how the second prince's bodyguard had seized my arm. You wouldn't think it to look at men so solidly built—that they could do *anything* so quickly—but there were Alcibiades and the bodyguard, both proving me wrong.

There was nothing so wonderful as being proven wrong. It gave one all manner of chances to adapt and solve the riddle, that one might be *right* the next time. I relished the thought.

Alcibiades' stomach made a loud and unruly sound.

"Perhaps," I ventured, "you might abandon your dreams of being recalled in favor of actually eating some dinner occasionally?"

"It wasn't even cooked!" Alcibiades proclaimed. A full sentence this time. Perhaps the hunger was forcing him to let his guard down. The theory, if it proved true, was rather a thrilling prospect. Why, by morning he would be speaking in paragraphs!

"At least you can rest assured that at breakfast there is very little likelihood of your bowl containing more fish. They don't seem like the type to repeat a performance—or a meal, for that matter."

Alcibiades rubbed his stomach, almost like the great shaggy dog I'd first imagined him to be. "I'd even settle for rice, at this hour," he said.

I looked out the window. I hadn't noticed it before, since it operated in much the same way as the sliding doors, yet wasn't made of rice paper but dark, polished wood. The moon hung like a slice of some pale exotic fruit in the sky. It was the perfect sort of night for a midnight raid on the kitchens. Granted, this wasn't my country estate, but it was always possible to sniff the kitchens out, and they were the one place in any country that never closed down completely for the night. What if the Emperor got peckish? It would never do to be caught off guard.

I didn't have much experience in raiding Ke-Han kitchens, of course, but I'd done that sort of thing often enough during my term in exile. Food was essentially the same everywhere you went, once you got right down to the bare bones of it. It didn't matter one whit whether the Ke-Han pantries were stocked with rice or with bread. Except, of course, to men like Alcibiades.

I stood up, quite glad that I hadn't changed for bed after all, even if my night set was brand-new, blue silk, to match all the rest.

It was the longest I'd gone without experiencing the need for some variety in my clothing, but I suspected that had something to do with the finery of the garments I wore and the utter foreignness of their shape and style.

Why, it might even take *weeks* to tire of them. If so, I had grossly overpacked.

Alcibiades looked at me with a carefully concealed measure of hope, as if he thought that I was finally going to sleep, and he could at last retire, or at least close the adjoining door between us. He'd been eyeing it for some time. Fortunately for him, I was in a generous mood, and of no mind to hold such a thing against him.

"Let's go and find some rice, then!" I said, with the air of someone embarking on a wonderful adventure. Alcibiades seemed like the type of man who needed that sort of nudge in the right direction.

"What?"

It was almost as if the man hadn't been following.

"Don't tell me you've *never* gone to the kitchens past nightfall," I said, though I was privately imagining that Alcibiades probably hadn't.

He grunted, which I took to mean that I'd imagined correctly.

"I'm used to eating my fill at dinner, that's all," he went on, after the fact.

His hunger was most promising if it meant that I wouldn't have to spend the bulk of my time translating Alcibiades' grunts into proper words. I wasn't any good as an interpreter. I slipped my hands underneath his arms and tugged him to his feet. I'd have never managed it if he hadn't been so surprised, but then I'd rather been expecting him to be heavier than he was.

It was far too early for him to be wasting away to nothing in any case.

"The sooner we leave, the sooner you eat," I said.

The palace halls were darkened when we slid the door to my room open. At one junction, far off in the distance, I could see a lantern-bearer, his lamplight reflecting in the mirrors set at each corner of the corridor and lighting their way like a staircase of stars around the twists and bends of the narrow corridor.

"Do you think they ever get a terrible scare, seeing their own reflections in the middle of the night?" I asked.

Alcibiades looked at me, then looked at the lantern-bearer. He shrugged his shoulders. "Maybe," he said.

I nudged him with my elbow, fishing again for an entire sentence. "Wouldn't it frighten you?"

"I'm not afraid of *myself*," he said. "Or the dark. So I guess not, no."

I nodded, taking his arm in a swift gesture. "I didn't think so."

It wouldn't have scared me, either.

As we passed the palace servants, the lanterns lit the change on their faces from a nearly uniform expression of utter boredom to one of concern and slight confusion. Perhaps if they'd known the words to ask us what we were doing, they would have done so. As it was, they merely watched us, hiding their bafflement as best they could after their initial shock. We must have seemed like ghosts in the night to them, unused as they were to our presence.

That cemented it. While I was there, I would almost certainly have to learn the Ke-Han language more idiomatically. It was nearly unbearable to think of all the gossip I might miss out on over something so silly as a language barrier.

I drew close to Alcibiades once we'd passed the lantern-bearers, and the hallways grew dark once more.

"Don't you think this will put us under suspicion?" I asked him. "Two men from Volstov, out and about in the night, sneaking through the halls of the palace? If anything untoward should happen, they'll surely blame us!"

"Don't sound so delighted about it," Alcibiades muttered, trying to shake me off. Then, as if it were an afterthought, one too good to pass up simply through stubborn reticence, "I'm not too used to exile, that's all."

"And I am?" I asked, still too cheerful at the thrill to be annoyed by the insult. I was used to people insulting me. They did it all the time. The best thing of all to do was act as though you hadn't heard it, or even worse, as though it didn't bother you. The one thing gossips and rumormongers enjoy the least is feeling ignored. "Well, I suppose you're right about that."

That time, when Alcibiades grunted, I took that as an inquiry as to how it had been, living in exile since I was fourteen. I had sixteen different tales depending on who it was doing the asking, but for Alcibiades, I thought I would be indulgent and go with the honest truth. Some men appreciated the strangest things.

"How kind of you to ask," I said, peering down one tight, dark hallway. I could smell rice. At least, I hoped that was what I could smell. If it wasn't, then I was very confused. "It wasn't all that terrible, really. Mostly, it was just boring. You know how that is."

Alcibiades looked at me with a baffled expression, as though he felt we were occupying and acting out two very different conversations. "What are you talking about?" he asked, confusion getting the better of him.

I liked it when he frowned. "Exile, of course. Terribly boring. One must depend solely on the kindness of others, to write letters and answer them in return. I was restricted to an estate in the old Ramanthine countryside. You can *imagine* what that was like. Or perhaps you can't, in which case you ought to be terribly thankful. In any case, you really must pay better attention, my dear, or else we'll never get anywhere."

"This is ridiculous," Alcibiades said. "I'm going back to bed."

I held up my hand in protest. "But we're completely lost. And besides, I was just about to tell you about the dog."

"The—what?" I'd got the better of him at last, though who knew how long I'd manage to continue coaxing responses out of him? It was best if I pressed my advantage right then.

"Why, the one you remind me of, that is," I said. I ducked quickly around one corner, sensing the sound of footfalls somewhere in the distance. From behind a closed door, I heard someone yawn; I could see, through the squares of rice paper, a candle as it was snuffed, followed by murky darkness. It was beautiful there, if a little damp, and the wood floors were very smooth beneath my slippered feet. It was possible, in a place like that, to traverse the entire hallway without making any sound. What a delightful prospect that was. All manner of people could sneak up on one that way, or listen to what one was saying. I felt sorry for them if they were listening to us. *I* was being amusing, while all Alcibiades could manage or muster were a few pained words here and there, and noises that sounded unpleasantly as though he had indigestion. "He died a while ago," I went on, shaking my head. "The dog, I mean. But he was yellow, and before he got very old and started relieving himself on the furniture and I absolutely couldn't stand him anymore, I liked him very much. The dog and all the letters: That was how I entertained myself."

Alcibiades just stared at me. I could make out his broad, simple features in the darkness. I smiled.

"During exile," I repeated, for his sake. "I did have parties, of course, but with the most impossibly boring people, without any imagination. Once I ordered tigers from the jungle and had them in cages and one woman fainted! Of course, that was *after* I let the tigers out, but they didn't really eat anyone. For tigers, they were disappointingly tame."

"You wanted the tigers to eat people," Alcibiades said. It didn't really sound like a question, so I could only assume he'd made his mind up about the matter.

"Not at all," I said. "Well—not *really*. It would have made a mess, and it's hard to keep good help in the countryside. Ah! Here we are, I think."

Alcibiades nearly crashed into me as I stopped short in front of another one of those beautifully crafted sliding doors—these weren't papered, but solid wood, and looked more native to the palace—more solidly, fiercely *Ke-Han*—than the other, flimsy creations had.

"I thought we were lost," Alcibiades said.

"Oh, we are," I agreed. "But now we're lost by the kitchens."

"Oh," said Alcibiades. Then, as if I were suffering from the same lack of attention toward this conversation *he* had been suffering from, he added: "I'm starving."

"Yes, my dear, I'm quite aware," I told him. I had no intentions of sleeping in such close proximity to a man whose stomach was infinitely more talkative than he was. It was far worse than the tigers! "That's why we're here, isn't it?"

"I don't know, do I? This wasn't my idea," Alcibiades retorted, though he didn't sound half as cranky as he had a moment ago.

Perhaps the prospect of food was placating him. "Smells like food, anyway."

"See? No matter what else people say about me, I'm very good with directions."

"*After* we were lost," Alcibiades reminded me mulishly.

"Well, we made it here anyway," I said, in a tone that I hoped might dissuade Alcibiades from pursuing any further argument in the matter. "Shall we search the premises?"

He nodded, and I slid the door open. It was heavier than it looked.

Alcibiades stepped past me once the door was open, then stopped and turned about.

"Thanks," he said gruffly. He seemed about to start rooting through the various wooden cupboards both above and below the countertops, so I thought it prudent to step in after him and look for a lamp—instead of falling into a dead faint at his attempt at manners, however stilted and reluctant, which was my other option.

"You, General Alcibiades, are very welcome," I informed him, standing on the tips of my toes to skim the top of the cupboards for a lamplight.

The kitchen was rather a small affair considering it served the entirety of the palace, but it was immaculate, and—judging by Alcibiades' sounds of pleasure as he stuck his head into the nearest cupboard—it was well stocked.

"Shouldn't call me that," he said, crouching down to slide open a small grain closet. "There isn't anything to be a general *of,* these days, and promotions after the fact don't count for nothing."

"Don't count for *anything,*" I said helpfully. "Aha! Here, wouldn't you rather search with some light?"

"There's a lamp over there," Alcibiades said, though his voice was mysteriously muffled.

I heard a suspicious rustling sound from the cupboard.

"Please don't tell me you're planning on eating uncooked rice," I began. Then my ears detected a sound that was decidedly *not* Alcibiades filling his stomach with all manner of indigestible foodstuffs. It sounded like a whisper, in the soft, foreign tongue that I'd come to recognize, if not understand. A light passed just in front of the door, pale and faltering. Not one of the lantern-bearers, then.

I was glad I hadn't yet lit the lamp. Curiosity propelled me toward the half-open door when abruptly I felt a hand on my arm, wrenching me back.

I hadn't heard him move, but Alcibiades was standing with his back against the wall, and he had his hand over my mouth. As if I would be *so* consummately foolish as to *speak* at a moment like that! I wanted to bite him. Perhaps I would settle for making him dream about uncaged tigers the whole night long—though that, I recognized, was not the sort of thing a man did to a new friend. I *had* grown uncivilized from my time in exile after all, knowing now the proper time to use my visions for revenge and when not to.

From what I could see through the crack in the doorway, there were two men standing in the hallway. They wore plain robes the color of the sky at midnight, but their sashes were all embroidered in the same style as the Emperor's robes. They were no servants.

The silver of weapons glinted at their sides in the faint light. Was that what Alcibiades had seen? Perhaps, ever the soldier, he might even have been able to smell it. I could think of no other reason for his curious bout of discretion since he was hardly likely to fear that our little pantry raid would cause an international incident. Then again, *we* were in no way armed. If not discreet, then at least Alcibiades was prudent— or maybe simply practical.

The men outside the door bent their heads together in murmured conversation. They seemed to be conferring over something very serious, whatever it was, since they hadn't even employed the use of servants for light and were instead carrying their own. I could feel Alcibiades breathing against the top of my head, even and slow, as though he was willing his stomach to keep from growling. I only hoped he wasn't going to get any rice in my hair.

In unison, the men lifted their heads. One of them, with neatly manicured facial hair, lifted his hand and made a hurried gesture. There was the soft sound of clanking metal as the two men broke into a slow run. To my surprise, they were followed by at least five more, all of them similarly outfitted. Each was carrying a sword.

I didn't hold my breath as the strange procession went past, but I could feel the beat of my heart positively hammering in my chest with curiosity. Had the servants who'd seen us alerted the Emperor to some foul play?

The only damper on the occasion was Alcibiades, who was still holding on to me like a farmer with an errant stoat. I bit his hand. It tasted like rice.

Alcibiades cursed, using a word I hadn't heard before. That was unexpected. Then he dropped me, which I *had* expected, and gave me an awful look.

"You needn't look so wounded," I told him. "Anyway, I'm certain they're just the guards. Perhaps we'll be at the center of another incident! And all before morning, too."

Alcibiades didn't seem nearly as thrilled at the prospect, but then, I was rather resigned to the fact that nothing at all seemed to thrill Alcibiades.

"I thought that no one was supposed to carry a weapon," he said. "Not us, and definitely not the Ke-Han."

"Perhaps they're guards," I said. "Perhaps they were told there were mice in the pantry."

Alcibiades wasn't amused by my little joke. He had yet to grow accustomed to my particular brand of humor. I shrugged it off as he peered around the half-open door, searching the now-dark halls for any further signs of armed men.

It was curious, I had to admit; or, at least, I was unused to living in a place where the halls needed patrolling in the middle of the night. I could feel all the hairs on the back of my neck stand on end—a truly pleasant sensation.

"Now, now," I murmured, "it isn't that surprising, really. No doubt they're here to protect us, as well as the royal family."

"I'd rather they let us protect ourselves," Alcibiades snapped back at me from over his shoulder.

"Do you think they would be so foolish as to disarm every man in the palace completely?" I asked, tapping the corner of my mouth with my forefinger. My thoughts were always crowded, and the smallest physical reminder always helped me to organize them. "That would leave them open not to foreign attempts, but native ones. I hear that the royal family has a history of near-death experiences with assassinations. Why, there is the oddest custom—the first son, of course, is the heir, and must be raised in his father's image with the strictest of manly pastimes, whatever those are. But should there be a second son, or more, they dress them up as little, wide-eyed daughters until they're of an age where people will start to notice something's not right, almost as a policy of insurance. Apparently, among the Ke-Han, there is a general rule floating about: that it's completely unnecessary to assassinate daughters."

"How fucking pleasant," Alcibiades said, biting the words out.

"Actually, it's quite clever. All things considered."

After a long pause, during which I could practically *hear* the wheels in my general friend's head turning, Alcibiades managed to speak again. "So you're telling me," he said, a little slowly, and a little disgusted, too, "that the prince we met tonight spent the first five years of his life thinking he was a girl?"

"Well, I don't know the exact details," I admitted, "but I'm sure it was something like that."

"This place," Alcibiades said, shaking his head and brushing rice from the corner of his mouth, "is three-ways fucked."

Even though I could have told him that it was the same in every country and every culture—that shock was only a matter of what type of fucked you were and weren't used to—I was inclined to agree with him.

CHAPTER THREE

MAMORU

Of the years of the dragon riders, those years of chaos before my father's empire fell, I remember one thing more clearly than the rest: the color of a raid night. The fires came close enough to scorch the air, and the air was made heavier still with sweat and fear. No man knew if—when—the dragons would come to the capital itself. How could we tell what those mysterious creatures were made of? How could we know what they would be capable of, given enough time?

But what I remembered most of all was the city after the final battle, when that which we were all dreading came to our very doorstep, and the dragons tore down each age-old wall with one flick of their massive, metal tails.

In the quiet aftermath of destruction, after the damage had been contained and the last of the fires extinguished, the sulfurous air choked our throats; no amount of burning incense could quite blot out the smell. It woke you in the night, or haunted you like a ghost, clinging to your clothes and your hair and even your skin. It impregnated all the silk. Most of it, my father had burned.

In the streets, animals from the ruined menagerie wandered, dazed as we were, uncaged but uncertain where to go. They reminded me of the returning soldiers—men who'd belonged in the capital once but no longer knew how to employ their own freedom.

It was a strange thing indeed to see lions hiding behind the wreckage of an old wall, or watch peacocks spill forth from the broken doorway of an abandoned house.

By some extraordinary chance, the palace itself had been relatively spared. Perhaps it was because it stood in the shadow of the great magicians' dome to the west, now a broken, hollow shell. One of the topics under negotiation was whether or not our magicians would even be able to continue under the circumstances, with so few of their prior number and the seat of their power all but destroyed. Our society was not so based in magic as that of the Volstovics, and perhaps in times of peace the magicians would not be so needed. What had hurt us most was the loss of the dome, what it symbolized to our people and our gods. Their dome had existed ever since I could remember, since before my father's era, and before my grandfather's. It represented the pinnacle of perfection in architecture—an auspicious shape from all vantage points, and one that complemented the power of the elements as it harnessed them for our magicians' use so that they might approximate the gods in power. There was great debate even among our lords whether such an edifice could ever be re-created.

Perhaps the delegation from Volstov would not allow us to. And, I wondered privately, with what magicians would we fill it? Only a bare handful remained.

The shrill cry of a peacock pierced the night air, indignant as any lord whose sleep had been interrupted.

When I'd been a child too young to venture from the palace, my father the Emperor had deemed the menagerie unsafe. There was too much open space where assassins might make their move and prove lucky. I, however, had longed more than anything to see a *real* lion, or a *real* peacock, and put up an impossible fuss, unbearable for all the servants whose misfortune it was to be assigned to me. I was so adamant that at last Kouje had resorted to playing a lion, in the days when I'd been too young to understand what a dishonor such behavior was for a warrior. I had never had what one might consider a proper nursemaid. Instead, after outgrowing my wet nurse's care, I'd been entrusted to Kouje, both my body and my mind, so that I might learn from him a warrior's capability and effortless strength.

There were days when I doubted that the plan had worked as well as my father had hoped. But Kouje was strong and patient, and when I was a child, he did not leave me much room to doubt.

After I'd been deemed fit to serve in my father's best interests, I'd led the men under me with as much wisdom and strength as I knew. Being a prince meant that everything I did reflected back on the Emperor, and thus on our people—but it was more than that. Numbered among the men who served under me was Kouje, there to aid, or to make certain that I'd taken all his lessons to heart. My brother Iseul always spoke of pleasing our father, and of what was good for the empire, but I had always had a dual purpose—proving myself a credit to Kouje's teachings as well as to my father's bloodline.

Perhaps, in the end, that was why I did not share my brother's strength of character. A man divided could never be as strong as a man with a single purpose.

At times, it seemed a favor from the gods themselves that Iseul had been the firstborn, since any man among us could see that he would make a much better emperor than I. I wondered how he would conduct the talks the next day, and whether he would inspire fear in the men and women from Volstov in the pale morning as he'd so clearly done that night.

"Do not lower yourself to speaking their language so easily," he'd chided me after the talks. "Or do you not see what it means, that they have not yet taken the time to learn ours?"

"It is an insult." I bowed my head, knowing that it was the only thing that could have caused Iseul to grow so quietly angry.

"You do what you think is best," Iseul said, with an imperial wave of his hand. He'd learned that from our father, but had only just begun to employ the gesture. It spoke more than his words. "But if you continue to bow so low, you will be a discredit to this house; you will poison our name."

Iseul had never spoken to me so coldly before, but I could only assume it was the strain of his responsibilities weighing on him. Not only did he have to adjust to his new role as Emperor, but he had to supervise me, as well, to make sure I committed no dishonor to our house.

It was a true gift and a boon that I had not yet done so. At least even Iseul admitted that I had some head for strategy. But if I did, it was all through Kouje's teachings and through picture scrolls of the histories. I could use a bow, but none so well as most of my brother's men. I had no cleverness with a sword, nor strength, either.

"You are like a prince of old, when we were more than warriors," Kouje once told me. I might well have been no more than thirteen at the time.

"When we were less, you mean," I countered.

"And what skill have I with the brush?" Kouje asked. "Were I given twice my own age to master calligraphy, do you think I could manage it?"

Kouje had no hand for the arts, that was true. His broad palms were callused, and his fingers blunt and strong. Yet the Emperor, I knew, would not accept my watercolors—unfolding images of cranes and clouds, of imagined mountains.

"I'm going to run away to the mountains," I told Kouje firmly, in the clutch of a terrible sulk. How he bore with me during those awful years, I'll never know.

"Will you be needing my services there as well?" he asked, not daring to smile at me. I was not entirely insufferable, but I had my moments of jealousy, same as all children. "There are demons in the mountains, you know, with long, terrible claws. They like to kidnap beautiful young princes—never to be seen again."

When I had nightmares that night and for weeks after, he regretted it, but I refused to let him apologize. He'd rallied my spirits, at least, as he always did.

In the many years since then, I'd done my part. All I wanted was to keep my men safe, or feel Kouje clasp my shoulder after a well-chosen tactic proved invaluable. My brother was the warlord, and I was in awe to see him Emperor, so fiercely proud, recognizable, and yet suddenly a complete stranger to me. He'd changed in an instant, as though the brother I'd known had been but a shadow cast from the future.

It was a hard night for sleeping. My thoughts were too tangled. I could feel the cool breeze stir against my face, as on so many nights before.

It was then that I mourned for my father.

Kouje was not there. He would not see me in my moment of weakness, and I was glad for that. We were long past the time when I could allow him to comfort me, and my unhappiness would only trouble him, without allowing him any means to undo it.

My father had not, in his way, treated me as most fathers treated their sons, second or no. But that was to be expected. My father was not a man: He was an emperor. I hadn't been the son he wanted, but I was the son he'd been given, and while he and Iseul were better suited for each other—silent even at private dinners in the same grave manner, with wills as swift and fierce as the gods—he had been the father I was given.

Had I ever thought that we would lose? What haunted me was the question that implied: Had he?

It was thus that I fell asleep, or must have, with my cheeks streaked by tears as though I was once again a child. It had been a very long time indeed since I'd last cried myself to sleep—and then Kouje had been there, one hand on my back, the other making shadow creatures dance across the far wall.

Sometime later, I heard the sound of the door in my room slide open. It was Kouje, or must have been, protective as he was, come one last time tonight to check on me before at last allowing himself to sleep. No footfalls followed, but Kouje was quieter than a cat when he chose to be. Those times were either of utmost importance, or to see to it that he didn't wake me. If he ever differentiated between the two, I didn't know.

I wished, distantly, as though through a dream, that he would simply go to sleep, but the sound of the door sliding shut with his exit never came.

My father and my brother after him had instincts. They could sense, as a great cat in the mountains could sense its prey, a coming storm, enemy troops, an assassin in the house. For the first five years of my life, I'd been raised far differently than they; it was because of this that I could not sense my own danger like a warrior's scars aching during the rainy season.

I was just drifting back to sleep when a hand, rough with use of a sword, closed over my mouth.

I could no more see in the darkness than I could scream around the suffocating palm. Something smelled familiar, but I couldn't distinguish it. Then, I was being dragged to my feet, out of my bed, and into the darkened hall.

KOUJE

During the time of the dragons, I'd spent many a night indulging in the barest artifice of sleep. I would lie prone, the covers over my body and one hand on my sword, but I would not sleep. It was what my body required for rest, but I could not term it restful.

The day they came over the wall, flying straight for the center of the city with fire all around them, was something I dreamed of often. The war had ended, but I still had not found my rest.

When the palace was first designed, it was built with separate, smaller corridors for the use of servants, so that the Emperor might never have to trouble himself with encountering one in the hall. They had long since been closed over, boarded up when it was decided they were too much an invitation for assassins, but there was one less closely guarded than the rest. It was the passage the hostlers used most often when conveying news of their lords' horses to the main palace, and was tolerated only because the door was impossible to find unless you knew it was there.

It was my duty to know the palace better than I knew the veins lining the back of my own hand.

That was the way I took my lord Mamoru, my heart pounding fiercely as though it sensed the wrongness in my current actions. It beat as a fish's heart must, upon finding itself on dry land for the first time. Perhaps what I was doing would prove just as fatal, but I could no more will myself to choose another course than I could will myself to sleep at night.

I kept my hand over Mamoru's mouth, half-carrying him through the passageway and half-dragging him. He'd stopped kicking and beating at my shoulders with his fists, but whether it was because he'd caught sight of my face and calmed somewhat, or because he'd gone rigid with terror, I didn't know.

It had been so long since I'd last comforted my lord that I'd forgotten the art of it. And, admittedly, kidnapping him in that fashion was something beyond a sad tale, or a bruised shoulder. Besides, we hadn't the time for it.

The stables were dark, filled wall to wall with foreign horses, all of which were exhausted from the ride over the Cobalts. It was there that I released my lord, catching his arm as he stumbled and gasped shallowly for breath.

"Kouje!" he cried, still wide-eyed with fear. "You nearly scared the life out of me. What are you doing?"

I wished that I could tell him without harming him. I wished, too, that I knew fully what I was doing.

Instead, I bowed as low as I could—as low as I knew how to. The straw littering the ground scratched at my nose and the smell of horse overwhelmed me, but I pressed my hands flat to keep them still.

"Forgive me, my lord. I would not do such a thing—I would never have dreamed of it—only..." I trailed off, for I could not find the words to tell him. After all, I knew, better than anyone, perhaps, how deeply Mamoru admired his brother. One would even have to say that Mamoru loved Iseul. If that day had never come, I might never have had the need to express my own, more private concerns about the reciprocity of those feelings. I had always known that Iseul was cold, ruthless in a way that his father had not been, and hard in a way that was difficult to understand. Perhaps in giving him the benefit of the doubt—any man my lord loved as much as Mamoru did Iseul could not be without merit—I had missed the signifiers up until that point. I had failed in my duty to protect him from the closest threat of all: that of his own brother.

I could not find the words. My lord had only just lost his father. To eliminate what family he had left in one fell swoop, with a handful of overheard words, was truly too cruel.

It was not a servant's job to abide by what he found the most desirable, however. It was a servant's duty to live only for his lord's existence. To do what he could to ensure that existence. To keep his lord strong.

I could hear Mamoru's breathing begin to even out and the soft sound of his slippers against the straw as he paced, confused and upset at having been so disrupted.

"Kouje," he said, imploring me with everything in his tone to offer some explanation for my actions. He knew that I was not prone to flights of fancy. In fact, on more than one occasion, he'd rebuked me for being overly serious. Perhaps he thought now that I'd gone mad. It had happened to other, stronger men during the course of the war. "Kouje, *please*."

I had to give him some explanation. I'd known that all along, but I hadn't prepared myself properly; I hadn't had the time.

"My lord," I said, lifting my head, "your life is in danger. We must leave the palace at once."

Mamoru shook his head, his face clouded with bewilderment. It took him a moment to speak—how I longed for the days when he was too young and my duty was to shield him from knowledge of the attempts, not inform him of them. "We must tell my brother," he said at last. "The Emperor must be informed of all such threats. He'll protect me. I know Iseul hasn't been emperor very long, Kouje, and he's been distracted with the negotiations, but...I still trust him to execute his duties. We must go to him, and you will tell him what you know."

The words clogged my throat, threatening to choke me. I could not speak, not yet.

"Kouje," Mamoru tried again, more gently. "If it troubles you, then I can speak with Iseul. You may tell me, and I will have an audience with him."

I shook my head. Something in my eyes must have frightened him then, for he took a step away from me.

"It isn't a member of the delegation," he said, his own eyes widening. "It couldn't be that you think—Oh, Kouje, the talks—the treaty— it will all be ruined!"

I could not let him labor under misimpressions any longer. If I did, the subsequent truth would be crueler still. At last I stood, and took my lord by his thin shoulders. I could say it all at once; they were only words. "My lord," I said, willing my voice to be like iron, without flesh or blood behind them, "the Emperor is the one who made the decree."

For a moment, Mamoru looked at me as though I had gone mad. Then his features changed from disbelief to confusion.

"You've misunderstood something," he said, his voice not quite so steely, but with its own, stubborn conviction. "Or I have. What is it that you think you know?"

I did not blame him if he didn't believe me. I had never lied to him—but then, I was only a servant. It was not unexpected that he would believe his brother's character before my word, no matter the situation. But his was not a situation that allowed choice. I'd already made the decision for him. It went against my Emperor and my country, and it meant my life.

"I will take you from here by force," I said. I could not bear to look at him. "If you will not go willingly, then I have no other choice."

"Kouje." My lord was nearly pleading with me. If it were any other place, and any other time, I would have looked toward him sternly; he would have known that now was when he commanded, rather than implored. Perhaps he remembered my old lessons, for after a moment he straightened, set his shoulders, and looked me in the eye. "Kouje, you will tell me what you know."

My lord's command was law. It was almost a relief to obey it. "Earlier this night, the Emperor called his council," I said, my hands in fists at my side. "It was by accident that I heard them—you may punish me for the breach in conduct as you see fit, but only once we are away from here. The Emperor spoke to his seven lords, and accused you of treason." If I separated each word before I spoke them, then I would not hear all that I was saying. It was easier, that way, to break my lord's heart. "The Emperor spoke of a plan. He said that his younger brother was conspiring against him, and for that, he had forfeited his life."

Mamoru shook his head. "But Kouje," he whispered, "I have done nothing."

I bowed. I was always grateful for protocol in moments of uncertainty. "I know that, my lord."

"He must have misunderstood," my lord continued, as though he hadn't heard me. "Earlier, he reprimanded me for speaking the diplomats' language—perhaps that's why he thought . . . ?" There, my lord paused for a long moment. One of the diplomats' horses, in a stall close by, snorted and stamped his hooves. I considered, for a moment, stealing one of them—for the men at the gate would not recognize the foreign horse, and it might ease our escape.

When my lord spoke next, it startled me from my thoughts. There was new strength in his voice, new purpose.

"We must go to my brother at once," he said, and his words caused my heart to sink in my chest. "We will explain to him—*I* will explain to him—I will *prove* that I am loyal. If he asks for any trial, I will give myself over to the test. He will know that I serve him, even if it—"

"Even if it kills you," I said. My own voice had no color to it; the sound made the Volstov horses uneasy.

"If he thinks I'm guilty of this crime, then I cannot run from him," Mamoru confirmed. "A guilty man flees. An innocent one returns to prove his innocence."

Everything that he said made sense. It was calm and reasoned, the way I had endeavored to instruct my lord to make all his decisions. Mamoru was able to see reason where I could not.

Yet what I had neglected in my teachings was how reason gave way in the face of madness, and to Mamoru it surely must have seemed madness that had led to Iseul's decision.

I could not give voice to my deepest fear, since I had no proof to make it manifest. My lord had no eyes with which to look upon Iseul's faults, his unreasonable qualities, the terrible things he'd done during the war, all for the good of the Ke-Han. As he proclaimed this latest decree to be, only now it gave me reason to question all the others.

What manner of monster had the Emperor held in check? I could only wonder at how Iseul had changed since his father's death and brought his true self to light. I had only my instincts, shaped over the years to know always what action was necessary, and to sense when something was wrong in the night. I had protected my lord's life with a sword and a ready hand for all my adult life. There was nothing I knew so well as my duty, but the argument that I wished to give my lord was one I trembled to think on.

I have done nothing, my lord had said, and I had told him that I knew it.

The cold timbre of Iseul's voice as he had given the order had told me that *he* knew it, too.

"My lord," I began carefully.

"I need to speak to my brother," Mamoru said. There was a cold glint in his eyes that for a moment reminded me of the Emperor's iron will.

Before I could stop him, Mamoru had started back into the passageway. He moved at a swift run, and I cursed myself for not having the foresight to prevent that from happening although I do not know if I would have been able to bind my lord's hands and feet even if I *had* been gifted with such foresight.

I ran after him, as silently as I could, and sent a prayer to whatever gods that might still be watching over the prince that no one would hear us.

I caught up to him as the passage made a crooked turn to the left, just before it emerged into the palace. He turned as if to shake me off, then stopped at the soft murmur of voices from up ahead. I didn't put my hand back over his mouth, nor did I wrest him away from the wall and carry him bodily back to the stables, which was what I longed to do. Instead, I held tightly to his arm just above the elbow and listened.

"Maidar has already roused his men," said a man with a strong, harsh voice like wood being chopped. "Do you really believe there's any point bringing yours as well?"

"I believe in not taking chances," said another man. His voice was familiar to me, since I'd heard him issuing orders to his servants from the high table all night. It was Lord Temur, of the western prefecture.

"Come," said the first man, "do you truly think it will be all that difficult? There was a time when you couldn't say it, may the Emperor's spirit rest peacefully, but the prince is weak. It's like sending wolves in after a lamb."

My lord let out a startled breath, and I tightened my hold on his arm. I wished that I could have protected him in some better way. If only I could tighten a hold around his chest to keep it from bursting at the knowledge.

"He was clever enough to conspire against his brother," Lord Temur pointed out. He'd sat next to my lord at dinner, and I'd done nothing. The knowledge was nearly unbearable. I had my sword with me—earlier, I'd thought to carry Mamoru away with me, and would never have left without some means to protect him. I could have done something, and I wanted to, but for my lord's sake, I held back.

The other man laughed—a quiet, shriveling sound. "You don't believe him capable of something like that, do you? No. I think the Emperor has his reasons, and we merely abide by them."

I felt a tugging at my sleeve in the dark. Mamoru had wrapped his fingers tight around the fabric, and was holding on with all his strength, as if he feared he might faint otherwise. I grasped his shoulder with the hand I'd left free. Sometimes even the strongest of lords needed help to stay on their feet.

"Yet," there was hesitation in Lord Temur's voice, even if it was slight, "of all the men who believed this change in power might affect them poorly, I never believed it would be the younger prince on whom the Emperor would turn his sights first."

There was a silence from within the palace, and I wished dearly to be able to see what was happening. Then the other man spoke.

"Who can fathom the will of emperors?"

My lord turned to me, his face hidden in the close shadows of the passage. When he'd been younger, I had always known what my lord was thinking simply by the expression on his face. As he grew older, and the necessity to hide his thoughts became unavoidable, I had developed other ways of knowing: from the tilt of his head or the way he held his shoulders. I had always known what my lord was thinking, even before he told me.

Standing with him in the dark, still robed for sleep and with his hair loose, the braids scattered, I felt only an overwhelming sense of loss radiating around the pair of us.

I didn't know what Mamoru was thinking. Without the experience, I couldn't.

Once again, no sound issued from the palace, no footsteps approaching or receding to alert us to the presence of the lords who'd spoken. If I dared, I would have offered some words of comfort to my lord, but the walls in the palace were thin for a reason. It was then that Mamoru released my sleeve and turned back the way we'd come—back toward the stables.

My only relief came with the knowledge that the lords we'd overheard had not spoken as if anything were amiss. No one had yet discovered my lord's flight. If I could be glad of my actions at all that night, I could at least commend myself for acting quickly.

It was time we needed to distance ourselves from the palace. I didn't know how Iseul would hunt us, though I knew as well as any how clever a general he'd been in the war, and a fiercer man in battle, besides.

I was a mere servant by comparison, but I would die before I let any harm come to Mamoru.

That was the choice I had made.

My lord looked very small in the large, airy stables. He stood next to one of the Volstov horses, his head bowed in deep thought, or in deep sorrow. I would have cut out my own heart before ever I harmed my lord's so, but to save his life, such hurts were necessary. I could only trust that he would be strong enough to survive them, that I had not been weak in training him. At least, I thought, with the wild desperation of a man who has abandoned one duty for another when he'd once been able to serve both, my lord had made his decision. We were there in the stables; he was determined to flee.

"My lord," I said.

"We'll take this horse." Mamoru lifted his head, his voice that of a commander on the battlefield—the very lord whom I'd served under for years. In his face, I saw the Emperor himself, a resemblance that had never shown itself before.

If I could have comforted him the way a hostler comforts a horse by touch, I would have been glad to do it. But my lord stood some distance away from me, remote and unapproachable. I'd brought dreadful news to him, and he might yet blame me for betraying his brother and his empire simply by favoring my loyalty to him.

"If you permit me to make a suggestion," I offered, as though we were playing a game of stones, or he were laboring over a troublesome page of calligraphy. I'd thought things through almost too well, and my lord knew it; his eyes on me were keen and sharp.

"Go on," he agreed.

"I would not suggest it under any other circumstances . . ."

"Go on, Kouje," my lord said again.

Use the old trick against the men who invented it, I thought to myself. It seemed fitting, a small and private revenge, but I couldn't phrase my words that way for Mamoru. "A disguise," I explained, as carefully as I could. "In order to make it past the gates. If we are dressed as servants, then even when questioned, no man will truly think to take note of us."

"Two men riding out on the eve that the prince and his retainer disappear?" Mamoru asked. "Kouje, I don't think—"

"We do not necessarily have to be two men riding out, my lord," I said. "They are poor clothes, and hardly fitting for a prince, but the woman who wore them first kept them clean and in good repair. They should fit you well."

"And for yourself?"

"Something less fine than my banquet clothes," I admitted. It was a shame to acknowledge how much I had prepared without first consulting him, but fear for his life had panicked me. At least, I told myself, what mattered was Mamoru's safety and not how able I was to be proud of myself.

"You've thought of everything," my lord said, his usual sweet mirth replaced by a dull dispassion. He moved like a little ghost, away from the horse, to rest one hand against the wall. "What if I had not come?"

"I would have returned the garments to their proper place," I replied. "No one would ever have noticed them missing."

"They'll notice them now. Perhaps someone will piece together the mystery . . . ?"

I shook my head. "My lord Iseu—The Emperor will not truly have the time or the inclination, if you are missing, to listen to a servant complain about her missing garments, my lord. I should have left money, but I was . . . I didn't think of it."

Mamoru stepped forward. His feet were bare, and I should have put my hands beneath them where he walked to keep the soles from being pricked by hay or sullied by dirt. Before I could offer myself, or at least the maid's cotton slippers, my lord had moved away from the wall to rest that same supporting hand against my arm.

"You have truly thought of everything," he said, and this time, it was more in gratitude.

"I thought that we might tell the men at the gate that you've taken ill, and I was charged with the duty of taking you from the palace as quickly as possible before day broke and the diplomats heard of it," I said, offering my lord the clothes. They were thin, and he took cold easily. I didn't like it, but I could bring his finer robes with us, and perhaps barter with them for something warmer, and shoes that would better serve him. I had no further plan yet. My sister had married a fisherman. Perhaps, if all else failed, I would learn to fish. It was ridiculous and implausible; my lord was a prince, and a fisherman's hut would kill him soon enough, or crush all the beauty out of him. For now, it would serve as a transitory destination. I was rescuing him. That was all I could think of. "While the delegation from Volstov is under the Emperor's care, he cannot allow even the smallest of threats to escape his notice."

Mamoru reached out to me for the maid's clothes, then hesitated. "The Emperor will find us," he said.

I could not hope to protect him, or so he must have thought, against his brother's far reach, against the age-old network of spies, against the soldiers he would send to search us out like wild dogs. Yet I was bound to serve my lord as always. Perhaps I was being too prideful, too sure of my abilities. I *was* no more than a servant, and the gods favored Iseul. In his veins ran their blood.

In Mamoru's, too, I told myself, as I handed him the maid's clothes.

"It will take him some time to send any men after us," I reasoned, as my lord stepped behind an empty stall to undress; I could hear the sound of silk moving against silk, and the crunch of old, brittle hay beneath his feet. I wondered if I had time to go back and find boots for him, and knew even as I thought it that I did not. "He will be busy with the delegation and the treaty, and it will take some doing for him to explain why you are missing. It will take longer still for him to gain permission to send armed men after us, since with the delegation present he will be reluctant to act too precipitously."

That, and my lord had made a favorable impression on the delegates, where I had read nothing but fear and discomfort on their faces while conversing with Iseul. That manner of impression would not have harmed him in the Ke-Han way of thinking, but it might just work in our favor when it came to the delegates' being comfortable with lending Iseul free rein. He was Emperor still, but we were under the thumb of Volstov until otherwise notified.

I could see my lord's eyes in the darkness. They were very pale, and very bright, and dark all around with shadows. I stepped into a shadow of my own to change, careful not to dirty my finest clothes. They'd be worth at least one pair of boots; that way, I would keep Mamoru's fine things for as long as I could.

"Diplomatic talks are always impossible," Mamoru agreed. Though he sounded subdued and resigned, there was faint strength remaining in his words, and an almost desperate humor. "It would take them days just to decide whether or not to open a window, much less—Much less chase down an errant traitor-prince."

"You know them better than I," I said, allowing a tight smile. That was no time for jests or laughter, and so of course we needed them more than ever. It was much akin to battle humor.

After a minute, Mamoru stepped out from behind the stable wall. It was easy enough to see that, despite the shabby clothes, he was every inch the prince, from his posture to the grace of his hands to his very complexion. He'd drawn his hair back clumsily, and covered it with a shawl. I felt my ribs tighten around my heart. My lord was never clumsy. It meant that his hands had been shaking.

But perhaps his clumsiness would work to our advantage, though it hurt me to think of using my lord's distress for any good. There was a certain cruelty in such resourcefulness, despite its practical uses. Iseul was resourceful that way in battle, and though it won him much acclaim, it still sat poorly with lesser men.

I smiled again at my lord, this time mastering the attempt.

"My lord, do you remember the theatre groups who would entertain at the palace?"

Mamoru looked at me with confusion, but nodded. "I do."

"I thought that perhaps, if you thought of this as...something similar, if you imagine yourself an actor, you might affect the posture of a servingwoman, and one who is ill, besides."

It was the only way that I could think to counsel my lord against betraying himself with his movements, his very being. I could not tell Mamoru to be anything other than a prince, but if I could see it so clearly, then others certainly would. Therefore, he would have to think of his disguise as more than that. It was a role, and one that our very lives depended on his playing. I could only trust in my lord's skills, as he was trusting in mine.

"Ah, I see," my lord said. "I do not yet look the part."

"My lord," I began, "it isn't—"

"If I do not, there is no need to spare my feelings," my lord chided. "Here: I will try it better." After a moment's pause, he crossed his arms over his chest and bent nearly double, as though attempting to shield himself from a great wind. The parts of his hair that hung loose from the braids shielded his face, and gave him a rather haphazard and common appearance, very much like a servingwoman who'd worked nonstop throughout the day, with no time to pause and fix her hair once more into its proper place.

He was better at adapting than I had even hoped. Perhaps the gods, in their own way, were on our side after all.

"That's very good," I said, warm where I hadn't allowed myself to be before. "Nearly *perfect,* my lord."

Mamoru lifted his head. In his eyes, I could see the shadows of a faint gratification at such praise, even in the midst of such a situation as ours. "Thank you, Kouje," he said, and I knew it was not entirely for my compliment.

"My lord is a virtuoso," I said, turning my eyes to the various horses, some of which had awoken at even our quiet conversation, and stared at us now with baleful eyes. Best to take one of the diplomats' horses, I thought, since it would not be so easily recognized by the guards who manned the gate at night. They knew all the lords' horses, and I did not trust my lord with a lesser beast. Perhaps the horse we took would even give Iseul some other, more pressing matters to deal with, since a member of the delegation from Volstov would surely question the loss of his mount. Iseul could not give the impression of caring too little for his guests, and so any affront dealt to them would have to be managed most publicly, and with all his resources.

I didn't truly believe that a missing horse would be our miracle, but my lord and I were in need of help wherever we could ask it. At best, it would provide a momentary distraction.

"I think we should take this horse," my lord said. It was the one he'd suggested earlier, a strong-looking animal with a russet coat. Indeed, it looked more like a farmer's draft horse than a lord's mount: perfect for two servants traveling out of the palace.

My approval must have shown on my face, for my lord did smile then, though it was a small and fleeting thing. I saw it as a victory all the same.

My plan would not work without Mamoru behind it. If he did not believe in me, it made no sense for us to leave in the first place.

"Give me your robes," I said. "If my lord will mount first, then I might walk alongside the horse."

My lord looked as though he meant to protest, but he merely turned to retrieve his robes where he'd hung them across the low wall of the stable and handed them to me. I took them, wrapping the fine robes carefully within my own to shield them from any harm, and bundling those again in a plain workman's cloth, the kind in which a servant carried his few belongings. I waited for Mamoru to mount, then secured the bundle behind him, so as to help along the artifice that my lord was a sick servingwoman ejected from the palace until the time came when she was well again.

"If you agree, I think it best that I do most of the talking," I said, easing the stall's gate open. "At least until my lord learns how to speak as a servant."

"Ah, but isn't that a counterfeit statement?" My lord looked down at me from the horse, his hair all in disarray and his clothing plain and mended countless times over. It hurt my heart to see him so transformed, but there was a hint of a smile still upon his lips. "Servants do not speak at all, so how can I ever hope to speak as one?"

I found myself smiling, too, as I led the horse through the quiet of the stables, even as I struggled to lift the beam that sealed the door at night. My lord was clever, and he learned quickly. I did not dare to guess at what result our venture would bring, not then and perhaps not ever, but Mamoru could survive as something other than a prince. I was certain of that, if of nothing else. Perhaps he would never learn the self-deprecation inherent in our words, the coarse grammar and the apologetic tone, but he *would* survive.

The courtyard was silent and empty, though the spare shapes of the rock statues in the sunken garden rose up in crescents and spheres to our left. White sand crunched beneath the horse's mammoth, shaggy hooves. Ahead, the main gate was lit with tall torches, and white paper lanterns lined the main path. I found myself holding on to the reins with an unnecessary force, though I did not speed my pace any, and I kept my breathing steady. Even so, the horse could sense the tension in my hand, and he shook his head, whinnying faintly.

I didn't dare to look up at my lord more than once, but he had his head down, his arms crossed in front of him, as if in the clutches of some uncomfortable affliction. I could not tell whether he was as nervous as I was.

Perhaps I was betraying his trust in me by being so nervous myself.

Then we came to the palace gates, and there was no more room for nerves.

The guards didn't ask any questions. They were trained to be as silent as the servants were. Rather, they stopped us, and waited on protocol. I was the one who must speak, to give them my statement as to who we were, and where we were going.

I'd been practicing it since the moment I'd heard Iseul's pronouncement, though I hadn't realized it then.

"This one's taken ill," I said, hardening my voice; I sounded like a fisherman, and I forced myself to ignore the shame of my lord hearing me speak so commonly. "My lord wishes for me to take her out of the palace before the diplomats get wind of it. The last thing we want is for the talks to be ended over something so foolish as *her* sneezing in someone's breakfast. Or worse, if you take my meaning."

The guard eyed my lord with some trepidation, as though worried the woman in question was going to be ill right then and there. He stepped back to confer with the other guards, who had been listening some distance away. The torchlight flickered and played off the shadows on their faces, the overhang of their antiquated helmets, which combined to give their expressions a masklike quality. If we were a theatre group, and my lord the leading actress, then the guards would be played by men in demon masks, pale white and blood red.

I felt a soft touch at my hand against the reins.

My lord was looking at me, his eyes filled with something like pleading behind the curtain of his hair. In the years during the dragon raids, there had been men who went mad with the fear and the anticipation, of waiting night after night and wondering, *Would they come?* There were no more dragons now, but in Mamoru's eyes I recognized some of that same fear. He did not know how long he must wait, or even what he was waiting for. It was why he had reached out to me in the first place.

I closed my hand over his and held it tight while we waited.

The guard we'd spoken to broke away from the rest to stand in front of us once more. He looked at me, then the horse and then my lord, all with a scrutiny that I would never have allowed if we had been our true selves.

Then, just as I'd become certain that Mamoru would bruise my fingers with the grip he held them in, the guard nodded, and the gate began to open.

"Get out," the guard said, with a nod toward the gate.

I fought down the urge to take him to task for speaking so rudely to my lord, but Mamoru gripped my hand with his own pale fingers and hunched over the horse's neck with a quiet groan. Instead of reprimanding the fool, I thanked him.

Then we were outside the palace.

The last time we'd ridden out of the palace together, my lord had been on his own horse. The sun had been high in the morning sky, the air crisp with the fall of autumn, and he had led his own company of foot soldiers and flag bearers, nearly seven hundred men in all under his command.

My lord shivered, and I led the horse on in silence until the palace walls were the vaguest of shadows behind us, and farther still. I couldn't be too careful.

The road we were on led deep into the heart of the city; if we continued to travel on it, we would reach the old dome by dawn. If we'd but had the time, I would surely have stopped and offered up a prayer there, for our safe passage. It was a familiar route, and a well-traveled one.

I led the horse off the road and under the bower of a maple tree. Its leaves looked black as dry blood in the pale moonlight.

"If you will permit me, my lord," I whispered, as Mamoru bent his ear to my lips, "I must join you on the horse for now. We will travel faster that way, else I would never suggest it—"

"We are no longer in the palace," Mamoru replied. I could see only half his face, the shape of a scythe moon; the rest was turned away from me. "Act practically rather than on protocol."

"My lord," I consented, and swung myself onto the mount behind him. The horse protested for a moment, but merely out of laziness; he was a mammoth beast, and after the first huff of annoyance, he settled into an easy trot. I wished to ride him faster, but the path was a trail too easy to follow. I urged him instead to the trees. It would be a while before we reached the mountains, but we had a better chance of hiding there than in the larger towns along the main roads, and the idea of being caught out in the open did not sit easy with me. I was a servant first and foremost, but I was also a soldier, and one trained to look to the skies, at that.

The Emperor was a different enemy we were fleeing, but Iseul was as formidable as a dragon and twice as clever as its rider.

After a few moments' stiffness, still curled like the ailing serving-woman around himself, my lord relaxed. Sometime after that, he allowed himself to lean back against my chest.

"It seems like something out of an old play," he said, very softly, but even the sound of his own voice seemed to startle him, as though he hadn't known how loud a whisper could be in an empty darkness.

When I'd comforted him on the eve of his first battle, he'd had the strength of an army and his birthright behind him. He was fighting for an empire.

I was silent now, the wind blowing his hair against my neck, the horse moving at a steadfast gait. I wondered how he would run, if pressed to it, for he wasn't a horse built for racing but rather for heavy loads. It was lucky in some ways and a worry in others.

No one will learn we are gone yet, I told myself. We needed only to disappear, and that required subtlety, not speed.

Sometime in the endless night, I heard Mamoru whisper, "Have we chosen the proper course?"

I had no answer for him, and said nothing. Soon enough, he fell asleep.

CHAPTER FOUR

ALCIBIADES

So, the prince was missing.

Caius woke me that morning by shaking my shoulders and laughing delightedly; I was too dazed and too damn tired to ask him at first why he'd come in, much less why he was sitting on my bed. He was the one who broke the news to me, and how he'd known it first before everyone else, I don't know if I'll ever find out.

"Isn't it incredible?" he said, beaming from ear to ear. It was the sort of smile that looked like it hurt. "If you don't get out of bed now, my dear, then we're going to be late."

All I could think about was how we'd been out of bed last night, and how delighted Caius had sounded at the thought of our getting blamed for one scandal or another. The day had only just started, and already I was out of sorts.

I managed an undignified but satisfactorily indifferent grunt; it must have sounded enough like a question that Caius continued as though I'd asked him, pretty as you please, to explain himself more thoroughly.

"The Emperor has called an emergency meeting! Well, wouldn't you? I suppose he wants us all to be there so he can make sure we're with him when he acts. I imagine he knows we don't trust him enough yet that it might spoil the talks to have him hauling off and acting on his own over something this important. He says that the poor young thing is a traitor—can you imagine? A traitor! And I was only just complimenting him on his choice of jade—and that he's been plotting against us all this time."

"Doesn't make sense to me," I managed, watching as Caius launched himself from my bed and began combing his hair—with *my* comb, in front of *my* mirror. "Maybe all that dressing him up like a daughter made him mad or something."

"Oh, who knows," Caius replied. "I can't imagine that sweet little creature betraying anyone. Still and all, we're all to be the Emperor's counsel in the matter. Of course, he can't decide what to do about Prince Mamoru on his own, now that we're in attendance. Alcibiades, *we're* a part of the Emperor's grand council!"

I'd barely got out of bed, and suddenly I was supposed to decide the fate of some idiot Ke-Han prince who'd overstepped his mark? The Ke-Han could do whatever they liked, for all I cared, so long as they left me out of it.

"No thank you," I said. "I'm going back to sleep."

Caius was back at my bedside in an instant, wearing a look of pure horror on his face. Perhaps he thought to rap my knuckles with my comb, which he still held. "You can't be serious," he said. "It's a direct order!"

"So we're taking orders now, is it?" I asked, turning my back on him and wishing there were a proper pillow to be found there—that I might either cover my head and drown out the sound of his voice, or hit him square between the eyes with it. I had an awful crick in my neck from the little wood block that served as my Ke-Han pillow, and I hadn't slept all that well, either, with my head nearly falling off it every time I turned this way or that. A man had to be comfortable, and I was in no mood to be ordered anywhere by an emperor whose culture had come up with a pillow like that. It was remarkable they were able to sleep at night, much less conquer whole countries and give our armies such a good run for such a good long time.

Or maybe this pillow was just reserved for special guests, in which case the second prince could assassinate every last member of the Ke-Han council, and I'd be right behind him on it.

"I don't see *why* you insist on being so *peevish*," Caius said, in a tone that suggested he might have been pouting. I didn't want to know what a pout looked like on that precocious little face. "Since we both know you're coming and that's final, it doesn't make any sense for you to put up such a fuss. It's only embarrassing for you later when you think of the scene you caused, and all for nothing!"

"Get out of here while I get dressed, then," I snarled, ready to fling the rock-hard pillow at his head if necessary, but he was already skipping out of the room.

"Ten minutes!" he cooed back at me, like a songbird.

I rubbed the back of my neck, which was stiff *and* sore, and thought about whether or not I could barricade the adjoining door at night with what meager furnishing my room'd been allotted.

Anyway, that was how I'd wound up in a grand council—and I'd never seen a more mismatched, ill-suited group of surly and impassive faces all crammed together into the same room—listening to the Emperor give some speech about how his brother was a traitor and in some cases you had to cut off your own right hand for the greater good of the rest, should it fall to rot. Josette looked about ready to fall to rot herself, like she'd still have been asleep if it had been up to her, and she kept twiddling at the fancy Ke-Han hair ornament that she'd pinned up her curls with. Marius, seated next to her, seemed wide-awake, but he was frowning down at the table like he wanted it to be the Emperor.

I wasn't the only one who didn't like what I was hearing, then.

Sure, it was the Emperor's own brother, and he probably knew the situation better than I could from the outside. But the point remained—and here was what stuck in my throat—that I just wasn't ready to sit back and eat everything he fed me. There was something about the way he was talking, something about the way he held himself, that stank.

Even Caius, crooked in the head as he was, could tell that the second prince wasn't the sort of man who would just up and betray his brother out of the blue. He'd been blushing the other day at the banquet, just because he'd managed to pronounce a few Volstov words right. And it'd been his bodyguard, not he, himself, who'd gone for it when Caius got too close.

The sort of man who wasn't on the defensive in the slightest wasn't the sort who was plotting something.

In short, the Emperor was selling—and pretty hard, too—but I wasn't buying. Not yet.

Then I thought I caught my name, which made me snap to attention quick as anything—though part of that was to do with the elbow Greylace had thrown into my side. He was a sharp little lizard, and I was going to pay him back for that. Just as soon as I figured out what was going on.

One of the red-faced lords seated next to the Emperor was speaking. He looked like a kettle ready to whistle, trembling slightly with the force of his words. Or maybe it was just his reaction to the Emperor, who was looking at him with intent interest. I was real glad that the Emperor'd never had cause to look at *me* like that, but I was even more glad that I wasn't the man next to him, who seemed to be experiencing his own personal rainstorm of spittle.

"Not that I wish to cast aspersions," he went on. "I merely wanted to bring it up as a matter of course so that we might dismiss the possibility up front and get along with our business."

I was still lost. Casimiro snorted, his hands folded against the table. Josette was staring daggers at me, and Greylace was sitting still as a little doll, neat and unhelpful as you please.

That was just great.

Fiacre opened his mouth to speak, then seemed to think the better of it and turned to me.

"General Alcibiades, I imagine, can explain himself quite capably."

Just as I was thinking that I might have to toss pride aside for sense—and kick myself for it later—Josette shifted in her seat and sat up straight.

"This is all so silly," she began, drawing a fan out of her sleeve as though she was embarrassed, which was about the most ridiculous thing I could imagine, since I was pretty sure Josette hadn't been embarrassed since the day she was born. "I'm afraid it's my fault, only General Alcibiades is too much the gentleman to place the blame on a woman. The fact of the matter is we were all up quite late together, the three of us, discussing what a lovely reception we'd been given in your honored palace. I quite lost track of the time, so that it was well past midnight when I sent him and Caius Greylace back to their rooms."

The Emperor raised his eyebrows and settled back into his seat. There was a smile on his face, but it wasn't a kind one.

"They were seen near the kitchens," he pointed out, as if commenting on some minor mistake Josette had made in an equation, and not like he knew she'd just spun that whole story out of nothing, which she most definitely had.

"Surely you can't expect everyone to have memorized their way through your magnificent palace already," Josette said coyly, but with a hint of steel.

The Emperor tilted his head, resting it against forefinger and thumb while he gazed at Josette like he was trying to decide whether or not to have her removed from the room. Caius laid his hand against my arm underneath the table, and I was so keyed up I almost hit him. Tensions like that always made my blood run hot—it was like the calm before a battle.

Then just like that, the Emperor nodded and shifted to sit up straight once more.

"Lord Jiro, I thank you for your concern, but I do not believe any man or woman from the delegation was responsible for the disappearance of my brother. We are all . . . united in our wish for peace, and such an act would make our talks impossible."

Fiacre nodded, not betraying one way or another how he felt about the matter, but I was pretty damn sure he was going to be chewing Josette's ear off the next time we adjourned.

I tried to catch her eye, but she was waving her fan back and forth and wouldn't look at me.

"Back to the matter at hand," the Emperor said, leaning to one side to reach for a sheaf of papers.

When he moved, his jewelry swung, and I caught sight of something he hadn't been wearing the night before. It was a strange little necklace, with what looked like a red pendant at the end of a thin silver chain. Except that as I caught sight of how it refracted the light, and how the color changed depending on which way he moved, I realized it wasn't a pendant at all, but a little vial of blood dangling pretty as you please and resting just over his heart.

That was just creepy, any way you sliced it. I'd have to ask Marcy later if she'd seen it.

". . . in the best interests of Volstov," the Emperor was still rattling on. His translator was hard pressed to keep up with him. "Gentlemen and ladies, surely you must understand our distress. We have done our best to prepare for your arrival, only to encounter such a betrayal. We will do all we can to protect the terms of the provisional treaty. If you give your permission—for in the spirit of the relationship we hope to foster, we would not act without it—we will employ all our might to unearth the traitor and bring him before a bipartisan court—a court both Ke-Han and Volstovic, for we would have none other."

Caius, sitting next to me, sat up straighter. No doubt he was just excited about the idea of getting to decree a real, live Ke-Han beheading. Across the table from me, Ozanne looked rather pale.

"Of course we understand your position," Fiacre responded, when it was our turn to speak. He had a nice, friendly voice, but it sounded smart, too; the sort of man you wanted to be head of your peace talks because he was slippery but he didn't sound it, at first. Real smooth. And he'd shrewdly chosen a translator who managed to echo his diplomat's tone. "And we do not wish a traitor of any kind to run loose in your kingdom. And yet we question the wisdom of releasing so many soldiers in pursuit of him. Surely, to show such an armed presence will merely..."

And so it went, on and on, long past what should have been breakfast and even through what I could only guess was supposed to be lunchtime. By the time there was any kind of pause, my stomach had turned into a tightened, empty fist and it was making the kinds of noises that were sure to offend some petty Ke-Han lord having a real bad morning—one who was just looking for a fight.

"Lunch?" Caius offered, and for once, I actually agreed.

Back in our rooms, we ate our rice—I was going to get sick of that very soon, I could tell—and, glad to have something in my belly at last, I made the mistake of asking him if he'd seen that queer necklace the Emperor had been wearing. Marcy'd disappeared, and I guessed it had been on my mind more than I'd thought.

"He wasn't wearing it last night, as far as I could see," I added, trying to shovel my rice into my mouth straight from the bowl with those infernal sticks. There was no other way to use them, I was sure of it.

"He wasn't," Caius agreed, then, on sudden inspiration, jabbed his own sticks excitedly toward my face. He was going to have to stop tempting me to hit him and call it simple reflex. "Oh! I know what it might be. Have you heard of the Ke-Han blood magic?"

"Rumors," I admitted, however grudgingly. Those were the kinds of stories that had been told around the campfire—born of fear and breeding more fear. A soldier told those stories to other soldiers so it was easier to hate the enemy. "Blood magic" had a definition that varied, depending on who was telling the story that night, and though it might've had some grounding in truth once upon a time, it'd grown beyond that. One time it had to do with killing lions and drinking their blood; another it had to do with how the magicians in the lapis city worked their magic by using blood as ink when they practiced their calligraphy. I'd stopped listening to the stories a long while back since I didn't need any more reason to hate anyone, especially the Ke-Han.

It was the sort of information I'd needed to purposefully put from my mind in order to embark on this trip without taking my grievances up with th'Esar himself. As a reward, I might have said, for all my good services to the crown, d'you think I could have had a damn vacation and not some more fucking work? And, promptly, I'd've been banished from my home, which, after years of fighting, was the last thing I wanted. So I'd swallowed the memories and kept biting my tongue.

Only the very phrase brought back campfire nights, in the belly of some mountain, listening to the rumble of the dragons overhead, or the howl of the trebuchets as they let each new fireball loose.

"You're wearing a curious expression," Caius said.

"Don't like the rice," I answered.

"Hm," Caius said, not entirely satisfied, but clearly not yet willing to be deterred from imparting what he saw as vital information. "In any case, I read all about it when I was in exile, you know. Fascinating people, the Ke-Han, with their odd little rituals and their quaint ideas. If Iseul's wearing that vial of blood—oh, if only we could ask him!—it probably isn't his."

"All right," I said. "How d'you figure that?"

"Because the magic is very simple, really," Caius said. "In many ways, it operates as a microcosm of the way in which they poisoned our Well: If you poison the river, you poison the whole ocean. Contaminate the source—in this case a mere few drops of blood—and it's possible to kill the man who owned it. Or so the book said. I'm sure that's vastly oversimplified, but until I can learn to translate Ke-Han texts..." He shrugged delicately. "*Brilliant,* though, isn't it?"

I thought of lying prone in the Basquiat, wondering how long it would take me to die, listening to the god-awful coughing move like it was catching from cot to cot, and how I had a power in me—something to do with water, *real* useful Margrave Royston had said, then never bothered elaborating on, the horse's ass—that I'd never asked for and didn't want, running like blood through my veins and making it easier to strike me down without so much as a warning.

Brilliant wasn't exactly what I'd call it.

Twisted, maybe. Tortured. The product of a people we'd been fighting and hating—both, maybe, for equally good reasons—for generations. And *fucked*. I put my rice bowl down.

"Not hungry?" Caius asked, though something in his eyes suggested he'd sensed his blunder and was actually perplexed as to how he'd offended me this time. I didn't bother acknowledging it and just looked away, since, sitting so close, it was easy to see how strange his eyes were. They were different colors, one of them green and the other one, carefully hidden behind the fall of his silky hair, a pale, murky white.

"Finished," I gritted out.

"Good!" he said, all good cheer suddenly restored. "Because we're going to be late."

The last thing I wanted was another few hours of listening to Fiacre and the Emperor go back and forth, with the occasional addition by Josette or another member of our merry band, while the rest of the Ke-Han warlords kept silent as the grave. But that was what I got. I was going to fall asleep in the middle of it all if it went on too much longer, and that was a hard enough task to manage, since they had us set up in parallel lines facing each other down the length of a long, stuffy room, sitting on nothing more than uncomfortable pillows. It was worse than Volstov diplomacy, which was sheer torture if you caught the men from the bastion on a day for arguing taxes. But at least, in Volstov, they had the decency to provide you with chairs.

One of my legs had lost all feeling, and I'd stopped listening entirely, when suddenly everyone was putting something to a vote.

I looked around the room, desperate for some clue. What were we deciding on? It was still only the first day of deliberation, so it couldn't have been anything that crucial, but the look on the Emperor's face implied otherwise. He looked determined behind that stony mask, a statue carved out of pure iron will.

"Don't worry," Caius whispered. "It's for whether or not we should spend the rest of the day trying to decide how many men should go after the prince, or retire for now and finish the day that was planned for us, before this . . . unforeseen event arose. The Emperor himself isn't voting, however—it's bad form."

The way I saw it, the Emperor was clearly hoping for the vote to go toward the former. If he could keep us trapped there even an hour or so longer, he'd probably wear Fiacre down into agreeing on a number. If we started afresh the next day, new stubbornness would have set in after the night, and it would be harder to convince our men of anything.

I already knew which way I was voting.

The other men and women from Volstov must've been thinking along the same lines as I was, since the vote came down to retiring for the night. Maybe they were just tired; I didn't care. I took grim satisfaction in being able to think I'd thwarted the Emperor. Maybe it was petty, but then again I'd never told anyone I was the man for this sort of job. It'd just been decided for me, and I was going to play it the way I saw fit, short of getting into any real trouble.

"Ah, fresh air," Caius said, standing next to me and breathing in deeply before letting out a fluttery little sigh. I'd heard women make that kind of noise. "Well! What do you think we should do now?"

"What should *we* do?" I spluttered, since I'd been looking forward all day to finally shaking him off once night rolled around.

"I thought," Caius went on blithely, "that we might request guidance to the menagerie. Of course, it won't be what it was before the war—so many of the animals were lost or killed, you know, during the final attack of the dragons on the capital—but I still hear it's uncommonly beautiful. Just the sort of relaxation we need after a hard day deliberating, don't you agree?"

I didn't, and I had half a mind to tell him exactly what I *did* agree to. And none of it involved him.

Except he'd turned his back on me almost immediately and, in the midst of the crowd—stony-faced warlords and passive servants and stretching men and women from Volstov, all of whom suddenly looked just as tired and uncomfortable as I felt—he was waving down some hapless creature.

"Menagerie!" he said, gesturing wildly with his arms. I thought he looked like a bird—but that was probably what he was going for. "Animals? We'd like to go there."

The servant shook his head. No doubt he thought the pale-skinned sprite was mad. He was right.

Caius sighed, and said something I didn't understand. Half of it sounded like a question and half of it sounded like a command, but all of it sounded like the Ke-Han.

"Seems you're a little too fluent," I said.

"Oh, I know the odd elementary phrase here and there," Caius replied.

"And 'Would you take us to see the menagerie' is one of them?"

Caius's lips twitched unevenly, the left corner lifting higher than the right. He looked like an imp. "I learned what I thought I'd need," he said. "And as you can see, it's served us both. This patient young man is going to show us the peacocks."

"You're going to see the menagerie?" Josette asked, suddenly beside us. "You know, I think that's just the thing I need this evening. Is it very far?"

Caius tapped the side of his jaw with one finger. The nail was a perfect oval, manicured like that of a woman at the Fans. "It isn't too far a walk, from what I recall. Certainly the sort of brisk evening stroll to put color on a lady's cheeks."

"You should enjoy it too, then," Josette said wryly.

I'd never minded Josette, at least. If I was lucky—which I wasn't, but I still liked to hope—then he'd talk to her all night and leave me right out of it.

"You will pardon my intrusion," a Ke-Han-accented voice said from just behind me, "but if you are going to the menagerie, then it is only fitting you should be taken there by a guide, and not a servant."

I turned, not liking the way he spoke—he was too confident at it, for one thing, and a confident man of the Ke-Han set off all kinds of alarms, no matter how much I'd supposedly trained myself out of those old soldier's reactions.

It was the lord who'd sat to the left of the Emperor. He'd been introduced the night before, and when I tried to remember, the name came back to me as one of the most important in the quick tutorial the 'Versity students had given all the diplomats who didn't know their asses from their elbows: Lord Temur.

Caius, of course, was ecstatic.

"Would *you* offer your services to us, my lord?" he asked, like a blushing maiden entertaining her suitor. "I've been *so* looking forward to seeing the peacocks!"

He was laying it on a little bit thick, I thought, but Lord Temur proffered a faint, unreadable smile. A civility, as far as I could tell, but at least he was trying. His hair boasted more braids than the young prince's had, but fewer than his formidable bodyguard's. I was starting to judge men by the quality of their hair—a peculiarity I didn't altogether enjoy noting in myself, but it was useful there. Lord Temur looked fierce, but fewer braids meant that he was more of a diplomat than he was a soldier. Or maybe he had men to do all his soldiering for him. I didn't know, and I didn't plan on making polite conversation with the man until I could find out.

"That's very kind of you to offer," Josette added, ever the diplomat. I thought that the lord hadn't so much offered himself as given a shrewd counsel, but that was the danger in coming too close to the swirling tornado of conversation that was Caius Greylace. Even an important Ke-Han warlord wasn't immune to getting swept up, turned all about, and spat back out again whenever the storm grew tired of its latest plaything.

But Lord Temur didn't seem too concerned about that though he couldn't have realized the danger yet. Instead of running for the hills, he extended to Josette the same thin smile he'd given Caius and offered his arm. There was just enough time for Josette to look surprised then flattered before Caius launched himself into the gap between them like a small, very well-groomed dog doing a trick with a hoop.

"You are *too* kind," he murmured, beaming that grin that made him look more like a jack-o'-lantern than a person. He laid his hand delicately on Lord Temur's arm like he was used to getting that sort of treatment. "Oh! What a lovely fabric."

I didn't think that Lord Temur was the sort of man who concerned himself with what fabric his robes were made out of though there was no way of telling that from the expression on his face. Disregarding that smile, I hadn't ever seen his face lose its calm, blank stare. Not even during the talks.

"The menagerie is this way," he said, and bowed, before turning around and starting off. Caius looked pleased as punch.

"Now, you mustn't think me rude, but are you quite certain that *all* the lions are safely within their cages?" he asked.

Like Caius Greylace didn't know already he was perfectly capable of handling a lion or two. If I could trust the stories—and I was more and more sure than ever that I could—then he'd already handled his fair share of them.

Lord Temur said something in a low undertone that I didn't quite catch, but I gathered from Caius's tinkling laughter that it was the height of Ke-Han wit.

Josette gave me a baffled look, which was as clear an indication as I was going to get that she thought Caius as nutty as I did. Maybe it was best to let our fine Lord Temur deal with him all night, though it'd give him a really odd cross section of the diplomats.

If anytime, that was my chance to escape.

"Oh, no you don't," said Josette, a suspicious look in her eye. "You're not bolting and leaving me here with Greylace and one of the seven Ke-Han warlords."

"I think he likes you," I said.

Caius and Lord Temur were walking up the white sand path, and coming to the garden that contained all the strange stone statues. We were going to have to run to catch up to them. Surprisingly, I didn't mind the idea. I'd been waiting all day to stretch my legs.

Josette gave me a look that suggested if she hadn't been such a diplomat, she'd have punched me square in the jaw for that last remark. Then she started off down the pathway, leaving me to catch up with her. I didn't offer her my arm when I did, but she took it anyway.

I didn't really see the purpose in going to a zoo at night, especially when it was nearing dark already, the sky stained a mottled blue-purple, like the ribbon Caius was wearing in his hair. (Knowing him, he'd probably calculated what night looked like, and picked out a ribbon that morning to match.) At least the air didn't get a chill in it as soon as the sun went down, the way it did in Volstov. That was one positive thing I could say for the Ke-Han and their country though I wasn't going to be making a habit of it or anything.

Up ahead of us, I could hear Caius's fluttering laughter as they discussed the price of tea, or the artwork in the diplomats' rooms, or the quality of silk, or all the trivial what-have-yous that Caius liked to talk about. I couldn't tell from Lord Temur's voice whether he was bored out of his mind or just plain bemused. From what I'd heard of the Ke-Han language, it was common to speak all in monotone. I guessed it went along nicely with not having any expression on your face, so that nobody could ever tell what the hell you were actually thinking. I couldn't even imagine what he thought of Caius's theatrical Volstovic.

Josette pointed to a distant hill, some ways outside the garden where a bunch of fat, colorful flowers was growing. "Oh, look!" she cried, sounding more like Caius than I'd ever heard her. "Chrysanthemums!"

Lord Temur turned around at that, his eyebrows raised. I didn't like how he understood everything we were saying so easily. Some might have looked at it like a gesture of goodwill, but to me it just felt like spying. The 'Versity scholars had explained that the Ke-Han language was one that took years to perfect, and that speaking it halfway was loads worse than not speaking it at all, but I couldn't help feeling like we were at a disadvantage, since the Ke-Han could retreat behind their soft, hurried consonants, and we had nowhere to hide at all.

"They are a symbol of the Emperor's reign," said Lord Temur, shielding his eyes from the setting sun to look up at the chrysanthemum garden. "No one else is permitted to cut them."

"Ah, I see," said Josette, and she looked more disappointed than I'd have thought, over a handful of too-big flowers.

"He's better than a guidebook," I muttered under my breath.

Caius shot me a reproving look. It figured that he would have freakish hearing on top of his freakish everything else.

"We have nearly reached the menagerie," said Lord Temur. "As I have assured your companion, all the lions are safely within their cages tonight."

It wasn't so much the lions that gave me cause to doubt, but then I supposed there wasn't much harm in going to look at a bunch of animals, of all things. Besides, there were three of us and one of him, so if things got ugly, we could just feed him to something that liked fresh meat and hope for the best.

The gates of the menagerie were wrought-iron bars, shaped into a graceful and purposeless design, the way the Ke-Han seemed to like best. The stone walls were a clean white—the sort that only *stays* clean for a year or so, maybe, before the elements get to it.

Then I remembered how Caius had been prattling on about the menagerie being destroyed in the dragons' last attack on the city—at least I thought that was what he'd been talking about, since I'd been trying to get to sleep at the time. The reason everything looked so new and shiny was because they'd only just rebuilt it.

They'd done a decent job, I supposed. There was white gravel all along the pathways, and bright, spidery-thin vines that draped down the white walls on the inside. There were dainty orange flowers blooming here and there, and a white sign at a fork in the path that said which animals were in which direction. At least, that was what I assumed it said, since the thing was written in the Ke-Han language, which meant that it looked like a game of noughts and crosses to me, but there were shadow-pictures of animals next to the foreign words, so my guess couldn't be too far off the mark.

In the distance, I heard the sharp call of a bird that wasn't a peacock.

Caius looked thrilled.

"Which should we see first, my dears? The lions? I see there are *leopards* also, how fearsome!"

"Yes, terrible," said Josette. "I'm sure we'll find ourselves all aquiver."

"What sort of bird was that, do you suppose?" I asked, since it didn't matter to me one way or another which animals we saw first. Though it wasn't the sort of thing a person could say outright—for the sake of diplomacy and all—I would rather have seen the menagerie just after it'd been destroyed, with the animals running every which way, loose and fierce and proud. They wouldn't look the same in cages, and, as much as I didn't like the idea of lions roaming free all around me, I liked the idea of them behind bars even worse.

"There is a section devoted entirely to the songbirds," Lord Temur explained, patient as anything, like he hadn't just been sitting through the same bastion-damned long day as the rest of us. "They were the young prince's favorite. Ah." He paused, apparently remembering what the talks that day had been all about in the first place, and turned toward the other fork in the pathway. "Perhaps my companions would like to see the cats of prey? I regret to say that we have not yet replaced the white tigers that were lost to us earlier this year, but we have all the rest."

Things were changing pretty fast there within the Ke-Han, you had to admit, and it was a miracle most of them were able to get up in the morning and go about their business properly, much less keep those blank looks on their faces and hold their heads up high. I didn't envy them their position one bit, but we'd given them what they deserved. They'd taken enough land, conquered too many people, and got greedy. All we'd done was make sure they didn't get any farther than the Cobalts. Took us long enough, too.

"The black panther was once considered a god," Lord Temur continued, to the sound of Caius's delighted "oohs" and Josette's sharp "ah!" "A long time ago, though he is still respected in deference to the old ways. You can still read of his mighty place in some of the historical scrolls."

"Do you think we will be allowed to see the libraries?" Caius asked delightedly, missing the point entirely. "My grasp of your language, my lord, is rudimentary at best, but perhaps you would be willing to allow me to usurp your time for the cause of history?"

"It would be my pleasure," Lord Temur replied, because he had to.

Meanwhile, I was watching the black panther. If he had once been a god, then it looked like he still knew it—somewhere, anyway, beneath all the lazy indifference. He was lounging on a low-hanging, stout branch, one paw dangling over the edge and his graceful tail just brushing the ground. He was watching us like we didn't matter to him one way or another, and it wasn't because of the bars that he felt so easy.

But the bars were still there, after all, and he was still behind them. God or no, he was a zoo animal, and we were there to make a show out of him, not pay our respects.

Volstov had its own menageries, of course, and its own fair share of caged animals. Still, as the panther lifted its half-lidded slit eyes to me and yawned, I didn't like the feeling the whole thing gave me, not one bit.

MAMORU

The dim, terrible happenings of the night before—as remote and impossible as the actions of puppets on the stage—should have dissolved the moment I opened my eyes. They felt like a nightmare.

They were not.

When I woke, I barely knew where I was; all I did know was that I was cold and that my arm was stiff and twisted beneath me. Something soft was beneath my head, but the rest of my body felt as though I were lying on a bed of twigs.

I moved, my arm useless, as though I were a veteran of war who'd lost it in the fighting.

Kouje was somewhere, close by as always, and he would tell me where we were and what news the morning brought. I didn't remember falling asleep. The last memory I did have of the night before was the steady rhythm of the Volstov mount beneath me and the rustle of the wind through the trees all around us, like women gossiping at court.

Were they already gossiping about me?

I sat up, brushing leaves out of my hair while my hand tingled back into feeling. I'd been lying on the ground, underneath the protection of a maple tree; the bundle of my clothes, wrapped around with Kouje's and then with a plain workman's cloth, had been under my head to serve as a pillow. The horse was nearby, tethered to a low branch, stomping lazily and poking his nose into the underbrush. He was hungry. My stomach tightened in sympathy. I was hungry, too.

There was a soft rustling from the bushes near us, and I felt a sudden fear take hold of my chest, causing my heart to pound double where it had been nearly calm. Moments later, Kouje emerged from between a parting in the brush, two rabbits held within his hands and a look on his face that suggested he wished for the quiet surroundings of the palace, where there were no bushes at all to rustle and signal his approach. His braids were undone.

"I hope I did not wake you, my lord," he said.

"You should have," I countered. It was true, not merely a childish fit of willfulness. If everything that had passed the previous night was true, then I could no more afford to sleep in than I could allow Kouje to go on indulging me as though I were still a prince. I'd conceded all rights to that title the moment I'd left the palace.

I felt a curious melancholy throbbing in my chest as the beat of my heart slowed, but I paid it no mind.

Kouje put the rabbits down and knelt in front of me beneath the bower of the maple. For a moment, it would have been easy to close my eyes and imagine we were back at the palace, or even on a campaign for the war, and had been separated from our men by a storm the night before. But my clothing was rough and unfamiliar under my fingers, and my back hurt from sleeping on the hard ground, and I could not hide the truth from myself.

It would only make the inevitable conclusion worse.

"Rise," I told him, swallowing down my darker thoughts. "We don't have time for such formalities, Kouje. *Please* rise. I see you've brought us breakfast."

Kouje lifted his head, looking apologetic where he might have looked proud. After all, he'd woken before me, and had managed to catch us a meal while I continued sleeping. If anyone should have looked apologetic, it was I.

"I know it is a meager offering, my lord," Kouje began, "and we have nothing to season them with, but I thought . . . if you were hungry . . ."

"They look very fine," I said, not allowing him to continue. "Why, I'm quite sure we had worse fare in the mountains, come to think of it."

Kouje laughed quietly, making me feel infinitely better about my small joke. There had never been a worse time to make light of a situation, I felt sure, but that was what drove me to it. I knew that Kouje would never indulge in such humor, but in doing so myself I kept him from becoming overly somber.

It seemed all the more important that we look after one another, and all the more important that I coax Kouje out of the habits that the palace had bred into him. Such deference from him to me, as I was clothed, would certainly lead to us getting caught; if not there in the forest, then inevitably somewhere else.

"I shall prepare them, then," Kouje said, and rose once more.

I watched him first twist what remained of his braids back out of his eyes, then roll up his sleeves. He bent to gather dry moss and sticks from the underbrush, bundling them together in his fists until he had enough to strike a fire with the flint from his pouch. I looked away when he pulled out the knife, hating to display such weakness. Tomorrow, I told myself, feeling my own hair as one snarled knot at the nape of my neck. Tomorrow, I would be the one to prepare breakfast.

"Kouje?" I set my fingers to the careful task of working the knots out of my hair, one by one.

I wasn't looking, but I heard the pause in his work. "Yes, my lord?"

"I've been thinking. If I am truly to master this disguise, then you mustn't bow to me, not even in private."

"My lord," Kouje began, sounding strangled, as though I'd just suggested he cut off the heads of all seven warlords.

I pressed on ruthlessly. I had to be ruthless. That was what Iseul had always wanted from me, though perhaps it was a joke of the gods that events had driven me to it at last. "And you mustn't call me 'my lord' anymore, either. Don't you see, Kouje? We're bound to . . . give the game away when it matters most. You're so in the habit of it already; I am as well. I need you to help me, or else I fear we'll never—Well. I believe it's for the best if we both learn to unlearn what was customary at the palace."

Kouje was silent after that. I could hear the crackling of the fire and the sizzle of the rabbits on their sticks, but there was no reply to what I'd said. I turned once I'd completed my braid, with the sinking feeling that I'd gone too far or said too much.

Kouje knelt in front of the fire, his eyes closed, buried deep in thought. His hands weren't tending to the rabbits anymore, but to his own hair, methodically removing each braid from its place and undoing them, one by one. All at once, I felt a fierce rush of grief run through me, for the loss of my father and now of my brother, too, the subjects and lands that had been ours to shepherd and protect. My friends. My room in the palace. The walk by the gardens. The way the light came in through the window and woke me.

We had lost so much over the course of the years, then had finally faced true defeat at the end of the war. I'd earned my braids alongside Kouje, fighting to honor my father and our country. I'd stood with him as he earned braids of his own. Watching him as he removed them from his own hair was like watching the magician's dome destroyed in a blaze of dragonfire and smoke. It was like having the years of my life, each triumph, scattered worthless at my feet, so many broken twigs upon the forest floor.

The fire snapped, sending a hiss of sparks up into the air. The rabbit was dripping fat into the flames. I felt as though I couldn't breathe.

"Your breakfast is ready, my lord," said Kouje. His hair was kinked from its long confinement, and loose as I had never seen it before. He offered me the smallest of smiles, his own habit from our days at the palace; this, however, was one we could allow. "I apologize. Mamoru."

The air was awkward between us, and we were separated suddenly by more than just the sound of the fire. Still, for now, this awkwardness would have to serve. Eventually, Kouje would grow better used to speaking my given name, and I would grow better used to hearing it.

No one ever called me by my proper name, save for my father and my brother, but one was dead and the other wished for me to join him. There was only Kouje left to me.

It was the strangest breakfast I'd ever eaten, which was not to say it wasn't satisfactory; it was merely that fresh meat in the morning wasn't my usual fare. I thanked Kouje for it nonetheless, and ate my full share. Anything less would have made him worry. Besides which, I *was* hungry.

What I wouldn't have done, though, for a bowl of rice.

After that, Kouje obliterated all signs of our presence, brushing leaves this way and that and destroying the fire he'd set to cook the rabbits. He spoke very little, save to ask me if I would like to bathe. He must have sensed my reluctance, as well as its reasons—we were too close to the palace yet and I didn't want to risk any delay. He didn't mention it again.

Then, we rode.

The farther we went, the more I was certain we were straying farther still from any path I'd ever known. I felt as though I were running away because I very much *was,* but the loneliness I felt beyond that was not simply due to all I had lost: It was due also to all I didn't know. Even the trees were unfamiliar to me, and I began to realize that I would evermore be the stranger.

"Where do you think we'll go?" I asked, loud enough to distract myself from my thoughts. I was sorry for it when the birds above us in the tree branches flapped their wings, a few of them even taking sudden flight.

Kouje didn't admonish me, though I thought perhaps he should have. His silence told me everything.

After a little while, however, he did speak. "We'll travel as far away as we can from the palace," he said, his words more quiet and more circumspect than mine had been. I was glad to listen to him talk; if only he were a man better suited for idle conversation. "It takes us a considerable distance out of the way, but . . ." He paused for a moment, listening to something deeper in the woods, then relaxed. I would have to do my best to distract him from his own worries, I realized—even if I was able only to chatter on foolishly about the weather. He was tense as a drawn bow behind me. "I'd thought to take you to a small fishing village near the mountains," he concluded at last. "I should have consulted you, but it seemed the best plan last night."

"It's better than hiding in the mountains with the tricksters and the foxes," I pointed out.

"I suppose that was my thinking yesterday," Kouje agreed.

The horse's hooves beat out an inexorable rhythm beneath us. I couldn't bear to listen to it, the amiable beast bearing me toward an unnamed *elsewhere*. I pressed on through the thicket of conversation for that reason alone. "This fishing village," I said. "How do you know of it?"

"My sister married a fisherman," Kouje said, after a long, taciturn pause. "She lives there. It would . . . be something, for a time."

I harbored a momentary warmth. "Have you been there before?"

"Never had time," he admitted. "But I do know where it is, well enough, at least, to find it."

"Will we . . . will we stay there, do you think?"

A mosquito buzzed by my ear, and a moment later sang at the horse. He whinnied unhappily, flicked his tail once or twice, and Kouje reined him in, guiding him in a sudden, sharp turn left. We were going west if we were to draw close to the mountains.

The mountains were where Iseul had fought; I'd been beside him in battle once, but they were foreign and remote to me, the distant and jagged symbol of separation. Men who fought in the mountains came back changed, and only on a very clear summer's day could you even see the top of the range from the palace. They were like the great wall of an old tale, a boundary marked out by nature. My people knew them better than the soldiers of Volstov, but I myself had no knowledge of them, although some nights, when I was much younger, I would dream of being caught in the mazes that wound their way through the rock— trapped, as Iseul once described it to me, by the shifting of ancient stone.

I wondered how anyone could dwell near the mountains without living each day in their massive shadow terrified some change in the earth or breath from the gods would send them crashing down.

"I wouldn't know how long we could," Kouje said. "I've no idea how to catch fish for a living. Besides, just think of the smell."

It took me a moment to realize he was teasing me. I hid my laugh against my rough cotton sleeve—an affectation of the court and one I'd have to shake off as well, though it seemed more than awkward to laugh into my palms. Besides which, the latter barely muffled the sound properly.

After that, we rode comfortably enough. Kouje pointed small things out to me along the way to keep us talking—such as the osmanthus trees that grew in a scattered fashion among the hardier trees, and bloomed delicate clusters of white flowers against evergreen leaves. When a bird cawed above us we would play a game to guess which type of bird it was, or if there was a rustle in the bushes that frightened us we'd guess as to whether it was a rabbit or a fox, and so on.

When we stopped at last to give the horse some rest and stretch our stiff legs, I no longer had any idea where we were, nor any idea how Kouje knew.

"How can you follow the sun under so many trees?" I asked him.

"I'll teach you," he said, and I agreed. After all, we had the time.

We mounted once again after no more than a brief respite and began the jostling trip anew.

It was senseless, mindless, numbing; we traveled toward a destination I'd only just begun to envision, and one which was farther away than even imagination could calculate. I wondered what the little houses looked like, if they were made of wood or straw or clay, and how the people dressed. I'd never seen a fisherman or, for that matter, a fisherwoman.

When it began to grow dark, the mosquitoes swarmed around us in earnest—whirlwinds of them that whined and stung. Kouje waved them away as best he could while I told the beginnings of the story of the monkey god and his quest to find the setting sun. We, too, were traveling west, and the story was one of Kouje's favorites.

At last, when it was dark enough that the owls were hooting and my stomach was cramped with hunger, we stopped again by a stream where the sound of running water drowned out the cries of the night birds. Kouje led the horse to drink.

"Are you hungry?" he asked. I sensed that he was not.

"I ate very well at breakfast," I replied, resting a hand over my stomach in the darkness to quiet it. If I said I was hungry, then Kouje would never have thought twice before he went chasing noises through the shadowy bushes. It was better if we both slept now and ate after the sun rose. "I believe I'm able to manage until morning."

Whether Kouje believed my lie fully or not, he didn't press the matter. I lay awake for a long time after that, hearing an errant mosquito flit past my cheek now and then, listening to the water flow over the rocks and to my stomach growling.

For the second time, I woke to find Kouje gone.

Cursing myself, I washed my face in the stream and drank from it, then washed the dust-coated hem of my stolen maid's costume. There was dust between my toes, so I washed my feet, as well, and did what I could to clean the dirt from under my fingernails.

When Kouje returned, again with rabbits, my own shame was momentarily silenced by my hunger. Matters were less complicated in the woods. I didn't apologize until after we both ate.

"Next time, you must wake me," I said, helping him to destroy the site of the fire. "It isn't a command, Kouje, it's . . . it's a request."

Kouje looked at me as though the word was something entirely foreign to him. Perhaps it was. Then he bowed his head, but the gesture was more a concession than a display of worship. It would have to suffice, for now.

"My lord—" He stopped himself, looking frustrated and ashamed in equal measures. "*Mamoru.* I believe we might be best served at passing through one of the villages. We're far enough away now that there is little chance of being caught out; littler chance still of being recognized. We might barter for better shoes for you there and . . . if there is any news from the palace, I would like to hear it. Thankfully gossip has more foot soldiers than your brother."

I twined my fingers together tightly in my lap, doing my best not to betray any weakness at the suggestion of news. It was cowardly of me not to want to know anything, and to want to forget the capital existed at all, now that we'd left it.

Kouje seemed to sense my discomfort, for he stretched a hand across the distance between us and rested it against my shoulder. "We will not listen to idle gossip," he told me. "I would not suggest we listen at all, except that . . . if there is any way to know how the Emperor plans to hunt us, I would like not to be caught unawares."

Of course. I couldn't quite bring myself to say it, though I nodded, and hoped that it might be enough. I could not help my loneliness, could not help feeling as though I were being left behind somehow. Kouje was adapting to the situation much more quickly than I could hope to.

I would have to work twice as hard, I vowed, so as not to become a burden on him.

This time, when Kouje set to work dismantling the rest of our crude camp, I helped him. We dragged branches across the earth to hide where we'd slept and tossed the stones of our fire pit into the stream where I'd washed my hands and face. Kouje patted the horse down, then we were away once more. I felt the beginnings of a lingering ache in my backside, the result of near-ceaseless riding, and pushed it to the back of my mind. I would not admit such weakness, when I did not know how far off our destination was. For Kouje to think it safe, it would have to be a great distance from here, which meant a great deal more riding.

"Will your sister teach me to fish?" I asked, when the birds had fallen silent and we had no more games to fill the time.

I felt Kouje's laugh more than I heard it behind me. "After she teaches me, perhaps."

I tried to imagine what it would be like. It wouldn't be like the stories, I knew that. There would be no giant peaches to fish from the ocean, no life-changing fortune sent to benefit the hardworking fishermen, since we would be fishermen in counterfeit only. It would have to be for the joy of fishing that we worked, then, and not for the hope of anything greater. We would rise early in the morning, perhaps, when a gray fog still clung to the ocean and the sun was merely a promise on the horizon. Then we would get into our little boat, and—Kouje's sister having told us all the best fishing spots—we would go to our very favorite of them all, casting our hooks and nets for bonito and flounder. We might well spend all day long underneath the sun, out on the water, waiting for the fish to come. By then, Kouje would have learned to speak easier, and we would talk about whatever came into our heads until the fish drew our attention by tugging at the nets. Perhaps, on very good days, we would come back with eel, and Kouje's sister would say that we were naturals at it.

Was that a life that Kouje could be content with? Was it a life that *I* could be content with?

I didn't know the answer to that, yet. But I was determined to find out.

"Is there a village near here?" I asked idly, tucking hair behind my ear.

"The last time I came this way, there was," Kouje replied. I refrained from asking him when it was he last traveled through those parts. Remembering would be too raw, yet. We could save the tale for another afternoon.

Soon enough, the trees began to thin out as we approached the village of which Kouje had spoken. It was one of the many little stopgaps between the bustling hubs of activity that were the larger cities, governed by warlords, and the capital itself, the greatest city of all. I had never been through one of these smaller villages, since the main road used by our forces to get to the mountains did not run through such inconsequential places, only past them. I couldn't help my curiosity, then, overpowering the feeling of strangeness. As Kouje guided the horse down the open dirt path that must have been the town's main road, I lifted my head to peer inquisitively at the shabby wooden buildings. Some of them looked as though they'd fall apart at the first strong wind, but some of them hung cheerful cloth pennants from their doorways. Now and then, the banner would proclaim this building as an inn, and that one as a teahouse.

All at once, I felt such a sharp longing for green tea that my mouth felt wet with the taste of it.

Men and women lined the streets. Here a middle-aged man swept the dirt from the street in front of his shop, and there two young women were carrying baskets laden with dirt-covered vegetables. There was a fish vendor with a head like an ax who was selling fried eel on sticks to a group of children, all of whom clamored and pushed at one another to be the first-served. In the alleyway next to his stood a woman with a parasol. Her robes were a pale mauve.

Kouje stopped our horse in front of what I judged to be a noodle house. The smells emanating from it were enough to make my knees weak, even though I'd eaten my fill of rabbit earlier that morning. I felt my stomach give a traitorous growl. Behind me, Kouje dismounted, and I found myself hoping he hadn't heard, that he wouldn't think me ungrateful for his efforts.

"Perhaps I might try to strike a better bargain for my formal clothing," he said, "if you are ever again to eat something besides rabbit meat."

"Oh, no," I protested. "I couldn't. Really. It's best just to have shoes, as you said, and not to waste money on such things." I didn't know how long a man could go on eating rabbit once a day, but I vowed that I would do it until our situation improved, or at least until I learned to catch my own fish.

Kouje was wise, but he was also tenderhearted when he did not have to be, and at these times it was up to me to preach sense. We would need sturdy shoes to travel as far as we were going. It was hardly so urgent that I be spoiled with hot noodles.

"I did not mean to suggest we waste money, Mamoru," Kouje said, and I was pleased that he'd remembered to use my given name. It was still a surprise to hear it sound in his voice, but one that I would overcome soon enough. He held out his hands, and I took them, getting down off the horse.

It was rather a relief to be on my own two feet once more. I resisted the urge to rub my backside, endeavoring instead not to stand up too straight, as Kouje cautioned me earlier. Those who worked all day long for their living tended to stoop, as though a great yet invisible weight bore down upon them, the memory of their physical duties. I could manage stooping well enough, but I noticed that none of the women in this village wore their hair in one long braid, but rather kept it pinned up underneath a wrap of cloth, or looped back under as a bun. I touched my own braid with a sudden self-consciousness. Perhaps I would be better served to imitate the women, that I might blend in with our surroundings all the more.

Kouje had tied his own hair back in the simple style I'd seen worn by the tradesmen who visited the palace on occasion. He'd got his hair to behave for the most part, no longer kinked from years' worth of wearing war braids, and I wondered whether he'd doused it with river water that morning, before I'd woken up.

"Come," Kouje said, offering me a smile I did not recognize, until I realized that it was a companionable smile, the smile of equals. Without any warning, Kouje was playing a role, and I was expected to play along.

On sudden inspiration, I took his arm.

"One can learn everything there is to know in a noodle house at noon," I said, "because at that hour, it is only all the people too important to work that frequent the place."

"That is from the story of Aoi the Underhanded," Kouje said, naming one of the legends of a slippery trickster who amassed his wealth from the misfortunes of others. He was more of a highwayman than a man to be respected or immortalized in tale or song, but as children my friends and I had enjoyed his stories best of all. If Kouje knew them better than I did, it was only because he was the one who'd told them to us, so many times over that we'd grown sick of them.

I didn't know what had made me think of it, since they were stories for children, and I was no longer a child. But as we entered the shop, it was immediately clear that Aoi the Underhanded's sage advice was as timeless as that of any mountain ascetic.

In other words, it was a time of day where men and women more important and better-monied than we were eating. And over their food, they gossiped.

Perhaps not surprisingly, they were gossiping about me.

It didn't surprise me for a moment that the story had overtaken us, spreading faster than a fire in the capital. News traveled more quickly, it seemed, than single men could, and anyone traveling along the main roads would have passed the word on with greater alacrity, covering more ground than Kouje and I were capable of with our circuitous and covert path through the trees.

I thought of the other scandals I'd lived through during my time at the palace—when young lady Ukifune had been courted, all too successfully, by Lord Kencho; or when Lord Chiake lost his heart, and his entire year's stipend, to a young man from a brothel. Those sorts of stories kept men and women alike gossiping for months at a time in their separate rooms, and the subjects of their gossip could never enter a room again—that is, if they hadn't been exiled from court for their behavior—without all the fans going up, and all the ladies there whispering behind their sleeves.

I'd always felt a mixture of unhappiness and pity when I thought of poor Ukifune, Lord Kencho, and Lord Chiake, and all the men and women who'd fallen afoul of gossip in our court.

When, if ever, would the gossip over Prince Mamoru cease?

"If you'll excuse me," Kouje said, suddenly halfway into the noodle house, standing with a deferent posture by the side of one of the busiest tables, "but you say there's something happened to the esteemed younger prince?"

One of the women at the table, wearing periwinkle blue, gaped at him. She had broad, unrefined features, and especially vulgar lips. She reminded me in many ways of a bullfrog Kouje had caught for me once. I averted my gaze and stared, as so many servants did, at my feet.

"You haven't heard about the trouble with the prince?" the woman asked, overly familiar.

One of the men slapped Kouje on the arm—which at first shocked me, until I realized it was actually a companionable thing to do—and laughed in disbelief. "You must've been on the road a long time, eh?"

"Sit down, and bring your girl," another man said, taking a mouth-watering slurp of noodles from his bowl. Unconsciously, I licked my lips, then felt my cheeks coloring. At least my disguise was working well enough. "We'll tell you everything."

Kouje gestured me over, his pale eyes sorry for the crudeness of the motion. It was necessary, though, and I hurried over, still keeping my eyes fixed to the floor and my shoulders slightly stooped. It seemed the appropriate posture, for no one looked twice at me as we both took our seats.

"He's stolen a diplomat's horse and run away from the palace," the bullfrog-woman said, clearly delighted to be the first one to break the news. "Can you believe it?"

"*And* he's a traitor. Was going to kill the Emperor in his sleep."

"*I* heard it was with poison. Isn't that right, Jin?"

"Kamiya down at the teahouse said no one knows what the plan was." The bullfrog-woman slapped me in the arm, and it was all I could do not to wince and to look, instead, appropriately shocked and delighted at once at all the spectacular gossip. Kouje stiffened at my side. If this were the palace, that would have been an offense so great, I wouldn't have been able to stop him from striking her. Here, it was a rite of passage.

I didn't think I would be able to summon the strength or the camaraderie to slap her back, however.

"But you know what it probably is," the bullfrog-woman went on. Her three companions nodded, and suddenly we were all bent over the table while the delicious aroma wafting from the bowls of food made my stomach seize up with hunger.

"It's the Emperor getting rid of him," a man with a mole on his right cheek confirmed in a whisper.

"It's been done before," another man agreed.

The bullfrog-woman drank from a cup of tea with a noisy gulp, then put the coarse little cup back down on the table, obviously satisfied. "I wonder where the prince is now?"

"His retainer's gone with him," the man with the mole added. "Loyal to the last, I say, right?" The other two men grunted in agreement, while the bullfrog-woman merely looked smug.

"Whatever the reason," she said, taking control of the conversation once more, "the Emperor seems to think they'll be taking the quickest route to Volstov."

One of the men spat on the floor at the mention of Volstov, which earned a laugh from his companions. Kouje joined in too, after a moment. I couldn't place what was so odd about the sound at first, until I realized that I had never heard Kouje laugh in such a loud and unfettered fashion before. It was nothing at all like the soft and courtly laughter he permitted himself in my company.

It made me wonder what else of Kouje I didn't know. For the first time, I was coming to realize that, for someone whose company I'd kept through my entire life, there were great gaps in my knowledge about him.

"Why would they be heading to Volstov?" Kouje asked, his tone full of contempt for the doings of royalty and the suggestion that good decent people wouldn't be able to fathom them.

The bullfrog-woman shrugged, and nodded toward the man with the mole.

"Shen here had trouble even getting into the village from Hojo last night," she said, naming one of the main cities, to the south of the capital and facing the water in the direction of Tado. "They've set up checkpoints along all the main roads, and they've already reinforced the existing checkpoints between prefectures. He says it takes *hours* to get through now, especially if you're traveling alone, or worse, with only one companion."

Shen—the man with the mole—nodded, and took another slurp of his noodles. I held my hands rigidly in my lap, and willed my stomach not to give me away.

"You'd be better off if you had another woman with you, if you don't mind my saying," Shen pointed out, looking me up and down in a way I truly didn't care for. "This one looks as if she's liable to drop any minute from starvation. She's not much for conversation either, is she?"

"It'd certainly aid the numbers problem," said the other man, who must have been Jin. He laughed, slapping his thigh at his own little joke.

"Actually," Kouje said, that one word so like iron that for a moment the man stopped laughing, and the bullfrog-woman raised her eyebrows in surprise. Out of the corner of my eye, I saw Kouje lower his head in contrition. "What I mean to say," he began again, his words so deferential and so scattered with interruptions that it was all I could do not to stare at him as he cleared his throat and added extra, unnecessary phrases for sheer politeness' sake, "is that I am hoping to find someone to barter with, that I might prevent her from—as you said—dropping dead of starvation."

I lifted my head in protest. I was already the subject of gossip in the smallest of road-stop towns. I would have something to say against being discussed like that right to my *face.*

Shen only laughed, and held up his hands in the sign meant to ward off bad luck. "I didn't mean anything by it, little miss, and you've a pretty enough face when you hold it up that way."

"I'm here for bartering," Kouje said. It was a gentle enough reminder, and perhaps I was the only one who could hear the steel behind each word. It wasn't a threat if it didn't have to be, but it lingered in the air along with the scent of the noodles and strong, hot tea.

The bullfrog-woman sucked her lower lip in, thinking. I found myself wondering whether or not she would emit a croak, then almost immediately felt contrite.

"It all depends on what you're looking to sell," she said at last.

"Some garments," Kouje told her. "Belonging to a former master of mine."

Her eyes flashed with amusement. "Stole them, did you?"

Jin shook his head. "Don't mind her. Old Mayu doesn't understand that not everyone's got a closet full of skeletons."

"Jin, that's a lie," she began.

"Just last month, weren't you trying to convince us all that the paper-hanger who works for Ketano was stealing from him?" Jin asked, laughing.

"And the year before," Shen chimed in, "when you said that Suzu was in love with a married man one town over?"

I wanted to tell them that Kouje wasn't the sort of man who would steal things from anyone, let alone his own master, but I was faced with the new and terrifying knowledge that it was not my place. I'd only just begun to grow comfortable with my place as a prince over my most recent birthdays, after the battles in which I'd won my braids, and now I was unlearning each lesson as Kouje had undone each braid.

The idea of having to adapt to another role was almost more than I could bear. I kept my head down.

"Well, what of it?" Old Mayu was sulking now. I could hear it in her throaty, smoke-worn voice. "Mark my words, that's why she hung herself in the end."

I wondered if Suzu had been the topic of all their gossip up until I'd fled from the palace. I wondered if anyone would guess at the truth of why she'd done it, or if that elusive thing—the truth—had died along with her.

There was no argument from Jin or Shen, who both seemed to sense that they'd gone too far. It wasn't the sort of remorse that comes from genuine regret, though, but more a fear of what would happen once Old Mayu had got over sulking and decided she was angry.

"Try the potter," Old Mayu said to the pair of us. "Down the road from here, next to the inn's stables. He's been prospering of late, and his wife's the sort who's always bothering him to dress up once in a while. He'll be your best bet for unloading your garments, stolen or not."

I lifted my head just in time to see her wink at Kouje.

"Of course if he isn't interested, you two come right back here and see me. I can't imagine what I'll do with only these two for conversation. It's not every day you meet someone so interesting!"

I didn't think that Kouje had said all that much, by way of conversation. In fact, most of the conversation had been carried by Old Mayu herself. I thought that perhaps her definition of "interesting" was different from my own.

"Thank you," Kouje said. He stood, and didn't wait for me before starting out of the noodle house.

I knew it was just an act, but I'd been caught unawares again, and found myself rushing after him into the light of the street outside. Kouje was standing by the horse, untying the bundle of our clothes. He looked up when I came out, and though he didn't say anything, there was a penitent look in his eyes.

"What interesting people," I said, to see if I could make the apology fade. "I'm glad they were so helpful, aren't you?"

"You did very well," Kouje said. "I almost lost my temper."

"Only once or twice," I said, shading my eyes against the sun and looking down the street, as though that held the secret of what the potter's house looked like.

"When she touched you . . ." Kouje began.

"We'd best see the potter," I said. "Should I stay with the horse?"

Kouje looked down the street, the same as I had, but with a different purpose. My gaze had been curious, but his was challenging and defensive at once. Perhaps, if I looked hard enough, I could see things the way he saw them: most of them threats and all of them gossipmongers.

"You'd best come with me," he said at last, taking my hand. "News has traveled fast. We can only hope the Emperor's riders haven't moved so quickly."

CHAPTER FIVE

CAIUS

I was feeling sorry for Alcibiades, because that morning he'd found out that the horse Prince Mamoru and his retainer had stolen was his. Or, at least, it *had* been his. Now it was Prince Mamoru's, and a lucky horse it was, riding all across the Ke-Han countryside, having adventure after adventure while Alcibiades glowered and sulked and, it was obvious, secretly missed him, the poor dear.

It was the sort of luck I felt was visited upon Alcibiades often, but the point remained that he was completely unapproachable, steaming mad and muttering to himself and not being a gentleman about the matter at all. The Emperor himself had apologized to him, but instead of being fascinated by the whole affair—there was a special ceremony for it, and two of the special Ke-Han-bred racing horses had been given to him, one as compensation and one as a gift—he'd locked himself up in his room and refused to come out, or even to answer me as I spoke to him about how the talks were going that day.

"They've decided to set up checkpoints to look for him," I explained, which was, I thought, a very gracious gesture. "You might have your horse back yet, my dear, if they do manage to catch him. I would have thought that right now you'd be there, leading out a Ke-Han search party yourself to find the young rascal! Then you'd be a hero of the Ke-Han people, as well as of Volstov. You're missing out on quite the opportunity. And don't you even want to see your new racing horses? *I* want to see them!"

Nothing at all emanated from the other room, though I could still hear him from where I was, my ear pressed up against the door and dreadfully bored, muttering away to himself like a madman. Eventually, the muttering stopped, but Alcibiades hadn't yet emerged from his room, and he'd barricaded the adjoining door.

There was no question in my mind that the man needed a bit of cheering up. He was simply making it very hard for himself and me.

Inevitably, I screwed up my resolve—determined to face any obstruction that might confront me—and I managed to slide the door open. It was only halfway, but that was sufficient.

"Good afternoon!" I called, over the rolled-up sleeping mat he'd piled up as a blockade against me. He was trying so hard; I thought it quaint. "Have you had lunch yet? I'm famished!"

Nothing at all again. I fancied I could hear the sound of a quill against paper though I had to concentrate very hard to hear it.

Alcibiades was writing a letter.

I could only imagine the sort of adorable dialect he employed while penning his epistle. And to whom could the man have been writing? I was shocked, in fact, at the very idea that he could write at all. How utterly delightful! I simply had to read it.

The blockade Alcibiades had set up against me was easily scaled, and I clambered up the side of it until I could at least see over the top. I rested my chin against the top and grinned in my most alluring manner.

"Are you writing a letter, my dear? Shall I call for our lunch to be brought to our rooms?"

Alcibiades startled, nearly spilling his poor inkwell before throwing his arms over the letter and glaring in the direction of my voice.

"You look like a bloody jack-in-the-box," he informed me.

"How jolly," I said.

"I *hate* jack-in-the-boxes."

"Mm," I said. Not my best rejoinder, admittedly, but I was quite busy in maneuvering my way down the other side of the barricade, and I wasn't altogether keen on losing my footing. When I reached the bottom I felt a warm satisfaction at a job well done. "Now, what do you say to some hot lunch?"

"I'm *busy*," Alcibiades said. He hadn't got up from his rather undignified position at the desk, arms crossed over the letter as if it were a state secret, and not some plain piece of paper with writing on it.

"I know, with the letter." I nodded indulgently. Then, trying to make it seem as though I'd only just thought of it, I gasped as if with a sudden brilliant idea. "I might read it over for you, if you like!"

"No," said Alcibiades. "You mightn't."

He'd propped the small desk his room had been equipped with—one which he dwarfed quite amusingly, and which no doubt would have given him an awful crick in the neck otherwise—up atop a chair, so that it was at least better suited to his size and stature. I thought that the furniture was delicate, handsomely crafted and exquisitely simple, but I had to admit that it did make Alcibiades appear a giant bear of a creature. It couldn't have been very comfortable to work at.

On his desk were a few pieces of paper blotched with ink and a collection of old pens. Underneath the half-full inkwell, however, was the true prize: not the letter Alcibiades was currently writing but the one to which he was replying. That was my goal. Who could it be? A sweetheart back home? He didn't seem the type. A frail and aging mother might have been more likely, or perhaps a brother; he didn't strike me as the sort who cultivated friendships so carefully as to write letters. He wasn't a man whose behavior encouraged you to send them.

I put my left slipper back on—it had fallen off as I scaled the barricade—and sidled closer, feigning disinterest by observing my fingernails.

"How *is* everyone back home?" I asked, looking at the screen set up by the far wall. His had cranes upon it, whereas mine had a splash of maple branches. "Your mother? Your father?"

"Wouldn't know," Alcibiades replied curtly.

I cast a quick glance at the desk, only to find that Alcibiades had put his shoulder squarely in the way, blocking my line of vision. I could see the back collar of his shirt very well, but nothing at all beyond that, not even what his handwriting looked like.

That shift, however, was his undoing. It was a fatal strategy, very inadvisable; I'd have to rebuke him for it afterward. It protected the letter he was in the midst of writing very well, of course, but it left open his entire left flank—where the letter he'd received was resting underneath the inkwell. It was very common paper, brown and heavy, and the penmanship was round and flowery, so it was almost certainly from a woman, but adorably hesitant, as though the writer didn't often find herself in the position of having to write anything at all, much less something so long as a letter.

I would have to act quickly—and carefully, too, unless I wanted to spill all the ink.

"I say!" I exclaimed, feigning a great deal of interest. "That woman has fish spilling from her hair. Did you know that your room has a print of the sea goddess?"

Alcibiades grunted, but didn't look up. That was good, since I couldn't risk any change at all in his posture. Not when he'd left such a perfect opening for me. I inched closer, *so* pleased I'd decided to have some slippers made up in the Ke-Han style, since they were so perfect for moving silently across boarded floors.

"Mine only has a winter landscape," I said in a desolate voice. "*Do* let's switch! I think mine would suit your room much better, what with the cranes and all. I'm surprised they mixed sea and air in the same room anyway. It must have been a mistake. Will you help me to take it down, my dear?"

Alcibiades wasn't even listening to me anymore, though he'd hunched his shoulders more tightly, as though even then he was work-ing to create a barricade against me with his own body. His pen scratched away dutifully against the page. I almost felt sorry for him, but then, he was a soldier, and it would do him good to remember that one had to go on the offense, occasionally.

I plucked the letter nimbly from the desk and scanned it eagerly.

Alcibiades whirled around immediately, the most murderous of ex-pressions on his face. "Put that *down*," he growled, grabbing for it.

I slipped just out of reach, still reading the letter. It was the sort of thing that would have been aided by the use of two good eyes, and not the one I had to make do with. Fortunately, Alcibiades was the sort of man you didn't need *any* eyes for, only a good sense of hearing, since even when he was in his own room he refused to remove his boots and he made terrible thundering noise everywhere he went.

Dear Al, the letter began. That was as far as I'd read before Alcibiades launched himself at me like an enormous beast, and I was forced to dart around behind the desk to read further.

"'Hope you are eating well,'" I read delightedly. "'No one cooks·like your Yana,'" was that a word from country dialect? I'd have to look it up, "'but you should eat anyway on account of your little fat belly not going away.'"

I paused, breathless with delighted laughter. Then, Alcibiades overturned the desk with a tremendous crash and I was forced to wriggle out from underneath the chair to keep from being crushed.

"'Do not allow your temper to run away with you like one hundred angry fire ants,'" I read on, pressing myself flat against the wall. It was to avoid Alcibiades' wrath as much as it was to hold myself up while laughing. He threw the inkwell at my head and I scampered away. It shattered against the far wall, splattering ink everywhere.

"Your temper, my dear! Your temper! It says it in the letter!"

"I'm warning you, Greylace, just give the letter back and no one gets hurt."

I had never seen Alcibiades so excited about anything in my life. His face was red, and his eyes were alive with the prospect of having me spitted and roasted over an open flame. I simply *had* to keep reading.

"'Do your Volstov and your Yana proud. It is great honor to be chosen for such special journey. And feed your horse nothing but apples, apples are the chosen food for the King of Horses,'" I managed, before I choked on my own laughter. From what I'd learned of the Ke-Han court, it was appropriate to hide one's laughter behind a sleeve or a fan, whichever one happened to have on hand at the time. However, survival instincts bid me ignore that particular rule, so that I was set to laughing quite openly in the center of the room, in a way I didn't normally make a habit of. It was a most unseemly display, but for a very special occasion.

Alcibiades swore, and kicked at one of his crescent-shaped chairs that had fallen over in all the commotion.

"'Wear your socks!'" I shrieked. Tears were beginning to roll down my face. This was better than a holiday, better than *ten* birthdays, and I found that I didn't care at all that my face might have been as red as Alcibiades' by that point. "'Otherwise'! 'Your feet get cold'!"

"It's summer," Alcibiades groused. "And humid as fuck here anyway. There isn't any cold to be found. Give the damn thing back."

He still had that murderous gleam in his eyes, but he was losing steam. That was the problem with men his size, they tired themselves out too quickly stomping about and making a dreadful ruckus. I darted up to the dais from which Alcibiades had moved his sleeping mat and collapsed there, out of breath and out of laughter.

"'Take very seriously this mission of diplomacy. Take very seriously your health, or else you will sprout mushrooms from your ears and become like a mossy stone that has no rolling left to do.'"

Alcibiades sat down on the floor, clearly plotting my demise for a future date. It was almost sweet really. He was so *earnest* about it. Perhaps he'd realized that I'd nearly finished the letter anyway, and there was no point in trying to keep me from reading the rest.

There was an enormous black inkblot on the far wall. If I squinted, it looked something like a butterfly.

"'Listen to your Yana, and you will always be happy, healthy, and fat. Yana Berger.'"

I sighed, feeling utterly emptied of everything and tremendously satisfied with myself. I would have to find a comb very shortly, and I would have to go over my clothing very carefully to make sure no errant drops of ink had landed on the silk, but all in all, it had been a very successful venture. I rolled my head to face Alcibiades, peering at him over the rumpled paper of the letter.

"Who's *Yana*?" I asked, in the tones of someone about to break open a terrible scandal.

"No one," Alcibiades grunted. He crossed his arms over his chest like a sullen child.

"Oh, come now." I sat up. There was a faint freckle of ink on my right sleeve, but I'd already decided it was worth the sacrifice. This outfit was a new one, and not entirely as flattering as it might have been. I was going to call the Ke-Han tailors soon, in any case. Now that everyone bent over backward to make sure that Alcibiades, the diplomat with the stolen horse, had everything his heart desired, I would tell them Alcibiades had sent for them, and they were sure to come more expeditiously and do a better job, at that. "You're telling me that this kindly soul, whoever she is—who took the time to write you this very... unique letter full of heartfelt sentiment and best wishes for your health—is no one? This lovely dame, who counsels you so very wisely to hold your temper because it is—so true, so true—like ants? Can this delicate flower be no one?"

"All right," Alcibiades said in an exasperated tone. His cheeks were still bright red, though whether it was from exertion or embarrassment, I couldn't tell. He was a fascinating creature. I was beginning to think of him less and less like the dog I'd once owned; although he'd just set to ruining a room like a misbehaved animal, he was far more difficult to train. "Just don't talk about her, all right? I didn't mean she's no one. Just that she's no one *you'd* know."

"I can't tell whether that's a jab at my station or an outright lie." I tapped my chin to order my thoughts where they'd got loose from me in all the excitement. My robes were creased—another mark against them. "I'll take it as a lie, I suppose. Perhaps you are . . . *embarrassed* to speak of her? Your dear, sweet Yana, who cautions you to wear your socks? How heartbroken she would be to learn of your reticence when it comes to speaking of her!"

"She as good as raised me from a sprog," Alcibiades finally said, though he spoke as though the words were being dragged from him by torturer's hooks. "After my parents were carried off, what with one thing or another."

"Carried off by one thing or another?" I asked. "Were they eaten by mountain birds?"

Alcibiades gave me a filthy look. Perhaps my excitement over discovering Yana had caused me to overstep my bounds, and I attempted to look appropriately apologetic. "My mother had bad lungs," Alcibiades ground out at last, "and my father had a wound from a threshing accident that he never quite got over. After that it was just Yana to look after my brothers and sisters and me. We never did quite figure out what country she hailed from, but my mother had her in to help with the twins when they were born, and she never left."

"How ghastly!" I said, imagining Alcibiades as a chubby young man crouched in a hovel with an army of brothers and sisters around him, all clamoring for food. It was very clear the lady was foreign from the way she wrote, but possibly he hadn't also noticed that she'd taken leave of her senses. "I didn't know you were a farmer."

Alcibiades looked at me sharply. "Didn't say I was."

"Well, I assumed," I clarified. "From the accident with the thresher."

"That was my father," Alcibiades said. "I've been a soldier since I was old enough to leave home, and I haven't looked back."

"Ah, of course," I said. "That explains a great deal."

Alcibiades gave me another dirty look. "Not every one of us can be raised like th'Esar's little lapdog," he said, a bit more unkindly than he ought. After all, I'd presumed that we were only having a bit of fun.

"I *am* sorry about your parents," I managed, very generously. Perhaps that would placate him. "Here, would you like your letter back?"

I held it out to him, as a peace offering between us. After a moment of staring warily at my hand, he snatched it back. I noticed, with a touch of affection, that he smoothed out one of the crumpled edges when he thought I wasn't looking.

"Well, that was fun," I continued, when he showed no signs of replying. "We ought to do that more often. Have you told our dear Yana about me yet? I am, after all, a significant part of your life here during the Important Diplomatic Mission."

"I've told her I'm being driven insane by a tiny madman named Caius Greylace," Alcibiades replied.

That would have to suffice. "I do hope she approves of me," I said helpfully. Alcibiades merely shook his head and sighed, as though he were afflicted by some incurable disease.

That was when the Ke-Han guards burst into our room.

Alcibiades, ever the soldier, nearly killed one with his chair, and there was a great deal of shouting from all parties in their respective languages, and pointing, and more chair brandishing, while I stood behind Alcibiades and offered words of encouragement and tried to decipher what the guards were saying, before we were able to determine what was going on. My ability to speak their language was shaky at best, and with all of them yelling at once it was impossible to understand half of what they were saying.

Thankfully, Lord Temur arrived to sort things out. He did so in an extremely dashing manner, stepping into the room with one hand held up palm forward, and roaring a command loud enough to make the sliding doors shake in their grooves.

The guards stopped shouting. Alcibiades almost put the chair down, but then thought the better of it. I remained where I was, although I waved to Lord Temur over Alcibiades' shoulder.

"Now," Lord Temur said. "What seems to be the trouble?"

"We're being attacked, that's what the trouble is!" Alcibiades growled.

"Well, that is," I explained, translating from Alcibiades into more common speech—the sort that human beings employed when success-fully communicating with one another—"we were having a bit of a romp, you see, and then all of a sudden there were guards everywhere, can you imagine?"

Lord Temur paused to make a careful assessment of the situation. His eyes flicked over the room, surveying the ink spot on the wall and the shattered inkwell beneath it, the overturned chairs, the desk perched on the stool and the sleeping mat barricade by the door sepa-rating Alcibiades' room from mine. At length, he turned to one of the guards and spoke with him quietly, before focusing once more on us.

"There has been fighting here?" he asked.

"Oh, no," I said. "We were just being friendly."

Lord Temur surveyed the scene before him once more, then looked to us again for some explanation.

"I tried to keep him out," Alcibiades said gruffly, as though I were a wayward kitten that had to be kept out of the room lest I get at the drapes. It was dreadfully unfair of him. His neck was red, and I could see his pulse pounding at his temple, but at least, finally, he *did* put down the chair. I was glad. It was frightfully embarrassing to be in the palace with a companion who insisted on using furniture as bludgeons. What would Yana Berger have said?

"Ah," Lord Temur replied, as though this had explained everything. "I see. Yes."

Alcibiades breathed a slight sigh of relief. "Sorry for, ah," he at-tempted, "any disturbance we might have caused."

"It is a lucky thing I was passing by," Lord Temur said, waving a dis-missive hand at the guards, who bowed low to us, then to him, and filed out of the room one after the other. "Else who knows how long this ... misunderstanding ... would have continued."

"The inkwell was mine," Alcibiades added, rubbing the back of his neck. "And the— No furniture was broken. I don't think."

"No need to apologize," Lord Temur assured him. I wanted to point out that Alcibiades had very nearly ruined my new clothes in his fit of pique, as well, but it didn't seem to be the time. "We will send for some-one to take care of the mess. Should we instruct the maids to leave things as they are"—he gestured toward the barricade—"or return things to their usual place?"

"Might as well return them," Alcibiades said. All the anger had drained from his voice, leaving it hoarse and almost demure. "Didn't work, anyway."

"I can see that it did not," Lord Temur agreed. "I was in fact just coming to call upon your companion, Lord Alcibiades, though now that I find you together I will extend the offer to both of you."

"I'm not a lord," Alcibiades said, managing to make it sound almost like a gentle correction and not something gravely rude. It must have been my influence. Or perhaps it was merely the reminder of dear Yana so close at hand.

Lord Temur bowed. He cut a very fine figure in his dark robes, but it was not a color that I could wear with my complexion. "My apologies," he said. "We have a title for diplomats in our language, but there is none for it in yours. 'Lord' was the closest approximation I could think of, and therein lies my mistake."

"Oh! No offense has been taken," I assured him, coming round to stand beside Alcibiades now that the guards had left. "That's merely Alcibiades' face when he's happy; one grows accustomed to it. You mentioned an invitation, Lord Temur?"

"It was an *offer*," Alcibiades muttered, but he fell silent after that.

Lord Temur smiled cautiously, as though unsure of the resulting expression it would leave on his face. "Yes. I was under the impression that Lord Caius was interested in learning more about our culture. I might recommend the libraries as a place to start, but the artists' district within the capital is something to behold."

"The artists' district!" I clung to Alcibiades' arm with excitement. "We'll go at once, won't we? The scholars didn't teach us anything about that."

Lord Temur bowed again. "They might not have found any merit in the teaching. The artists' district is not for the...upper class, the people of the palace. But it has many fine works of art, and it is a place full of entertainment, despite its reputation for scandal. If we are to share our culture, we cannot merely offer tours of the palace. It is..." He paused, searching for the proper words. "...one-dimensional."

It was as though he'd known exactly what I'd been thirsting for. Perhaps the delicate network of servants had relayed such information to him, or maybe it had been one of our fellow diplomats. Whatever the reason, Alcibiades and I were about to be escorted to a place of *questionable repute* by one of the *seven warlords*.

Josette would simply die when she found out.

"Sounds all right," said Alcibiades, though I caught him casting a longing look back at the desk and his unfinished letter. It was all right, I wanted to assure him; he could tell Yana all about it later that night. I didn't think he would appreciate the effort, though, so I merely patted him on the arm. "Lead the way, then."

Lord Temur led us through the halls with little conversation, pausing here and there only to point out a particular element of architecture or relate the history behind a particular room. Soon enough, we were outside the palace and flanked by two fearsome-looking men who must have been Lord Temur's retainers. Alcibiades kept glaring at them and muttering what I had no doubt were unpleasant things under his breath.

"Your temper, my dear," I murmured, low under my breath.

Alcibiades merely made a noise in my direction in reply—half grunt, half growl.

Lord Temur paused at the main gate to explain our destination to the guards. I bounced on the balls of my feet, eager to see the city we'd only been able to view previously from carriage windows. It had been so scintillating, those mere glimpses, the smells warm and exotic, the sounds of a foreign people going about their daily lives without realizing how absolutely and extraordinarily *different* they all were.

"Stop all that bobbing up and down," Alcibiades said. "You're giving me a headache."

"Don't be so sour," I admonished him. It was time for mollifying him. "Just think of all the interesting things you'll be able to put into your letter *now*."

Alcibiades just stared at me as though trying to assess whether or not I was making a joke.

"Perhaps you might even purchase a watercolor," I added. "To send along with your letter. A piece of the scenery, perhaps? Yana might like the memento."

"Right." The harsh lines of Alcibiades' face smoothed out somewhat, making him look less monstrously cranky with the world; the whole effect made him look miraculously much younger. "I could do that, I suppose."

"Gentlemen." Lord Temur beckoned us and his retainers over with a regal sweep of his arm. He had *such* presence. "Your pardon, but the gate is open."

A carriage—in the Ke-Han style, of course, a deep blue color that made Alcibiades snort when he saw it—awaited us.

The road from the palace stretched out for miles. All the city lay open before us. The scholars had given us maps before we left and explained that the lapis city was built with the palace as its hub, that formidable building set like a jewel in the very center of the glittering crown that was the capital. Buildings radiated outward from it like the sun's corona, illuminating the glory of the palace itself. Closer to the palace were the larger houses, set far apart from one another; these were the lords' homes, when they were recalled from duty to sojourn at the palace. The farther from the palace you traveled, the closer together the houses grew until, just in the distance, I could glimpse the cramped quarters of the town, the circumference of a great hexagon, which provided the framework for the entire city. The roads, the buildings, the lords' houses, and the blossoming cherry trees were all planned down to the last seed or stone. It was nothing at all like Thremedon in Volstov, which resembled a handful of buildings flung together piecemeal and multiplying without proper planning, all scattered down the mountainside.

This was the most beautiful place I had ever seen.

At my side, Alcibiades snorted.

"Isn't it lovely?" I said.

"That poor bastard up ahead just fell off his horse," said Alcibiades.

So he had. I didn't blame him, either, for as we drew closer and closer to the outer city, the streets grew more and more crowded; wealthier men, perhaps prosperous merchants, rode on horseback, while commoners scattered as we passed. Everyone bowed. It was crowded and full of noise, men recognizing one another and calling out greetings, women doing the same, or urging their children to keep up—and all completely different from the serene beauty of the palace and its environs.

I was somewhat disappointed with Alcibiades for being unable to recognize the great beauty laid out in perfect geometry before us.

"There are certain parts of the city, of course, that would be most unsuitable for our esteemed guests," Lord Temur explained. I peered past the bamboo-curtained window of our carriage out onto the street, and saw a sprightly pickpocket flee the scene of his yet-unnoticed crime, purse in hand. "I would not dream of taking you there."

"But what are they?" I began, perhaps too eagerly.

Alcibiades cleared his throat. "Understandable," he said, and Lord Temur nodded.

"As it stands, my lord the Emperor would not approve of my giving our esteemed guests such a tour," he continued. "This part of the city is not nearly of the same caliber as the palace itself, and there are places here that would shame us in your eyes. And yet..."

The carriage turned a corner, and suddenly we were up against the famed wall—passing, I noticed with some interest, a section of it that had not yet been rebuilt. A young man, dressed in common work clothes, had paused against the broken gap to pass his arm across his brow and eat a stick of fried dumplings. They smelled delicious. Perhaps Alcibiades would have enjoyed them.

Alcibiades must have caught sight of the same thing I had, now that I was holding the bamboo curtain up with one hand, and cleared his throat.

Lord Temur bowed his head, as though it were the only way to express momentary discomfort at the faux pas. "We must pass through that which is unseemly in order to come to the true artists' district," he explained. "There, you may see our culture as the artisans understand it. We have a wide variety of sculptors, calligraphers, and printers, and it would bring great honor to any man whose craftsmanship pleases you."

The words, I recognized, were rehearsed, yet I was nevertheless delighted by them. So few had been chosen for this venture, and, not being a soldier or a combat magician, I would never have found the opportunity elsewhere to see these people for myself. It was better than being in a museum, for the exhibits were living and breathing, shouting from windows and bowing down as we passed by, children lunching on dumplings or chasing kittens, an old man stooped with age but laughing nevertheless.

My eyes caught Alcibiades' in a moment of shared realization. We were so eager to watch these common people because they wore what we had so missed in our Ke-Han companions at the palace: expressions.

"Something smells good," Alcibiades said suddenly, as though the connection unnerved him and he felt compelled to say something rude again to diminish the moment.

Lord Temur paused for a moment—his only indication, it appeared, of discomposure—then nodded in understanding. "Ah," he said. "A street vendor. Stop the carriage."

The two guards reined in the horses, then opened the door for us.

"After you," Lord Temur said.

Alcibiades stepped out first, and of course completely ignored me as I held my hand out to him for assistance. Sighing—when *would* the man learn some decent manners?—I lifted the hem of my garment and alighted. The road beneath us was dusty, and my slippers were sure to be ruined, but it was for a worthy cause.

"Lord Alcibiades is hungry, I believe," I explained to Lord Temur. "His palate is somewhat unrefined. He comes from the country, you see, and isn't very adventurous when it comes to foreign spices."

"I see," Lord Temur said. "I, too, am from the country, but I have always enjoyed these dumplings. Perhaps Lord Alcibiades would honor this vendor by sampling them?"

"I told you," Alcibiades began, but I silenced him effectively by offering him the delicacy in question—sticky dumplings served most cleverly on a wooden skewer.

"My lord Caius," Lord Temur said, offering me a skewer of my own. They smelled simply heavenly, and I accepted, nibbling daintily at the one on top. They were filled with something sticky and sweet; Alcibiades was sure to approve, since after all, no fish were involved as far as I could tell.

"Good," Alcibiades managed, after a long while of chewing, since he'd bitten three dumplings off at once.

"I believe you don't eat the stick," I said helpfully. The dumpling vendor, meanwhile, only looked deeply relieved, as though we had come to cart him away to the gallows and pardoned him, instead.

"If you will follow me," Lord Temur said. He'd secured a dumpling stick of his own, and another for Alcibiades—which was quite thoughtful of him, really. "The artists' district is very close by."

"Well, if the art is anything like the dumplings," Alcibiades said, apparently in a better mood now that his stomach was full. If I could have kicked him, I would have, but Lord Temur would have been sure to notice. I'd reprimand him privately later. Lord Temur was a sensitive man; the Ke-Han's was a sensitive culture. They valued works of aesthetic beauty nearly as much as they valued a man's strength and prowess in combat. To compare art to dumplings was the height of rudeness.

While Alcibiades' churlishness was endearing in private, it was dreadfully inappropriate before others, especially after Lord Temur had gone out of his way to take us on such a fascinating tour.

Thankfully, Lord Temur pretended not to hear him, and we carried on by foot, one retainer waiting with the carriage, the other following behind us.

The houses were built almost too close together, as though they were all vying for the most room possible, and all of them were somehow losing. Awnings overhung us, and brightly colored banners with words I could not read—it was one thing to memorize a few Ke-Han phrases and quite another to learn their complicated, pictographic alphabet—hung outside of doorways. Most important, however, was that the people were staring at us. Of course they were; we were so obviously foreigners, and Lord Temur so obviously an important member of the upper class, that they must have wondered what purpose drew the three of us there.

"The streets are too crowded to continue by carriage," Lord Temur said. "And we must pass by one or two of the theatres. My sincere apologies."

"But I love the theatre," I said. "There's nothing to apologize for. Do you think we might be able to attend a play?"

"I shall see what I am able to do," Lord Temur said, the stilted formality of his words still betraying nothing of his emotions. "We will have performances at the palace in our esteemed guests' honor, of course, but I sense that you in particular, Lord Caius, are searching for a more...authentic experience."

"Exactly that," I confirmed. "How wonderful! Is that one of the theatres?"

It was a tall, imposing building with a sloped roof, and the first one I'd seen in a while that wasn't fighting off the crush of other buildings around it, as though all the houses on either side were making way for it. I thought it looked like a member of royalty among the commoners.

Outside the building, a few young men stood in idle, relaxed poses, looking for all the world like the images from a storybook. Hands on their hips, ebony-black hair slicked into complicated chignons, their robes far more colorful and garish than anything I'd seen at the palace, they loitered outside the entranceway with their faces painted white and their lips daubed bright red, their eyebrows thick and high. After a moment of closer inspection, I realized they were painted on for dramatic effect.

They must have been actors.

"In a manner of speaking, that is a theatre," Lord Temur said. "But it is a common one; much too common for our esteemed guests."

One of the actors cast a glance in our direction, indolent and slow. If he was surprised to see a nobleman guiding two foreigners down the street, it didn't register on his face. He wore his makeup like a mask, and merely shifted his weight from one side to another. I realized then that he was deciding which one of us to rest his gaze on, and it was only then that I understood what, exactly, they were looking for.

"Oh, I *see*," I said, taking Alcibiades by the arm. "Come along."

"What?" Alcibiades asked. He still carried his stick with one lonely dumpling on it and seemed more concerned that my sudden attentions might make him drop it. "I thought you *wanted* to see the theatre."

"Yes, well," I said. He really was an infuriating man, making me explain it to him. I could tell from the way Lord Temur held his head, looking straight down the road, that he wasn't the sort of man who required such explanations. "Another time, perhaps."

"It'd be something to write in a letter," Alcibiades said, like he was granting me a favor in being this interested and wasn't instead being hideously obtuse. "Maybe I could get an autograph."

"Hurry *along*, General Alcibiades," I said, for one of the men had taken notice of him, and was smiling in an overly familiar way. He looked like a young lion stalking its prey.

"Look," Alcibiades said, his attention drawn by irritation, as I had known it would be. "I told you not to call me General, either. What's with this sudden relapse?"

"I'll tell you once we have reached less . . . outgoing climes," I said, and hauled determinedly on his arm until we'd passed not only the theatre, but the building that stood next to it, and the narrow, winding road that separated *that* from an archway hung with colorful banners.

"This is the artists' district," Lord Temur said. He paused, in order to give us a chance at catching up with him. His expression, as usual, betrayed nothing. I was starting to wish that my Talent was in mind reading and not visions after all, since it seemed the only way to figure out what the lords of the Ke-Han were thinking, but *velikaia* of such Talent were never allowed at talks such as these, for obvious reasons.

My particular Talent would have come in very handy if these talks were less diplomatic—or if they needed to be coaxed along some—but until then I was compelled to keep things under wraps. A pity, since it tended to make my head a very complicated place. "Perhaps another day, I might take you to a more fitting theatre."

"That one didn't seem so bad," Alcibiades said.

I made a note to take him aside later and point out that not everything was a slight at commoners, and therefore at him. I had no idea what provoked him to be so contrary all the time, but I felt certain that if I didn't come to the root of it, it would poison *all* our fun in the capital. And I couldn't have that.

"I thought we might begin at one end of the alley and work our way back along the other," Lord Temur continued thoughtfully. "There is a great deal to see, and I would not like to think I'd neglected any small detail."

The artists' district was arranged much like a market in Volstov, with wooden stalls crowding in on one another and lining either side of the street. Some had the same colorful banners that I'd deduced doubled for shop signs, but others were simply bare, with nothing but wind charms and little mascots of folded paper nailed to the supports.

We stopped first at a booth that featured no signs, only a wind charm made of glass, which tinkled merrily in the breeze that whispered down the street. I thought that I recognized the shapes in it from the patterned robes worn by one of the warlords attending our diplomatic talks, but I wasn't certain. We hadn't brought up the topic of the Ke-Han wind magic yet, if only because it would surely bring all minds around to the broken outline of the dome, still a gaping wound in the perfectly crafted city. I'd learned in our intensive course predating our arrival that the Ke-Han did not specialize in wind but rather all four elements. They took their magic from the land itself, and perhaps the only reason we were so familiar with the wind aspect of their skills was because it had been the one we were confronted with most often. Perhaps there was something particularly easy about that one element to harness. Or, perhaps because of the dragons, they'd had enough of fire to last a lifetime, and earth was too dangerous an element to toy with high in the mountains.

Then again, I reflected, that had rarely stopped our soldiers, or so the stories had told me.

It was doubtless still a wound in the hearts of the people, as well. As it was more a symbol for the people than anything else, it was something best left out of negotiations completely, though it was the subject first and foremost on everyone's mind.

A man dressed in short robes and leggings hurried up to the front of his stall, as if drawn by the fall of our shadows over his beloved artwork. The artist's fingertips were stained with ink, as though he'd just been working on a new piece when we interrupted him. He wore a thick white cloth wrapped around his forehead, to keep the hair out of his eyes, and when he saw his customers were two foreigners and a lord from the palace, he stopped short, jerked to a halt by an invisible chain.

"Welcome," the artist murmured, eyeing us warily. "Please let me know if there is anything I can help you with."

"What did he say?" Alcibiades had the decency to lower his voice when he nudged me about it.

"He said, don't lick the drawings, they're made with lead paint."

I saw Lord Temur give me a puzzled look out of the corner of his eye, and I offered him my most winning smile. It would never do to be the only man with a sense of humor in all of Xi'an. I would have to work much harder at being winning.

This particular artist's specialty seemed to be women in teahouses, for each picture featured a beauty with porcelain skin and ruby lips, her delicate fingers curled around a cup of green tea. Their robes were as varied as the flowers in a garden, of all different colors and textures, the patterns sometimes overpowering the women beneath them so that the subject resembled nothing so much as a ghost dressed in the most extravagant finery.

Alcibiades picked one up and examined it as though he really was trying to decide whether or not to lick it, specifically because he'd been told not to. The artist watched him with keen eyes, not altogether liking his delicate prints in the hands of such a large and foreign bear. From his perspective, I couldn't precisely blame him, since Alcibiades had the sort of hands that were clearly meant for destruction and not the careful handling of art.

"Does it remind you of dear Yana?" I asked.

He rounded on me with such sudden ferocity that for a moment I was certain the picture *would* be destroyed. The artist cried out plaintively, and Lord Temur cleared his throat.

"Perhaps," he said, "it would be best to move on to another stall."

"Fine by me," Alcibiades muttered. He put the picture down and stuck his hands into his pockets like a child who'd been scolded.

I clucked my tongue in disapproval and threaded my arm through his in order to keep a closer eye on him. It was rather like having a large and angry pet, one whom you needed to keep on a leash at all times.

"If you will," Lord Temur said, and he wore his peculiar version of a smile. "There is much to see yet, not to mention my own personal favorite."

"Oh *really*?" I couldn't imagine what sort of pictures would be Lord Temur's favorite. He'd said that his family had originated in the countryside, so perhaps his inclinations favored natural landscapes? Or perhaps he would surprise us both by enjoying something more risqué. One could never tell with these Ke-Han warlords, for they kept everything hidden beneath the sash.

We stopped at countless booths, some of which did indeed seem to specialize in natural landscapes. There were drawings of the Cobalts, done all in inky blues, with the Ke-Han name for them written in their fascinating script underneath it. There were drawings of the Xi'an coastline, with trees that grew bent-backed in the wind, and fishermen who grew bent-backed from years of hauling up their nets.

My very favorite was a picture of the lapis city at springtime, every street seeming to blush with the pink of cherry blossoms, and two women standing gossiping under a parasol to ward off the sudden rain of petals.

I was horribly disappointed that we hadn't come to Xi'an in the spring.

I glanced at Lord Temur as if to question him, but he merely shook his head. The natural landscapes were not his favorite.

Next, we came to a section of stalls that seemed entirely devoted to the supernatural. There were women with the tails of foxes, and small imps that crouched in a merchant's carriage wheels, waiting for the perfect opportunity to send him and his wares sprawling. One booth had another ocean scene, but this one showed that the cause of the fearsome wind was a creature with golden scales that blew the fishermen round in their boats until they were forced to return to shore. I saw the picture that Alcibiades had in his room, of a water goddess with fish spilling from her dark hair.

It seemed to me that Lord Temur was much too stolid to appreciate tales of the fantastic, but since I was curious, I glanced at him again. Once more, he merely shook his head, though this time he was smiling, and I felt tremendously pleased with myself.

"This is rather like a game," I murmured happily to Alcibiades, who was looking increasingly like one of the bored husbands you saw in the Volstov shopping district, dragged by their wives from hat shop to dress shop to hat shop again. He'd even given up trying to shake me off his arm.

"Wonder if we'll be able to have another stop at that dumpling stand on the way back," he said, looking suddenly hopeful at the prospect of more fried food that didn't contain any fish whatsoever.

"Oh honestly," I said, pouting only slightly. "You aren't even *trying* to guess."

Alcibiades sighed like a dying man. "Maybe it's that one," he said, indicating a stall at the very back. While most of the artists seemed to jostle for a good position, declaring their whereabouts to passersby on the streets by whatever means necessary, this stall seemed almost to cower behind the rest, hiding its wares away from potential customers. It stood half-obscured behind a booth that featured pictures of men in furs riding over a mountain range that wasn't the Cobalts, and it featured no distinctive markings whatsoever. It was utterly plain, without even so much as a wind charm to alert one to its presence.

In fact, I was rather under the impression that if one didn't know it was there to begin with, one wouldn't be able to see it. Perhaps Alcibiades' instincts weren't to be dismissed entirely, after all.

Lord Temur turned halfway around once he'd reached it, as though beckoning us over. I felt at once that we were about to be privy to some magnificent secret, so that I was almost disappointed to see that the drawings looked very similar to the others we'd already seen. These were of people, true, and not natural landscapes or sea monsters, but I had been hoping for something more.

"That one looks like the Emperor," said Alcibiades.

Lord Temur glanced around the street once, his eyes keen as a tiger's, then nodded once, like a confidence among the three of us. He seemed almost pleased.

My eyes widened in delight. "You mean these *are* of the Emperor?"

"Some of them," Lord Temur admitted. "It is not technically illegal, but the portraits are rather ... frowned upon, in any case."

"This one's of that lord who's always shouting," said Alcibiades, pointing out an exact likeness of one of the diplomats privy to our talks, but with an exaggerated coloring—his face was painted a bright red.

There was another of Lord Ochir, who had particular skill for lisping his words, and whose head was painted onto the body of a snake. Another was of a man I recognized as Lord Kencho with a *much* younger woman, both subjects smiling foolishly for an unseen artist.

"Where're you?" Alcibiades asked, looking at Lord Temur.

"Ah," he said, in a tone that was very nearly intimate. I thought he almost sounded amused. Perhaps it was the palace itself that made the men and women in it so quiet and expressionless, and one needed only to remove them from it in order to witness a metamorphosis. "I believe there is one just there."

I plucked it from the rest before Alcibiades could get his hands on it. The picture showed Lord Temur dressed as a country peasant, standing in the middle of a rice paddy. I thought that it was fairly mild, as far as satire went, though perhaps Lord Temur was relatively well liked among the people, and anything crueler wouldn't have been as popular. Of the caricatures we'd seen, it was only Lord Temur and the red-faced lord who had managed to keep their dignity more or less intact.

"I think I shall buy this one," I said. "How much is it?"

But Lord Temur was no longer paying very much attention to me. His entire focus had been caught by another sheaf of porous rice paper, freshly painted and framed in the center of the artist's display by all the other caricatures. It was of two men, both of whom were incredibly familiar, although I had to admit it took me a few moments to recognize them: the young prince and his overzealous retainer.

Even Alcibiades didn't have the presence of mind amidst his shock to say anything inappropriate that would spoil the glorious wonder of our discovery.

The scene depicted was a dashing one—if I hadn't known any better, I would have thought the young prince was a hero of the people, and not a traitor who'd turned on his brother, then fled. But perhaps this artist knew something we did not. He had painted—with loving, haunting colors—the image of the young prince on a small, sleek boat, helmed by his retainer, cutting through a dark sea in the midst of an even darker night. All around them, the only splash of color was the white foam of the waves, which looked more like apparitions and ghosts than the roiling of a common ocean storm. The closer I examined the print, the better able I was to see that in the swirls of foam were sharp, accusatory features—they were, dare I even say it, almost *imperial*—but the expression the retainer wore was fierce and determined, and the prince, the focus of the piece, seemed to draw strength from his posture. Ultimately, I was given the unshakable feeling that the two men, though caught in the midst of a deadly maelstrom, would reach their destination—an opposite shore, which the artist had chosen, quite wisely, not to include at all.

"The Ke-Han have an interesting way of choosing their heroes," Lord Temur said finally, breaking the silence. "I doubt they have reached the sea yet, in any case."

Then, in an action that seemed to surprise us all—even Lord Temur himself—he swept the print in question up in one hand and crumpled it with a sudden show of animosity that rose, from nowhere, like a crushing tide.

"The cost," I began, but he held up his hand for silence. I felt like one of the men under his command in the war, though I had no reason to; it made all the soft hair at the back of my neck stand on end.

"We must return to the palace," Lord Temur said.

Even Alcibiades plainly felt there was to be no arguing with him. We left the prints and all of the artists' alley behind us without purchasing anything, and without paying for the print Lord Temur had destroyed.

CHAPTER SIX

KOUJE

One matter weighed heavily on my mind, more than all the rest: There was no way to reach any kind of haven without crossing the border between prefectures, and there was no way to cross the border between prefectures as two travelers without being caught.

The first night after we heard the rumor, I could not sleep, and it was not because of the owls hooting or the mosquitoes humming by my ears, or because I had, shamefully, grown used to a soft bed during so much time spent at the palace. My thoughts haunted me the way fireflies haunted the bushes; the moment I thought I'd managed to quiet them, another worry lit bright and fierce in the corner of my vision, and I was wide awake once more, my throat tight and my heart pounding.

I did not know whether or not my lord slept. It seemed he always did, sometime toward morning, but managing some sleep and being well rested were miles apart from each other.

But if the arrangements did bother him, he hadn't yet complained.

That morning I watched him for some time as he slept, the distant light very pale as it rose not quite high enough yet to crest the trees. Mamoru wished for me to wake him when I began the hunt, but he was sleeping more peacefully now than before. It seemed a shame to disturb what little respite he had. Yet, if we were to be equals, I should honor his request as a friend the same way I had once honored his commands as a prince.

"Mamoru," I said, touching his shoulder.

He was awake at once, with such a look of terror on his face that I could barely hide my remorse.

"Oh," he said at length, leaves tangled in his braid. "Are we hunting rabbits?"

We did, and he was quiet at least, if not skilled enough to catch them himself. I taught him how to skin them, and though his mouth grew tight and his eyes widened, he was not sick at the sight. He was being very brave, but to tell him so was to patronize him. So I said nothing; and in that fashion, things between us were just as they had been at the palace.

"Your hair," Mamoru said, when we'd eaten our fill. "It isn't right."

"My lord?" I began, confusion making me forget myself. "Mamoru," I added hurriedly, forcing myself not to bow in apology.

"It isn't the same as the other merchants wear theirs," Mamoru explained, motioning for me to turn my back to him. I did as he wished, though I turned to look at him over my shoulder. "It's merely something I noticed yesterday in town. People of—People of our standing don't wear their hair down. The women plait their hair, but the men twist theirs back, I assume so that it won't get in their eyes, or perhaps to keep the backs of their necks cool while working. It's very clever, for otherwise it gets in the way."

"I have no knowledge of how to fix my hair in that fashion," I admitted.

My lord smiled evenly and with his eyes. "I think I might be able to approximate it," he said, brow furrowing. "It's a small detail, but it might help us in some way. It *is* clever. It's just a matter of what is most convenient." He came closer, the leaves and grass crunching under him, and knelt behind me, undoing the haphazard knot I'd used to sweep at least some of my hair from my eyes. He combed his fingers through my hair once, almost as though he were about to return my warrior's braids; then, his fingers began a different and unfamiliar task, twisting my hair up and back and doing his best, with a braid strap, to affix it in place.

"Now turn around," Mamoru said.

I did so, and faced him hopefully. I'd barely asked "How is it?" before my lord began to laugh at me.

"I've done it wrong," he managed, after he'd regained composure. "It's all to one side. Either that or it hardly suits you, Kouje. Here, let me try a second time. I'm doing *something* wrong."

It took three more attempts before Mamoru achieved a topknot that didn't send him into fits of laughter, but by the time he was done both our moods were much improved.

"Now," I said, making an attempt at restoring what order we'd lost in our laughing, "I think it might be a good idea, Mamoru, if we were to bathe here. We are near the river and we might not get another chance for some time."

My lord's eyes brightened with a laughter he kept hidden, this time. "Are you suggesting that the need to bathe has become rather dire, Kouje?"

I bowed my head, but it was a friend's gesture, meant to hide embarrassment and not to offer supplication.

"That's quite all right," Mamoru said. He waved his hand as if it were a courtly fan in front of his face. "It *is* becoming rather dire, all things considered. I'm surprised we managed to sleep at all last night."

It seemed that he'd made a joke, and so I allowed myself to laugh. "I am glad we're in agreement."

"So long as you keep your hair out of the water," Mamoru stated, as firmly as he had ever issued a command to me before. He was smiling as he rose. "I shouldn't think it a valuable use of our time if I have to try and master it again. We'd be here for days."

I nodded, joining him in the joke. "Indeed, it would seem that you will have to style my hair every morning from now on."

"I shall accept it as my lot in life," Mamoru said, and placed a hand over his heart in an overdramatic gesture favored by actors from the theatre.

My lord had a curious sense of humor at times, but a lively one. I found myself laughing on the path down toward the river more than I had in all my days since the war's end combined. Without the palace to press silence in at us from all sides, I was finding myself caught up in conversation with my lord more and more, and I was pleased to learn that we understood one another well enough to wish to continue speaking of nothing at all.

I had always known that my lord was kind, that he was clever and eager to learn, but I had never known him to play the fool quite so often. I would have been able to rest at ease knowing it was his wish only to make me laugh, but I couldn't help wondering if he weren't venturing at so many jests to hide his deeper feelings.

We had not spoken of Iseul since leaving the palace that fateful night. I still feared that forcing my lord to confront the truth would break something inside of him, something that I would not be able to fix, but he seemed well enough, laughing at my side all the way to the riverbank.

Still, as we sat by the water and shed our rough costumes, I resolved to keep a better eye on him—a closer eye, if I could. My lord was strong, but I would die before I failed him.

The day would be warm, but it was still early and the heat was manageable. I felt a moment's regret that we didn't have the luxury to wait until noon, when the sun would be at its fiercest, and my lord might be able to warm himself on the rocks when we'd finished bathing. Then I pushed it aside. There was no room for me to feel regret, especially not when my lord behaved in a way that would set an example for the most noble and virtuous of men.

I entered the river first. The water pooled around my legs and waist, the current of the river strong against my chest and bitterly cold. That particular river was one of the many that ran down from the mountains in the west; the glacier-melt from the snow and ice was what made it so, even in the height of summer.

I heard a splash, and a yelp from my right, which announced Mamoru's presence far better than he could have if he'd intended it.

"The water's cold," I said, feeling a rush of apology once more. My lord had never bathed in anything but the heated baths at the palace, and the great tubs that one could build a fire under during the war. He was used to those hot baths, and to servants who passed him bath oils and lotions to scent the water and soothe his skin; it was not private, by any means, but the ceremony obscured the vulnerability of nakedness. Here, we were completely bare, and both pink-edged with the chill, our fingertips wrinkling.

I should have warned him sooner.

"It's . . . it's all right, Kouje," my lord said, though I could have sworn

I heard his teeth chattering. "Really. It's very bracing. A good start to the morning, I expect."

My stomach tightened as a crow cawed overhead, and I strained to listen for any rustling in the bushes, *any* sound at all. It took flight over our heads. I watched it go.

"Do you find it a good start to *your* morning?" I asked my lord, taking a cue from his fondness for making jests.

He cast me a baleful look, for a moment resembling some pale river spirit and not my lord at all.

I laughed, softer this time, for the crow had reminded me that we were not alone in the woods. "You'll feel much better once you are clean and dried," I promised.

Mamoru nodded, pressed his lips together bravely, and ducked his head under the water to wash his hair.

I allowed my body to drift with the current, trying to put my thoughts into the same ordered flow. We would come to a checkpoint at the border of our prefecture sooner or later. We would have to cross more than one, if memory served, to get to Honganje prefecture and the fishing village where my sister lived. I thought it likely that Mamoru's disguise would get us safely past at least one checkpoint, since the guards had doubtless been instructed to stop two men, and not a man and a woman, but what would happen after that? My lord could not very well live out the rest of his life under such a disguise, despite his admitted experience in the practice. Such times were past. He was a young man now. More than that, he was a *prince*.

I remembered a time when my lord had been just three months shy of his fifth birthday. Awakened by nightmares in the middle of the night and unable to sleep on his own, he'd roused me as well. His eyes had been very grave while I tried to comfort him in all the usual fashions, and finally, I had abandoned protocol that I might ask him directly what was the matter.

"Kouje, why do I look different from Iseul?" he'd asked me. "Is there something the matter with me?"

"No, my lord," I'd told him. "There is nothing at all the matter with you." And then, because I could not help myself, I added, "Things will change for you soon enough."

How could I ask my lord now to return to such a state of isolation?

I had already taken him from his home, from his very station. I would take no more from him than that.

A shout and a loud splash interrupted my thoughts—Mamoru, in danger—and a current of fear cut through the very center of me. My short blade was on the riverbank. Could I reach it in time? I scanned the land for any sign of movement while yet holding one hand out for Mamoru to take, that I might draw him behind me.

"What is it, my lord?" I asked.

"My ankles," he cried, and pointed.

Beneath the clear, swirling water, I could see the dark shapes moving with the current and between the larger rocks, their long whiskers swaying beside them.

"Catfish," I said.

"Catfish?" he gasped, splashing himself and me in a poorly-thought-out attempt to run in water that swallowed him from the shoulders down. "It was *enormous,* Kouje—did you see it?"

Relief made my knees go weak. "A catfish," I repeated, just to be certain.

"It was the size of my arm!" Mamoru cried, looking about with wild eyes. It seemed cruel to mock him, when he was so clearly apprehensive, but the words were out before I could stop them.

"Your arms aren't very big, Mamoru."

He looked at me in surprise and utter confusion. I couldn't blame him. I'd never had much practice at telling jokes, and perhaps I'd misspoken. Then my lord was laughing, all the louder for how anxious he'd been a moment ago, and I felt my heart resume beating at a normal speed.

That afternoon, we had catfish when we stopped to rest the horse, and my lord wore a particularly satisfied look on his face as he chewed.

It was deceptively soothing to ride the daylight hours into dusk as we were, with my lord in front of me. We were travelers, and the steady pace was like a lullaby. While we were under the cover of trees, or passing by the rice paddies, or winding our way on narrow, empty roads that encircled the hills, it was easy to imagine we *were* all alone in the world. But soon enough, we would come to a resting stop by the side of a larger road, or crest a hill to find a small village laid out before us, and we would learn fresh news of our very own flight toward safety.

"What shall we do at the border?" Mamoru asked me, shooing a mosquito away from his cheek. Thankfully, it was not their season. Nevertheless, he would feel the itch and the burn soon enough, and I would have nothing with which to soothe him.

"For the crossings," I began hesitantly, "I thought we might avoid closer scrutiny by continuing dressed as we are."

"I might pretend to be your sister," Mamoru offered. If it troubled him to return to that mode of disguise—one so familiar and yet so remote—he did not show it.

"Two men are suspect," I agreed. "A man and a woman... That is not the quarry they seek."

My lord nodded, satisfied. "Yes," he said. "They would never think..."

He did not finish the thought. I wagered a guess as to why, and did not press him. At least he was not dressed as some lowly creature of burden, but a simple common woman. I knotted my hands in the horse's reins, and we rode on.

It was late in the day, the sun already beginning to sink below the distant horizon, when the dusty back road we were on opened up without warning, and we found ourselves riding into the roadside rest stop.

There was a tea-and-noodle house, and a sheltered bench just outside it for rainy days, should any unlucky traveler be caught out beneath a sudden storm. Only two horses were tethered outside the shop, and the door was closed, but we could hear well enough the sound of a few voices from within—no doubt belonging to the shop owner and the few travelers who were stopped there for the night.

In front of me, Mamoru breathed in deeply, as though he were trying to calm the quickened pace of his heart. After a moment, however, I realized the truth of the matter: he could smell food on the air, the simple, clean scent of white rice in the pot. There was a hunger in his eyes I'd never seen.

We had some money from my old clothes; I'd spent most of it on new shoes for Mamoru and then, when he insisted, on sandals for myself, as well. There was a little coin left—enough for a night spent at a roadside inn, a bowl of rice for each of us, and some left over.

Mamoru's fingers tightened against the horse's mane, and the creature whinnied. I thought of my prince sleeping on the forest floor, of his bathing in the forest stream, of skinning rabbits for his breakfast.

"I'd like to sleep in a real bed tonight," I said. Perhaps it was weak of me to give in so easily to the mere sense of what my lord desired, but how was I to know when we might get the same chance again? Honganje and my sister's cooking were both a great distance away from where my lord and I found ourselves.

"Kouje," Mamoru said, but the protest was weak.

"Only if you think it wise to grant my wish, of course," I said. "It was merely a suggestion—and perhaps it was an unwise one?"

My lord looked at me over his shoulder, his eyes bright with the conflict. He wanted a simple bed that night—we could only hope a decent business was being run there, and that there were no fleas between the sheets—and, more than that, I knew, he wanted a bowl of rice. Yet he also wanted to do what was most practical. It was better that I make the decision for him, so that it would not be his to regret. If I was treating him like a child, then I would allow him to grow resentful at my actions—but better that than to resent himself.

After a long pause, Mamoru made as if to speak, then shook his head. "If you think it wise to stop," he said, "then you know full well I would not argue against it."

"Then it's settled," I said.

We saw to the horse—or rather, I saw to the horse while Mamoru stroked its nose and murmured wordlessly to it; he was gifted with the creature in ways I was not. It was a slow night, with few travelers. When we entered the rest house, there were only two men sitting at one of the homely tables and the shop owner serving them. The latter was glad enough to see us there, and as I haggled, Mamoru kept close by my side.

The other two travelers ate and watched us to the point of staring. Just as I thought I would have to better inform their poor manners, one of the men broke into a wide smile and waved us over.

"Lonely night," he said, "isn't it?" I nodded. "Jiang and me were beginning to think we'd stumbled into a ghost story."

The one named Jiang shrugged, arms folded over his chest. "The old man," he said, nodding toward the shop owner, "keeps talking to himself. You never know, on a night like this."

It was, as I understood it, as much of an invitation to join them for dinner as we'd ever get from people like them. Mamoru and I sat with them as we waited for our rice—and if the shop owner took longer with it, I thought, then he really would be a ghost; I'd see to it.

"Traveling long?" the man—not Jiang—asked, looking pointedly at the dust that had gathered on our clothes and settled, it would seem permanently, in our hair. Of the two, he was clearly the more outgoing. I wished that he were not so friendly, nor Jiang so laconic, and I wished that both of them would stop staring at Mamoru.

"And farther still to go," I said.

"Your wife?" Jiang asked, nodding this time at Mamoru.

I swallowed my temper, forcing it back down into my chest, and balled my hands into fists under the table. Mamoru patted one of my hands; I could feel how nervous he was simply by sitting beside him.

"Not your wife, then," the friendly one said, breaking out into a wide grin. "No need to explain to me, friend. I see how it can be. Times are changing, eh? The name's Inokichi, but they call me Kichi for short."

I offered up our predetermined aliases. After that, the rice was finally brought, and they paused, almost respectfully, for Mamoru and me to eat. I saw him try not to wolf his food down, but it was a struggle, and he was finished quickly enough that it was plain how hungry he had been. I offered him what was left in my bowl, but he refused, even if he was sorely tempted to accept it. I ate it as quickly as I could after that, so he would not have to sit and watch me eat longer than was absolutely necessary.

"Hungry, eh," Kichi said. It wasn't entirely a question, and he looked too amused by it for me to feel any traveler's companionship for him at all. Besides which, he'd said it to Mamoru more than to me, and I didn't like the tone of voice he was using, or the slant of his mouth.

I edged closer to Mamoru on the bench. "We've been riding hard," I said, trying to find some comfortable medium between too vulgar and too polite. I was a common merchant, if that; I was dressed in a servant's clothing, and it was better that I spoke like one. Yet to embrace the coarser speech Jiang and Kichi so readily employed, or to speak of Mamoru the way they did, was also a poor option.

"Riding hard, eh," Kichi said. "Heard about the young prince, have you?"

"Gossip, mostly," I said. "Have they caught him yet?"

Jiang snorted, and Kichi burst into laughter. "Caught him?" he said, slapping the table. "Giving the Emperor a run 'round the bush at every turn. They don't even know where he is, I'm telling you; he's given them the slip and they'll be lucky if they ever find him. Making life damn hard for the rest of us, though."

I feigned concern. "How?" I asked.

"Imagine this," Kichi explained. "You're minding your own business, just trying to sell your goods, when all of a sudden you can't even get past the borders—that is, if you're a man traveling alone or two men traveling together. And they search *everything.* My friend Hanzo was stopped for two whole hours, just 'cause he had a regal look about him."

"Ah," I said. "I didn't ever think I'd say it, but... It's a lucky thing we're traveling together." I nodded toward Mamoru at that, and he patted my hand again; perhaps he was trying to assure me that being disrespectful in a place like that and under those circumstances was all right. I wasn't going to be unless I had to, though. My nails dug into my palms, but I offered a companionable smile to our new friends.

"Well, you'd think that, wouldn't you," Kichi said, "but they're searching women now, too. Apparently the prince could be disguised as anyone, so they're stripping women who fit the bill right there at the station. Naked as babies, Hanzo tells me. I tell you, brother, I was born into the wrong job—am I right?" Here he slapped at my arm for agreement, and I laughed with them, all the while wanting to slap him back.

I feared that I would do it too hard, and would then have yet another apology to make to my lord, on top of all the others I felt I owed him. Next to me, Mamoru smiled politely, so that even he looked more good-humored than I. Reluctantly, I allowed a quiet laugh to escape my lips, as though I were either too polite or too slow to have enjoyed the joke properly. Still, knowing what they'd told me now, it was rather difficult to laugh. If they were stopping anyone with even a passing resemblance—if they were going so far as to strip women naked at the station—then my lord and I would soon have a very serious problem on our hands.

How to get past the prefecture checkpoint without being detected?

My worry must have shown plainly on my face, for Kichi slapped my arm again, this time in a manner that was meant to be reassuring rather than crass. Or, at least, that was what I thought. "Worried about your lady friend? I'd be too, if she were mine. *Very* beautiful. There's no telling for certain whether or not they'll see a hint of royalty in her. Or maybe the looks of her will leave 'em feeling... particularly dutiful."

That time, Mamoru put a hand on my arm before I could move,

else I might have lost my temper entirely. He cast his eyes down, for all the world like a shy maiden. His cheeks were flushed with embarrassment, and I could not ignore the sharp pang in my chest of a duty neglected, no matter how I had resolved to shun that duty for another.

Had we been our former selves, I would have killed anyone who humiliated the prince so. Now I was forced to laugh with them and call them friends. Breathing slowly, I endeavored to be calm.

They seemed like decent enough men. Perhaps I was judging them altogether too harshly.

"Yes," I said, edging the words out until I could make them sound natural. "That thought had crossed my mind."

Kichi nodded. "I don't blame you one bit, either. You get a woman like this for yourself, you don't want anyone else seeing her naked."

"She's my sister," I said finally, hoping that would put an end to some of the joking once and for all. I had a sister and I knew well what clarifying that relationship did to dissuade discussion of their beauty or any other . . . attributes.

"Ah," said Kichi. "Say no more, good sir. It's your protective instincts as a brother that put such a fearsome spark in your eyes. I understand completely. I've got sisters myself, two of them—both with faces like radishes, though. Never have to endure such talk."

"We've been trying to figure out how to get past ourselves," Jiang said, without warning. I'd almost forgotten he was there, for all that his loquacious companion overshadowed him. "Not that either of us looks womanly enough to be stripped bare, mind you, but I'd rather keep my belongings private and not laid out on display if you know what I'm saying."

"Been at this game as long as we have and you're still nervous as a newlywed on her wedding night. They're hardly going to keep *us*, brother." Kichi laughed, slapping his companion on the back. I was glad it wasn't me this time. "Not with a face like yours."

"I'm less worried about *my* face, and more worried about *your* mouth," Jiang said, with a long-suffering eye toward the pair of us, as though he weathered such abuses every day but only rarely entertained a sympathetic audience for them.

Kichi stroked his long face thoughtfully. He looked like a painting of the monkey god come to life, I decided, only his beard was short and black instead of long and white.

"We *could* travel *with* you."

I nearly didn't recognize my lord's voice as it came so sudden and clear from my side. He bowed his head when the three of us craned around to look at him, as though suddenly conscious of how he'd managed to capture everyone's attention when he had meant to do anything but.

"What I mean to say is, that if they're more suspicious of groups traveling in pairs, wouldn't it make sense to go along as a bigger group? They might not scrutinize each of us so thoroughly, which would save you time, and I might escape with my dignity intact."

Kichi gave Mamoru a look that was admiring, and Jiang surveyed him with something else besides that in his eyes, something I was sure I disapproved of.

"I like the way you think," Kichi said, smiling his monkey smile. "Sensible *and* clever. You'll want to watch out, brother, or some devilish man's going to take her from you."

"I'll keep that in mind," I said, gritting my teeth together. My lord's hand was still on my arm. He gave me a pat that was equal parts warning and reassurance.

"Anyhow," said Kichi. He leaned back in his chair as though he meant to get up, and perhaps he'd sensed my animosity after all. "It's a fine plan. Your sister's got a fine head on her shoulders. If you want company for this leg of the journey, you've got it, right, Jiang?"

He stuck out his hand without waiting for Jiang's confirmation. I got the impression that all their decisions were made in a similarly one-sided fashion.

I could feel my lord's hopeful eyes on me, and despite what misgivings I had, I knew what the decision would have to be.

I put my hand in Kichi's and shook. The radiant air of his smile did nothing to assuage my misgivings.

"That's agreeable of you," Jiang said, getting up from the table. He didn't seem to bear his companion any ill will for his brash nature, or for his willingness to make decisions on his own that affected the two of them. Perhaps he'd grown used to it. "Just the spirit of brotherhood—sisterhood as well, you'll pardon me, miss—that's been lacking in these parts of late."

Mamoru bowed his head and, if he felt any remorse at the mention of brotherhood, he kept it to himself. I waited until our colorful bene-factors had left before I dared to turn to Mamoru, my contrition writ-ten plainly over my face.

"They have the right idea, don't you think?" Mamoru said mildly, ignoring what apologies I might have made altogether. "Perhaps we'd better turn in."

I wanted nothing more than for Mamoru to enjoy what comforts he could while he could. If I had the means to provide us both with soft beds for the evening, then it only made sense for us to take full advan-tage of them. Who knew how early Jiang and Kichi would expect to leave in the morning?

For that matter, who knew when we would ever get the opportunity to sleep so well again?

"It's a fine idea," I said, allowing myself to praise it as my lord's own and not Kichi's. I paid for our dinner, then ushered Mamoru up the creaking wooden stairs ahead of me.

Our room was just off the landing, second on the right. I was al-most gratified to hear that the floorboards creaked as loudly as the stairs did. No one would be able to surprise us in the middle of the night; naturally, it was not a building built with the same niceties of ar-chitecture as the palace, and for that I was grateful.

I slid the door open for Mamoru out of habit, managing not to bow only as a cursory remembrance. My lord was doing so well at playing his part. It dealt a great blow to my humility to think that I was not.

Our room was plain, with two narrow mats stretched out in the center of the room and a lamp set on the back table. It flickered uncer-tainly from time to time, as though unsure as to whether or not its presence was welcome. Outside the window, the moon waxed like a ripening fruit, pale and elusive.

Mamoru slipped his new shoes off and began to undo the tie that held his hair. Out of habit, I paced over the length of the room, search-ing into all the corners and listening to the sound of the floor as I walked it.

"Kouje," Mamoru murmured, his voice as soft as a moth's flutter-ing, "I do not think you'll find any assassins here."

"Mamoru," I said, fighting the urge to bow. "I did not mean to dis-turb you. It is merely a habit. If you find it offensive..."

My lord smiled warm in the lamplight. "No. You needn't stop. I find it almost reassuring, truth be told, and . . . I am in need of some reassurance tonight."

He drew back the thin, summer-season coverlet. It was imprinted with a design of trees, ones that held the most elegant of songbirds. My lord had always enjoyed listening to the songbirds in the menagerie. On some occasions, if the night air was right, he said that you could hear them singing all the way from the palace.

I knelt on the mat next to my lord's. "Everything will be well tomorrow," I told him, "now that we're traveling in a larger group. No one will take any notice of you."

"My face," he said, touching one smooth cheek thoughtfully. "That man said that they were stopping everyone with a regal air about them."

"I shall counsel you to amend your posture," I said firmly. "And leave your hair uncombed in the morning. And perhaps we might cover your face in dirt," I added, as an afterthought.

"Kouje!" Mamoru looked at me for a moment, stunned and amused in equal measures. "Surely our companions would notice something peculiar about such a thing?"

I shook my head. "It was unwise to bathe when we did. I see that now."

My lord sighed fondly, in a way that did not betray his exasperation in the slightest. "Next time, I'm sure we will both think twice, and learn to live peacefully enough in each other's stench."

"Indeed," I said, allowing myself the smile I'd been holding back. I couldn't help looking around the room once more, since there were other habits a man accumulated during his lifetime, ones less easy to break than the familiarity on the tongue of a certain title. "Is there anything I might fetch you, before the day is out?"

Mamoru cast his eyes toward the window, and the moon that had risen high over the trees.

"I believe the day is already out," he said, then, "I've everything I need, Kouje. Thank you."

I rose to extinguish the lamp, trying and failing to make my feet sound noiselessly against the floors, the way I could at the palace. That I couldn't was some reassurance, but some loss also. I heard a quiet sigh, and the shifting of fabric as Mamoru tucked in underneath the coverlet. I tiptoed back as softly as I could to my own bed and pushed the covers back in the dark.

"Thank you," my lord said again. Already his voice was coming slower, half-ragged with the pull of sleep.

"You have nothing to thank me for," I assured him in a whisper that would not break the tenuous threads of sleep forming around him like a spider's web. "I merely felt the need for a proper bed. You have forgiven me for my indulgence, and I'm very grateful. There's no more to say on the matter than that."

"No more to say on the matter," Mamoru murmured, the words nearly swallowed up in a yawn worthy of the menagerie lions.

"Good night, my lord," I said.

A quiet snore was his only response. I lay awake after that for some time, listening to the creak of men and women walking the halls, finding their rooms for the night or leaving them. Gradually the noise subsided as the rest stop closed down for the night, and then there was no sound at all but for Mamoru, sleeping peacefully in the bed next to me. In such a small roadside stop as this one, there were no gamblers or pickpockets roaming the streets at night, so there was only silence from the road beneath as well. I lay on my side, staring at the wall across the room before turning over, noiselessly as I could so as not to wake my lord.

There were no crickets to chirp and buzz in the night, and no frogs to hum their mating calls to one another from the streams. The bed was soft beneath my back. I should have been able to sleep, but I couldn't.

The only way I realized that I'd eventually dozed off was when the light woke me in the morning, striking me full in the face like an unwelcome hand. I was up at once, looking about the room with considerable confusion before I realized where we were, and recalled the arrangements we'd made to slip past the border checkpoint later in the day.

My lord was still asleep, even after I'd gone to the window to judge the relative position of the sun. It was early yet. If I hadn't promised to wake him whenever I myself was awake, then I might never have found the heart to do it, but I knelt at the side of the bed and took gentle hold of his shoulder.

"Mamoru," I said, as softly as I dared.

He was awake immediately, in his eyes the same dread as the

morning before. He seemed to calm when he saw my face, though, and relaxed back against the futon with an odd, sleepy smile.

"I had the most wonderful dream," he said, in a voice tinged with melancholy.

"When we're on the road," I promised, "you may tell me about it."

Memory passed across his face like a shadow and he sat, his hair something of a mess. Had he slept restlessly during the night? I didn't remember the sounds of his tossing and turning, but he might have begun to sleep poorly after I myself had managed to drift off.

Mamoru left no time for concern, sitting up at once and tucking back the hem of the coverlet with delicate regret, a dreamy grace. "Well," he said, after a moment's pause, beginning to pull his hair back into a clumsy braid. "Let us attempt the border crossing."

ALCIBIADES

The more time I spent with the Ke-Han, the more time it looked like I was going to have to spend with the Ke-Han.

If I'd said it once, then I could say it a hundred times: I wasn't any kind of diplomat, not even a piss-poor one, and I didn't see how decisions that shouldn't even need to be discussed could take hours, sometimes whole days, to go over. Were we ever going to get to the real meat of the problem? How much longer was this nitpicking—and some on both sides of the debate had perfected nitpicking like it was a bastion-be-damned *art*—going to take?

Forever, maybe. And I had to sit through all of it.

Also, I was starting to feel like we were being horsed around—really taken for a ride. But Fiacre liked negotiating so much that he hadn't caught on to it yet, and the only reason I had was because I didn't. We hadn't discussed any of the particulars of the provisional treaty yet, let alone anything to do with the new one, and all because the new Emperor was so hell-bent on tracking his brother down that he'd kept us on the topic for the better part of a week. I was starting to think he was just doing it on purpose.

We'd finally agreed to adjourn the talks when Ozanne had fallen asleep right at the table and knocked over his cup of frothy, bitter tea. I'd have done the same if I'd thought I might get away with it, but for all

I knew two cups of spilled tea in one night spelled a diplomatic incident for the Ke-Han.

They'd never have stood for it in the war. When you were a soldier—especially when you were a soldier who knew what he was doing well enough to get promoted beyond the ranks of miserable, Ke-Han fodder nobodies—you made decisions. Sometimes they weren't the right decisions, but you didn't have the time for sitting around and weighing each option, and making sure all the factors had been carefully considered when most of those options were irrelevant anyway, like what the weather was like and how much cotton was going for these days and whether or not your maiden aunt had a hangnail or what you were having for dinner that evening.

Maybe I was there because I was a soldier, and maybe I was there because th'Esar liked to keep a few trump cards up his sleeve, and maybe I was there because I was paying penance for all the men I'd killed during the war without weighing each option, but at the rate these talks were proceeding, we'd be staying in the Ke-Han for ten years at the least, and only then would we move on to deciding what tile we should use in rebuilding.

Didn't anybody just want to *do* something? Didn't anybody see reason?

But Fiacre was in his element, and Josette, too; their parents must have raised them to be mean little quarrelers, for they could talk circles around the best of them, and if it hadn't been driving me so crackbatty, I would have been a little proud.

The way I saw it, though, was that we didn't *have* to argue about these things. We'd won the war; the Ke-Han'd lost. But then, I didn't understand the finer points of diplomacy, and maybe it was better to set up a system that worked rather than having the whole thing collapse on you ten, fifteen years down the line.

Whether it was due to it being so damn hard to work things out or due to an unnecessary number of nitpickers all having a field day with each other, I didn't know. Like I said, I wasn't cut out to be a diplomat, and now that I knew what diplomacy consisted of, I was damn sure I wouldn't be making it my life's work. Even though I'd been pressed into joining the delegation.

Someone, somewhere, was having a real hard laugh at my expense, that was certain.

And meanwhile, I was going stir-crazy.

During the war, I hadn't had the time to sit still for all of an hour, much less days. I woke before dawn and tucked in early, and a man got used real quick to his specific routines.

In the palace, the finer men and women woke late and turned in even later, on account of all the goodwill everyone was determined to show, meaning that every night we were forced on pain of death to attend stultifying parties.

The one thing I really didn't get was the Ke-Han music. It was three notes howled at you over and over by a woman who sounded more like she was choking on her dinner than singing. It gave me a splitting headache and it could last for hours if you weren't lucky.

The dancing was all right, though.

But underneath all the assurances of goodwill, things were tense. The second prince was still missing, the Emperor was still working on us to let him send out veritable armies to hunt down his brother—all while we were getting nothing done—and I could tell I would've been privy to some of the nastiest gossip in at least a hundred years if I only spoke a word of Ke-Han. Good thing, then, that I wasn't a gossip.

Caius Greylace, the carnivorous little flower, was having a field day picking up Ke-Han turns of phrase right and left. Didn't matter to me, I figured, since the more time he spent gossiping, the less time he spent bothering *me*.

Most of all, I just wanted my horse back.

After over a week of getting pins and needles in my own damn backside, of being restless at night for lack of doing anything proper during the day, I figured something had to start changing, and that something was me, since it sure as bastion wasn't going to be the situation. I was out of shape enough already. There was only one half-decent solution.

I started rising when the peacocks woke me.

An interesting thing about peacocks that not many might have known was that the ones in the Ke-Han woke up just like roosters did, like they thought morning light was some alarming sign that everyone needed warning about. It happened every day like clockwork; the ones that ran wild in the Ke-Han palace courtyard shrieked like their tails'd been stepped on with the first light of dawn. Normally I just pulled my jacket over my head, since that was what I'd been using for a pillow in place of the wood block the Ke-Han had outfitted every room with. A man would've thought the Ke-Han could make small pillows, since they knew how to make large ones, but apparently not. Everyone in the palace slept so late that there didn't seem to be any point in doing anything else.

That was when I'd had my brilliant idea. Instead of going back to sleep, I started going through some of the exercises we'd been taught in training camp during the years before a man became a fit enough soldier to fight on the battlefield. It was the sort of thing every man practiced in the lull between battles, so they wouldn't get rusty in the interim. Being rusty meant life or death—usually the latter, when being in shape counted for something. I was rusty as an old iron gate just by letting myself go so long, but that was what living among the Ke-Han did to a soul, I supposed. Especially with a madman next door.

The only exercise I'd had lately was avoiding Caius Greylace at dinner, or barring the door against him with whatever I could find to wedge it closed.

It was hard to practice without a weapon. I'd had every man from th'Esar on down try to explain to me just how it was a good idea to visit a country that still loathed us without any arms to speak of, but no one could see the wisdom in what I had to say. Instead, they'd told me that was what we had men like Greylace for, whose weapons weren't the sort that could ever be put down. And men like me, though I didn't like to think about it, and probably wouldn't unless I fucking had to.

So what it amounted to was, th'Esar wanted us to give the appearance of being unarmed. Still, we had *some* backup defenses, just the kind that were invisible, and not the kind used by those who'd done any actual fighting in the war or anything like that.

Not having a sword threw off my entire balance in the exercises. A sword's got a certain heft to it that a soldier had to get used to if he ever wanted to catch the enemy napping. Without a sword, my hands moved too quickly. Without that added weight, I overcompensated once or twice and stumbled over the crescent-shaped footstools that were strewn around my room once more, like the maids were trying to box me in. I'd requested them, and now they too were working against me.

On the third day this happened, I heard a quiet tutting sound from the next room over. I nudged the footstool aside with the toe of my boot and went on, ignoring what I'd heard—though by now, I knew the sound all too well.

Maybe if I ignored it, Caius Greylace would just go back to sleep. If luck was with me, I'd be able to finish *and* sneak in a quick bath before everyone else woke up.

Luck, as it happened, had abandoned me yet again. I heard the unmistakable sound of the door sliding open, soft as a whisper, and before I had time to pretend I hadn't seen him, Caius Greylace was standing in the doorway, wrapped up in a cocoon of white silk robes with the front pieces of his hair pinned back like a woman's. It was disconcerting to see both his eyes so clearly, since he normally took great pains to hide the one he'd lost the use of during the sickness. He peered at me sleepily with one green eye, the other one murky and white and without any focus or direction.

"I daresay, my dear, that you could wait until a decent hour to begin moving furniture around." He yawned, his little pink tongue reminding me of a cat's, and looked around the room. All at once, his expression changed from bemused and sleepy to curious, and I felt a sinking feeling within my chest, as though I would never have a moment's peace again.

"What *are* you doing?" he asked.

"Nothing," I said, though the battle was already lost.

He ignored me, and wandered in to perch himself on one of the small chairs I hadn't managed to knock over yet. It figured that *he* wouldn't be too big for them the way I was, even though they'd been put in my room to begin with. Then he yawned again, covering his mouth like a Ke-Han lady did with a fan.

"Carry on," he said, with what he probably imagined to be a regal air.

"If you're so tired, then you ought to go back to bed," I told him, but I knew it was hopeless to try to talk Caius Greylace into doing *anything*.

Best just to get on with things.

I did, doing my best to ignore Caius the way I ignored how wrong the exercises felt without a proper sword in my hand. I told myself that the most important thing was working up a sweat, and feeling that sweetly uncomfortable ache in my muscles that meant I was using them, not sitting around on a cushion all day while my ass got a little more numb and my arms and legs turned to cooked Ke-Han noodles.

I was just about finished when Caius started to clap. I'd done a pretty good job at forgetting he was there, so that the noise startled me out of the neat routine. Try as I might, I couldn't get my peace of mind back enough to remember what came next. It was hard work, sparring without a partner.

"Oh, that was *marvelous*," Caius said, twirling a loose bit of hair between his fingers. He looked thrilled to the bone, and too excited to sit still. "I've never seen soldiers training before. This explains all the noise you've been making. Do you plan on doing it every morning? Perhaps you should; it really does look as though you're in need of some practice."

"Looks better with a sword," I told him, wiping the sweat from my forehead with my sleeve. "Works better, too."

"Ah, I see," Caius said, nodding. He rested his chin on one hand, watching me with his off-putting, mismatched eyes.

"Also," I added hastily, not knowing why I felt compelled to explain myself to him anyway, "it's better with two people. That way you've got someone to fight back against. It keeps you thinking."

"Fascinating," Caius said, drawing the silk of his robes more tightly around him. Then he stood up as though he'd heard some wake-up bell I hadn't. "Shall we dress for breakfast, my dear?"

He turned and swept through the door that joined my room to his like a little lord, his robes trailing down past his feet in a way that was probably planned, if I knew him. And I did, unfortunately.

The next morning, he showed up before I'd even started my warm-ups. He was carrying a sword. It was a strange blade, thin and curved at the very end, like the sword-maker had got distracted and pulled away too soon. He was holding it all wrong, bundled up in his arms like he thought it was a baby or a cat, and not a real metal blade, sharp and nastiest at the tip.

"Where did you get that?" I asked. It was nearly as big as he was.

"*Well*," Caius said, looking ever so pleased I'd asked. He was wearing green robes that morning, and his hair wasn't clipped back over his bad eye, which meant that he must've been planning to interrupt and not just jarred cruelly from his beauty sleep. "I asked around, you know, and that charming lord who's always shouting—Lord Jiro, I believe—said he had a son about my age, and it was every boy's duty to carry a sword, or something to that effect. I admit my understanding of the conversation waned toward the end of it. Anyway, his servants dropped by my room later that night, and they were *ever* so kind enough to provide me with this."

He held out the sword like it was a dead cat; only it was heavy, because he was holding the hilt with both hands, and swaying under the weight of it. I wanted to laugh, but what I wanted to do even more was to take the sword. I did.

I was surprised to find that it was lighter than any blade you'd have found in Volstov, and thin like I'd thought it was. When I pulled it out of the sheath, I saw that there was one blunt side and one sharp. All the more useful for when you wanted to maim your opponent rather than kill him, I supposed. I was surprised, also, that the Ke-Han could ever decide which side to use without summoning a council of a hundred, but then maybe that was why they'd lost the war.

Caius sat down on the crescent seat again, watching me expectantly. I swung the sword through the air experimentally, making a pass here, a block there. It was a good sword.

"It's still better with two," I said, calling out to Caius the same way I'd called out the city boys who'd gathered around the barracks to lean over the fences and watch us fight. If he was going to sit in, he might as well learn something from it—if he could.

Caius's eyes went wide, as though I'd genuinely shocked him.

"I'll go easy on you and everything," I said, though privately I was thinking, *not that easy.* His being a magician, even a reluctant watery one, meant that I'd heard my fair share of rumors about Caius Greylace in my time, and despite his looks, he could definitely take care of himself, spoiled lightweight or not.

"Oh my," he said, fluttering like a lady just asked for her first dance. "Wouldn't the guards think the worst of us again? I'd hate to cause any commotion."

Ever since my little mishap with the guards, I'd noticed, they tended to patrol up and down our hallway with greater care, and took their time loitering right outside my doorway since they didn't know the truth of it, that the whole thing had been Caius's fault. All the other diplomats had their theories as to why, since no one knew the real reason except me, Caius, and Lord Temur, and there wasn't one of us opening our mouths on the matter. Still, we were wasting time, and I wasn't about to be put off from the one thing that kept me sane by a bunch of overexcitable, unintelligible guards.

"You can use the scabbard," I said, holding it out to him. "It's about the same size as the sword."

"That's hardly fair; it's not really the same at all," he said. "And you're such a great brute—you'll have quite the advantage over me!"

He took it by the end, like a fishmonger carrying his catch of the day. I waited for him to do something—maybe stand a little straighter, or hold it up as if it were a real sword. Anything. *Something*. Instead, all I got was a coquettish look.

"My dear, I do believe you're staring at me."

"You're holding it all wrong," I told him, as if that was completely obvious, which up until then I would have said that it was.

"Oh," Caius said, looking at me and then at the sword. "Well fancy that!" He adjusted his grip, fiddling for a moment with his long, wide sleeves before settling on something that looked marginally more normal.

"Haven't you ever held a sword?" I asked him. I was getting that sinking feeling again.

"Well, I haven't ever had to," he said. "I've held knives. Well, they were more like letter openers, but they were decidedly knife*like*. You needn't worry, I'm sure I'll pick the trick up sooner or later."

I began to reevaluate the situation. "Maybe you'd better sit this round out," I said.

"Well, if you insist," Caius said, and went back to his perch. I noticed, though, that he held on to the scabbard—probably because it was the same color as his outfit, and he liked that sort of fussy little detail.

Eventually, after a couple of days, I was able to forget that Caius Greylace was there at all. He kept quiet—the only place he ever managed to—almost like he actually respected what I was doing, though there was no real way he could've appreciated it properly, since he'd never been a real soldier, himself. Maybe the true understanding was lacking, but at least he was able to hold his tongue, like maybe he thought he was watching a performance at the local theatre, and he didn't want to disrupt the performer. I was no more than entertainment to him, though; that much was certain.

"I daresay you look much happier with that awful thing than in the company of your friends," Caius said, after the third morning.

"What friends?" I asked, but I was grinning while I asked, and wiped the sweat off my brow.

The next morning, Caius was dressed all in blue—just to spite me, I figured, since there was no other reason for it. He opened the door and clapped his hands together. "Wonderful news," he said, and immediately I was wary. "Well you needn't look as though I've gone mad," Caius continued, pouting enormously. "It's only, I've found a better place for you! So you won't break any more stools."

"I've only broken one," I said. The remnants of the stool in question—I'd stepped on it the day before—were piled in the corner of the room, far enough out of the way that I wouldn't splinter the wood any further.

"Two," Caius corrected me.

"Now, that's not fair," I said. "The other one's barely cracked. It doesn't count."

"Nevertheless," Caius said, "I've the solution to the problem. Why ever do you refuse to trust me?"

Because you're a two-wheeled carriage, if you know what I mean, I thought. It didn't matter whether I said it or not; Caius Greylace could sense an insult as sure as if you'd really spoken it.

"Well, you might as well just *see* it," he reasoned, taking me by the arm and dragging me toward the door. "And I do believe you *will* like it."

Letting Caius surprise me was a piss-poor idea, I thought, but suddenly, I was curious. He'd been almost tolerable the past few days. What if the Ke-Han air was getting to him, making him ... sane? Well, saner, I thought, because he was still dressing like the belle of the ball, but there were some problems no amount of good weather could cure. Little lord Greylace was cracked.

But, as it turned out, I'd misjudged him.

"There," Caius said, satisfied, after leading me through the twisting halls of the palace, enough so that I'd got thoroughly lost.

I didn't know how he'd done it, but we were in a quiet, empty garden; the walls of the palace shielded it from the rapidly rising sun, and the ground was covered by bleached white stone. In fact, it looked a lot like he'd brought me to a place where I could train in the cool morning air, in private, in peace. Whether or not he'd done it for himself—giving me a better stage to make the show more entertaining—didn't matter much to me.

"I *thought* so," he said, judging by my lack of response. "And what's more, I've brought visitors!"

That was where he lost me. For a moment or so, I'd even been grateful.

"Visitors?" I asked.

"I just couldn't help talking about it," Caius went on, as though I didn't need any further explanation, even though, between the two of us, I wasn't the *velikaia*. "Even though you do break stools, it's quite enjoyable to watch. You see, my dear, I was in the middle of a fascinating conversation with Josette about Lord Jiro's battle history—she is so wonderful to talk to about these things; you ought to try it sometime—and I happened to let it slip that you were in the midst of preparing for another war, or so it seemed, the way you were behaving. Then, because she looked rather alarmed at the prospect, I had to explain everything... which was when Lord Temur overheard our conversation and suggested that, instead of practicing inside your room and breaking all the furniture the Ke-Han had to offer, you might prefer to practice somewhere you can do it properly, and without splinters."

"He suggested I practice here," I said, caught up in the whirlwind of illogical progression that was just Caius's way of going about his everyday life.

"Something or other like that," Caius agreed happily. "Aren't you delighted? They should be along any minute now, so you mustn't look foolish or stumble and disappoint them. That would be awful; I'd be hideously embarrassed. And after I praised you so sincerely! Lord Temur is a war hero, you know, and trained in all manner of the martial arts. He'll know whether or not you're performing to the best of your capabilities. I think, if you're subpar, you'll be letting all of Volstov down." With that, he smiled a very smug smile, obviously pleased with himself.

If he was trying to goad me, anyway, then it was working. The idea of looking like a fool in front of a Ke-Han warlord really got my blood hot.

Something told me that Caius had orchestrated the entire scene just to watch the audience interact with the actor; so that he, the grand director, could sit back and clap at our quaint performances.

But I'd wasted enough time already standing around and chatting with him. Whether Lord Temur came or didn't come, I wasn't going to let it stop me from taking advantage of the new space I'd been given, and I wasn't about to stop practicing, when it was the only thing I could call my own in that forsaken place.

I hefted the sword—it still wasn't heavy enough, but I was getting used to it, even though it meant I had to relearn all the steps to compensate for the shift in balance. That was what a good soldier was supposed to do. Improvise and adapt. This was the sword I had, this was the time I'd been given, and it hadn't been so long since the end of the war that I'd forgotten what being a good soldier meant.

I began with the easiest steps, while out of the corner of my eye I saw Caius step back toward the wall—nowhere to perch and watch me here, just wide open space and the bleached white gravel beneath my boots. After that, I forgot all about Caius Greylace being there, and the possibility of Lord Temur stepping in to size me up. If I let anything distract me, then I'd let myself down, and that was that.

The gravel crunched loudly beneath my boots with each step, but at least there weren't any stools around me to break; Caius was right about that being helpful. And, that way, I could swing a sword freely without worrying about getting it stuck in the beams above my head or the wall or something like that. Breaking a stool was one thing; cutting up the fancy room that the Ke-Han'd given me was another, a less pardonable offense, considering how prim and proper they were and how meticulously they'd decorated it with furniture meant for tiny children.

It felt good to be out in the fresh air, and it was early enough yet that it wasn't humid. Still and all, I'd worked up a considerable sweat by the time Josette and Lord Temur did arrive, their footsteps on the gravel alerting me to their presence before I could pause in my routine to look up.

"That is Lord Jiro's sword," Lord Temur said, once I stepped out of the old motions, pausing to wipe the sweat out of my eyes and acknowledge my new visitors with a nod. Caius clapped happily and offered me a sip of water—he really had thought of everything. I accepted.

"Suppose it is," I agreed.

"It is different from a Volstov blade," Lord Temur added thoughtfully. "It cannot possibly suit you."

"I'm learning it, anyway," I managed.

"We hear you're very diligent," Josette said, looking composed and wide-awake, despite how early it was compared to the diplomatic mission's usual waking hour. "Caius has been telling us all about it."

"Has he," I said. "How . . . gratifying."

"We've been keeping tally on how many stools you've broken so far," Josette added, for all the world like a schoolgirl teasing a poor country boy. In a way, maybe she was. It was just a different face from the one I was used to seeing her with, her politician's face, gracious but humorless.

"I believe it was two at last count," Lord Temur said. "If I recall the right number."

"The general doesn't think that the second chair counts," Caius reasoned, almost as if he were taking my side in the matter but still managing to drive me crazy by insisting on calling me by my title. "But that's neither here nor there, really; stools are replaceable, and we've distracted the good general long enough."

Lord Temur bowed his head in brisk acknowledgment, and Josette went to stand by Caius's side, next to the high white wall.

"Of course," Lord Temur said. There was no hint of mischief at all, either in his voice or on his face, when he added, "I merely thought that a practice sword might be of some use to him. They are, after all, slightly heavier." And, like he was saying, "And I just so happen to have brought one with me—what a fantastic coincidence," he produced one from behind his back: a heavy-looking wooden thing that'd been polished to within an inch of its life, except at the hilt, where it was rough enough that it wouldn't slip right through your fingers. Maybe the polish was useful for practicing, though, since if you could hold on to something so shiny and slippery as that, you could probably keep proper hold of your sword in the midst of a battle, when everything, especially your hands, was slick and wet with blood.

"Delightful!" Caius said. "He's been complaining about the weight all this time—haven't you, my dear?—and I'm sure he'd be ever so grateful. Aren't you, General?"

I gave him a look, even though I was beginning to realize the futility of it, and allowed myself to accept the offering from Lord Temur with grudging thanks. I had to admit, it *would* be helpful. He was a man who understood what it meant to be a soldier, at least, and I had to respect that.

"And," Caius went on slyly, like the little snake he was, "he is often complaining of how it isn't proper at all to spar without an opponent. I'm in perfect agreement, of course—but then, I'm no match for the general, so my opinion is rather worthless, don't you agree?"

You could've cut the tension in the air with one slash of Jiro's sword. Josette was giving Caius a look that I recognized all too well—it was the look I always gave Caius—so it seemed we'd figured everything out at about the same time, namely why Caius had been talking to her about my practicing and why Lord Temur had just happened to be close enough to overhear him while he was discussing it. The whole thing had been orchestrated like we were all puppets on a single string, one that was wrapped around Caius's crooked little finger.

For someone who hadn't been a soldier himself, Caius Greylace sure knew how to manipulate them. Then again, he probably knew how to manipulate anyone, but this was something real special. This was something else.

At the same time, from the look in his eye, I didn't think the whole thing had been the result of an impulse that was purely selfish. In his own way, I realized, Caius thought he was doing it for me as some kind of a present or favor. I'd complained about having no room and no one to spar with, so he'd given me a better place to practice and someone to practice with.

The only variable in question was Lord Temur. What kind of pride did the Ke-Han have? And just how rash could they be when that pride was aroused?

Lord Temur was a soldier, and so was I. Caius had set things up pretty as a picture.

"General," Lord Temur said at last; I could hear Josette's breath leave her in a short, excited burst. "It would do me a great honor if you would deign to practice awhile with me." And he bowed deeply.

I couldn't see how there was any way to refuse, since we'd come that far. Josette would probably call it a setback as far as diplomacy was concerned, and Caius would sulk for days if I ruined all his best-laid plans, so I bowed to Lord Temur, just as low as was courteous, and not an inch below that.

"The honor's all mine," I said, thinking that if I was going to do this, I might as well do it right.

As it turned out, the sword Lord Temur wore at his waist was another practice one, made of dark, polished wood and about as lethal as the footstools in my room. I guessed looks were more important than function when it came to the Ke-Han way of things. Besides, there was that rule we all had to follow—no weapons carried by the diplomats, and even the warlords had to abide by that. That was probably why Lord Jiro didn't miss his sword too much by letting me borrow it, *if* he knew I had it. Knowing Caius, that didn't seem like a foregone conclusion.

But a wooden sword was better than no sword at all, I decided, if you came right down to it.

The gravel didn't crunch as loudly under Lord Temur's feet as he settled into a ready stance across from me. Being light on his feet that way meant he was going to be fast, but I felt the weight of the practice sword in my hand like some kind of reassurance against what was coming. I didn't know how Ke-Han warlords fought in one-on-one combat, but I had a sword that suited me, and I was about to find out.

Lord Temur swung high first, the movement startling me so that I only just managed to bring up my sword to block it. It was that expressionless face that made it a surprise. The lords of the Ke-Han were normally so quiet and still, I hadn't expected such a swift and sudden movement from him. It was a stupid mistake, and one I wouldn't be making again.

He swung his sword next to the side and I parried it more easily, feeling the gravel shift and give way beneath my boots as I stepped back. Whoever kept the garden so neat and tidy was going to have their work cut out for them when we were through, I thought, and brought my sword around to swing at Temur's ribs. He stopped me before I could get there, the sharp smack of lacquered wood against lacquered wood ringing out through the courtyard. I thought I almost saw a faint smile flicker across his face—and that was one mystery solved, at least. If you wanted to get an expression out of the Ke-Han, all you had to do was put swords in their hands.

"You fight very well," he said, and there was something different in his voice this time, none of that underwater calm that all the diplomats radiated, like they were half-asleep.

I didn't answer. It wasn't Volstovic custom to talk during a battle, and I'd been trained to focus all my energies on one thing: looking for an opening.

It seemed as though Lord Temur had been trained to focus all *his* energies on one thing, too, except that thing was: Don't show an opening because your very life depends on it. His sword crossed mine at every turn, like we formed the warp and weft of some violent tapestry. He drove at my skull and I knocked him away, feeling the strain in my arms like an old friend, long absent and well missed.

I might have shouted with the sheer joy of it, but I was too busy with each thrust and parry.

Lord Temur's fine warrior braids had fallen in front of one of his eyes, and I was starting to feel like there was nothing I'd rather do but wipe my forehead since the sweat dripping down was starting to impair my vision.

I shook my head once, quick like an animal drying off, and out of the corner of my eye saw the sword arcing toward me.

I caught it hard on my forearm, stronger than the other one because it was used to bracing such blows with a shield, but I felt it all the way up to my shoulder, numb and strange all at once.

I heard Josette gasp—I knew it was Josette because it sounded concerned, rather than excited, the way it would have sounded if it'd been Caius—but Lord Temur only drew back as if to attack again, and I swung my sword hard back against him, searching for the opening I knew I'd find. It was only a matter of time.

I'd noticed one thing, at least, and that was the Ke-Han style of fighting focused on three parts of the anatomy—the head, the belly, and the hand. Lord Temur's attacks were varied, but they had all the same targets. It wasn't single-minded so much as it was damn stubborn, but almost beautiful in that. It was like he just assumed, sooner or later, he'd hit his mark, so there was no need to shift the target. Stubborn and determined and fierce.

I could live with that.

My arm was numb but my blood was hot, and I wasn't so out of shape that I didn't think I could take him. It was just a matter of figuring out his style. He wasn't just some common Ke-Han soldier, and it wasn't the kind of desperate free-for-all that a real battle inspires in a man. We weren't fighting tooth and nail; it was kind of like a dance, only we were both hearing different music with different rhythms. It must've been something pretty to look at from the sidelines, each of us acting out his own steps while all the while trying to figure the other one out.

For example, we were even crouching different. Lord Temur was lower, and he held his shoulders back; that changed everything, from his lunge to his swing. He put more from his legs into it, while I swung a sword mostly from my back.

I got revenge for my numb arm and tingling fingers soon enough when Lord Temur went for the head and I went for the stomach. All the air left him in one satisfying whoof of surprise, and he stumbled back, the gravel scattering every which way around his sandals.

"One–one," I said, figuring that we were even.

Lord Temur's eyes narrowed—and I knew that we were about to really start fighting. I tightened my hold on the unfamiliar hilt of the wooden practice sword, bracing myself, the blood pounding between my ears.

"Gentlemen." I didn't recognize the voice, but I was pretty annoyed that anyone would try to distract us when I was clearly so close to getting the upper hand.

"Oh!" Josette said, sounding shocked in an entirely different way than she had a moment ago.

Lord Temur didn't seem all that inclined toward listening to the voice either, for all he stepped back swiftly to get out of range of my sword before darting in again, close and hard like he was through with being polite. I could understand why he'd be sick of it. He'd probably been polite all his life.

"*Gentlemen*," the voice said again, and this time I thought I *did* recognize it, after all.

"Oh, your Imperial Majesty, isn't it simply thrilling?" Caius said, sounding like he'd never seen anything *more* fascinating in his entire life—and like it was nothing out of the ordinary at all to address an emperor like that on a lovely morning while watching two diplomats go after each other in dead earnest during peace talks.

Lord Temur stopped short. I had to wrench my arm back into a feint at the last minute to avoid cracking his head open with the wooden blade. He dropped into a low bow immediately, which was what gave me time to turn around and see for myself what everyone was on about.

The Emperor was standing in the courtyard, flanked as he always was by his seven surly-faced bodyguards. I hadn't even heard the gravel crunch with their approach. Was it later in the day than I'd thought? I wouldn't have pegged the Emperor for an early riser, but maybe he had to get up early just to have the time to dress in all the layers he did. That day's special ensemble was green on gold, which meant that he was wearing gold ornaments in his hair along with the jade. It was the sort of thing Caius would wear every day, given the opportunity and enough time to grow his hair.

I didn't think Caius had the time or the connections to organize that little turn of events, but with Caius Greylace, you never knew what he had the time or the connections for. I looked at him warily, just to check, but there was pure shock on his face. For him, this was just a happy accident.

"The guards informed me that there was fighting in the gardens, between the diplomats from Volstov and one of our warlords," the Emperor said. There was something fiery in his eyes that made them bright where they'd always been lusterless during the talks. "I was resolved to put an end to such nonsense, but now I see that you fight without real swords and with an audience in attendance, and my misgivings have been put to rest."

"It's only practice," I said, since it didn't seem like Lord Temur was going to stop kissing the gravel and defend himself anytime soon. What a waste of a perfectly good soldier. He'd ruin his back, bowing all the time like that, then he wouldn't be good for fighting anymore.

"Ah," the Emperor said, turning his eyes on me. Just then, he reminded me a little of Caius for reasons beyond his clothing, because I thought I saw a spark of madness in his expression. "I see. You practice at fighting, but do not deem it necessary to use real swords."

Josette sucked in her breath, like she knew what was coming, and, even worse, that she couldn't do a thing to stop it. That alone should have made me think twice, but my blood was pounding so hard from the fight that it made it real difficult to think even once.

"I *had* a real sword," I pointed out. "Only it was borrowed, and it just seemed like good manners not to get it all banged up practicing with someone else."

"Good manners," the Emperor repeated, only in his voice it sounded like something soft and slithery, a snake sliding through dry leaves.

"Yeah," I said, tapping the sword against my leg. I caught Caius's eye from where he was standing up against the wall. He looked like a puppy in a box, trying to keep his composure but still too wriggly and excited to actually manage it. I wasn't going to get any help from him in squirming my way out of this conversation, and I was starting to wish I'd just gone and bowed like Temur so as to placate the Emperor so he could've gone on his way and let us be. There was something about the way he was looking at me that I didn't like. I felt like a beetle pinned under a 'Versity student's lens.

"Well," the Emperor said, "a real soldier of the Volstov should fight with a real sword."

I couldn't get my head around why that sounded like an insult before he'd undone something at the front of his robes, and was shedding all the fine, heavy layers like the most elaborate cocoon imaginable. Underneath it all, he was wearing plain black robes, just like his servant-bodyguards. It was then that I remembered he was still in mourning for his dead father.

Emperor Iseul snapped his fingers, and one of his entourage started doing something with a cord to tie back his sleeves.

Beside me, I heard the shifting of gravel as Lord Temur got to his feet. For the first time since I'd met him, he looked flustered.

"Correct me if I'm wrong," I said, feeling a sudden inexplicable companionship with someone who'd until now been my enemy, "but—to me, I mean—it looks as though the Emperor wants a chance at fighting me next."

Temur eyed me, as though trying to choose his words very carefully. "I would lend you my sword, had I been permitted to bring a live blade."

There were too many things I wanted to say to that. Did that mean that yes, I was going to have to fight the Emperor? Did it mean I was finally going to get what I'd been wishing for—right when I really didn't want it—a real fight? And most important: Was I going to end up like the second prince if I caught one of the Emperor's fancy jade hairpins on the edge of my sword in the heat of the skirmish?

Before I had a chance to answer, one of the Emperor's guards unsheathed his sword and handed it to me. I guessed whatever rules applied to us about swords didn't apply to them. There was something about the weight of the gesture that was like a sudden cold wind up the length of my back. I didn't like how this was going, not at all.

Caius waved to me from the sidelines. He looked as though he'd just been told there was going to be a festival in his honor, with lanterns and streamers, dancing girls and fireworks.

"Good luck, my dear!" He smiled that creepy jack-o'-lantern smile he had. "Do us proud, would you?"

At least he had his priorities in order. I wasn't expecting the same kind of encouragement from Josette, who had to be diplomatic now that the Emperor was there, but she'd pressed her lips together into a thin line, like she was afraid that she would start cheering if she didn't remind herself not to.

I swung the guard's sword, testing the weight of it against what I'd just been using. It was heavier than Lord Jiro's sword had been, maybe even the same weight as the practice sword. I was thinking maybe that I should have thanked him, but when I turned around he'd already retired to the sidelines and so had Lord Temur, who was standing next to Josette and murmuring something in her ear.

If it was a bet, I was hoping Josette'd forget to be diplomatic just long enough to put it all on me. It was a matter of patriotism, after all.

The Emperor stepped out into the open area we'd made our sparring arena. His long, ornate sleeves were tied back with a thin, ropy cord, and he had a fierce look in his eyes. Somehow, I thought, he looked a little like the paintings we'd seen of the warrior-gods, smiling cruelly, their hair braided with the bones of their enemies or something.

However preposterous he looked all dolled up in traditional Ke-Han fashion, this was a man who'd got rid of his own brother for questionable reasons. A man who'd dressed in his finest to greet us the afternoon we arrived, when only that morning his father had killed himself for the sake of honor. I was starting to get the feeling that this—everything—had been a really bad idea, when he swung his sword up into a waiting position. It was the same stance Lord Temur had adopted yet different all the same.

In the time it took me to follow, the Emperor's expression changed from bloodthirsty to amused.

"I was a warrior myself, General," he said, "before I was an emperor."

With that, he brought his sword down lightning quick, and when we clashed it was with the crisp, dangerous ring of metal on metal.

It was one thing sparring with Lord Temur, who was more or less, in the scheme of things, my equal. I was a general; he was a warlord. We'd probably both been in the same position during the war, and we were the same age, more or less.

It was another thing to spar with the Emperor of the Ke-Han, who was, by my understanding, a good five years younger than I was.

All I could think was that Emperor Iseul was lucky he *hadn't* been Emperor during the war, or during my time fighting in it, anyway. *That* Emperor had a lot to answer for, and, with a sword in my hand, I might've been tempted to make him answer for it right then and there, and peace treaty be damned.

The first meaningful thing I learned about Emperor Iseul was that he was *fast*.

He came at me like a poisonous snake lashes out to bite, whip-quick and light. He looked more at home in plain clothes than he did all trussed up in emperor garb, and he looked pretty regal then.

And it wasn't anything at all like fighting Lord Temur, partly because they were two very different men and partly because having a real sword in your hand changes everything. I was more than just plain grateful that I'd had the practice fighting Lord Temur to learn a little more about swordplay in the Ke-Han style. In fact, I didn't have any proper words for just how grateful I was.

Knowing what the Emperor was aiming for helped me to parry the first ten or so attacks, but not knowing what direction he was coming from wasn't doing me any good. I couldn't read anything in his face beyond the glint in his eyes. He'd wanted to strike out at us for a long time, ever since we'd arrived and probably before then, too. I just happened to be the poor bastard standing in front of him, holding a sword.

I thought about Volstov. I thought about how many years I'd fought, and how many friends I'd lost, and the battles I'd been in with that man on the other side.

It was hard to get past the defensive, but there was something as angry as fire in the air and it was coming over me now, same as it'd come over the Emperor himself. I didn't even know what we were fighting for anymore, but we were fighting honestly, like two starved lions in the ring.

I brought my sword down, hard, aiming for his shoulder, and he parried, throwing all his weight against the attack. I could feel the clash in my jaw, it was so sudden and so hard, and then he was on the offensive again, while I had to keep blocking his attacks at lightning speed, or else. He was moving fast enough that I didn't know if his swings were the sort of thing he could stop in time—that is, if he did break through my defense—before he sliced my arm off, or worse.

Head, belly, hand, head, hand, belly. He fell into a pattern that was deceptively easy to follow, striking out with rhythmic diligence. It wasn't anything like fighting an ordinary soldier. I wasn't good enough, and we both knew it. That didn't mean I wasn't going to make him sweat—and fighting, I knew intimately, wasn't always about who was good and who was better. It was about luck, too, and tenacity, and about reading a person.

Only it was impossible to read the Emperor. The more I fought him, the more I realized he was fucking insane.

There was sweat in my eyes, pouring down the back of my neck and staining my shirt and my chest, my shoulders, my underarms. I wished to bastion I had my own sword—a mean, heavy Volstovic number that could've broken his blade in half with the right swing—and then we'd've seen how good he was, with two pieces of a sword and me bearing down on him.

I could hear my breath turn ragged, was starting to recognize the pattern of the Emperor's breaths, too—how he breathed in when he attacked, breathed out when he parried. Our swords met, over and over, me fighting like a Volstovic soldier, him like the Emperor of the damn Ke-Han.

Then I slipped on the gravel. It was the only opening Emperor Iseul needed—the opening, maybe, he'd been waiting for this whole time. It was my boots, or the fact that I wasn't used to fighting like that on the gravel, or how out of practice I was. Any number of things could've caused the slip, but they were all worthless excuses. It was a mistake, pure and simple, and I was going to pay for it. It was only a matter of how.

My thoughts came pretty quickly in that instant, right before the Emperor's sword came down.

I managed to stop the blade from slicing me open, cracking my collarbone and heading toward the lungs or the heart, but it took all my weight—at least I was a bigger man—to keep Iseul at bay; I had no chance to push him fully off. He'd attack again, and quickly. The second strike would likely throw me off-balance.

I braced myself for it, down on one knee and thinking through all the unfavorable situations I'd been trapped in, all the scars I'd won. Was I really going to let some Ke-Han bastard get the best of me, Emperor or not?

So instead of just waiting for the attack, I brought myself up to meet him as his sword came down the second time. The noise was so loud I thought I heard Josette shout behind us—less like a scream of fear and more like a vote of confidence. Or, at least, I chose to read it that way.

It surprised the Emperor, as much as he *could* be surprised, anyway, and I pressed my advantage without much finesse. Strength might win me this one, not technique. If only I had my fucking broadsword.

Iseul parried my every move, but at least I was driving him backward.

Pride undid me. I was too pleased with myself, and that blinded me to the possibility that the Emperor could be as strong as I was. That maybe he'd been holding back some cards for the very last round, the way they had in the war, so that by the time we'd got them figured, it was nearly too late to stop them.

And, just like that, I was on the ground, flattened out, dazed and aching and wondering how I'd got there. I'd lunged too quickly, pressed my advantage too fully, and Iseul had caught my blade with his own, then...

Then, he'd tripped me.

Still, I always knew the Ke-Han fought dirty. I should've been expecting it all along.

I could hear the sound of a sword coming down, could hear it sing through the air with such grace and speed that I knew two things. One, that the Emperor was a master swordsman, and at least I'd been bested by a worthy man. Two, that the Emperor was going to kill me.

You didn't swing a sword like that unless you were aiming to kill, and I was down, moving too slowly. I brought my sword up, but my bad arm was numb, and there wasn't enough strength in my hand to stop Iseul; he'd just drive my own blade into my neck with his own.

Shit, I thought. Caius Greylace had really done it this time.

"My Lord!" Lord Temur shouted from the sidelines. There was something in his voice I recognized—a little bit of the same desperation I felt, although not as much, obviously, since I was the one Emperor Iseul was about to slice open.

The Emperor stopped as if on the blade of a knife, the tip of his sword a bare inch away from my face. My life didn't pass in front of my eyes or anything like that—I was used to almost dying—but the morning sunlight glinted too brightly off the metal of the Emperor's sword, and my heart was pounding so hard I could scarcely hear anything else.

Then, just as neatly as you could turn a Ke-Han sword from sharp side to blunt, Emperor Iseul's face lost that mad spark, so that even when I looked for it, I couldn't catch the barest hint. He removed his sword in a deliberate gesture, graceful, as though it had all been a part of the dance to begin with.

Except I'd heard the panic in Lord Temur's voice. *That* hadn't been a part of any dance, Volstovic or Ke-Han.

"I overestimated your skill," the Emperor said, as if that was his idea of an apology. Close to, the sharp planes of his face made him look less like a warrior-god and more a man wearing a demon mask. His eyes were lined with kohl, making them seem longer and thinner, like the eyes of some great cat that toyed with you before pouncing. The ornaments in his hair clinked together like the wind charms we'd seen in the city. "If it is your intent to practice here in the future, I will inform the guards that you are not to be disturbed."

I didn't know what the proper response to that was. How did you thank a man who'd just tried to kill you? Did you show you were grateful, just because something—fate or Lord Temur's voice or a combination of both—had intervened? All I knew was, I was flat on my back and I wasn't about to turn over just to bow.

"It seems as though I'll be needing the practice," I said instead, wondering a bit too late whether or not the humor would translate.

Emperor Iseul stretched his lips in a humorless smile. "Indeed, you do."

He turned and walked off the yard to where his servants were waiting, muttering to themselves in a language I still didn't understand, though I thought I caught one or two words that were starting to sound familiar to me. Maybe one was the Ke-Han word for "Volstov," or "little blond shit-stirrer who dresses like a woman."

As it didn't look like anyone was going to rush over and help me up anytime soon, I got up myself. I brushed the white dust from the gravel off my trousers and rolled my shoulder a couple of times, stretching out my bad arm gingerly. With my luck, it'd stiffen over the course of the day and get worse overnight. Either way, there was no doubt in my mind it'd be sore as hell in the morning.

Emperor Iseul's servants were busy dressing him, tying on the colorful robes that hid his private mourning, and all of them silent as the grave before Iseul started barking orders and they began to talk among themselves, hesitantly at first. Who knew what they were saying? Maybe they didn't like the way I'd been manhandling their Emperor, but if I could've spoken the language, I would've assured them that it was *me* who needed the fussing over, and not Iseul. I'd been the one flattened—and my pride felt it too, just the same as my back and arm.

One of them shuffled over to take the sword back, which I handed over gladly. I'd had enough of real weapons for the time being.

"Are you all right?" Josette had finally broken away from the wall to ascertain my well-being—after having waited a properly diplomatic interval, I was sure. "That last looked quite . . . forceful."

I shrugged, regretting it when my arm started to tingle after the movement. "It was good exercise. And that's the whole point. Force."

"Well," she said, looking between Emperor Iseul and me, "think of the story this will make, though. Fiacre will never believe it. One of our own, sparring with the Emperor of the Ke-Han!"

All at once her face changed, got all excited and flushed the way Caius's did when he contemplated some new fabric or a particularly beautiful formation in his tea leaves. At least she didn't sound so thrilled by the fact that I'd almost had my neck sliced in two. Maybe she didn't realize it.

"I have to go and tell him," Josette continued. "I'm sorry, but if I'm not the first to break the news, I'll be sorely disappointed. I'll see you at breakfast, though! And Alcibiades . . . perhaps you'd better bathe first."

I followed Josette back to the wall, where Lord Temur was standing uncertainly in the middle distance between Caius and the Emperor, looking rather unsure of himself for the first time.

I still couldn't shake the sneaking suspicion that Lord Temur had saved my life by recalling the Emperor to his surroundings the way he had. I guessed that meant I had to be grateful to him. What surprised me was that I didn't really mind.

"Lord Temur," Josette said suddenly, as if she'd just had a brilliant idea. "Would you like to accompany me back to the palace?"

Temur blinked, and I thought I saw a hint of a smile in his eyes. Maybe the Ke-Han had expressions after all, and you only had to know where to look for them. Or maybe it was just the remnants of the fight still in him. Either way, he held out his arm, and this time, Caius didn't dive between the pair of them to take it away.

In fact, Caius was being oddly still for someone who'd been all but doing cartwheels in the courtyard earlier. With his one good eye, he regarded the Emperor's servants refitting his train, and he didn't even look as excited about the clothes as he might have, nor was he tapping his cheek in fake concentration, a gesture that was rapidly becoming overly familiar.

I joined him by the wall, standing by way of blocking his view, since as far as I was concerned he'd orchestrated this whole thing in the first place. Even if it had started out as something of a favor, it'd ended up almost killing me.

"My, my," Caius said, coming to life suddenly as though he'd been in a daze all this while. "What a dreadfully exciting morning, don't you think? You'll be the talk of the palace for months, my dear, as the diplomat from Volstov who tested the Emperor himself!"

"Yeah," I said. "It's been some kind of morning, anyway."

"It's so splendid that I don't know how I shall bear it," he murmured, his eyelids fluttering shut. For him it might've been all some grand, gay dream. For me, it'd ended up as anything but.

"He tried to kill me," I said, not because I thought I could trust Caius, but more because I didn't have anyone else to tell.

Caius opened his eyes again, and I could see the milky outline of his bad eye through the fall of his hair.

"Oh, my dear," he said. "I know."

CHAPTER SEVEN

MAMORU

Of all the things I'd managed to prepare myself for in the past few days, the one thing I wasn't anticipating was Kouje's behavior that afternoon on the road to the border crossing.

Ke-Han land was partitioned according to the pattern originated by the old domains hundreds of years ago. When my ancestors swept across the land on horseback, consolidating their power and subsuming each territory into our vast empire, what had once been separate castle towns and the land that surrounded them became prefectures. To this day they remained cordoned off by the great walls, which transected the Xi'an landscape like the stitching in a farmer's patchwork cloak. Now, the prefectures were run once more by lesser lords and defended by their retainers; the only difference was that the lords each answered to the Emperor, and their duty was to serve the empire first and not themselves.

The greatest wall of all, which surrounded the capital city, was nearly thirty feet high. Until then, it had been the only one I'd ever seen with my own eyes, though I was told that, because of the walls, our country itself was one of the greatest wonders of the world.

As apprehensive as I was about crossing the border, I did wish to see that great wonder for myself, to observe for myself the famed checkpoint towers. I was no child, but it struck me as somehow sad that I, once a prince of the Ke-Han, had so little knowledge of what had been my own land.

Up ahead of us, Jiang and Inokichi had stopped by the side of the road to rest and water their horses; Kouje and I dismounted to do the same. It was a beautiful road, if barren and somewhat lonely. There was something to be said for the comfort of a road well traveled, though I was glad we'd passed so few riders that day. As much as it had unsettled me to live like a wild demon in the forest, I missed the shelter of the trees and was unaccustomed to so much open air, and so much sun.

"Here," Kouje said, wringing out a cloth in the stream and offering it to me. I pressed it against my burning forehead, and sighed in relief. I wanted to ask him if the sunlight bothered him—if he felt on fire from the inside out, or suffered the pounding headache that came from a long morning riding through the heat, or if he was sore all over from riding—but I felt uncomfortable speaking in front of Jiang and Inokichi, so said nothing.

"Little flower you've got yourself there," Kichi said, and though Kouje stiffened, I attempted to remind myself that it was his own peculiar way of paying me a compliment. I didn't understand it—there was no poetry at all within it—but I would have to accept it. "Real delicate. Ladylike. Is she married?"

"She's still young," Kouje managed, tension lacing his voice. I allowed myself to pat him gently on the arm.

"My brother is quite protective," I said, hoping to defuse the situation somewhat. I could allow myself, in this disguise, to speak with *some* of the delicate language from the palace. After all, I was a woman, and I felt no need to become someone like Old Mayu just yet.

"Ah, say no more," Kichi said, winking at me in a way that I supposed was meant to be congenial.

It occurred to me that I had very little understanding of the way that men and women communicated with one another in an informal setting. I had a great deal to learn. And perhaps Kouje did as well, for I could practically feel the tension radiating from him in waves. If we could have had a moment alone, that I might have asked him frankly what the trouble was, I would have felt marginally better.

As things stood, though, I was unsure as to whether Kouje was simply having trouble adjusting to the way of life we'd taken up, as I was. At the palace, he would never have tolerated anyone speaking to me with such familiarity; the sudden change must have been a great strain on him.

I squeezed his arm where I'd patted it, trying to convey my meaning without words: that it was quite all right and that he needn't worry so.

Kouje looked at me, and I could see his frustration quite plainly, mingled with the knowledge that this was what we had to accept. To be perfectly honest, I was surprised at the difficulty he was having in adapting. I'd always assumed that Kouje would undertake any task with the greatest of ease while I would be the one left struggling.

It had been so ever since I was young, after all, with Kouje set as the bar for everything I aspired to become.

Of course, there were many things I had to learn on my own since Kouje, for all his fine attributes, was not a prince, but he praised me in my learning of those other subjects too, even if he did not understand himself the particularities of poetry or calligraphy. In some ways, Kouje had been like a second brother to me, not as proud or as stern as Iseul, but one who would give me comfort when I'd done poorly, and encouragement when I'd done well. Such needs were only an indication of my weaker character, for Iseul had never required a brother to offer him anything—but then again, that was where the difference between us lay. I was a second son, born weaker than the first, and nothing could be done about it.

"My friend," I murmured, softly enough that I didn't think Inokichi or Jiang would hear me.

Kouje nodded, his eyes saying what he could no longer speak aloud: *my lord.*

It was an agreement, though I'd not asked anything specific of him, to try harder. I could tell by the troubled expression on his face that he, too, was concerned by his conduct. He would have to take better control of himself, rein himself in as he did our horse.

Some way from us, Jiang and Inokichi sat beneath a tree, playing a game with knucklebones. Rather, Inokichi was playing, and Jiang was looking bored, casting a glance toward the horses every now and again to see if they'd tired of drinking yet. I gazed at the stream with some longing myself, for all we'd bathed the day before. Had it only been a day ago? My clothes were coated in traveling dust, the hem of my robes stained with the damp of early mornings in the forest and hunting for rabbits. I could no longer recall what it felt like to be clean, even though I remembered the sharp cold of the water in the river and the slither of catfish around my ankles. How Kouje had laughed at me then, and rightfully so. I smiled to think of it, new memories that were not so sore as the old ones and were heartening to think back on.

Time had passed in a curious fashion since we'd left the palace, first so quickly and then impossibly slow, so that I was no longer certain of the day or time. By my calculation, though, it had been less than a week. Four days? I would be missing the summer festivals in the city, that much I knew—but had they already started without me?

"We should be moving on soon," said Kouje aloud, for everyone's benefit. Then he took the cloth from my forehead and patted it against my temples. I realized that he was as concerned about getting me out of the sun as he was with furthering us to our destination. Or perhaps he was feeling the effects of it as badly as I was and only thought to save himself a splintering headache.

It was very likely the former, but I tried now and then to pretend Kouje was also looking after himself.

Kichi stood up all at once, like a theatre puppet pulled to its feet. Jiang followed at a slower pace, looking less than amused at his friend's antics. It was a kind of exasperation that was born of real affection, though, which made sense when one wondered how they could have put up with traveling together so long.

"Wanting to get it over with as soon as possible, hm?" Kichi stretched his arms over his head. He was overly tall, as well as overly cheerful. "Can't say as I blame you. Never know who you're going to end up stuck behind. And if there's some poor bastard with a royal air about him ahead of you, the crossing could take all day. That is, if the guards don't take an irrational dislike to you with no warning."

Jiang snorted. I got the feeling that perhaps Kichi was the sort of man that guards took an irrational dislike to.

Kouje seemed to think so, too, but I saw him clench his hands at his sides and breathe in deeply instead of saying anything. I laid a hand against his back, to comfort him as much as to draw strength from his resolve.

At the palace, I would have been ashamed to draw on any outside comfort, especially now that I was of age, but I'd never before seen a side of Kouje that faltered, that was ever anything but completely certain. It frightened me more than the imminent border crossing, and I was glad to see him taking control of himself once more.

"One more little border town and we're at the crossing," said Jiang. "We thought we might stop there for lunch. Kichi crosses better on a full stomach."

"What he means is, I'm less likely to ask the guards what they're having for lunch and end up on the wrong end of a sword," Kichi said, smiling as though he shared an enormous joke with me.

"Sounds all right," Kouje said curtly. I could tell that he was wondering whether or not we'd have the money for lunch. We still had some left over from the night before, but it seemed prudent to save it for a time of need rather than on another bowl of rice so soon after the first.

Jiang and Inokichi mounted while Kouje helped me onto our horse. It was an unnecessary gesture, but one we'd thought might aid the illusion that I was his maiden sister, younger and inexperienced. It made me wonder about Kouje's real sister, the one upon whom we were pinning all our hopes. I wondered if she was like the sister I played at being, or if she was more like Kouje himself. I hoped at least that she would forgive us for using her home as a place to hide—for the trouble it could bring her, and the disgrace if she were ever caught. I hoped that she hadn't already branded me as a traitor or blamed me for her brother's downfall.

More than all the rest, I hoped that she would like me.

I fell into a restless dozing on the bright, sunny road that led to the border crossing. When I woke, I was rested back against Kouje's chest, my neck bent at an uncomfortable angle and my head pounding from the heat. The only comfort I found was the shade cast over my cheek by Kouje's profile, but my neck felt raw, and was no doubt red as summer beets.

I licked my dry lips, and lifted my head gingerly.

"Where are we?" I asked.

Kouje shifted behind me, as though he'd been reluctant to move before. How long had I been sleeping, I wondered, and how uncomfortable had it been for him? "I didn't want to wake you. I believe we're almost at the town."

"Oh," I said, squinting down the road ahead. Inokichi and Jiang were riding some way in front of us. I could hear Kichi's laugh ring out sudden and sharp, startling birds into flight at regular intervals.

"Kouje, how long have I been asleep?"

"Not long," he said, quiet as though I was sleeping still, and he was trying not to disturb me. "Not longer than half an hour. Does your head trouble you still?"

I nodded, regretting the movement seconds later. "I think that, even if we do not partake of lunch, I am sorely in need of some water."

"And . . . what of lunch?" Kouje asked.

We both knew how hungry I was; Kouje, surely, must have been hungry as well. "Full still from the night before," I said, offering Kouje what I hoped was a reassuring smile. "Perhaps I might fashion some sort of covering for my head before we ride out next."

"An umbrella would work best," Kouje said.

"Mm, yes," I agreed, "and an armed escort—perhaps a stroll in the gardens, or a palanquin?"

Kouje flushed, and laughter sparked momentarily in his eyes. "Perhaps we'll figure out some kind of veil, then," he agreed. "Though I don't know if it would suit you."

"It would cover my face," I pointed out. "Which might be useful, all things considered, for reasons beyond protection from the sun."

"Still," Kouje said, "it wouldn't suit you."

It might, I thought, allow me to avoid any further comments from Kichi as to what a delicate flower I was, or how it wasn't fair of Kouje to be so dead set against my receiving compliments. After all, I wasn't *that* young, and Kichi was certain there'd been a young gentleman or two— probably, he added with a wink, more like a whole army of them— knocking down Kouje's door to be the lucky bastard who could convince my brother he was worthy, and was that what we were on the road for, hm? Running away from all my blockhead suitors?

I was grateful, at least, that I was convincing in my part. When Kichi went on and on in that fashion, it was easy enough to blush and duck my head, for all the world acting like the delicate flower he thought I was.

What I was most worried about was being *too* delicate. Even though we were a party of four, I couldn't run the risk of being too aristocratic.

Occupied by my thoughts, it wasn't long before we crested a hill and Kichi reined in his horse for long enough to wave back at us and gesticulate toward the horizon. What I saw there took my breath away.

One of the many great walls lay before us, large gray stone weathered by time and bleached by the sun, and a thriving wallside town in the valley below. It was a busier place than we'd seen in a long time, more people than we'd been among since we left the palace, houses and shops crowded together beside the protection offered by the wall.

"How tall do you suppose it is?" I managed to ask Kouje once I'd regained my breath.

Kouje paused for a moment to appraise the height, with the horse whinnying and snuffling below us in annoyance at our strange whims.

"Fifteen feet I'd say, at the least," he answered finally. "Can't tell for sure until we're closer."

"Are you gonna spend all day staring at it?" Kichi howled back at us, though it was clearly a good-natured demand. "Or are you gonna get a move on? Hicks!" He let out a cheerful whoop and spurred his horse suddenly on, tearing off down the hill, leaving Jiang to give us a long-suffering look and follow after at a more dignified pace, with us trailing behind him.

The town wasn't nearly so big as the capital, but it was large enough for me to realize how much I had missed city life—even though most of my opportunities to observe it were through a palanquin window, it was still the knowledge of its bustling presence, its constant activity, its arts and pleasures and luxuries, that I'd been missing. We might have grown accustomed to our isolation in the woods, to sleeping on beds of leaves and to hearing the owls hooting in the night, but I'd never once stopped missing what I'd lost. All that became painfully clear the moment what I'd lost was, in some ways, returned to me—the noise and the light and the excitement of a real city. I could smell dumplings cooking, ducks being roasted, could hear the commotion of shop owners chasing orphans away from their doorsteps or calling to the passersby, trying to tempt them inside. My stomach grumbled so loudly I knew Kouje must have heard it—I didn't like that he should have to catch me out in a lie, no matter how necessary it was—but he didn't say anything, and I willed the grumbling to be silent. We barely had any money left, and I tried my best not to stare at the children by the roadside eating their dumplings, entirely oblivious to just how lucky they were.

"Fried eel," Kouje said, almost without thinking.

The smell was torturous, but I breathed in deeply anyway, storing the scent and trying to let the memory of what fried eel tasted like fill my stomach. It didn't work as well as it might have, but it was the only taste of eel I would have for a long time, and I savored it.

All around us, people were talking in the cruder dialects I was coming to understand better and better, slurring their conjugations and elongating their vowels. Sometimes they used words I didn't even recognize, which left me scrambling after the meaning of what I'd overheard, trying to piece together what the word must have meant by the context of the other words surrounding it. If I was to be a commoner, then it was necessary for me to understand their language, though their slang often made me blush.

What I recognized most of all, to my shame and growing agitation, was my own name, usually spoken in loud whispers; the rest was gossip, each tidbit more ludicrous than the last. One of them had Kouje fighting mountain demons in the north; another had me already in Tado, across the ocean, in talks with the royal family there. Where had I found a boat, I wondered, and how had I got across the water so quickly? And yet, when I thought of the guards at the checkpoint, I wished that I *were* in Tado, dining at the royal court, speaking with them of true treason.

Yet—and this was the strangest thing—the men and women on the street, when speaking my name or Kouje's, uttered them without any animosity at all. I was a runaway and, for all they knew, also a traitor. I ought to have been vilified. Men should have spat on the street when they spoke of me, and women should have looked up to the heavens in apology when they acknowledged my existence. Why didn't they loathe me? There was some piece of the puzzle I was missing, and I didn't know how to go about understanding it.

Kouje reined the horse in suddenly, to avoid trampling a group of small children as they darted out across the road and almost directly under our horse's hooves.

"*I'm* Lord Kouje," the child in the lead called back over his shoulder, waving a short stick in a way that intimated it was not, in fact, a stick at all, but rather a great sword.

"*You* were Lord Kouje last time!" one of his companions accused, deeply affronted by his friend's selfishness. "And Sanji was Prince Mamoru last time, too!"

They disappeared past us down a side street in a chorus of shouting and laughter, leaving Kouje and me baffled in their wake.

"Imagine that," was all Kouje finally said, and we hurried along, so as not to lose Jiang and Inokichi in the crowd.

We stopped at last in front of another noodle shop—and spending so much time near noodle shops without buying any noodles, I realized, was going to drive me mad sooner or later. My favorite noodles had been the wide, flat rice ones, served hot, usually in broth; Kouje preferred buckwheat noodles, served cold and sprinkled with sesame oil. Just thinking about it made me ache all over.

"My old friend runs this place," Kichi said, after we'd dismounted. "He'll give us the best noodles for cheap. Can't find better noodles, not even in the capital!"

"We're not hungry," Kouje said, a bit too quickly. I understood the reason why—the longer he hesitated, the more difficult it would be to refuse.

Inokichi looked at us, mouth wide open in shock, like a dead fish's. "Not possible," he said finally, pointing toward me. "I've been listening to that one's stomach grumble for miles now."

I felt the blush rising in my cheeks almost before I could duck my head. Of course I knew that Kouje's stomach must have been empty too, and that there was no shame in so simple a thing as hunger, but I couldn't help wishing for a little more control over the noises that made it so evident to everyone else.

Kouje looked at me with uncertainty in his eyes for the first time. It was easier to believe that I was full when I had no one to contradict the lie of it.

Kichi sucked his teeth in a way that reminded me of a tutor I'd once had, and snapped his fingers. "Ah, so *that's* the trouble, is it? No worries; I'll cover the cost myself."

"That's not necessary," Kouje began.

Kichi shook his head. "What kind of man would I be, letting a delicate little blossom like that starve? If you're not careful, she'll drop all her petals."

"You're too kind," I murmured.

Out of the corner of my eye, I saw Kouje bow his head, his jaw clenched tight against any further protest. I hoped he wouldn't think the less of me for compromising his pride along with my own, but if there was a chance that I could silence my stomach's complaints—and if there was a chance that Kouje could have something to eat, as well— I knew that we had to take it.

I didn't regret it. I would have done it over again, given the chance. Besides which, refusing the offer a second time would be an insult to the man, and we couldn't afford to make any more enemies.

"It's decided, then!" Kichi slapped Kouje's back, looking quite pleased with himself. "I know we don't always see eye to eye, brother, but you've got to at least be flexible on the road. Think like a reed, and less like a rod, hey? There's other things they say about rods, but I can't tell that one to you with fine ladies present."

At once, I felt myself blushing all over again. Kichi laughed his raucous laugh and pushed aside the colored banners that hung in the open doorway. Kouje touched my hand with his own in a gesture of reassurance, and I held on to it tightly for a moment, wishing I were not *quite* so delicate as to be left out of all interesting conversation. It wasn't that I felt there would be any special merit in Kichi's joke. In fact, it wasn't even the joke at all but rather the spirit of camaraderie behind it. As things stood, I was in very nearly the same position of isolation as I had been in the palace. No one spoke his mind to a prince if he could help it, and apparently no one spoke his mind to the sister of a strapping young man like Kouje, either.

It was the most curious sensation to be surrounded by people and yet still feel so utterly alone.

"Are you all right?" Kouje asked me, the question soft between the two of us.

"Just the heat," I lied, knowing that Kouje would guess at the truth behind my words well enough. If I'd felt confident enough to explain it properly, perhaps I would have tried. Perhaps Kouje understood them anyway, and that was why he'd made the gesture in the first place. Whatever the reason, I found myself grateful beyond words, and I held on to his hand with both of mine as we stepped inside. Things were less lonely with Kouje at my side.

The restaurant was a small but friendly-looking affair, with a counter for customers who were only interested in drinking, and a kitchen just behind it that emitted puffs of steam and mouthwatering smells in equal measure. It was also very crowded, so that Kouje and I had to pause for a moment to get our bearings once more. It had been so long since we'd been in a place with so many people that I believed for a moment we'd almost forgotten the way of it. Then I saw the consternation on Kouje's face pass, and his grip on my hands relaxed. I allowed myself to breathe in deeply and concentrate not on the shouting or the jostling of the restaurant's patrons, but the wonderful smells emanating from the kitchen.

Jiang and Inokichi were already sitting at a table near the back. When Kichi saw us, he stood up and waved us over.

"We thought you'd changed your minds," he said. "Which would've been pretty stupid of you, really. I'd have to question your sanity in turning down a free meal like this one."

"My sister's just a little dizzy from the heat," Kouje said, as politely as I'd heard him yet. The prospect of the noodles must have been affecting him just as it was affecting me.

"The two of you are awfully private with one another," Jiang said. "Used to living on your own, are you?"

"Something like that," Kouje said, and he stopped just short of the table.

I looked up, to see what was bothering him, and then I understood. Jiang and Inokichi had sat down across from one another, so that there was no space for Kouje to sit next to me as he normally did. I let go of his hand, and made as if to sit down first to set him at ease. Perhaps I would have to speak to him later, just to reassure him that he did not need to be so protective there as he was in the palace.

"I'll sit there," Kouje said, ducking around me when I would have sat next to Kichi. "I like to watch them make the noodles," he offered by way of explanation, nodding to me and looking at no one.

I took my seat next to Jiang, remembering to smooth my rough skirts underneath me, and offered him a small smile, as if to acknowledge the common affliction we shared: companions with a vein of eccentricity run through the center of them.

It wasn't entirely fair to Kouje, but I was certain he'd understand. I would have done anything to ease the tension between us.

"We didn't want to take the pleasure of ordering away from you," Kichi said, "so we waited. As long as you make it quick, we should be out of here with enough time to pass through the border and still make it to the next village before nightfall."

"There've been reports of highwaymen out in full force now that everyone's caught on the roads between checkpoints," Jiang clarified.

Kouje sat up a little straighter, listening closely to memorize the information for later. He told Inokichi our preferences for noodles, and even smiled at the joke Kichi made about men who liked their noodles cold before he went off to order.

"Well," Jiang said. "Silence. Beautiful, isn't it?"

"It has its merits," Kouje agreed.

Things were a little less tense than when Kichi was around to say anything and everything that popped into his head, but it was hard, too, not knowing what to say while Jiang made no effort to hold up any kind of conversation.

I was just trying to think of something—anything, really—to break the silence when I felt something brush against my leg. Thinking immediately of the catfish, I swatted it away with considerable panic.

"My apologies," Jiang said, looking not at all alarmed by the fact that I'd just thought his hand was a rat or worse.

Kouje narrowed his eyes, but didn't say anything.

"It's very kind of you to help us across the border this way," I said, before Kouje had time to ask what, exactly, Jiang was apologizing for. I had no skill in conversation, at least none that would help me here, unless Jiang wished to know the seven accepted ways to write a poem about nature, or the preferred variety of tea they were taking in the capital these days. It was all the more reason for me to practice, since it seemed I would need the skills sooner rather than later.

Jiang shrugged. He had a look in his eyes that was mostly friendly, I thought, but with a thread of something else that I didn't entirely recognize. It was like coming up against a word I didn't know in country dialect—a foreign object in the middle of what should have been familiar territory.

"We're helping each other," he said. "It's the neighborly thing to do."

I didn't entirely know what to say to that, so I nodded instead. Across the table from us, Kouje cracked his knuckles. I wondered if they were sore from the strain of holding the reins every day, and if we shouldn't switch off eventually, as equals might have.

I resolved to ask him the next chance we got.

Kichi returned shortly thereafter to put us out of our awkward misery, bearing a tray with four bowls of noodles, one steaming hot and three cold.

"I can't believe you're eating hot noodles on a day like today, blossom, but who am I to argue? I got you some water as well, since your fine strapping figure of a brother seems concerned for your constitution in this heat, and I for one don't blame him."

I took the water from him, too grateful to be embarrassed, and downed the glass in greedy, messy gulps.

When I'd finished, there was water on my chin, and dripping down my front. Kichi stared at me in plain amusement, while Kouje looked down, hiding his own smile but not before I'd seen it. I wiped my mouth, feeling shy but much less thirsty than I had a moment ago.

"Well," Kichi said. "Eat up, then."

Conversation died down as everyone dug into his meal with equal enthusiasm. Kouje and I hadn't had any breakfast to speak of—a fact I was made all the more aware of now that I was eating, and eating something that I felt I'd been craving since the night I'd left the palace, though of course I knew that was impossible.

There was another moment when I thought that I might have discerned a rat against my leg, and I twitched, bumping the table surface from below and nearly knocking Kichi's bowl over. Jiang apologized, and I apologized, and Kouje narrowed his eyes further, looking as though he'd found something sour at the bottom of his noodle dish.

I was the first to finish lunch. Once my sticks had scraped the bottom of the bowl, I put them down and tried not to look too longingly in the direction of anyone else's meal, especially not Kouje's, since I knew that he would have given me whatever he had left without thinking twice about it.

"Want another?" Inokichi asked, grinning like a monkey.

"I couldn't," I said then, trying to muster more conviction, "really. Thank you, Inokichi."

"So polite," Kichi said, clacking his tongue against his teeth. "Man oh man. You've got yourself some sister."

I folded my hands in my lap and sat very still, listening to my companions slurp their noodles, and grateful that Jiang's hands were occupied with his sticks. I ought to have savored my noodles more, made them last, but I'd been too hungry. At least, I thought, I could let Kouje savor his without worry or anger spoiling the taste.

Kouje finished at about the same time as Jiang and Inokichi did. "So," Kichi began, talkative once more now that his mouth was no longer busy with eating, "guess we'd better move on. Don't want to get caught outside at night, 'specially when a lady like that's riding with you."

Kouje murmured his agreements. I would have done the same, save for the fluttering touch at my leg. Jiang's hands were under the table again, and it was growing harder and harder to believe he was touching me by accident.

My realization must have dawned on my face at about the same time Jiang gave my thigh a—what had he called it? Neighborly?— squeeze. I couldn't stop myself, and Kouje, who knew my face better than anyone, saw it at once.

He stood so quickly he nearly knocked the bench he'd been sitting on over, and Inokichi with it.

"Hey, hey," Inokichi said, struggling to keep his balance. He held up his hands, the only one at the table, now, who didn't know what was going on. "Did you see a rat or something? I swear, they don't make any difference to how the food tastes—"

"May I speak with you outside for a moment?" Kouje said, ignoring Inokichi completely. His eyes were burning.

"Stop," I said, reaching out toward him, but Jiang was already standing. When he didn't slouch, he was a little taller than Kouje, and he'd raised himself to his full height.

The other patrons of the restaurant had all gone quiet, save for a whisper here and there. This sort of thing must have happened quite often in a place like this, though it had never happened to me before. We were making a scene. The last thing we needed was to be apprehended by local authorities so close to the border crossing—one which my brother's loyal retainers were patrolling at this very moment, looking for me.

"My pleasure," Jiang said.

"I'll only be a moment," Kouje said, turning to me, his expression softening. "Stay here."

Suddenly, I was outraged. Had I asked to be defended? Couldn't this have been resolved some other way? My cheeks were burning hot; I was dizzy from anger and desperation and the long day's ride in the hot sun. I reached out to catch at Kouje's sleeve—perhaps I meant to command him to stay, which admittedly might have called further attention to us—but I was too slow. Already, he was stepping past the colored banners in the doorway, ducking outside into the bright sun.

"Traveling companions, huh?" Inokichi said nervously, craning his neck to look after Kouje and Jiang. "Can't travel without 'em, but sometimes you wonder if being lonely isn't preferable to being..."

"Stuck in a noodle shop while your brother defends your honor on the streets," I supplied.

"Yeah," Kichi said. "Something like that. Though, of course, your situation and mine aren't exactly the same."

I wondered if, all this time, Inokichi was the easygoing one—if he was the one who suffered from Jiang's more volatile nature—all the while putting on a good show. Was Jiang in the habit of doing this sort of thing often? Was Kouje in danger?

Likely not, I thought. Likely, Jiang had no idea the hornet's nest he'd just stepped into the middle of.

And, just like that, after a shared glance of mutual panic, Inokichi and I rushed outside into the street, with all the patrons of the noodle shop whistling and howling and crowding out after us.

The first thing I could think, upon seeing the scene before me, was that this wasn't the way Kouje usually fought.

He was a graceful fighter, calm and poised, taught by the same master as my brother and therefore in some ways stylistically similar. Yet, at the same time, Kouje was a vastly different man from Iseul when each had a sword in his hand. Both were stubborn, yes, and inexorable, and both grew fire-eyed and tiger-fierce, but Iseul became a punishing god, a vengeful deity. Kouje became the paragon of sword fighting, a man whose sword was merely one more extension of his body. Both fought uncommonly well, but in my most secret of hearts, I knew which style I preferred—Kouje's quiet strength over Iseul's wildfire fury.

This, however, was not a sword fight in the palace. I was not sitting some safe distance away, watching two men spar with wooden swords. Rather, I was standing a bare foot from Kouje as he sparred with

Jiang—or rather, as he toyed with him. They were hardly matched: Kouje, who had trained in the palace, and Jiang, a common merchant. Each wild swing Jiang attempted, Kouje easily ducked, whereas every blow Kouje dealt hit its intended mark.

It was a side of Kouje I'd never seen. I didn't even know how to stop him—after all, in the crowd that had formed, I couldn't even use his real name without giving us away. In his current state, too, I couldn't trust that he would respond to the aliases we'd arranged privately between us. I felt helpless.

Kichi swore. He stood a good head and shoulders above everyone else in the crowd, which had gathered round to jeer and holler instead of do anything useful, like stop the fighting. I thought that perhaps, if Kichi had wanted to wade through the crowd to get to Jiang, it wouldn't have been much of a problem for him. It wouldn't have been nearly so easy for me.

Kouje was handling himself quite well at the moment—it was obvious to anyone who knew what he was looking at that Jiang didn't stand a chance—but I couldn't just do nothing and wait for Kichi to change his mind and join the fray. Or worse, for the town's authorities to arrive and adjudicate the fight. I threw myself forward into the crowd, too worried now to wonder about offending anyone if I jostled or pushed them. Not for the first time, I cursed my size—for although it was helpful in the disguise we'd manufactured, it made me feel futile and small when surrounded by so many able-bodied men and women. An elbow connected with my side; another narrowly missed my nose. I nearly cried out in frustration, still buried in the crush of bodies that had poured out of the other shops surrounding the noodle house, and hearing nothing but the two men scuffle and the roaring approval of the crowds.

I couldn't get past.

"Hey!" A voice in the crowd shouted, slightly louder than the rest. It wasn't a very cultured voice, but it was the sort of voice men listened to all the same. "Hey now, make way for the little blossom!"

Inokichi's voice rang out over the heads of the onlookers. I had just enough time to prevent my knees from going weak with gratitude before my way became just a little clearer, and I hurled myself gratefully through the gap, running toward Kouje with a fervor I'd never felt before, as hot as fever in my blood. Someone in the crowd laughed as I burst through, as though this were a fascinating new development and their entertainment had just become that much more diverting.

My heart beat a wild anxiety within my chest. We couldn't afford a scene like that.

Jiang's face was white with rage. A cut on his lip was bleeding, but Kouje was being meticulous with his aim, and, despite how livid he must have been, wasn't swinging at Jiang's face at all. Now that I was closer, I could see that Kouje's face bore the markings of the fight as well. His cheek was swollen beneath his eye, and there was a sore-looking spot on his jaw that I knew would be a large, dark bruise by nightfall. All at once, I felt the noodles I'd been so grateful to have eaten stir unpleasantly in my stomach. I pitched forward without thinking, grabbing on to Kouje's arm with all my strength and dragging it back.

"Stop," I said, breathless with fear. I had never seen such a rage on Kouje's face before. I never wanted to see it again. "*Please.* That's enough! Control yourself—*stop.*"

Kouje strained against my hold for a moment and I threw all my weight into it, nearly dropping to the ground like a theatre actress pleading with the hotheaded hero. Then I heard Jiang stumbling backward, coughing wetly as the dust rose up all around in clouds from the road. The crowd around us muttered in disappointment, and Kouje caught me underneath my elbow, his stiff hands possessed of a sudden gentleness as he drew me to my feet.

"I'm sorry," he murmured, and bent low to see me face-to-face—but also because it was the closest he could get to kneeling. There was something in his eyes, in the absence of his rage, that betrayed a deeper misery. It wasn't that he regretted what he'd done. It was that he'd known what it meant to do it, had understood all too well what a risk he'd be taking, and had done it anyway.

It wasn't regret I saw in his eyes. It was shame.

I wanted to ask him *why* he'd done it if he'd known as well as I did how foolish it was. It didn't solve anything. It only made matters worse.

"Your cheek," I said instead, touching the bruised space just above the line of his jaw. "It's going to hurt something awful tomorrow morning."

Kouje bowed his head under my touch, and I knew that my acceptance of his actions was far worse than any scolding I could have given him. He swallowed something back, as if refusing to speak any words that weren't the right ones. I knew what he wanted to say, of course. It was what Kouje had always said, especially when he could think of nothing else. *My lord.*

"It's all right," I said, willing it to be. I didn't know how to shake him from his guilt without using his name, either, since it was all I'd ever used to recall him to himself. Instead, I squeezed his arm gently where I'd grasped it with such desperation earlier and repeated my useless words. "It's all right."

When Kouje lifted his head at last, he wore an expression I at least recognized. He was resolved.

"We have to get out of the street," he said.

I nodded, glad for some action, *any* action, that would take us away from here, where the crowds had dispersed, but continued to watch us, from windows and from doorways. The streets were as good as empty as we made our way back to the noodle house. I didn't realize how far we'd drifted from it in the chaos. I didn't see Jiang, or Inokichi either, but I hadn't really expected to.

I felt a momentary pang of guilt when I remembered how Inokichi had cleared the way for me to get to Kouje. I hoped that Jiang wasn't so stiff and sore that it stopped them from reaching their destination, or gave them any trouble at the border crossing.

My heart sank. The border crossing. I didn't know how we were going to get past it.

I followed Kouje all the way back to the front of the noodle house to where we'd tied our horse before I realized I was still holding on to his arm.

"We should leave," he said, "before there's any trouble." The apology lay unspoken between us again, but there was no point in casting blame between the two of us.

We were all each other had.

"Any more trouble, you mean," I said, trying valiantly to lighten the mood.

Someone snorted, the sound of it more like a laugh than anything else, and I whirled around, startled at the idea of having been overheard when I'd thought we were speaking privately.

Inokichi was standing with his back to us, brushing down the spotted horse tied up next to ours. I didn't know how to put my finger on it, but I felt as though something about him had changed. It was odd, since we'd been traveling together all this time and yet I couldn't shake the sense that I was looking at a stranger—a new man, somehow. He was still the same Kichi in appearance—unusually tall, his arms awkwardly long—but he didn't look at all clumsy or unsure of himself. I wondered, with faint awe, how he managed that. He scratched at fleas and his hair was unkempt, but I'd never seen anyone so perfectly at home with himself. I'd been raised as a prince, but I felt I could have learned a thing or maybe two from Inokichi's self-confidence.

"You take care now, little blossom," Inokichi said.

"About your friend," Kouje began, then stopped himself. "And the noodles..."

Inokichi shrugged it off, and when he turned, he was smiling his monkey smile. "A man's got to protect a lady like that, brother. I can't say I blame you for getting a mite carried away."

"Thank you," Kouje said, the words as heartfelt as I'd ever heard them.

Kichi nodded. "Good luck at the crossing. Maybe we'll meet up again in the next life, hey, brother?"

"Thank you, Inokichi," I said, wishing I could have offered him more.

He grinned and winked at me, then glanced at Kouje to make sure he'd given no offense before speaking again. "Not every day you get to help a lady out. Just think of old Kichi the next time you're at a roadside shrine, right? I didn't do it for anything but that ladylike smile."

"Thank you," Kouje managed, when I nudged him in the ribs with my elbow. And then, just like that, Inokichi was gone, sauntering down the street and leading the two horses behind him.

Kouje helped me onto our mount, then swung into the saddle behind me. I could see where his knuckles were bruised and cracked from the day's activity, and felt a pang of regret that I'd ever reacted to Jiang's wandering hands at all.

"What now?" I asked, looking toward the wall. It loomed overhead. Somewhere in the distance children were laughing—perhaps still playing their game of Lord Kouje and Prince Mamoru.

"I'll think of something," Kouje said. Then, against the back of my neck, he added fiercely, "I swear it."

All his good intentions, I thought privately, did little when we were faced with that wall. My brother's men were waiting to find me and, if I knew my brother, they were getting more thorough and more ruthless with each passing day. We had no time to waste. Yet I bit my tongue and said nothing as Kouje nudged the horse into a trot beneath us and led us soberly away.

CHAPTER EIGHT

CAIUS

Alcibiades deserved something special, I thought. After all, he'd only just narrowly escaped being killed by the Emperor. Anyone in his position would have needed a bit of perking up, me included. And even though Alcibiades hadn't spoken of it since, I was determined to make things up to him.

"Go on," I said, watching his face eagerly for some reaction other than mulish brooding. "Open it."

"It's not snakes, is it?" he asked.

Wherever did he get those ridiculous ideas? One had to wonder about his countryside upbringing. "Is that a custom among farmers?" I asked. "Wrap snakes up in boxes and give them to their friends? I'm not entirely sure I like it. Wouldn't it be better suited for your enemies?"

Alcibiades snorted. "So long as it's not something alive," he muttered ungraciously.

"Not last I checked, no," I said, trying my best to placate him. "Come now, or we'll be late for supper."

"Hm," was all Alcibiades deigned to grace me with before he tore into the wrapping paper without any ceremony. He was an awful brute sometimes, in need of far better training. Poor Yana. I sympathized with her deeply.

It had been awfully hard to come by, mostly because I'd needed to guess at Alcibiades' measurements. I'd thought about sneaking in to his room at night with some measuring tape, but one could never trust Alcibiades to react like a normal person under the circumstances. He *was* as angry as fire ants.

"It's...cloth," Alcibiades said finally, pushing aside all the extra wrapping paper. "Red cloth." The Ke-Han were exquisite gift-givers; the paper was thick, brocaded, shot with flashes of silver and gold. I'd gone for something particularly ostentatious, since Alcibiades was a simple man and might have been swayed by bright colors or the like.

"You're being deliberately obtuse, my dear, and it's making it very hard for me to be gracious," I said. "You might try unfolding it."

Alcibiades looked, at least momentarily, appropriately sheepish, and did as he was asked. Perhaps I might shame him into proper etiquette yet, though who could tell how long it would take to teach this old dog a few new tricks?

"It's a coat," Alcibiades said, unfurling it like a war banner. "A red coat."

I didn't think he would appreciate it if I told him how expensive the fabric was, and how delicate, and so I merely said: "Please, my dear, try not to wrinkle it. I thought you might wear it tonight."

"But it's red," Alcibiades said blankly.

"Well, you insist upon wearing the color anyway," I pointed out. "And it's better than that dusty old thing you refuse to wash. You're beginning to smell, and it disturbs Josette. In any case, *this* color will match."

Alcibiades' eyes instantly narrowed. "Match what?" he asked.

"Why, the outfit I've had made up for myself, of course!" He really was too slow. "One moment, my dear—it'll only take a little while to change, and meanwhile you can make sure everything fits in the shoulders and around the waist. I wasn't sure of the exact number, so I had to guess. If anything isn't right, then we'll send for the tailors straightaway, and they can make the alterations before dinner is even on the table."

"Why are you doing this?" Alcibiades began to ask, but I was already closing the door on him. If he couldn't figure out how to try the coat on properly, then he was on his own entirely and would receive no more help from me.

I'd tried to be considerate when having it made—nothing more than the simplest of cloth, and the reddest, as well. I thought that ought to please him, obdurate as he was. Perhaps I'd gone overboard with the epaulettes? Yet they offset all the red quite nicely, and were the same gold as the buttons. Besides, the collar on his old jacket looked as though it were too tight for him, especially during the talks.

And, most important, I thought he needed some reassurance. What better way to do that than to dress in his favorite color?

My own new outfit was quite different, though I'd had it in mind to match ever since I came up with the idea. We were similar in color only—according to my plan, we'd be two bright red cardinals tonight amidst a flight of bluebirds. Yet what suited Alcibiades, a proud Volstovic military coat in proud Volstovic colors, would hardly do for me. I didn't even like red; it made me look too pale.

I compensated for it by designing the shape in purely Ke-Han style, from high Ke-Han collar to long Ke-Han hem, to layer upon layer of red sleeves, to bright red Ke-Han sash.

I looked like a bloodstain, I thought, as I caught sight of myself in the mirror and smoothed out my robes. Alcibiades would no doubt ask me what, exactly, I thought I was doing wearing a dress to dinner; I was expecting it, but I would be sorely put out nonetheless.

"Sorry to keep you waiting, my dear," I said, sliding open the adjoining door. "I had a bit of trouble with the sash."

Alcibiades didn't turn for a moment—he was too busy looking at himself in the mirror. And, I was overjoyed to note, the coat fit him perfectly in the shoulders and in the back.

"Oh!" I exclaimed. "*Do* turn around, General, so that I may see the complete effect! Does it fit as well in the front as it does in the back?"

It was the first time I'd ever seen Alcibiades do something I'd requested willingly, although he could have stood up a bit straighter, and there was no reason for him to tug at the hem or adjust the collar as though the whole thing made him uncomfortable. It was made from the finest fabric by the finest tailors the Ke-Han had to offer, and I'd made sure it was in a style he'd like. If he'd only stop slouching and keep his hands still, he would cut a fine figure indeed.

After all, since he adored the color so ferociously, it behooved him to act more proudly while wearing it.

"Well!" I said. "Don't you look handsome? I would never have guessed it. Those epaulettes suit you—I *knew* they would."

"Why in bastion's name are you wearing a dress?" Alcibiades asked.

I sighed. "Since I am doing you the favor of joining you in this fit of pure bravado," I quipped, "I decided it might be prudent in some ways to dilute the effect by at least giving a nod to Ke-Han culture in some other fashion. Besides, the days are turning cold, and the wealth of fabric will help on those chillier nights. Are you satisfied with the explanation, my dear, or have you other complaints to make?"

Alcibiades was silent for a long moment, staring at me. I looked him over again in the meantime, wishing he'd thought to shave. He needed a bit of a haircut, too; his curls were growing unruly.

"You look all right," he said finally. "I mean, for a madman."

"Pardon?" I asked, surprised out of my examination for a brief moment. In my distraction, there was always the possibility that I'd heard him wrong; when it was something so close to a compliment, the possibility became a likelihood.

Alcibiades shrugged, looking at the epaulettes on his coat as though he liked the effect they created as he did it. "It suits you. Better than some of the others, anyway. *They* look like imposters. Uncomfortable imposters, besides."

"That, my dear, is the difference between a good tailor and a bad one," I said, feeling all over again that this idea had been one of my better ones. Why, I might even have ventured to say that it had put Alcibiades into a relatively good mood, which was more than I'd ever seen him exhibit.

He wasn't exactly smiling, but this was certainly a step in the right direction.

"I daresay I'll never outshine the Emperor," I continued, venturing to stand beside Alcibiades in front of the mirror. "Oh! We make quite a striking pair, don't you think?"

Alcibiades looked down at me as if I were a bit of grit he'd suddenly noticed on his shoulder. Or perhaps he was thinking of the Emperor, and how he'd nearly been killed, in which case I'd been terribly gauche in bringing it up. I'd only wanted to test the buoyancy of his good mood and what would cause it to sink down beneath the waves of reticence he seemed so fond of. His stubbornness made him very difficult and very easy all at once.

"We're going to stand out," he said at last. "That's for sure."

I took his arm, smiling at my reflection in the mirror. "My dear, that's entirely the idea."

To tell the truth, I'd been looking forward to dinner a great deal ever since Lord Temur had taken me aside after our afternoon break in the talks to inform me that a theatre company had been invited to perform that night. It was the first bit of good news I'd had all day since I'd long since begun to realize that the Emperor was using his brother's absence as an excuse to run us all around in circles every day. He didn't require our permission to *do* anything, though some saw it as a fine gesture of diplomacy. I thought it seemed more like a diversion myself, keeping us away from the meat of the treaty discussions over an issue so sensitive that even those of us who'd picked up on it felt loath to mention it.

I felt it accounted quite well for all the sour faces around the delegation room though. A play was just the thing I needed to feel refreshed and renewed.

The Emperor's chamberlain had arranged for a new form of entertainment to be put on every night for us, and while I'd enjoyed the singing better than Alcibiades—and while the dancing had been divine—it was the coming entertainment that I'd truly been anticipating. A real Ke-Han play, one of the classics, performed exclusively by the most esteemed theatre company the Emperor could find.

"What're you skipping for?" Alcibiades asked belligerently. "Walk like a normal person."

I sighed, slowing my steps so that I might be more of a pace with him. "Aren't you at all looking forward to tonight?"

Alcibiades snorted. "Looking forward to leaving the palace in order to get some real food, maybe. And I guess I'm looking forward to seeing some of those stuffed shirts at the high table fanning themselves into a fever pitch over our new gear. That'll be real entertaining."

It was the most I'd got out of him since the incident with the Emperor. If the coat took credit for his unusual loquaciousness, there was room for me to feel immensely pleased with myself over having found the perfect solution to our problem.

"Don't tell me you've gone and forgotten the play," I said, in tones suggesting the utmost consternation.

Alcibiades only looked at me as though I'd told him the Ke-Han were putting a permanent ban on fried-dumpling stands.

"Oh, honestly," I said, shaking my head. "It's our entertainment for tonight. You were lurking about when Lord Temur told me, same as Josette. Don't tell me you've forgotten already!"

"Huh," Alcibiades said, in a way that I knew meant that he had, in fact, done exactly that. "Well, at least it's not going to be singing. There isn't singing involved in these plays, is there?"

As it happened, we were among the first to arrive to dinner. This was because I'd left enough time for Alcibiades to decide if he wanted last-minute alterations to his coat, and when he didn't, there hadn't been much to do but leave for the dining chamber. Normally I would have abhorred arriving early at *any* location—it would have been deliciously dramatic to arrive late, clad all in scarlet—but there was a certain pleasure in watching the various Ke-Han warlords enter with their servants and take their proper seats at the high table. Before the meal was served there was normally some accompanying music to set the mood, which more often than not set Alcibiades to grumbling and shifting and kicking me—he *said* it was by accident—like a sullen child.

It took all my strength not to invoke Yana at those times—since, like all powerful weapons, her name retained its power only if used sparingly.

"I see Lord Jiro is already here," I noted. So far, the room was gifted with an overabundance of red—we hardly stood out at all yet—though the lord's coloring was sadly in his face and not his clothing.

"We match him, too," Alcibiades noted, and took a drink of his water before I could see if he'd actually cracked a smile. I would never know whether or not that had been a joke.

If it was, I was quite prepared to cede my anticipation for the play in favor of further such entertainment, the sort only Alcibiades and his peculiar nature could provide.

Lord Maidar entered next, seating himself with a space between himself and Lord Jiro, though the night before they'd sat next to one another and shared conversation quite comfortably. In Volstov, I'd followed the rise and fall of various courtiers as they all scrambled to reach the very tiptop of the Esar's esteem. It had been a game, and a tremendously amusing one at that, until the day I'd been condemned to exile myself, after which it became a very difficult thing to keep track of, so far removed from the playing field had I been. It was somewhat more difficult keeping track of things at the Ke-Han palace, since—like anywhere—the servants held all the best gossip, and I hadn't yet learned enough of the Ke-Han language to be able to communicate with them. I'd studied abroad—as abroad as exile could be termed in those days—but an education in the formal language was quite a different thing from knowing the ins and outs of all the common slang. I would pick up on it eventually, I was sure. I was determined, though; my time would come. Until then, I would have to settle for gossiping with my fellow countrymen.

I leaned close to Alcibiades, holding my cup out so that he might pour me some of the delightful jasmine tea we'd been enjoying with dinner. "Do you think that Lord Maidar is sitting farther away today because of their disagreement in the talks?"

Alcibiades glanced up at the high table, taking no notice of my teacup at all. "Don't know," he said. "Personally, I think Jiro's right, and there isn't much point in focusing all our resources on one lost prince who doesn't even seem all that menacing anyway. Better to see what he's planning and deal with it then, isn't it? And in the meantime, we can get our talks out of the way. It's a—what's it, a nonissue, some kind of smoke screen. Keeps us from getting to the real issues. The Emperor probably couldn't've planned it better if he'd worked the whole thing himself."

I shrugged, tapping the delicate base of my cup against the table ever so subtly. "Don't look now, my dear, but I do believe the good lord has taken notice of our patriotic garments."

Alcibiades followed the direction of my glance, though whether it had anything to do with the fact that I didn't want him to was another matter entirely.

"Let him stare," he said, then glanced at me as though suddenly confused. "Is there a reason you're banging your teacup against the table? Or did you just get inspired by the music?"

"Just enjoying myself, my dear," I said, and nodded in the direction of the doorway. "The fun, I believe, is nearly about to start."

Josette, dressed quite fetchingly in a pale shade of cerulean, was standing there; she'd seemed happy enough until she'd caught sight of the two of us. Then her expression changed completely. I was quite fond of her—and her temper. She reminded me of Alcibiades in that respect—and I was doubly pleased with her when she barely hesitated at all before charging straight toward us.

"What," she demanded, "do you think you're doing?"

"Eating dinner with the Ke-Han," Alcibiades said, as though a pat of butter wouldn't melt in his mouth. His lips didn't even twitch; he had quite a knack for deadpan delivery, and I was forced to hide my delighted laughter behind my sleeve. "Why, what's it look like we're doing?"

"As if fighting with the Emperor wasn't bad enough," Josette hissed, taking the empty seat beside Alcibiades and fixing him with a terrifying glare. "What are you trying to do—cause an international incident?"

"We won the war," Alcibiades said, better than if I'd coached him through his lines myself. He really was a fantastic creature, my new friend. "Don't see why we have to pretend all the time like we didn't."

"These matters are *sensitive,* General," Josette said, though some of the anger in her eyes was becoming suffused with a sort of admiration and wonder. "As diplomats, we must...we must do what we can to make sure things progress as smoothly as possible."

"Good thing I'm not a diplomat, then, isn't it?" Alcibiades said. He took a cool sip of his water and sighed. "Ahh. Hits the spot. Real refreshing."

Josette turned her accusatory glare to me. "This is your fault, isn't it, Greylace?" I had to give her credit for seeing right through our little charade. I understood her position, of course—I'd even been in agreement with her at the beginning of our sojourn in the palace—but Alcibiades was, for all his brute strength, something of a delicate creature. All the rules were stifling him, and I was merely trying to give him a little fresh air to breathe before he went mad and did something very foolish, indeed.

"I like to show solidarity," I said. "My dear, would you pour me a little more tea?"

"Gladly," Alcibiades said, and obliged. "That enough?"

"Perfection," I replied. "Perhaps Josette would also like some tea?"

"Josette most certainly would not," Josette said, scanning the rest of the guests. Perhaps she was waiting for Fiacre to appear, in hopes that he would have the inclination and the clout to put an end to our game. Or perhaps she was on the lookout for the Emperor's arrival, which, considering Alcibiades' current standing in his graces, would result in something of a situation. It appeared, however, that Josette was doing her best to pointedly ignore us, so I turned my attention once more to the entranceway, just as Lord Temur arrived.

His expression revealed nothing when he saw us—the Ke-Han warlords were dreadful spoilsports—but I was delighted when he strode purposely over to us and chose his seat at *my* side.

"Lord Greylace," he said, nodding in our direction. "General. Lady Josette."

"Lovely day, isn't it?" Alcibiades said. "Would you like some tea? Apparently it's delicious."

All this time, I thought, and the secret to success with Alcibiades was so simple as giving him something he wanted! People were such complicated animals, far harder to please than dogs and far harder to care for than horses. In many ways they were the most like cats—aloof yet dependent, with moods of so many shades and variations that it was impossible to tell which they'd be sporting next.

Lord Temur glanced at me, then to Alcibiades, then to Josette. Josette merely shrugged, a dainty rise and fall of her shoulders that might have been taken for anything else but was, of course, exactly what it looked like. *Who knows?* her expression seemed to say, and, *It's awful being even the slightest bit associated with them.*

"I see you have made use of my tailor," Lord Temur said, after a pause. "General Alcibiades did not wish also to try the Ke-Han style? It is much more comfortable when sitting cross-legged for the talks, I find."

"I'd look pretty damn silly wearing something like that," Alcibiades said, nodding toward me. "All due respect, of course."

"Of course," Lord Temur said thinly. "It suits Lord Greylace very well. He has caused quite a commotion among some of the younger lords, who think he has a poet's aesthetic taste."

"Do they *really*?" I asked. This evening was shaping up to be even better than I'd hoped. "Why, Lord Temur, I had absolutely no idea!"

"They are in quite the state," Lord Temur said. "In particular, I believe they are enamored of the color of your hair."

"Now, Lord Temur," Alcibiades warned, though there was only surprising good humor in his voice, "do you think it's such a good idea to let Caius know that? He's so little, and if his head gets any bigger, it'll snap his neck."

Lord Temur looked at Alcibiades mildly—an expression I was coming to discover implied some modicum of surprise. "I think I have misunderstood something," he said. "It is often the case when speaking your language—I understand the basic grammar well enough, but the colloquialisms, the less formal turns of phrase . . . I admit that I am occasionally lost."

"That's better than I am with your language, anyway," Alcibiades said, on the verge of sounding amiable. "It sounds like so many hens clucking at one another, if you know what I mean."

"You must forgive him," I interrupted, as smoothly as I could given the circumstances. "He was raised on a farm, and apparently by wolves. What General Alcibiades meant earlier was something of an insult. He was intimating that, if you continued to compliment me or relay such praise from other sources, I would grow too proud and puff up like a peacock."

"A red peacock," Lord Temur said.

"The best kind of peacock there is," Alcibiades agreed.

"The Emperor," Josette said.

Immediately, the air in the dining chamber changed. The Emperor had a certain fearsome presence that consumed all the air in any room he entered; even when he'd stepped outside to observe Lord Temur and Alcibiades as they sparred, he'd managed to steal my breath away. Of course, I didn't like him, not even for the barest moment. It was something about his eyes; he reminded me of a panther on the prowl, a beast of prey in the jungle, the sort that pretended to be sleeping up until the very instant before you found it at your throat. He moved with the same lazy, intentional grace. It wouldn't have surprised me at all if he had falsely accused his younger brother; he seemed just the type. The poor little thing, I thought, out in the wild with only his loyal retainer to protect him! It must have been dreadful, as accustomed as he was to all the comforts and luxuries of palace life. I did hope he'd managed to escape.

But all that was mere speculation; the pondering of an otherwise unoccupied mind. I didn't share my suspicions with anyone, not even Alcibiades.

Imprudence and pride had seen me banished from the Esar's court once before. I'd suffered long, dreadful years in the countryside, with nothing more to occupy my time than counting sheep and gossiping with dreadful chatelains, or teasing their equally dreadful sons and daughters. Despite my exotic new surroundings, and despite my exotic new companions—and though I could have been the center of such grand, infamous scandals without even trying—I wished to get through my stint as a diplomat with as little incident as possible.

Perhaps, I mused, I shouldn't have followed through with the matching red outfits.

Yet the decision had already been made, the coats exquisitely tailored, and there we were in the Ke-Han dining chamber as the Emperor made his appearance. I had, as they liked to say in the country, made my bed in the stables and had no right to complain about sleeping with the sheep.

As on all other nights, everyone assembled bowed low over the tables. Even Alcibiades was game enough to follow suit, though that might have been less because of his new coat and my unexpected showing of Volstovic nationalism, and more because he wasn't actually drinking water but rather the clear, sweet Ke-Han wine. It was meant, as far as I could tell, for those who were too easily affected by the redder, richer draft—for children and the infirm—but Alcibiades had been knocking it back as though it were water. It was bound to be an interesting night.

I knew the exact moment when Emperor Iseul caught sight of us, like two red peas in a pod. To his credit, his expression revealed nothing—though when, of course, had I ever expected it to?

It was a dangerous little game we were playing, for I knew by then that the Emperor was prone to fits of passion despite the rigidity of Ke-Han protocol. He was fastidious and immaculate and dangerously powerful, but just like the Ke-Han wrapping paper in that he was shot with flashes of silver and gold—the colors of obsession and madness. All great men, I supposed, in positions of great power, must have been in some form or another exactly like him. How could I, little Caius Greylace, presume to know what it was like to be raised as a second-in-command, the replacement for my father should anything happen to him in battle, trained within an inch of perfection, with all my servants whispering to me since birth that I was descended from the gods themselves?

Even I'd gone mad once or twice, so the gossip said, and I was merely an Esar's cat's-paw. It was a tragic fact of the Greylace family that we were bred for beauty and Talent but little true function besides that. My great-aunt had been a famed beauty, and my mother, the second Lady Greylace, had been the rival of the formidable Lady Antoinette before the former's mysterious and very private death. I myself was nothing so fancy: raised in the palace due to some lingering fondness for my mother on the part of the Esar, until one of his men had caught me practicing my Talent in the eastern wing of the palace.

I was seven at the time.

"Fernand tells me he saw you with a *tiger* in the eastern corridor," the Esar had said, his beard the color of spiced wine.

"Not a real tiger," I'd admitted, to my great disappointment. "I made him."

Looking back, I couldn't help but wish I'd announced the thing with more grandeur, but what does a child know of such artifice?

"Show me," the Esar had said. "If you prove yourself useful, then you may have all the tigers you could ever want."

Royal blood—whether you were inbred or not—was always distinctly corrupt.

I reveled in the Emperor's aura despite that, for I had never felt such a presence in all my life, nor seen such impeccable grace firsthand. He was better than any actor, with greater stage presence, and he dwarfed us all in comparison. We were not fit to sit in a room with him. He believed this, as did most of his men, and the sheer force of that belief was beginning to convince even me.

Beside me, Lord Temur bowed lower than the rest of us, and I had to wonder what punishment he had received, outright or oblique, for being carried away with Alcibiades the other morning. At least, bless his heart, he hadn't tried to kill the general. And Alcibiades was going to have to practice harder if he ever intended to be quick enough on his feet to present Emperor Iseul with any real challenge.

The Emperor ascended to his place on the dais at the far end of the room and lifted one hand, palm outward—the signal for us to cease formalities and commence eating. Lord Temur continued to keep his head low for a moment longer than the rest of us.

"This is the best water I've ever had," Alcibiades murmured to me, in what he may have thought—poor dear—was a whisper.

"Must be from the mountains," I said, patting him on the shoulder. "How does your new coat suit you?"

"Fits better in the shoulders," he admitted, and less grudging than I would have thought him capable of being. "Like the epaulettes, too. A bit above my station, I think, but not too much so."

"Are you doing it for a purpose?" Lord Temur asked, as calm as you like. He spoke our tongue better than he gave himself credit for, which I supposed was all part of his tactic to encourage us to talk more freely around him. "I do hope," he added, without turning to look at either of us, "that you do not mistake my question for rudeness. I have a genuine curiosity when it comes to such Volstovic displays. We are each proud countries, but in a different fashion from one another."

"Greylace here likes the color better," Alcibiades said. He'd even stopped tugging at his collar—though I realized a moment later and to my chagrin that he'd undone the top button while I wasn't looking.

"I like variety in my wardrobe," I confirmed, sipping meekly at my tea. "Besides, I always find it better to wear red near autumn."

"That way you match the leaves," Alcibiades provided.

"Yes, my dear, that's quite enough, thank you," I said.

"Lord Temur," Josette said, brown eyes keen as she reached toward Alcibiades' setting to confiscate the clear wine and, I noted, pour a little for herself, "I believe that my two companions are what is known in Volstov as 'characters.'"

"Ah," Lord Temur said, though I could tell he honestly had trouble with this new and unfamiliar idiom. "Characters, you say? Perhaps... from a play?"

"In a manner of speaking, yes." Josette set Alcibiades' bottle down on the opposite side of her own table, so that he'd need to make a clumsy lunge for it to retrieve it, and pointedly ignored his dirty looks. "They are—somewhat over the top in the same way. Do you understand that?"

Lord Temur regarded us for a long moment. At length, he replied, "Completely."

Alcibiades favored Josette with a look that suggested he thought her the worst of traitors, and gazed sadly at what wine was left in his cup.

I patted his hand, and used that extremely opportune moment to turn our conversation around.

"Speaking of characters, my dears, can anyone give me any more detail on this play that's slated for our entertainment tonight?"

Josette shook her head, and Lord Temur leaned forward, his voice pitched low and careful, though whether this was because it was taboo to speak about plays before they occurred, or whether he merely did not wish to spoil the surprise for the other men and women around us, I couldn't guess.

"It is one of the old classics," he said, "about the princess who lives in the moon."

"She must get very lonely," Alcibiades whispered loudly. His eyes were wide with inebriated sincerity.

Josette clucked her tongue in disapproval. "It's only a story, Alcibiades."

"No, in this case the general is correct," Lord Temur said, correcting her gently. "It is rather a sad tale, about one who has a home but can never return to it without feeling a great loss for the man she has fallen in love with."

"Ah," said Josette, sobering up considerably, despite her foray into the bottle of wine she'd appropriated from Alcibiades.

Lord Temur nodded. "In some sense, it is a story about homes and the loss of them. I do wonder at the choice of program; would not a comedy have been best? But likely it has no real meaning behind it. The play is one of our most popular. If at any time you are interested in learning more of our history, you will find it mentioned in all the classics."

There was a faint shadow of an expression on Lord Temur's face— one that I was beginning to associate with something very close to anxiety. I wondered if it were the poor second prince he was thinking of, who had certainly lost *his* home, though not for any love. If that was what the Emperor meant by showing us the play, then it was deviously cruel of him.

Somehow, this did not surprise me. Perhaps it was because I'd seen him fight that I felt with such certainty all the things I'd only been able to speculate upon before. I had no understanding of the way a prince of the Ke-Han was raised, of course, but when I thought of how that sweet little creature had smiled at Josette's joke without understanding the half of it, and the careful way he'd shaped his words to sound like ours, I thought perhaps that it wasn't the way they'd been raised at all. Some things were simply born in the blood.

"So wait," Alcibiades said, with more interest than I'd heard him exhibit all night. "This princess. She lives on the moon?"

"That sounds *lovely,*" I said hurriedly. "We've been so looking forward to seeing a theatre performance. Why, we were nearly to the point of hiring out a carriage and going back to the theatre ourselves, weren't we, my dear?"

"Yeah," Alcibiades said, rather startling me with his agreement. If that was the effect clear wine was going to have on him, I would have to have a bottle sent to his room every evening; then we could take evening constitutionals, or gossip about the day's events together. It would do wonders for our friendship. "Well, it'll be a nice change from all the singing, no mistake about that. Caius, what in bastion's name are you *kicking* me for?"

I smiled, hastily and winningly. "It was an accident, my dear."

"The food's coming out," Josette said, sounding as grateful as I felt. We couldn't have planned its timing to be more felicitous.

While I was rather enjoying this new side of Alcibiades, it was probably for the best that he find something to occupy his mouth with rather than talking. It was one thing to create a sensation just by the clothes one was wearing and quite another to be impolitic. I wasn't entirely certain that Alcibiades was on his guard enough at the moment to catch his little slips.

I would have to catch them for him, I resolved. Even if it did mean resigning myself to kicking him under the table all night long. That was what friends were for.

Alcibiades looked up hopefully at the twin rows of servants bearing food. Each was carrying our starters, which of late had been clear soups, or small bowls of white rice. His favorite, to date, had been a broth poured over hot, flat noodles that we'd not seen replicated, but hope sprang eternal in his simple heart.

It was rather sweet, really. He was so earnest.

That night, it seemed, we were all in for rather a lovely surprise, as what the servants put down in front of each of us was a round dish with three cooked dumplings in the center. They were floating in an inch of delicious-smelling broth, and looked plump, as if they'd burst as soon as you attempted to pick one up. They weren't fried, like the kind we'd enjoyed in the capital, but they looked just as mouthwatering. I sincerely hoped that Alcibiades would find three an ample number.

"You must be very careful with these," Lord Temur counseled us. He had a rather pleased look about his eyes and mouth, which I supposed passed for a large and winning smile among Ke-Han warlords. He knew as well as I did that dumplings were Alcibiades' preferred fare, at least when it came to Ke-Han delicacies. "The soup that they are filled with is quite hot, and you will burn your tongue while eating them, unless you take the proper care."

"Armphg," said Alcibiades, waving a hand in front of his mouth and reaching for the water pitcher like a man possessed. His cheeks were nearly so red as to match his coat.

Josette hid a laugh behind her hand and eyed her own dumplings with considerably more circumspection.

"That is most prudent advice," I said. "Thank you."

"You must eat them like this," Lord Temur said, once Alcibiades had emptied two glasses of water, and his eyes were less bright, his cheeks less crimson. "If you place it on your spoon, and pierce the wrapper like so with the end of your stick, the broth inside will fill your spoon like soup, making it far easier to cool with your breath."

There was a moment's silence after that as Josette, Alcibiades, and I all endeavored to follow Lord Temur's sage advice. After some demure—and not so demure, in Alcibiades' case—slurping, we'd managed the dumplings well enough; the broth inside was nearly sweet for a tantalizing moment, before it turned spicy, and we were all pleasantly surprised.

"I have endeavored to counsel the cooks in their choices for each evening's repast," Lord Temur said, before he set to work on his own dumplings. "I would not want our esteemed guests to go hungry."

"More dumplings," Alcibiades said, with a winning smile.

Lord Temur inclined his head in recognition of the request. "I shall take it under advisement."

"Seems odd, though," Alcibiades went on, not entirely tactlessly; he simply sounded curious, "that a man like you would be in the position of telling cooks what to do. Isn't that a little below your station?"

I saw Josette's fingers twitch in her lap, but Lord Temur merely smiled his diplomat's smile—the one that revealed nothing and which even I failed in attempting to parse. The Ke-Han warlords were impossible to read, rolled up tight as forbidden scrolls, and even more tormenting because of it.

"Since it seemed that you were having such trouble with our earlier meals, General Alcibiades, I only wished to make things easier on your stomach," Lord Temur declared. If I hadn't known better, I might have said he was enjoying our conversation—not because of the topic, mind, but rather because of its blunt honesty. Perhaps he needed a little more of that in his life. Perhaps we all did. "Noodles and broth and dumplings seem better suited to your tastes than some of the other, less familiar delicacies our chefs have to offer."

"I've eaten some pretty awful things in my time," Alcibiades said, "but at least it was Volstovic and awful, if you take my meaning."

"Somehow I think I do," Lord Temur replied dryly.

Our conversation was sadly cut short as the second course arrived, and then the third—rice and rice noodles and more fish, which Alcibiades was leery of until hunger got the better of him. Thankfully, the business of eating kept him momentarily quiet, although he did lean over and intimate to me, in the midst of a particularly tricky portion of catfish lined with countless little bones, that he missed a good tea-cake more than anything, and didn't these Ke-Han have proper sweets?

"I don't think you need any more sweets," I replied, delighted to be able to tease him properly.

"I'm not that out of shape," he grumbled, albeit good-naturedly. "Getting back into it, anyway. Any more of this Ke-Han diet and I'll be skinnier than you are."

"Who knows," I said. "It might allow you to be quicker on your feet."

"Like an emperor," he muttered, and we both glanced toward the dais, where Emperor Iseul was eating as though neither gods nor royalty ever deigned to get hungry. Alcibiades skewered some of the fish on his plate with hands too large for his sticks and the delicate fillet was flaked to pieces by his attempts. "Do you suppose he's ever cracked a smile?"

"I'm sure he has, my dear," I said, though it was a flippant response, and without real thought or honesty behind it. When we were in a group like this, then we were of necessity still diplomats. I was quite skilled when it came to lying, and by my understanding, a diplomat's sole duty was to lie through his teeth no matter what obstacles lay in his path. However, I would have preferred not to lie to Alcibiades, and so resolved to answer his question more seriously later in the evening, when we were alone and I could do so freely. I did so wish to speak of the Emperor—I did so wish to learn what Alcibiades had learned directly from the source, by fighting with him. Soldiers and warriors had instincts I barely understood.

Depending on whether or not Alcibiades succeeded in procuring more of that refreshing water or not, of course. It had worked so far very much in my favor; with its aid, I might even convince him to spend some time before bed discussing the day's events without him calling it gossipmongering. It wasn't gossipmongering simply to confer on occurrences of some interest to us both. But the wine was bound to make him somewhat more amenable.

After dinner there were no teacakes, but a pale, flavored gelatin that even Josette had trouble eating with her sticks. The problem was that it went all to pieces the moment you exerted any pressure on it, so that the safest way was to maneuver a soft hold. It required a control that I endeavored to mimic from Lord Temur's example. I'd never seen the like of such desserts in Volstov, of course, and after having eaten some here, I wouldn't precisely have called it my *favorite* of desserts, but it was delightfully mild and light, a palate cleanser as an end to the meal.

Dessert aside, there may have been some truth in Alcibiades' words about losing weight on a diet of strictly Ke-Han foods. Perhaps once we got back, I would recommend it to one or two of my friends, who had little success with heavier Volstovic fare.

No one stood after our sumptuous meal was through. It was customary to wait for the Emperor to make his move first, of course, but after dessert there was to be the theatre company's production, and though I'd imagined we might at least rearrange the chairs and clear the tables out of the way to make an empty space for the troupe to perform, no one moved.

Alcibiades stroked his stomach, his fingers feeling their way around the new buttons of his coat in a way that brought satisfaction to his face, I hoped; it was always possible his satisfaction was inspired simply by the fullness of his stomach.

"Let's have the play, then," he said, as if he'd taken leave of his senses completely and thought he was the Emperor. Then again, after their little encounter, I didn't think that the Emperor was the sort of man Alcibiades would be comparing himself to anytime soon.

"I'm certain that it will be starting at any moment," Lord Temur said, aligning his sticks neatly at the front of his bowl.

Then, as if summoned by some external force, a pair of servants went scurrying toward the front entrance to the dining hall, the way we'd all come in.

All at once the actors appeared in the doorway, and they were a curious-looking group by all accounts. The men wore their hair pushed back off their faces, and some of them kept it pinned back under skullcaps. The women wore their hair looped back in elaborate curling styles that were more fascinating than even the Ke-Han warrior braids. All had eyes lined in dark pencil, and the imperfections in their faces smoothed over with a fine patina of white stage makeup, so that each glistened more like a mask. Their clothing was dark and clung to their bodies in the style I'd seen in town—short robes and leggings. I could only assume that these were the finest actors in the capital. One couldn't mistake their graceful posture, or the way some of the older or more muscled members swaggered down the center aisle, as though not even performing for the Emperor himself could faze them.

"They are all men," Lord Temur narrated, in a low whisper. "Many years ago and well before my time, local authorities had . . . a great deal of trouble with members of the audience who grew overly excited while gazing upon such beauties."

"Oh, how wonderful," I said.

"Just like the prince, huh?" Alcibiades said, thankfully in a voice low enough that only I could hear it. "Maybe it's a Ke-Han preoccupation."

Behind the actors came their stagehands and costumers—men and women carrying cloth bundles on their backs, and large paper screens upon which were painted country landscapes at night. Their faces were entirely unremarkable to look at, and I wondered if any of them had signed on with the troupe in the hopes of being actors, only to have their poor little hopes and dreams dashed to pieces. There was all sort of hardship in the world waiting for those who were mediocre.

One or two men in our party craned their necks around with interest, as though they'd never seen so much as a common mummer's production. Others began whispering excitedly at the utter foreignness of the group parading before us. Whatever else I could say about the Emperor, he was at least a man who knew how to entertain his guests.

The costumers opened their bags behind the night-screens, so that all we could see were the shadowy outlines of clothing being removed—what I imagined to be the finest of robes kept hidden from the audience until the performers made their appearance swathed in them. As the actors prepared, the lights were dimmed, the lantern-bearing servants rearranging themselves and spreading out to the farthest edges of the chamber.

"I do say," I whispered, laying a hand on Alcibiades' arm. "This is the most delightfully eerie atmosphere for a play. I thought that it was meant to be a love story!"

"Nah." Alcibiades shook his head, but refrained from trying to shake me off as usual. "It's a play about ghosts, isn't it? I don't know of any real people who could've lived on the moon, anyway."

Lord Temur seemed to have overheard our conversation, as he leaned forward on his elbows, dropping his voice to a murmur. "In fact, our most traditional plays are meant to convey times past, so that in many ways they are all—just as you stated, General—about ghosts. They are simply the ghosts from and of our past, instead of those more supernatural creatures you might first imagine when you hear the word. In that sense, you are both correct. It is a love story and a ghost story both."

Josette shivered as though she'd felt a turn in the air. "Some of them looked like supernatural creatures. The actors, I mean. If you don't mind my saying so, Lord Temur."

He shook his head, smiling a diplomat's smile. I thought that if Lord Temur weren't careful, we'd convince him to start making expressions all the time, and he'd be lost for certain among his peers. Or, at least, he would begin to make a very poor diplomat. "They are not meant to look natural. If that is what you meant, then you are paying them a compliment."

"Oh." Josette nodded, not looking entirely sure that she'd meant it to be one. "Right, then."

"I wonder which one was the princess in the moon," Alcibiades said, toying idly with one of his sticks. As seemed par for the night, he was speaking far too loudly. "I hope it was the one with his hair all dolled up in curls." And then, as though it were the most scandalous piece of news he could have shared with us: "He winked at me, you know."

Across the table, Josette stiffened, and I had to hide my laughter behind my sleeve once again.

"I fear the language barrier would prove too much for you, my dear," I said, doing my best to console him. "Not to mention the difference in nationality. He *is* from the moon, and all."

Alcibiades snorted. "You don't need language for *everything*. Let alone worrying about a barrier. If he *was* a woman, I mean."

"Oh, I *see*," I said, just as Josette clucked her tongue angrily once again.

"The play's starting," she said.

I turned around immediately, glad for some excuse that would silence Alcibiades' tongue, at least until I could spirit him back to his room. I was interested in this new development, but it was decidedly unhealthy as far as diplomatic relations went. At the same time, I was rather amused. One would think a stubborn old soldier like Alcibiades would hold his liquor better; it all seemed to have gone to his head in a matter of moments.

In the absence of so many lantern-bearers, the light in the dining hall was diffuse and dim. It complemented the setting before us, of a pale noblewoman clad in robes patterned with red and gold chrysanthemums. Her lips were painted a bright crimson, her hair swept up and pinned back with delicate gold ornaments that tinkled as she moved. She—he—was very beautiful. I didn't know if the actor was the one that Alcibiades had taken an inadvertent fancy to, though.

A woman in plain dress sat at the front corner of the stage they'd set up, kneeling on a large, squat cushion. She held what I'd come to recognize as one of the traditional Ke-Han stringed instruments—with a long, slender neck, curved just at the top, and a stout, round body—and before I could think to warn Alcibiades, she'd swept the strings with her long fingernails and begun to sing.

Sure enough, I heard a grunt of displeasure at my back, though he was discreet enough to keep it subdued, at least. There was something to be thankful for.

"It is the . . . I am not sure what the word is in your language," Lord Temur said, no doubt sensing this new tension. I should have liked to get to know Lord Temur a little better, but it was impossible to know where to begin with these Ke-Han men. "The storyteller? Perhaps narrator is more accurate, though it holds a double meaning in our language. She begins the story for the actors and the audience."

"Lucky me," Alcibiades muttered under his breath, and I leaned back nonchalantly to elbow him in the ribs.

From our table, even above the screens that the theatre troupe had set up, the Emperor's face was visible. He looked neither entertained, nor bored, nor put out in the slightest by the music. I wondered if there were anything at all that could put an expression on Emperor Iseul's face. Then I remembered the duel between the Emperor and General Alcibiades and felt the keen prick of interest once more.

It was at times like that when I wished our instruction had been more specialized to deal with the current Ke-Han dynasty, and not simply the various ways one was expected to bow to them. What background, for example, had these men experienced? How many years of despising us had carved their features to be so fierce and so fine in our presence? What had Emperor Iseul been like as a child? I knew he had not been timid and uncertain, but more than anything, I longed for the intimate details of daily life, not the masks we saw, like so many layers of makeup, as though the Emperor might just as well have been a princess hidden in the moon, so remote from us was he.

"It'll be a little hard to understand what they're saying, don't you think?" Alcibiades hissed at me.

"It's about the mood, my dear," I said. "Please *try* to concentrate."

Alcibiades looked disappointed—perhaps he was expecting me to agree with him on everything, once I'd demonstrated such a grand display of solidarity—but he did as he was asked. If we were lucky, the wine's effects were wearing off, or he was doing his best to imagine himself in an indeterminate elsewhere, a simple place, undisturbed by Ke-Han song.

"Ah," Lord Temur said. "Here are the suitors."

They filed out one after the other, each more resplendent than the last. They held themselves with dramatic poise—an adopted nobility that in some ways echoed Emperor Iseul's posture or Prince Mamoru's elegance, but which were at the same time merely shadows of the real thing, reflections caught in a clouded mirror. The first suitor was dressed in scarlet—I heard Alcibiades snort with amusement at my side—the second in emerald, the third in rich blue sapphire, the fourth in silver, and the fifth in gold. Their faces were indistinct, all white with shocks of red at their lips and cheeks, their thick black brows high on their foreheads, and angled to create an imperious effect. There might have been the slightest hint of mockery in their precise motions—after all, they were mimicking the imperial class, without belonging to it—

but there was such delicacy in each step, each tilt of the chin or curl of the finger, that one was caught up in the beauty as if one might suddenly drown in it.

Without so much as the slightest cue, they all removed from their opulent sashes equally opulent paper fans and unfurled them all at once, obscuring their faces.

That was when the moon princess appeared.

There was no mistaking her—or him, I supposed, but it was impossible to remember that—though she was dressed in pale grays accented with lavender, the color of a fine morning mist hung low above the grass. She was not nearly so bright as her suitors were, but her poise was positively celestial. I found myself transfixed—I would have to order robes in the Ke-Han style of fabric in exactly that color at the very next opportunity—attempting, as best I could, to study the way she crossed the makeshift stage from right to left, then right again, as though she were floating bare inches above the floor.

"Beautiful," Josette said. I could do no more than agree with her. The only one of us who looked skeptical was Alcibiades, no doubt because he couldn't allow himself to forget her secret. It troubled him, I surmised, that anyone should appear as anything he was not.

She moved like a cloud crossing paths with the moon, her lips and nails the same deep, blushing red. The music, as played by the "narrator," fanned the fire in our hearts by quickening pace, though the woman who played was no longer singing. The words, I supposed, would have to be found in the princess's every movement, one hand lifting, then the other, changes so minuscule they should not have mattered.

What an artist the actor was. I never doubted for a moment that this was a woman before me, a princess fallen from grace with the stars, who would soon learn to live without them—only to be returned to the heavens once more, without a say in the matter.

"Wait," Alcibiades said, and I could have throttled him for the disruption. "What's that?"

I was just reaching over to quiet him by any means necessary, even if I had to go so far as to cover his mouth with my hand, when I, too, saw what he was talking about. How Alcibiades, still half-inebriated and hardly paying proper attention to the play itself, had managed to notice the knife hidden in the moon princess's fan, I'll never know. All

I did know was that suddenly Alcibiades had leapt to his feet, knocking our dainty table over in the process, and was suddenly part of the play in progress. Or was it that the play had suddenly become all too real?

Another woman, one of our party, gasped. Josette, whose composure was magnificent, especially for a lady of true Volstovic heritage, did not. I did, however, feel Lord Temur tense beside me, reaching for a blade that unfortunately was not strapped to his side.

But Alcibiades, bless his heart, moved more quickly than all the rest, more quickly even than the Emperor's guards themselves. I was more proud of him than I'd ever been of anyone, which was more proud than I had any right to be.

It was all over very quickly, though the moments etched themselves like scenes from a storybook, individual woodblock prints, across my vision. Alcibiades, breaking through the group of young actors portraying the suitors, who had, I saw then, cleverly formed a blockade against the majority of the diners to obscure the moon princess's actions; Alcibiades, grasping the moon princess's wrist, regardless of the dagger she held; Alcibiades, throwing himself between the Emperor and, it would seem, death itself, clad all in smoky, luxurious gray, while the music ended sharply on a jarring note; Alcibiades, acting as though that was what he had always been trained to do, and not, in fact, a terribly incautious whim.

The dagger fell to the floor, and the noise seemed to wake everyone from their slumber. Although I did not blame them, for I, too, felt as though I'd been caught in a spider's web of dreams, the food and the incense and the music a deceptive spell thrown over us all to keep us sluggish and too slow.

The Emperor's personal guards were the first to act, forming a ring around the Emperor's dais with provisional blades at the ready. The warlords were next, catching the brightly colored actors and musicians as they ran, presumably for their lives, now that their ruse had failed. Lord Temur leapt from his position beside me, quicker than all the rest save for my brave general, and caught one suitor by his carefully lacquered hair, and another around the throat. Josette, without so much as lifting a brow, tripped a musician as he ran past and I, in a fit of desire to contribute, finished him off with a soup bowl to the head.

It was Alcibiades, though, who had the distinct honor of presenting the would-be assassin to the Emperor, one arm twisting behind him, the beautiful fabric of his costume torn at the sleeve.

Emperor Iseul's nostrils flared.

"I am . . . in your debt, General Alcibiades," he said at length, when the commotion had died down somewhat, and all the members of the troupe had been rounded up. "You have done the empire a great service."

"I . . . ?" Alcibiades said, looking all around nervously, as though he'd only just realized what it was he'd done. The would-be assassin, the beautiful moon princess, struggled for a moment against his hold, then went entirely limp. Alcibiades held on to him in the same way he held on to all beautiful things—as though he were somewhat afraid of their beauty. None of us could bear to look at them, nor could we bear to look away from them. "Uh, I mean. Your Highness." All eyes were on him, and it was as though he'd only just understood it. It was also making him quite uncomfortable.

For someone who so obviously did not like to stand out in a crowd, I noticed that Alcibiades had a curious way of going about things.

"It is your honor," the Emperor continued, his voice ringing clear and purposeful, "to mete out adequate punishment."

"To . . . mete out . . . ?" Alcibiades began.

The penalty—I tried to mouth to him, as Josette dragged the fallen musician to his feet and held his arms behind his back—*for an assassination attempt upon a member of the Ke-Han royalty is death.*

Gruesome death, I added, remembering with an illicit thrill down my spine the level to which the Ke-Han had refined torture. They were even better at it than I was. *As gruesome as is humanly possible.*

"The penalty is death," Emperor Iseul said, inclining his head once in Alcibiades' direction. "It is your choice to decide how this traitor is executed. If you wish it, it is your hand that may do the honor."

"I . . ." Alcibiades began. He looked toward me, then, almost as though he were a drowning man casting about for a lifeline. I was surprisingly touched, until I realized he was probably looking to me because I was the only person he knew who had ever killed a man in cold blood, and he needed someone with experience to tell him what came next.

It was very curious that he was the soldier, and I was not.

"I," Alcibiades said again, "I think...your Highness, that is, I believe...since the attack was on your life, it would be better if you..."

"Ah," the Emperor said, stepping past his guards, and down off the dais. All eyes were now on him, including, I noted, the actors'. Theirs, however, held not a curious gaze, but one of steady, thwarted hatred.

Emperor Iseul, on the other hand, did not appear fazed at all. From what I understood of Ke-Han emperors and princes, such attempts were quite common; Emperor Iseul might well have grown used to them before he was ever past boyhood.

"I am yet further in your debt," the Emperor said, bowing his head more deeply. He walked calmly in a circle, starting by Alcibiades' side before coming to stand by the moon princess. The dagger—very nearly the assassination weapon—lay on the floor beside him.

I knew already what he would do next, but I held my breath nonetheless as he bent down to pick the blade up by the hilt, letting it dangle between them like a dead thing.

Then he slit the moon princess's throat.

One of the suitors cried out from where Lord Temur held him pinned. I could almost have imagined it to be a continued scene from the play, if I'd wished it, but this was far too remarkable to be anything but reality. My eyes went immediately to Alcibiades. That was not because I found the idea of blood distressing, but because I thought his would be the most interesting reaction. More important than that, I was feeling some modicum of concern for the poor man, who had brought himself to the Emperor's attention twice in such a short period of time. I couldn't even bring myself to be jealous, as I might normally have been under the circumstances.

Earning favor with royalty was one thing. Earning attention from a man who might remember your face above all others the next time he had a fit of temper was quite another. I felt rather alarmed for Alcibiades, his eyes trained carefully at nothing as the moon princess's blood was spilled, soaking the delicate gray and lavender robes to a dark, murky red. The color palette was completely ruined, and all the attention couldn't have been very healthy for Alcibiades.

The Emperor inclined his head toward our general one last time, before the doors at the front of the hall burst open, and the dining room was filled with fierce, blue-clad guards. The general didn't so much as flinch, though his mouth was set in an unhappy line.

Alcibiades was too honest to benefit from the Ke-Han skill of making a mask out of one's face, I thought, and at least Emperor Iseul was too distracted to notice how uncomfortable he'd made him, still clutching the moon princess's sleeve. At last, one of the Emperor's bodyguards—and they must have been cursing my brave friend, for what fools he'd made them all look—lifted the moon princess's limp body by one arm and carried her off. Josette turned her head aside as they passed in front of us, but I couldn't help looking, myself. It was curious to see the actor's face, registering blankness beneath the mask of makeup he wore, now stained and smeared with blood. The white makeup had been smeared just under the chin, revealing the shock of darker skin, surprisingly vulnerable.

The soldiers all moved aside for the bodyguard carrying the body, and he disappeared from the dining room. I wondered where he was taking it. I couldn't recall what the Ke-Han did with their honored dead, let alone their assassins.

"Take them all away," said Emperor Iseul, his voice loud but calm, as if he'd just spent the day in deep meditation. "I will dispose of them later."

The musician moaned involuntarily with fear. Or perhaps he'd simply become aware of the bump on his head from my soup bowl. Either way, Josette tightened her hold on his arms.

Gruesome death, I thought again, and pressed the pads of my fingertips together that I might not become lost in imagining it. Perhaps I might even offer my services to the Emperor. I would have to ask Alcibiades what he thought of the idea, if he ever saw fit to come back to our table. Indeed, as the guards streamed into the room, wrestling the captives away from the warlords, and from Josette, who looked almost disappointed she wouldn't get a chance to punish the musician herself, Alcibiades stood at attention in front of the Emperor's dais still, a pool of blood at his feet. The ruined screens were arranged around him like fallen soldiers in a failed battle, some of them with blood sprayed across their scenes of soft, dusky evening.

Perhaps he was waiting to be dismissed, I thought. If that were the case, he'd be waiting a very long time, since the Emperor had already swept away to speak in low tones with his captain of the guard, a man with fearsome eyebrows and an even more fearsome expression.

It was up to me to collect him, then. Resolved, I picked my way carefully around the guards, as they manhandled the would-be assassins out the door and the tables that had been overturned in the ensuing frenzy. I approached from the side, so as not to chance staining my slippers with blood, and slipped my arm through the general's, our hero of the hour.

"I do hope, my dear, that you haven't got anything on your coat," I murmured.

Alcibiades started, as though I'd startled him from some waking sleep. He took in the rapidly unraveling scene around us, then the puddle of blood at his feet.

"Let's get the hell out of here," he said, and pulled me with him against the current of guards robed in blue and into the hall, where the sounds of commotion and chaos were muted, distant through the night's tranquil silence.

CHAPTER NINE

KOUJE

My lord was not speaking to me. I would have liked to think that there were many reasons for that. We were both thinking about the best way to bypass the border crossing, for example, and did not wish to disturb one another. I had a feeling, however, that I knew the truth of the matter, which was that he had yet to forgive me for my fit of temper in the village. And there was no reason why he should have.

Even knowing as I did the insult paid to my lord by Jiang—filthy bastard *dog*—I could hardly excuse my actions. Better to have held my tongue, along with my hands, and have got us safely through the checkpoint.

Mamoru had done so well in adapting to his new station, despite his noble upbringing and the absence of all the things he'd once held dear. I could not afford to do less, to shame him by being unable to turn aside my duty as it was to protect him. The only difficulty was that I did not know what manner of man I was without my duty to Mamoru, first and foremost. Not when I had gone against the Emperor himself to fulfill it.

"Are you thirsty?" I asked. It was a cursory question, one that had as much to do with keeping my lord well as it did with ascertaining his temperament.

"No," my lord answered, managing to convey how angry he was with me by that one word, itself like a blow.

"Ah," I nodded, judging our progress by the distance from the wall. We would cross the border well before nightfall. There was that, at least, to be thankful for.

We rode on, the silence weighing heavily on my heart for all the times before when we had made games of guessing what birds there were in the trees above us, or what animal rustled in the bushes by the roadside. My lord had always been so cheerful in times past, and I had taken it away from him. I feared that if I allowed him to dwell too long on the things that made him unhappy, the well of his misery would rise up and swallow him whole. There was so much that he had lost, after all, and it was only his immutable spirit that kept him strong.

"We should stop here," I said at last. "Even if you are not thirsty, the horse will need to be watered."

My lord said nothing, only allowed his slender shoulders to rise and fall with grudging consent.

I dismounted behind him, leading the horse to the stream that was hidden just off the road. The clouds over our heads were a gathering dark, and I hoped that it would not mean rain before nightfall. When it came to helping my lord down, he took my hands—stiff as they were, the knuckles cracked from each unrefined blow—but refused to look at me.

In some ways, it was that which gave me the courage to speak again.

"Mamoru," I said.

"Don't," he said, less angry this time, and with a greater pleading.

There was another rustling in the bushes, which for a moment gave us pause. More than likely it was an animal, though, and one disappointed by the occupation of its favorite water hole. My lord stroked the horse's mane, as though in need of something to do with his hands. His shoulders were set against me. He was angrier than I'd ever seen him. I waited the barest of minutes before pressing on, heedless of investigating the noise any further.

"I must apologize," I said, speaking of need and not of duty, for apologizing was akin to drawing the poison from a wound, and even if it was to no avail, it must still be done.

"It does little good now," Mamoru whispered, as though by quieting his voice he might quiet his anger too. His fingers were knotted in the horse's mane. I could tell so easily how he wished for some barrier between us. He held himself rigidly still.

"I...cannot tell you how sorry I am," I added, for indeed, there were no words that would properly convey my regret in having disappointed him so deeply.

"Then why did you *do* it?" The words burst from him all at once. "You *knew* how important it was that we cross with another party. I don't need to be defended! I didn't tell—I didn't *ask* you to do it."

"He insulted you," I murmured, lowering my head.

"You didn't have to strike him!" Mamoru whirled around. His face was flushed, his eyes bright with hurt and anger. "We aren't...*there* anymore, Kouje. You don't have to shelter me so from everything. I would have borne his insult gladly if that was to be the price of crossing the border. We must both make sacrifices."

"You don't *know* what he expected as the price for crossing the border," I said, the words coming so unexpectedly that I didn't have the time to stop them. "For their *generosity* at the noodle house!"

Mamoru sucked his breath in sharply, perhaps in surprise at my sudden outburst, but the words were rushing from my mouth now, as if they'd found a hole in the dam that had always kept them back. I lifted my head to look him in the eyes.

"He said that he didn't know about Kichi, but that *he* at least expected a chance between your legs before we parted ways. That it was the proper thing to do—and neighborly. That you couldn't expect to get anything for free these days."

I could feel the bile rising in my throat, sharp and hot all over again just remembering Jiang's words. Even if the man hadn't known who he was speaking to, it didn't matter. My obligation to Mamoru ran deeper than the fealty I'd sworn. That had to be true, or else how could I have ignored the Emperor's command in the first place? The sooner I dealt with the troublesome rebellion within me the better. It was causing problems left and right. I couldn't tame it. It made me too sharp with him, too cross with myself.

"All the same," Mamoru insisted, though he looked troubled now, and his voice betrayed the fact that he was growing increasingly distressed. He had balled his hands into fists, and his voice cracked in places, like the spider-line fissures in the fine lacquer of an ornamental table. "I *didn't* know that, but as you are *not* my brother in truth, it is not your duty to protect my honor!"

"It is not for duty that I do it!" I said, raising my voice to be heard over his. I took a breath to rein my temper in. I could not afford to lose it again, so hot upon the heels of the first time. "Mamoru," I added, more softly. The name still sounded strange to my hearing, such a fine name on such an uncultured tongue, but I had to do my best to please my lord at his command when I could, as it seemed there were many areas where I could not.

I did not know what was worse. That it might become easier to say it, or that it might not.

My lord ducked his head down. When he lifted it, his eyes were bright with tears. They were not the beautiful, elegant tears that I'd seen the women of the court weeping, for the loss of their sons and husbands during the war, or even the restrained weeping done behind fans and closed doors for the death of the Emperor. These were messy tears, streaking down his cheeks and reddening his nose. His breath came in short, painful gulps, as though he was no longer able to control himself. I was reminded sharply of the boy he had been, back when the rules laid on our heads had not been so unyielding. I had allowed myself to comfort him, once, when it had been clear that mere words would not do the trick.

Did I remember the way of it now?

"Why?" my lord asked, the word nearly lost in his next wet intake of breath. "I don't understand it. *Why?*"

"Mamoru," I said again, counseling my voice to hold firm and steady. If I was to calm my lord, I would have to be the steady one. This I knew, above all else.

I reached out one hand to take him by the arm, to draw him close enough to put my arms around him. They knew the way, and it was not so difficult a thing to remember as I'd feared. I could feel the rough, homespun garments stretched thin against his back. He was trembling with the force of his weeping. I could feel it choked and wet against my neck.

"Perhaps what I hold for you is not duty, but something closer to friendship," I told him in hushed tones, willing him to understand what I myself did not. "Is that not how we are meant to conduct ourselves now that we've left the palace?"

It was not entirely the truth, since my disobedience had begun in earnest before we'd ever left the palace. How was I to explain that there were some things that were more important than duty to me, when all I'd known my entire life was simply that? It was everything that I'd been trained for, so that in the end I was shaped as keenly as a sword built for its wielder. Like a sword, I had no other purpose in life save what my wielder gave me. To act alone was unthinkable, and yet I had done it.

"You should have controlled yourself better," Mamoru told me, his voice slippery and filled with rebuke.

Before I could apologize, or try to put into rational speech the dilemma turning as a tempest within my head, his arms came up around my neck. It told me better than any words that he'd forgiven me.

"I know," I said, speaking to his former scolding. "I can offer no excuse for my actions. They were inexcusable."

"Still," he murmured, snuffling around the word for a moment. "I suppose there is room for a certain amount of irrationality within . . . friendship."

"If you are kind enough to allow it," I acknowledged, feeling myself immeasurably lucky once again for my lord's particular vein of kindness.

He sighed so deeply that I felt it in my bones. It was a sigh of great relief, from a man who had long been bearing a weight far too heavy for him. Perhaps my lord, too, had been in need of unburdening himself.

"Do you know, Kouje, I feel as though I've needed to get that out for ages."

"We'd best be on the move," I told him, running my hands sensibly down his back, in a movement meant to induce calm and clear-headedness. "Before the rain starts."

My lord blinked, and cast his eyes upward to the leafy canopy hiding the clouds that had formed above our heads. To my surprise, he smiled.

"It's been a dreadfully warm summer," he said. His face was entirely changed when he was happy. It was all I could do not to swear then and there that happiness was all I would ever seek to bring him. "The land could do with a little rain. I believe it is dry this season. So I have overheard," he added, and colored at his cheeks and ears.

"In that, you are correct," I said, ignoring the rest and releasing Mamoru from my hold.

My lord was thinner than he looked, but there was a core of steel beneath all his delicacy that any man would have been proud of. Perhaps it was presumptuous of me to be proud of him, and yet I found that I was anyway, for I had played some part in his upbringing.

"Kouje," Mamoru said, sounding almost hesitant.

"What is it?" I asked.

"Oh, well it's nothing really. It's only . . . your hair."

"Ah," I said, understanding at once the need for such levity. "Well, if you would be so good as to fix it for me, my friend, I would be forever in your debt."

A smile touched my lord's eyes at his new title, one more commonly acceptable outside the palace, and yet with a hint of the secret between us.

"You'll have to sit," he said, judging the distance between my height and his.

I did.

There was another rustling in the bush, some fox or badger rooting for its evening meal. Our stolen horse snorted impatiently, having finished his own rest and drunk his fill of water. If it was to be raining soon, then we would be better served to leave as quickly as we could. I felt cold dread in my stomach when I thought of what the border crossing might hold for us, but we would come to it sooner or later, and it was my firm belief that sooner was better than later.

That time, when I helped my lord back onto the horse, he smiled at me.

"It shouldn't be long now until we are at the crossing," he said. In his voice I could detect none of the worry I myself was feeling.

My lord was, as he'd ever been, determined to look on the future with hope. In that aspect, he was much braver than I, since it seemed far more realistic to plan for a situation that would neither be the best nor the worst possible outcome, but something closer to in between. It was far easier not to fix one's hope to either. I didn't understand how my lord could go on being optimistic without the disappointment of his losses eventually dragging him downward. My lord deserved someone who would not worry, as he did.

He needed a friend, and perhaps not a retainer, after all.

"Now then, brother," Mamoru said, with another relieved sigh. "Mount up."

We came to the road just as the rain began to fall, fat drops quickly mottling the road dark and light. My lord laughed, and turned his face up toward it, whereas I might otherwise have tried to shield his head from letting a single drop land. At the palace, Mamoru had always carried a parasol, alongside the other fine lords, so as to shield his skin from the sun and the rain alike. On the road, he had already suffered the attentions of the sun, so that his nose and cheeks betrayed a faint pink; the only time I had ever seen him colored so was when he'd been taken over by fever. Just then, it seemed that my lord was about to be rained on, without any recourse or parasols to better our situations.

I'd never have guessed he'd look so delighted at the prospect.

His laughter broke as the sound of wooden wheels creaking toward us caught our attention and startled us each from our more private thoughts. I felt a moment's reassurance, since that was evidently the sound of rustling I had heard. There was a large wagon approaching, led by a black-and-white horse and followed by a half dozen men and women, their livelihood carried in bundles on their backs. They seemed to me to be a troupe of entertainers, the sort of group of acrobats, dancers, and jugglers that went from town to town to try their fortunes with the crowds in a bigger city. They must have been coming from the border town as we were, since it was the largest hereabouts, and such groups didn't fare well in small villages, where the men and women had to hold on tightly to what coin they had.

Their caravan bore colorful markings, though as it approached I could see that the red paint was fading in places and one spiraling purple curlicue had all but flaked off. One of their wheels had been recently replaced.

They slowed as they passed us, and I felt my heart give an involuntary jump in my chest. Then, those who rode inside the caravan threw open their doors, and I realized that they had only just noted the rain, as we did, and thought to let their fellows ride inside after all.

One of them, a woman, eyed us curiously as the entertainers rearranged themselves, crowding in while the driver took this opportunity to check all three of the wheels they *hadn't* replaced. The woman wore her hair tied back with a piece of red cloth, and dressed in the style of the men she traveled with, leggings and a short jacket. One would never have seen such a thing in the palace, and even then I noticed that Mamoru turned his head aside just slightly—out of deference, it would seem to any stranger, but I knew well enough it was more inspired by shyness.

"Passing through the border?"

My lord half turned, as though to ask me what course to take.

I nodded, though I did not feel entirely secure in my decision, myself.

"We are," I told her. Then, the memory of my disagreeable temperament with previous people we'd met provoked me to add, "It's a shame about the rain, though."

She indicated the caravan with a nod of her head. "You're free to ride with us, if you like. We could tie the horse to the back."

"We wouldn't wish to impose," Mamoru said, though I thought that I heard a note of hope creep into his voice.

A drop of rain hit her square on her brow. The lady shook her head. "Wouldn't have asked if it was an imposition." She looked around for a moment, then stepped closer to our horse. "I've heard there's trouble for couples crossing the border. You'd do better to ride with us. Less trouble."

"Still," I said, waiting for that sense of unease to creep over me, "you hardly know whether we are worthy of such a kind gesture."

Mamoru laid a hand against my arm. She continued to regard us coolly.

"I get a sense about people, that's all. Goro says I'm better at that than I am in the troupe."

"We would be very grateful to accept your offer," Mamoru said, turning to eye me from the side. "Wouldn't we?"

"All things considered," the young woman said. "Less trouble, like I told you."

I smiled, beset from all sides. "I cannot see as how we can refuse now."

"Aiko!" The driver, seemingly finished with his inspection of the wheels, was waving us over, covering his head with his arms as he did so. The rain was falling harder now.

"Just a minute!" Aiko shouted back. She turned again to us, an enigmatic smile on her face. "Are you two coming?"

I was still waiting for that sense of unease to come. It hadn't; at least, not yet. Moreover, this was our chance—perhaps our only chance—at crossing the border without detection.

I dismounted, not waiting for my lord to hold out his hands before taking him by the waist and helping him down. Now that we'd made our decision, I didn't want to incur any annoyance by dawdling.

Mamoru grasped my sleeve, as if to ask whether I was certain that was the best course of action. I smiled, true as I knew how to, and sent him into the caravan ahead of me while I hitched the horse up to the back of the wagon.

"Is this all right?"

My lord leaned close to whisper the question as I moved in next to him, Aiko pulling the doors shut behind us. I nodded, reaching out to clasp his forearm warmly, just to reassure him that I'd taken his words to heart. It was as my lord had spoken. There were things the both of us had needed to get off our chests before they crushed us completely. In their absence, the air between us seemed much clearer, and the distance much smaller than before.

We'd made the decision together, as brothers on the road.

Inside, the caravan was dark and crowded, the men and women sitting close together with their knees drawn up to their chests in an effort to make more space. Nearer to the front there was a man telling jokes, and the crowd around him laughed uproariously at the latest punch line.

Closer to us was a musician tuning his instrument, murmuring a few bars of a song to himself before frowning and turning the keys at the neck a minute fraction over. The instrument howled sadly, but also out of tune, the rain no doubt affecting it.

"So she says, that's not a melon, my lord . . ."

". . . and hair of river-silk . . ."

". . . it's *two* for the price of one!"

The next line of the musician's song, about eyes that shone like lamplights in the gloom, was lost in the tide of laughter at the jester's latest joke.

My lord smiled shyly, taking in the scene with wide eyes, as though he'd never seen the like. Neither had I, if it came to that. The actors brought to the palace were classically trained, and even then came only to perform. There was no interaction between them and those who worked at the palace. This was an experience entirely foreign to the pair of us, and I could only hope that my bewilderment didn't show on my face as obviously as I felt it.

"So, where're the two of you from?" Aiko asked after we had given our aliases, straightening the edge of her jacket as though it was the hem of a skirt.

My lord glanced at me, and I smiled, bowing my head. "We lived near the capital, before. But my sister's taken ill, and she lives in the Honganje prefecture." It was a lie that came far too easily to my lips. What was worse, I was glad of it.

Aiko whistled. "That's a fair distance. You're traveling the whole way by yourselves?"

"We didn't hear about the trouble with the prince until it was too late to turn back," I explained, willing my voice to betray nothing, as my hands did. "Now it seems we'll have more trouble crossing the wall points than we thought. My . . ." I hesitated only the slightest moment. ". . . wife and I have had enough trouble with disreputable men along the way," I explained, swallowing thickly. "With the trouble at the bor-der—"

"He's more impulsive than I knew when I married him," Mamoru said wryly.

"Well," Aiko pondered, stretching her arms out in front of her, not seeming to mind when she almost slapped the musician in the back of his head, "that all depends. Your wife is pretty enough that she might get through, *or* you might get someone with an eye that decides she looks a little too much like royalty. She does, you know," Aiko added.

In comparison to what passed for women in nearby towns, I supposed that he did.

"Except it seems you've helped us quite neatly in avoiding that particular difficulty," I pointed out, not to be contrary, but because it genuinely baffled me. Were there people going out of their way to help one another on the roads, now that they'd been made so difficult to travel? I didn't know if I believed it. I didn't know if my nature would allow me to.

"Like I said," Aiko shrugged. "I get a feel for people."

"You can get a feel for me any day, Aiko," someone called across the caravan.

"Shut it, Goro," she said, seeming not put out at all.

"We're grateful," Mamoru said, with a glance toward me. "We . . . my husband's sister, her condition is very poor indeed. And they were so close when they were children. We're not certain how long she'll last, so we can hardly afford delays."

"Oh," said Aiko, raising one eyebrow as I turned to look at Mamoru in surprise.

He stared straight ahead, his expression betraying nothing but a restrained amusement around his mouth and in his eyes. He was enjoying himself. He would have done well in a traveling theatre group such as that one. I could only hope that my own surprise and amusement would not show too readily on my face.

"Yes," I said, shaking my head sadly to remind myself that, no matter what new turns this game with my lord took, I had a terribly ill sister. "I am fortunate, however, to have a wife so caring as to make the journey with me."

"Most would stay at home," Aiko agreed, though there was something in her voice that suggested she was not one of them.

"Oh, not at all," said Mamoru, taking my hand. When my lord had been very much younger, he had been vociferous in his approval of the actors who came to the palace, and more than once had declared it would be his calling in life. It pleased me to see him taking up the role with such enthusiasm, that I had been able to give him something after all, in the midst of taking so much away.

"I don't mean to imply that my husband is an untrustworthy creature, of course, but if you were married to one this handsome, would you think to send him on such a long journey unaccompanied?" Mamoru shook his head gravely. "Certainly not!"

Aiko laughed, not bothering to hide her amusement behind her hand.

"Oh, I see," she said. "Just married, I take it?"

"Why, what if he were to run into the prince and his retainer?" Mamoru went on, growing more excited. "I might lose him forever to his sense of duty."

Aiko's eyes sharpened at this. "What do you mean by that?"

Mamoru lifted his chin, looking so like the prince I knew that it hurt my chest. "My husband knows something about the character of men. You might say that he, too, has a feel for people."

Aiko leaned her head in closer to mine, and Mamoru did the same.

"What *have* you heard of the prince?" she asked us.

"Likely less than you," I said, feeling distinctly uncomfortable with the direction this conversation had taken.

"I've heard that his retainer is seven feet tall," she said, folding her knees beneath her, and lowering her voice to a whisper. "That he fights mountain lions in the north, and wrestles sea monsters into submission in the south at once."

"*Really?*" Mamoru asked, his eyes bright as he settled in closer. "Would you care to tell me more?"

ALCIBIADES

I had a splitting headache, like I was back in the Basquiat being held captive during the fever. And all the rest—the Ke-Han, our victory, the diplomatic mission, the plays, the bell-cracked Emperor, Caius—was some dream I'd come up with in my delirium.

The Ke-Han could've defeated us with their clear wine.

"Oh Alcibiades!" The all-too-familiar voice of Caius ever-loving Greylace—unfortunately *not* a dying man's hallucination—came singsonging to me. It got right between the eyes and settled there, lancing at my brain with remorseless good cheer. "It's mail time, and Dear Yana has written you again with news from home!"

I rolled over and buried my face against the pillow. *No,* I thought. Not "no thank you," and not "come back later," but an unflinching *no.* It wasn't just that it wasn't the time, but never. I'd never get used to him, nor to the way I felt; nor would I ever start feeling like a man again beyond the dull throbbing between my ears where my brains were supposed to be. They'd been there once, but the wine had done away with them completely, as evidenced by the fact that, just last night, I'd saved the life of the Emperor of the Ke-Han by stepping between him and an assassin's blade.

I didn't even like the man. Truth was, I hated him. It was something different from the way I felt about that little bugger Caius, who'd proven both how worthy and how infuriating he was on countless occasions, to the point where I was almost getting used to being driven up the wall by him, and *that* was frightening.

But I hated the Emperor of the Ke-Han with everything I had in me, for every man I'd lost and every friend who'd died, for every story

I'd known was false but had allowed to harden my heart against the enemy anyway. He wasn't human. He was a fucking monster; anyone could see that as soon as look at him, apparently even his own people. That actor'd looked at me right before he died and suddenly, we were on the same side as one another, except for one thing: I'd fucking stopped him.

"Bastion blast," I snarled at the pillow.

"I hear you in there, Alcibiades," Caius said. "Are you decent?"

"No!" I shouted, and meant it, and regretted it almost as immediately, when my head started buzzing like there was an entire hive of bees up inside of it.

"No worries," Caius said. "I can wait."

Maybe I'd get a commendation, I thought dizzily as I pulled myself from the bed and stumbled toward the bedside basin. Cold water in there, as always. I resisted, somehow, the urge to stick my head in it, hoping I could drown myself that easily. I might've done it, too, to get myself out of there, except I'd never yet run from a fight and that was the fight of my life.

I was General fucking Alcibiades of the fucking Glendarrow. I was a stupid kid leaving home so I could fight in a war I didn't even understand, so I could be hard and strong like every man I'd ever known, so I could take down the other side and be some kind of a hero or, if I was lucky, I could at least not be *dead*. I was a soldier, first and foremost, before I'd ever been a general, and I'd fought the Ke-Han Emperor hand to hand just before I'd gone and saved his bastion-damned life.

Only it wasn't *my* emperor. It wasn't the Emperor we'd come to hate but this young bastard of a crazy upstart, and all those stories faded in comparison to what I'd seen.

I'd always assumed the Ke-Han Emperor had his people behind him. Otherwise, what the hell were they fighting for? How in bastion's name had he managed to make them fight all these years?

Clearly his son wasn't half the man that he had been.

And between the two I was confusing myself between hate and respect.

The water in the basin was freezing and I was glad for it, splashing it all over my face until I couldn't feel my nose or my chin. Like being garrisoned up in the mountains during raid season, glad for the cold that meant no one could smell anything and no one had to get naked enough to bathe. Those were the ever-loving days—not a nightmare of being polite and wearing the right things and sitting at low tables while your legs cramped and your eyes crossed and everybody talked and laughed, polite as you'd like, with all the things we'd done to each other during the war boiling under the surface.

Peace? Everyone wanted *peace*? Was that what Emperor Iseul was thinking when he'd sliced open that poor bastard's throat, or was it something else?

I'd get on my horse and ride out of here first thing if my horse hadn't been stolen.

"Let's see," Caius called, from the partitioning door. Somehow, the Ke-Han had known this would happen; they'd divined the future and put us together just to make me crazy. "Yana says that the chickens are very healthy. You have chickens? How utterly delightful, Alcibiades! How *does* one go about raising chickens, I wonder? And don't they wake you up in the morning something *awful*?"

I bowed my head over the cold water and closed my eyes. All I could see was Caius standing, probably wearing some feathered night robe made of silk and sunshine, just next to the door separating us. He wasn't suffering from any headache—though, in all fairness, I couldn't have said he never got 'em, being *velikaia* and all—and he probably looked like nothing had flustered him in his entire life. However long it'd been so far, the little creep.

I sighed, felt myself smiling, and made a noise to cover it up—a hoarse grunt.

"Stop reading my private mail," I muttered, dragging my wet hands through my hair. "And come in or don't; just *pick* one."

"She also wants you to know that she's thinking of selling the wagon," Caius went on, having chosen *come in*, like I'd both known and feared he would.

There was something nasty to be said about my current situation when even a madman was becoming predictable. I didn't want to think what that said about me, about how I was being slowly driven 'round the bend by a pint-sized magician and his more-than-pint-sized appetite for entertainment.

"Also," he continued, coming closer so that I could see him in the mirror. I'd been right—not a hair out of place. Certainly nothing to suggest he'd indulged in as much of the clear wine as I had, which I suspected he had; but of course, it hadn't bothered *him* one ounce. He pulled a face, managing to look like a tragedy mask but not an actual human who happened to feel sad. "She wants to know why your brothers never write to her the way you do. You're the most diligent of all, it would seem. How many brothers, by the by? I can't imagine there being more than one of you—and all in the same house, no less. Your poor, dear mother—not to mention poor, *dear* Yana!"

"Don't know if the others *can* write," I grunted, head still ringing from my earlier shouting. Words were so *loud,* and Greylace knew so many of them. I didn't expect him to understand it, but *I* certainly wasn't going to be doing any more talking than was strictly necessary.

I lifted my head—a more difficult task than it should have been—and glared at my own reflection in the small, round mirror set over the basin. Everything was still vaguely blurry, since the pain caused by trying to force my eyes into focus just plain wasn't worth the trouble, but I still had both ears and both eyes and one good nose, however red-rimmed they all were.

It was more than I could properly say for the assassins, I thought. Even if we hadn't seen hide nor hair of them since their being dragged off, every soldier among us knew what came next. Torture. Hell, even Josette had known, judging by the firm, blank expression she'd pulled last night and the unhappy twist of her mouth later on, when she, the madman, and I had all gone back to our private rooms, nobody saying anything, and everybody thinking too much.

There was something to be said for the atmosphere when even a diplomat was expecting the worst.

Greylace was still reading my letter, holding it up in front of him like an official carrying an edict from th'Esar. Maybe he thought that falling silent would throw me off the trail, like I was some kind of bear trying to catch his scent in the woods. Unlucky for him that I'd been learning from our little encounters, and while to all appearances I was feeling my cheeks to decide whether I could leave off shaving another day, I was really watching my fine friend the snake with the aid of my mirror.

It was a Ke-Han trick I'd adopted to keep tabs on Greylace. That ought to have upset me, but with all there was going on in my head at the minute, there wasn't much room for feelings, upset or otherwise.

His guard was down. I was about ten times bigger than he was. That was my chance, my perfect moment, to reclaim what was rightfully mine.

I moved all at once, my muscles sore from their practice with Lord Temur, not to mention their not-quite-practice with the Emperor. I liked to think I'd learned things from that day too, though—like how to be sneaky when it suited my purpose. And when my purpose was to expropriate a letter from the hands of one Caius Greylace, sneaky was the order of the day. I turned and plucked the letter from his fingertips, not quite managing to keep from smiling with triumph as I held it very, very high above his smug little head.

As far as I was concerned, it was all worth it for the look on his face—pure shock and concern, as though I'd finally managed to get one up on him.

"I've been practicing," I reminded him, and smoothed the paper flat out of habit while keeping my body between him and the letter.

"Oh, my dear," he said, shaking his head so that I noticed he was wearing drops in his ears, some kind of red stones that caught the light and bothered my eyes. At least he was wearing red—had been wearing red, I admitted to myself grudgingly, for a few days. Out of misplaced camaraderie, probably not out of any feelings of nationality he harbored for our homeland. "There's something dreadfully wrong about this letter."

"Wrong," I snapped, eyeing him darkly. If he'd thought joking around was the order of the day when something was wrong back home, then I was going to crack his head open like an egg against the wall before breakfast. Finally, an excuse for it.

I glanced down at Yana's penmanship, scanning the letter's contents briefly. Reading was exactly the kind of thing I wanted to be avoiding at the moment, but—well, I didn't like that look on Caius's face, that was all. Yana'd never mention if she was sick, or anything like that, but there was always the chance that one of the others . . .

"Am I reading this right?" I asked, like it didn't bother me a heck of a lot even to have to ask for an outside opinion. As much as I hated to admit it, though, Greylace was the only other person who'd read one of Yana's letters, and in my current state I didn't know if I trusted myself to be the last word.

Caius pushed a hand through his hair, so that I caught sight of his bad eye before the strands fell back into place. Why didn't he just wear an eye patch? He could even put jewels on it, have different ones to match his every outfit. Hiding wasn't the sort of thing I associated with Greylace; it didn't suit him. Nor was he the type to fidget—at least, not so unconsciously. Everything he did—every movement he made—was calculated, planned out for a certain effect to add to the overall appearance. Much like that performance last night, and just as fucking deadly, too.

There were times when I figured he could easily have been raised by the Ke-Han, for all they were similar in most of their insanities.

He reached a hand out as if to take the letter, then withdrew it.

I didn't like this. Not one bit.

"I don't know," he said at last and sighed, producing a fan from inside his voluminous sleeves. He snapped it open in one smooth flick of his wrist and studied its ridged horizon with his one good eye. "Did you know that noble ladies sometimes carry weapons in their fans," he remarked, as though he imagined I cared. There was something serious in his voice, though, or maybe it was the *absence* of his usual unflagging delight.

"I didn't know that," I said, trying my best to rein in my temper. "I wouldn't doubt it, though. Women are dangerous. I was *asking* about the letter."

Yana hadn't even mentioned my temper in this one. That was another funny thing, besides. She never missed a chance to correct my flaws. It just wasn't like her.

In fact, the whole letter was off, like someone else had been writing it. Someone who didn't come from the country, who'd learned a long time ago the proper way of sentences, who wrote perfectly fine but without any real flavor.

"That's precisely what I meant, my dear!" Caius's gaze flicked up to me, that time. He looked wounded that I hadn't been able to follow the fevered ramblings of his brain. Like that was something new.

"Humor me," I said flatly.

Maybe he could give words to the feelings I had.

Caius closed the fan again and stepped up on his tiptoes to smack me on the nose with it, like a bad dog who'd made a mess of the kitchen. By the time I'd got over the shock—which didn't take me long—he'd danced out of range and into the center of my room. He wasn't laughing, but he'd opened the fan again and was holding it in front of his face.

It wouldn't've surprised me to learn *he* had a knife hidden in that fan. He was just the type for it.

His one good eye sparkled wickedly, like a chip of green madness in an otherwise mundane marble statue.

"You see before you an ordinary fan," he called out as I reluctantly followed after him. I sat on one of the too-small chairs, clutching Yana's strange letter in one hand.

All right. An ordinary fan. Whatever that had to do with anything.

I supposed I could agree with him on it, though. The deep reds of the silk and the pale wood of its binding were all I *did* see, and it seemed ordinary enough. Quite plain, even, for Caius Greylace's tastes.

"Watch carefully now," he counseled, while I privately resolved that he was going to regret it if he chose to hit me on the nose again. It was still sore. That crafty little bastard.

Instead, he pushed the fan shut with both hands this time. When next he opened it, there were small knives, thin-bladed and cruel, hidden in the fan like the spaces between fingers.

I lifted my eyebrows. Caius giggled a high-pitched giggle, and covered his mouth with one hand, quite carried away with his own success at managing the trick. He'd probably been practicing it, waiting for the right moment to reveal all to me, like the magician that he was, through and through.

My patience was wearing thin. There was indulging a man his peculiarities just so you could get to the point, and there was wasting precious time. I wasn't even sure why I'd been in the mood for the former, but I certainly wasn't going to allow the latter. Not where Yana was concerned. Definitely not with this bastion-cursed headache.

"I don't see what this has to do with the letter," I said, calm as I could.

"Oh, *don't* you see?" Caius cast the fan down in frustration, and I moved my feet to make sure neither of them caught a knife by "accident." "It is one thing made to look like another! The danger concealed in something quite ordinary. I *did* think I'd made it clear as possible."

He'd made it clear as mud, I thought, but I kept that to myself.

Caius paused, and I could almost see the change coming over him,

like some kind of invisible comb made to sort out and straighten anything that had gone astray in his momentary fit of temper. I made a
joke of it often enough, but there *was* madness in the Greylace blood. It
was common enough knowledge, and it was little things like this that
reminded me of it. Something just wasn't right—like a dragon with a
bolt gone missing. Couldn't trust him, even if you wanted to.

Which I didn't.

"My apologies," he said, in a low, calm voice. "What I mean to say is
that someone has clearly written this letter in place of your dear Yana."

His robes pooled elegantly around him when he ducked to pick up
the fan, and his knives. I defnitely wasn't anywhere near calm anymore.

"What are you saying?" I demanded. Not the most eloquent, but he
made it damn hard. "She's not in trouble, is she?"

"I should think not," Caius replied. "At first I thought that she
might have taken ill; that the unusual tone was the product of dicta-
tion, perhaps. I worried for her health, and wondered if I ought to
write to someone—have a doctor sent out to visit her in the country.
You absolutely *cannot* trust country doctors, my dear; we both know
that much. And since she's so very important to you—you've had so
much weighing upon you of late, I didn't want to worry you—I
thought to keep it to myself. Perhaps rewrite the letter so that *you*
wouldn't notice anything was off, either, while I took care of things."

"Wait," I said. "Greylace. Just how often are you reading my private
things?"

"You're welcome," Caius went on, smooth as buttermilk. "It *was*
very kind of me; but I do it because I've grown so fond of you, and
since you refuse to take care of yourself, the burden falls on those long-
suffering souls like myself and Dear Yana. However, Alcibiades, I do not
think that Yana is ill."

"Course not," I muttered, though I was relieved nonetheless. The
letter was crumpled and small in my hands, themselves stiff from so
much practice with a foreign blade. "She's got a constitution like a
bull."

"Naturally, as all fine women do," Caius acquiesced. "So it was with
a mixture of relief and dread that I continued to theorize. What sort of
change might come over a woman, a woman like Dear Yana, strong as a
bull and set in her particular grammatical ways, to alter her tone so
drastically as to sound like..." Caius trailed off, then waved in the

direction of the letter with a pained expression—the sort of face he pulled when he saw some kind of outfit that, he said, was indicative of poor workmanship. "Well, like *that*," he concluded at last, and chose that moment to take my favorite chair all for himself.

"I don't know," I said slowly. I didn't know. It could always have been the madness talking—except I knew that it wasn't. Caius Greylace was absolutely, without a doubt, at *least* three cards short of a deck, but he was smart as a whipcrack and he wasn't about to create a conspiracy where none existed.

"Exactly," Caius said. "Neither did I, really, so I don't blame you for being at a loss."

"Well," I muttered. "If you've got the solution, we don't need a dialogue about it."

"Humor me," Caius Greylace said.

"Don't I always?"

"Not really," Caius said, and clapped his hands together. "All right then, I *will* tell you, but only if you promise to have breakfast with me. I've already ordered it, and some nice soap that you can use when you bathe and shave today. How does that sound?"

"You're bribing me," I replied.

"Only a little bit," he admitted.

I sat back in my uncomfortable Ke-Han chair, eyeing the letter in question. The handwriting was exactly right, loop for loop; the paper was the same as always, coarse and from the countryside, heavy and stiff and nearly impossible to tear. But everything else was wrong. It just didn't sound like her—and Caius, of all people, knew why. How long *had* he been snooping through my things? And when had he found the time to do so? I wondered if he spent most of his time sneaking around my room while I was sleeping—last night, for example, when I was practically dead to the world—and the very idea made me shudder. At least I knew that he was on my side. It was clear now that he could have killed me, with one of those fan-knives, for example, at any time he wanted.

So he considered me quaint, like a pet. Worth keeping around for whatever happened next. Almost the same as I considered him, except I was sane and he was loopy as Yana's letters.

"Breakfast, huh?" I said.

"I think I have managed to procure us some fried eggs," Caius added. "I left extremely specific directions with the servants. And everyone is all too ready to give the great hero what he wants. You are a hero now, you know. I am sure the Emperor will wish to speak with you at some point today—I'll go with you, of course; I don't trust you alone with people."

"Neither do I," I agreed, almost overwhelmed. The headache was coming back.

Without speaking, Caius was suddenly standing and gliding across the room, quick as you like, to stand by me. He ruffled his fingers through my hair—he was actually touching me, but now that I'd finally started to get used to him, I was going to have to kill him—and pressed his thumbs against my temples, where the blood pounded all too hot.

Everything stilled and cooled; the world slowed around me. It was like the night before, with the incense and the wine and the music. It was like being in another place, on the bastion-damned moon, floating out into the night among the stars. For all I felt imaginary at that one moment, I might as well have been a painting on a standing screen: some bowlegged crane or a flower-dusted pine tree, bent and knotty with age.

He was pulling his mind magic on me.

"What're you..." I muttered, trying to struggle against it as he pulled a blanket up over my slumbering brain. "Stop that...Tickles..."

"I'll be more careful," he murmured. "It is only that I thought I might cure your headache. I've had my share of them myself, you know."

"Stop it," I said, but even I could hear my voice held no conviction.

"Besides," Caius went on, his voice hushed, "this way, we are closer, and I may speak to you in private. It is my suspicion that Yana Berger wrote to you as she always does, with the peculiar patterns she always did, but that someone has intercepted her letter to you and rewritten it."

I struggled against the sleepy heaviness in my head. At least it didn't hurt anymore, but that didn't make it any less impossible to think. "Why would anyone do that," I said. "It's just Yana."

"Someone paranoid enough to screen all our letters," Caius said.

A little shiver ran down my spine, the fingers of some unseen hand, and I didn't even once suspect it was part of Caius Greylace's Talent. "Tabs're being kept on us," I snarled. "Aren't they?"

"That was the very same conclusion I came to, myself," Caius said, "as I pondered this dilemma while *you* drooled into your pillow."

"Fuck," I said.

"Fuck," Caius Greylace agreed. "What a horrible word that is, but I suppose it will serve. In this instance only, mind; I don't approve of it otherwise."

"You're not..." I began, but Caius clucked.

"I'm not Yana?" he supplied.

"What about *my* letters to *her*?" I demanded. "Have they been changed?"

"That I have no way of knowing," he replied. "I do hope, however, you haven't been indiscreet, and that, if you have had any private information, any suspicions, you have kept them to yourself and away from her. We don't want to draw any further suspicion; you've already caused a great deal of commotion. And, exciting as it may be, now that all eyes are on the dashing hero Alcibiades, it makes it very difficult for us to investigate anything at all."

"Your," I managed, forcing my brain to work. "Your Talent—You're a *velikaia*. Why don't you find out who's pulling this shit, and we'll—"

"We'll what, Alcibiades?" Caius asked.

I snorted. "I've a few ideas," I said. "Just leave that part to me."

"My Talent doesn't exactly work that way." Caius sighed. For a moment I saw that familiar, fleeting pout pass over his features, and I was almost comforted by how familiar they were, the only thing I recognized anymore amidst all the smoke and mirrors, the hanging scrolls and the standing screens, the painted doors that slid open to reveal everything rotting away behind the gilded colors. "It is much more complicated than all that. If only things were different... But they aren't, and I am as I am, and we must do things more slowly. Perhaps that's for the best—it will give you time to cool your heels. Think of the bright side, my dear: Yana Berger is safe and sound with her chickens and your brothers, and we are the ones who may keep her that way!"

With that, Caius Greylace removed his hands and my headache from my head. I was caught with a sudden dizziness I couldn't shake off, and by the time my thoughts had cleared, he was once again sitting in the only comfortable chair. Damn him, I thought, but there was some respect there.

He was useful, anyway. And clever.

"So what now?" I asked, folding the offending letter and setting it down on the table beside me.

"Breakfast, I imagine," Caius replied, his lips spreading into a soft grin with a flash of pearly white teeth behind it. "And then we shall sit down to compose a long and detailed epistle to dear Yana telling her how *wonderful* things are in the Ke-Han Empire."

MAMORU

"You," the playwright said, waving me over. "That's right, *you*. I don't bite, unless I'm playing substitute for the fox. That man of yours keeps a close eye on you; we both know it. But I've a line or two that needs testing."

If Kouje had been beside me, he would have bristled at the tone the man chose to take with me, even if he didn't mean anything by it. As it was, most of the group had managed to rope Kouje into hard labor as we stopped for the night, hauling trunks of costumes and juggling sticks and the like from the back of one cart to another. He'd been given time enough only to cast one helpless look over his shoulder toward me before Aiko pulled him in the direction of working for our suppers. And, of course, the border crossing.

The wall rose high above us in the night, illimitable and fearsome. If we could just get across it, then we would be all right; I knew it deep in my bones. But for the moment it stood between us and our escape, and I was as frightened of it as I had been of the Volstov dragons. It was on the same scale and, beyond that, it meant just as much—a cruel, stark metaphor, the symbol of oppression.

Yet it was only a wall.

I'd been left to myself, or so I'd thought; apparently there were rare few among the group's number that were useless, and I and the playwright were together in that count. In the distance, I heard one of the actors shouting, and the sound of Kouje's voice answered him, clear and stronger.

"Well?" the playwright asked. "It's not like you'll be of any help lugging boxes. You'd break as soon as look at some of those coarse creatures—and I'm only talking about the women, ha-ha!"

I approached the playwright, who was in the midst of reading through a long scroll of rice paper and chewing upon a length of bamboo—which, I realized upon closer inspection, was actually serving as his pen.

"I'm not an expert," I began, but the playwright hushed me with one hand.

"All the better," he said. "If I can win you over, then I've got anyone on my side. You catch my drift?"

"Ah," I agreed, and, after a moment, sat upon an empty trunk, folding my hands in my lap. The trunk belonged to the playwright—whose name was Goro, I thought; or at least, that was what Aiko had called him—and he didn't seem to mind. Besides which, he was too caught up in the writing to notice anyone sitting on anything.

"The prince and his loyal retainer—not ours, of course," Goro intimated, brushing stray hairs back into his ponytail. "From back in the day; I'll find a reference, make it work, attract all the right sorts of attention and none of the wrong if I'm lucky. And if I'm not . . ." His eyes twinkled. "Be famous forever, I suppose."

"Go on," I encouraged, though I felt suddenly uncomfortable. There were stock plays, of course, familiar stories that could be repurposed for relevance according to current events—but they also worked to circumvent the law, since any writer could claim that they were merely staging a revival of an old favorite, and it had nothing at all to do with the current state of affairs. It also made the creation of a new play a relatively quick affair: The structure was all there to begin with. Perhaps I ought to give him suggestions.

Then again, perhaps not.

"They're in the mountains on this one, fighting a demon—you know what, I'll just set the stage for you. Where's Ryu? Probably off getting drunk as a lord and badgering all the women. It's nothing without the music. But think of it like this: They've just evaded the guards from the palace, and the two of them are making their way up the mountainside to call upon their ancestors for assistance."

As Goro spoke, his face transformed into a specter, a fascinating play of light and shadow upon features as still as though they were part of a blank mask. This was no ordinary playwright, I supposed; but it was nonetheless quite strange to see someone else imagining the very story I was living.

At least there had been no mountain demons. Not yet.

"The prince is caught," Goro continued, striking the hero's pose. "And I was torn on this line—do you think he ought to say 'Halt!' or something a bit more poignant? The poetic hero's popular these days, but with these country bumpkins—"

"All right, Goro, that's enough," Aiko said, coming up behind him. "You've got two good hands. Why don't you ever use them?"

"I'm creating something marvelous," Goro said, with a flourish and a bow. "There are men in this group that'll kill to play the prince's role."

"I'm far more fond of the loyal retainer," I said, almost quiet enough that neither of them would hear.

"Come on," Aiko said. Her gaze was sharp and clear; but that might well have been the starlight. "I'll save you from this ruffian. They've got your husband lifting the heavy stuff now. Little did you know we'd be kidnapping you like this."

"It was all a part of Aiko's cunning plan," Goro added, saluting me with his makeshift pen. "Then again, what isn't?"

"We're very grateful," I said quickly, hoping that I hadn't ruined their clever jesting with my own earnest interruption.

I had always loved playacting, but it seemed that I was still no good at playing anything but serious. It was all I'd been trained for.

"That's just because you aren't the one doing the lifting, am I right?" Goro winked at me, settling himself against the trunk I'd been sitting on.

"All right," said Aiko, slipping her arm through mine. "This one's not up for being recruited. You'll have to get your inspiration from the same place everyone else does."

I saw Goro throw his hands up in exasperation as Aiko pulled me, gently but insistently, away. It was hard not to feel just slightly regretful. Though I knew the idea was foolish, I couldn't help but wish that perhaps Kouje and I might stay on there awhile—among the sounds of people and not birdcalls in the night, rustling animals through the brush startling me awake at every turn. Laughter was a comfort, and so much sound was like a shield. Perhaps it would be too much to ask that Kouje act, of course, but there were many other talents to choose from. Perhaps he might be a sword dancer—one of those graceful yet deadly entertainers.

Yet, when I tried to imagine it, all I could conjure up was Kouje looking plaintively at me from the sidelines, as though even inside my own head he disapproved of the matter entirely.

I couldn't help but sigh. It caught Aiko's attention as we drew nearer to the fire they'd built, and the sharp, rhythmic sounds of trunks being unloaded or rearranged.

"They'll have him currying the horses next, if you aren't careful," she said, but she was smiling, so that I was *fairly* certain she was joking. Mostly.

I settled myself carefully next to her on the ground, arranging my robes with care. It had been ages since I'd last donned women's clothing; so long ago that I scarcely remembered it at all. I was perhaps fortunate, then, that my clothing at the palace had been infinitely more complicated than what I was wearing. I'd stand out awfully if I were tripping over my own feet everywhere we went.

"I don't think he'd mind it, to be honest," I said quietly, sharing a smile of my own. "He's used to hard work, and he has a fine hand when it comes to horses."

Aiko's eyes took on that bright, clever look again, that made me feel almost uneasy, as though I'd given away something I ought to have kept hidden. Something of my discomfort must have shown on my face, because the look soon softened before it disappeared entirely. Aiko stretched her legs out in front of her, reaching her feet toward the fire and tilting her head back to look up at the sky.

"Might rain tomorrow," she said. "Clouds make for a warmer night, but there's no telling what they'll bring in the day."

I looked up too, disappointed. It had been so long since I'd seen the stars. I ought to have been grateful for the opportunity to look at all.

"You'd be no good for the role, you know."

Confused, I turned my head to glance at her. How could she wear such clothes, I wondered. They would never have allowed that in the palace. And yet she looked so comfortable—as though she didn't realize it was improper.

"The loyal retainer," she elaborated, waving a hand to where we'd left Goro, bamboo brush pen stuck behind his ear as he muttered to himself. "You said you preferred him, didn't you?"

"Ah," I said, feeling the twist of anxiety in my stomach. Where was Kouje at that moment to rescue me? Probably tending to the horses. I would have to have words with Goro, and indeed with any and all playwrights we encountered from that day out—someone would have to correct all false impressions of the loyal retainer's impeccable timing and bravery where his lord was concerned. *Horses.* I'd never forgive him.

"Ah?" Aiko asked.

"Well, you see," I said, arranging my sleeves with the utmost care, as though I was embarrassed. It wasn't that difficult to feign. "He reminds me a great deal of my husband."

I lifted my head, half-dreading what I might see. To my relief, this seemed to be the answer Aiko had been looking for. She was nodding and smiling once more.

"Don't worry," she said, as though now we shared a secret between us. "My lips are sealed."

"Keeping secrets now?"

I heard Kouje's voice before I heard his footsteps, that same rigid training that he could not quite seem to erase from our days at the palace keeping his movements silent. Had there ever been a time when the most I had to worry about was the sound of servants' footsteps interrupting my thoughts? It was very difficult to imagine just then, seated in the shadow of the border wall.

Kouje took his place next to me, settling on the ground with a stretch and a yawn like one of the great lions in the menagerie. I couldn't help turning my head just slightly to stare, since he had never been so informal in front of me. Perhaps it was the influence of the actors, and no doubt his shoulders ached from all that lifting.

All at once I felt like a child, privy to the dressing room where actors removed their mantles and became the real people they'd always been underneath.

He looked first at me, then at Aiko, since neither of us had responded to his question. My own reply had been delayed out of surprise and delight, and likely Aiko was waiting for me to speak. It was my place as a wife.

I giggled, unable to help myself, and hid my face behind my sleeve.

"Oh, I see how it is. That's just fine," Kouje said, stretching once more and leaning back to lie on the forest floor. "I'm not invited to share women's talk, I understand. I was only lifting things all night with the thought that I might come back to the ministrations of my darling wife, but I see now that it was all for nothing."

I stared at him, gaping mouth hidden by my sleeve. He was acting not at *all* like himself.

"What's got into you?" I asked, though my question was not a part of our jest.

On my other side, Aiko shook her head. "The actors are a terrible influence. Rough lot. Not suited for finer folk."

Kouje smiled, and I caught his eye in the dark. Where had this skill in acting come from? And why had I possessed no knowledge of it until that very moment?

"Husband," I said, lowering my voice as other men trickled in toward the campfire, some of them toting blankets, "if you run away to become an actor, I shall be *terribly* cross with you."

"I have always wanted to play the hero," Kouje confided, eyes practically gleaming with wickedness.

I sighed. His enthusiasm was infectious, and I had always been particularly weak when it came to resisting enthusiasm.

"Aiko, what am I to do with this man?" I asked. "Who will explain to his dear sister, who once had such high hopes for him?"

"Every man wants to run away to become an actor at least once in his life," Aiko told me in the midst of setting up her own bed for the night. "It's the real fools who actually do it."

"We should worry about crossing the checkpoint," I said in a whisper, and the shadow of the wall came over me again, chill and sudden.

Kouje seemed to sense it, for he sat up, hesitantly putting a hand against my arm.

"Better to worry about getting a good night's sleep tonight," he said, low and calm, in the voice I recognized best of all.

"All right," I agreed. To the soothing cadence of actors laughing in the night, I slept.

I woke with the bump and jolt of the caravan in the morning, my face against Kouje's shoulder. I couldn't believe that I'd been sleeping so deeply as to miss our getting under way, but it seemed we'd commenced with me snoozing on like a baby.

Slightly embarrassed, I clutched at Kouje's arm and peered around curiously. I couldn't tell from our position inside the caravan how far along we were.

"Are we stopped?" I whispered.

Kouje half turned, his face bearing none of the impulsive humor from last night. "We are at the checkpoint," he said. "They're queuing up wagons and caravans to go through a separate gate."

"We've *got* all our papers," Goro muttered, "so what's the holdup? Morning, princess," he added as an afterthought just for me.

"There's a lot of people going through," Aiko said, sterner than she'd been the day before. "That's the holdup. No problems. We're in order."

I could feel Kouje go nearly rigid with concern next to me. I laid my hand carefully against his shoulder, leaning my head against his back to calm him.

"We'll be through," I murmured privately, for myself as much as him. I could feel my heart hammering like a hunted animal's, but I willed myself to ignore that. We'd made it that far, hadn't we? That much had seemed impossible, once.

Our carriage moved with miserable slowness, inch by aching inch, as though with each passing moment we grew farther from our goal. The countless ways in which we might be caught ran through my mind—something like a play, I supposed, though one which Goro would never have the inspiration to write—and I could hear Kouje's heart hammering in his chest from where my ear was pressed, up against his back.

Where was his skill with playacting from the night before? The disgruntled husband, snared by the allure of the open road? And where had my laughter gone?

"Hey," Aiko said, pausing for an instant before she covered my soft hand with her own rough fingers. "If they see you looking like that, they'll never let any of us across."

Our eyes met, and she pulled her hand away from mine as though she'd been burned.

"Sorry," she added. "I'm needed up front."

The carriage—if it could have been dignified by such a name, held together as much by the will of its inhabitants as it was by craftsmanship—rolled to a stop, and Aiko disappeared into the front. I could hear the sound of guards and Goro's laughter changing seamlessly into obsequious apologies and formalities.

"We are sorry to have troubled you," he was saying, and I closed my eyes.

The image of the guards—perhaps they were even men I had

known and trained alongside; friends of my brothers; members of the extended family—seemed more terrifying to me than any quarrelsome demon perched in the trees above on a steep mountain pass. I could imagine the border guards in full theatrical regalia, the vivid red makeup denoting the villains' roles stamped clearly across their white faces. I could even see Goro playing the wicked captain as he drew back the curtain and peered inside the carriage.

I was not ready for the stage, though I did have a moment where I paused to wonder if I would one day be in the audience, watching my own antics being reenacted. Yet in that play, I knew, the villain would not have been any mere captain of the guard. He would have been my brother. *Iseul.*

The door in the back of the carriage was flung open and one of the guards, a face I was relieved not to recognize, barked out orders in a tone that *was* familiar. Even Kouje had used it more than once during campaigns.

"Out," the guard said.

One by one, we filed into the sunlight; before us, the guards were arranged in immaculate order while we, a ragtag group of the commonest caliber, milled together uncertainly.

"I know I'm an awful playwright," Goro began, but the guard had only to hold up one hand, and all was silence thereafter.

"These?" the guard demanded, nodding toward two jugglers who stood together.

"Brothers," Goro replied, his head lowered; he was on the verge, I realized, of kowtowing, dragging his brow through the dirt. "We picked them up a year ago, my honorable lord."

"And these?" the guard continued.

"Actors," Goro deferred. "Very poor ones. Of no interest to you, my honorable lord."

"And these?" the guard asked, stopping before us. I lowered my head in a stiff bow, every bone so brittle I knew they were certain to break. Beside me, Kouje was doing the same, both of us hiding our faces by means of simple custom.

"The man's hired on for the season," Aiko said, in the smoothest lie I'd ever heard. Even I, for a wonderful moment, believed it. "The woman's a seamstress. Fixes our costumes, my honorable lord."

There had been no need to lie, I thought dizzily. At least, not as far as Aiko knew. I didn't lift my eyes as the guard took me by the chin and lifted my face toward his, inspecting it.

"A fine woman, cast among this lot," he said, and for a moment, I recognized what I saw behind the steady mask that obscured his finer emotions. He was regretful. He was only a man beneath it all, and it pained him to think that I, "a fine woman," had been reduced to traveling with such a crowd. No doubt the times troubled him as much as they troubled anyone else with capacity enough to think beyond orders.

I missed home when I saw his face, but in that moment I was equally grateful to be away from it.

"We've often said so," Aiko said, in a tone I couldn't quite place.

"And these," the guard asked, moving down the line toward the next suspicious couple. They were the last, and cleared as actors as well. It was, I supposed, just that easy. I almost wished to apologize to the guard—for it was my own fault that he was stationed there, away from his family and the finer life he craved, searching for someone who had just slipped through his fingers.

"There," Aiko said, once we were settled back in the carriage and leaving the wall behind us. "Told you lot, no problems."

"He took a fancy to you, princess," Goro said, grinning as he chewed, somewhat nervously, I thought, on his bamboo pen. "Pity you've already hitched your carriage to another horse. He might've made a real lady out of you."

"She's a real lady already," Kouje said quietly. For the first time that morning, I could feel him relax.

After that, Ryu began to tune his instrument, and Goro began to sing the prince's solo—something about, as I'd suspected, the cruelty of fate and the loss of palace life—and I could not even see the border crossing disappear behind us, as one by one the actors and the jugglers and the musicians and even Aiko began to laugh and joke again, about nothing and everything at once. They were relieved. We all were. And we were in the next province; the first border crossing was finished and done.

"You'd best not run off with a border guard," Kouje murmured. "They live a hard life, you know. It's not all palace living and fine parties."

"I hadn't once thought of it," I replied, gripping his hand. "Besides, I've heard the women at the palace can be so *cruel* to one another."

"And he'd never be home," Kouje added. "Always off for this or that."

"All right, you lovebirds," Aiko said, clapping Kouje on the back. "No need to make us all jealous. We'll be stopping in town soon enough, and we're expecting a performance this evening, so prepare yourselves for some hard work. You too, seamstress," she added, but she didn't quite look at me—as though she were unable to meet my eyes.

CAIUS

I'd done something wonderful, but of course Alcibiades wasn't going to be pleased.

We both needed something to take our minds off trouble "at home," or at least "at the palace." I could have grown used to living in such a place—except for the spying, of course, which didn't bother me as much as it did Alcibiades, yet nonetheless was a point of some concern for both of us—but that was neither here nor there where Alcibiades was concerned. We'd been here a day short of one month precisely. A distraction was necessary, and I had just the means for it.

"The theatre," Alcibiades said flatly.

"The theatre," I repeated. Sometimes it was very difficult to get anything at all through his head.

"You want me to go to the theatre," Alcibiades said.

"I want you to go to the theatre," I confirmed. "Don't worry—I hear it's all very exciting. I'm sure you won't fall asleep right away."

"I hate the theatre," Alcibiades said. "I hate the theatre in Volstov, and I hate it here." He leaned against the wall of my room and glowered at the ceiling, very much like a little boy in the midst of a good, long sulk.

"You can't possibly know that if you've never been," I tried to reason with him, though why I thought reason would be effectual, I'll never know.

"Yes," Alcibiades said, "I can. I'm not going, and that's the end of it."

The door separating our rooms snicked shut behind him as he left, but it was no fun sulking without an audience and I knew he'd be back. I didn't have to be a *velikaia* to see very clearly exactly what he was doing in his room: checking his cheeks in the mirror to see whether or not he needed a shave in general, and whether or not he needed a shave now that he was going to the theatre with me tonight. His brow was furrowed beneath his unkempt hair while he pondered the best way to agree to the theatre because he truly was interested, even if he refused to admit it. For now that he'd been so adamant about not attending, capitulating was quite difficult.

I knew him so very well. It was a pity he didn't know himself better.

Five minutes later, just as I was setting out that evening's outfit for him, I heard the door slide open.

"What's it about?" he asked. "The play, I mean. Some stupid history? If there's singing, I'm *not* going."

I whirled around, trying my very best not to look as though I'd been expecting that. My face was the very picture of surprise. At least, I hoped it was. I was an appreciator of the theatre, but never an actor myself.

"Oh, *do* come and get dressed," I implored him, not entirely answering his question. I had a tragic dearth of knowledge when it came to Ke-Han theatre. I only knew what I'd managed to squeeze out of Lord Temur, that there were familiar stories, changed and updated according to the tastes of the people but never truly *different*. There was something delightfully traditional about it, and wicked as well, since as I understood things, it was a clever way to get topical political commentary past the censors. My only concern was that I had failed to ask whether or not there would be singing.

He glared at me, then at the clothes I'd set out for him. They were neither red nor blue, but a delightfully stony *green* I'd discovered after I'd been fortunate enough to run across the palace tailor making his way from the Emperor's chambers. Some explanation of my situation, as well as my dear friend Alcibiades' predicament in terms of suitable attire, had been required, and after that it had only been a matter of slipping into the general's rooms in order to purloin an outfit of his for the purpose of measurements.

"What's that," he asked, regarding the clothes as though they might well contain poisonous vipers.

"They're your clothes for the evening, of course! You don't expect to wander into the heart of the city dressed in that awful old coat, do you? We'd be turned away at the doors. Come, come."

I took it upon myself to pick them up, pressing them into his arms and shooing him from the room so that *I* could get dressed appropriately, myself.

"So what *is* it about?" Alcibiades bellowed through the wall between us. "I've had about enough of moon princesses, if you know what I mean."

"Oh no, my dear, it's the most scandalous thing," I replied, delighted by the informal nature of speaking through the wall in this fashion. Like something out of a story. "It's a *new* play. Said to be about the prince and his retainer! Though it's not *said,* of course, since that would land everyone in a spot of hot water, but it seems quite evident to the people themselves. Or so I've heard. From my *sources.* By which of course I mean our delightful tailor! They've been popping up all over the place since the prince's disappearance, so I suppose one can't call it *new,* precisely, but it's the latest thing in the theatre district and I mean to experience it."

I heard a confused swish of fabric, and what was doubtless Alcibiades trying to sort out the layers of his outfit. I did hope he wouldn't be *too* angry with me procuring something in the Ke-Han style for him, but truly, it wouldn't kill him to blend in every now and again.

"Are you quite all right, my dear?"

Alcibiades grunted, and I heard a loud thump that sounded as though he might have kicked a footstool toward the adjoining door between our rooms.

"You stay on your side," he said. "Anyway, how'd you get tickets for this thing, if it's supposed to be so scandalous or whatever?"

"Oh, they're advertising it quite enthusiastically in the streets," I informed him. "It's merely at the palace that we have to keep things so tightly under lock and key. It seems we're worlds apart up here from the glorious goings-on down there."

"Right," he said, as though he didn't believe me. "Well, I can keep my mouth shut, in any case. Seems to me that—hang on a minute."

I went to the mirror to don my earrings. Pearl drops, this time, to complement the dusky grays and bright whites of my own outfit. I did hope that Alcibiades had been speaking only in jest when he'd claimed to be sick of moon princesses.

"Do you need help with the sash?"

"No," came the indignant reply. "Just a minute!" Another thump, perhaps moving the footstool from where it had fallen, and the door between our rooms slid open. Alcibiades lowered his voice to a hoarse whisper. "What I was going to say is that it seems to me if there's something the Emperor doesn't want us seeing, then it's our job to go out and see it."

"So it's our duty to attend the theatre!" I turned once more, clapping my hands in delight. "And don't you look *handsome*."

"Don't I?" Alcibiades asked, sounding grumpy about even that. He'd done the knot in his sash all wrong, bless him, but it really was a good effort, and the color suited him marvelously. I felt a flush of pride in my own handiwork once again.

I'd train him yet.

"You do," I assured him, extinguishing all the lanterns in my room. "I'd invite Josette in to agree with me, but I didn't think to get the poor dear a ticket since she's been so busy with Lord Temur these past few days, and it would be dreadfully rude not to invite her, don't you think?"

"I guess so," Alcibiades said, as though agreeing with me was something very difficult for him to do. "Wait, what was that about her spending time with Lord Temur? How *much* time?"

I slipped my arm through his as we left the room, taking that opportunity to readjust the sash before he noticed what I was doing. All in all, I felt quite accomplished. "Oh, I wouldn't worry about that, my dear. Josette's Volstovic through and through. I believe she's just absorbing some of the local culture, which I might add, it is high time *you* did. In fact, it is what we are about to do right now!"

"I think I've absorbed enough local culture," Alcibiades said, rude as ever. At least he'd had enough sense to keep his voice down. That time.

I hadn't been able to make the connections necessary for arranging a carriage into town. The only man we'd encountered with such power was Lord Temur, and though I felt sure he liked us as much as his upbringing permitted him to, I felt equally sure that Alcibiades and I would *not* be able to enter the city without at least some questioning. I wouldn't have blamed him in the slightest for it, either, but by my thinking it was much easier just to bypass the entire difficulty. I had an excellent sense of direction, after all, and we'd traveled the route once before.

Besides, it was a warm evening. Perfect for walking.

It seemed that I was not the only one with that idea, since the streets were teeming with people young and old, men and women, finely dressed and shabby alike. Here they were all allowed to intermingle—ourselves included in that tally. I held firmly to Alcibiades' arm, confident that with such a large and forbidding companion, I would not find myself the victim of pickpockets or their like.

"You sure you know where we're going?" Alcibiades asked with an expression of mild concern, as though he believed he knew the directions better than I.

That was just like him.

"Yes," I answered, doing my very best not to be exasperated with him. He was coming to the theatre, after all. Perhaps there was just so much room for change or surprise in Alcibiades, and he'd used up his quota all at once in agreeing to come with me. "Just follow along, my dear. I shall lead the way."

The sun was just setting. Some of the street-side vendors seemed to take this as a sign to begin closing up shop, while others remained open, confident that the warm night would bring them yet more customers. It was true that the closer we drew to the theatre district, the more vendors I saw lining the walkways. Perhaps it was common to buy food to enjoy during a performance?

I was just about to ask Alcibiades if he would consider sharing some sweet dumplings with me when I noticed that his head was already lifted—like a dog detecting scents on the wind—and that he was already cutting his way through the crowd to absorb some local culture of his own. The fried dumplings. I ought to have remembered.

I stepped quickly to keep up with him, since it was either that or be dragged away through the crowd.

"I'll have one of those as well, my dear," I said, examining the stand to see if there were any distinctive markings, or whether I was going to have to use Alcibiades' excellent nose whenever I wanted to track down the fried dumplings for myself.

He looked down at me, almost disappointed, as though he had wanted to keep the entire cart for himself.

"All right then," he said, holding six fingers up to the vendor. "We'll take six."

"*Six?*" I repeated, aghast.

"You'll hold these for me, won't you?"

Then, without waiting for a response, Alcibiades took two sticks in each hand, and handed two to me.

I told the vendor thanks, and then hurried after my companion, lest he become caught up in his feeding frenzy and do something inexcusable like wipe his hands on his new clothes.

"It's good food," he said, around what must have been three dumplings in his mouth, judging by the empty stick.

I felt my mouth twitching in laughter before I could help it. Perhaps through dumplings, I would convince my friend to enjoy his stay there after all. At least, if the matter of Yana's letters could be resolved.

Alcibiades had gone through two more sticks of the dumplings by the time we reached the theatre, so at least my hands were free to reach for the tickets. I'd made certain to leave enough time for us to find truly excellent seats, and once inside the theatre proper I took off like a shot, slipping away from Alcibiades so that I could examine the stage from every viewpoint, in order to decide where it would be best to sit.

Fortunately, whoever had designed the theatre had kept in mind the comfort of all the patrons; there was no one seat, no matter how far removed from the stage proper, that would leave its owner with a poor view of the play. There were also wooden walkways, suspended just above the general seating area, that bisected the audience—and which, I realized, must have allowed for the actors to come out into the audience; to join with them, however momentarily, as one. The theatre itself was not so large that sitting far removed from the stage would ruin our view; the question was merely whether or not we would be able to find two seats together amidst the crowd.

"Quit swooping around like a bat in the belfry and just sit," Alcibiades said, crossing his arms like he was rethinking the entire night out.

"Eat your dumplings, my dear," I told him. There was nothing to do when he got into these moods except pay him no mind whatsoever and go on with my business. That was precisely what I intended to do.

It seemed that eating his dumplings was a course of action that Alcibiades and I could both agree upon, since he fell silent after that, munching away like a contented monkey.

Truly, there were so many animals the general resembled that it was very difficult to characterize him.

I came to a rise just left of the center, set so that one could see *all* of the stage, and just the *tiniest* bit of the area backstage, where Lord Temur had told me the actors might congregate before they were ready—that is, if they chose to enter through normal means. The theatre in the Ke-Han style, Lord Temur had also told me, was in this particular incarnation enamored of unorthodox entrances: Puffs of smoke were not uncommon, nor was it out of the question to expect an actor to appear from the rafters above us, dropping directly onto the stage as though he had leapt from the heavens.

It was perfect.

"Here!" I called, settling delicately down against the cushions and sitting straight up with excitement. Alcibiades followed me to where I'd settled, looking somewhat mollified by fried food and the prospect of a large cushion to sit on.

"More comfortable, anyway," he admitted, peering forward to try to catch a glimpse of the goings-on backstage. We both saw a flash of red at the same time, the flutter of silk and a pattern I could just barely make out: three golden diamonds, nesting one inside the other.

"Who do you suppose that was?" I asked, and gripped Alcibiades' sleeve. "I do so *love* the theatre."

"Hm," Alcibiades replied, in a way that intimated he was just as excited about what came next as I was.

The shows began in the morning, much to my disappointment, and could last as much as the entire day. That was typical of plays in the capital, I'd learned, whereas the more provincial shows in the countryside resembled an evening of Volstovic theatre and took place only at night. Sadly, I knew that it would be quite impossible to trap Alcibiades into a full day of cultural activity, from dawn to well after dusk. His constitution simply wouldn't allow the affront. And thus I was left to pick my battles very carefully; he would have been immensely impressed if he had known what a clever strategist I was becoming, just for him. The final act was what I was most curious about.

The audience was far more rowdy than the pristine palace would have led anyone to believe the Ke-Han people could be. But there, gathered in the theatre with us, were the merchants and umbrella makers, the artists and the farmers, even peddlers with an extra coin or two to spare for their entertainment. Whoops and calls emanated from the audience in the native, if slurred, Ke-Han tongue. From what I could understand of the situation, they were all calling for the appearance of one man—an actor—no doubt the star of the stage that night.

"They are waiting for it to grow dark outside before they light the lanterns," I whispered to my companion. Alcibiades grunted, and looked up to the ceiling, where the fat paper lamps hung in two straight lines, bisecting each other at the center.

The entire place was full of the scent of food and sweat and, my very favorite, anticipation. We were all as one, every member of the audience, leaning forward as we waited for the moment that the lanterns were lit: And then we were bathed in the golden glow of atmosphere, the perfect, supernatural experience just before smoke began to roll across the stage, and a howling voice began its narration.

"What's he saying," Alcibiades hissed, as the cheers and cries quieted and the audience fell hushed with momentary reverence. From what little I already knew of the Ke-Han theatre—Lord Temur had warned me against going due to all this vulgarity—that silence would not last.

Fortunately, where my knowledge failed in the common slang, I was quite capable of a rough translation of such formal language.

"'Long have I traveled this dark road,'" I translated. I kept my words no louder than the barest of whispers. "'Long have I searched for a port in the dark storm. But I am cast out from my home—who will be loyal to me now?'"

I was given no further opportunity to continue, for with a sudden explosion—miniature fireworks, how utterly exquisite!—an actor appeared on stage, body frozen in a sharply angled pose. He looked more like a statue than a man, so still and so expressionless. His robes were made of the deepest cobalt blue and I caught on his back the three golden diamonds I'd seen before.

My fingers twitched at Alcibiades' sleeve, and he was so distracted by the glorious display he even patted the top of my hand.

"'My lord calls,'" I whispered, wishing I did not have to translate for the general. Nonetheless, it wasn't particularly unexpected that he wouldn't know this, the most formal dialect of the Ke-Han, reserved now only for the classics and performance scripts. "'I hear him upon the wind. Who needs now the presence of a man loyal when the world is not? It is I, noble warrior! We fight as one!'"

The actor's face began to change, but not through any motion he made. Rather, it was through the subtle changes of *emotion*. I knew at once that he was the loyal retainer. Even I, stranger that I was, could feel the purpose behind his performance.

"Uncanny," Alcibiades muttered.

The cheering from the audience began.

" 'Never shall we be separated,' " I continued, savoring each word. " 'I have pledged my life to thee, and thine it is, no matter who chases us down.' "

"I know who chases you down!" someone shouted from the audience. He was followed by such a chorus of hooting and jeering that I wondered what sort of training the actor must have had to ignore it completely—to carry on as though he were alone in the world. Indeed, alone like the prince and his retainer upon the high mountain.

" 'Is that you, Benkei?' That must be the prince, offstage," I said, as I leaned closer to the stage. "I wonder how he'll appear—I wonder if he's as beautiful as the one we were so lucky to see for ourselves—"

"Shh," Alcibiades hissed. "You're being rude."

My cheeks were hot with amusement and pleasure, and the close atmosphere of the theatre, the heavy air made damp and close by all the bodies pressed together, waiting for the prince to arrive.

"Benkei, my sorry ass," said a man sitting next to us, before he settled back to scratching the back of his neck as though he might have had fleas.

" 'My lord, I have brought you your sword,' " I whispered. " 'By your side I shall be as your sword. We shall fight as one, and safety under the gods will be ours.' "

"A little bit much, isn't it?" Alcibiades murmured, shifting uncomfortably. It was either because he'd finished his dumplings or because the emotions of the people there had finally caught up to him. "A little bit queer, too. In Volstov, he wouldn't be such . . ." Alcibiades trailed off, chewing the words over while he observed the actor, imposing and fierce and lit with glowing lamplight. "Well, such a damn hero."

"Unless there was some good reason for his change of loyalties," I added.

"Ch'. Foreigners," the man sitting next to us said, casting us a disapproving look.

"My sincere apologies," I said. It meant only that I had to settle myself closer to Alcibiades so that we would disturb no other patrons of the arts with our commentary and with my translation, which I did. " 'Here you have come to complete your training. Even the spirits of the wind and trees respect your plight, and weep for it.' "

"This," Alcibiades said, "is downright insane. How do they get away with it? What in blazes does their esteemed Emperor think?"

"They've given them different names, you see," I replied mildly. "I think that makes it all less obvious."

"Huh," Alcibiades snorted, then, "*bastion.*"

The prince had appeared.

It was not with fanfare and fireworks, as had his lord Benkei. It was not even with a shower of tinsel or through a trapdoor. He had merely come onto the stage as though he owned the stage, gliding across it like a spirit of the wind and trees himself. He, too, was dressed in blue, though it was scattered across with gold and silver, like light upon a deep lake. He was beautiful—though not, I noticed with some interest, as otherworldly as the true prince had been, the prince upon whom this entire madman's charade was based.

I thought of Emperor Iseul's eyes as he bore down upon Alcibiades, as though he meant to kill him. Indeed, he was not a man who would allow something so simple as substituted names to stop him from killing the playwright behind this insult and the actors who perpetrated it. Perhaps not even the members of the audience were safe, on account of their tacit participation.

It was much like being in the lion's den while the lion was out. At any moment, the great beast might return to reclaim his territory, but for the moment, it was ours.

"The prince!" someone called from the audience. The cheers began in earnest over the dialogue I could barely translate properly when it was all I could hear.

"I've heard he's got an army of spirits up north," a nearby patron told his companion. Then, his voice hushed, he added, "*Prince Mamoru.*" The tone he used to speak the name was almost reverent.

"They've made him into a deity," I told Alcibiades, my eyes wide with wonder.

"No," Alcibiades replied. "They've made him into a god."

I was about to correct him—to tell him the two were one and the same—only then I didn't. He was right. A deity was too small for what the second prince had become onstage, moving past his retainer with the grace of a moonbeam. Alcibiades was right. He *had* become a god.

I couldn't help wondering if he knew it, the poor dear creature. At least he had someone with him. Someone as loyal and as unfaltering as time itself, as the narrator might have said. I felt a thrill run up my spine at the prospect; and, at the same time, I wondered where they were hiding themselves. If they truly were still alive.

It was as though Alcibiades and I had become caught up in a story, a tale of heroes and villains. There was something about the city that night, the smoke and the stage, that made reality seem very close to the stories. It was almost difficult to tell the difference between the two.

The smoke rose once again over the stage, and I thought I saw the flicker of screens being changed, the apparition of another face in the gloom.

"What now?" Alcibiades murmured, craning his neck to see.

There was a figure emerging onstage. He was taller than the prince, but more slender than his retainer. He stood rock-still at the center of a platform as it rose from somewhere below the stage, his eyes cast down, his arms stretched out to either side of him. His palms were upturned, as though awaiting adulation, and through the smoke I thought I saw a flash of the same crimson red we'd seen backstage. Indeed, even his face it seemed was painted in harsh, thick lines of the same color, and his robes were the color of blood. It was Alcibiades' Volstovic red: the very same hue.

There was a sudden rush of movement from all around us, as everyone in the audience suddenly began to stir, whispering to their companions or stretching to get a better view. I sat up straight as I could, wishing not for the first time that I might borrow just a *little* of Alcibiades' height.

The narrator was wailing again.

"'My search is nearly over,'" I translated hastily, while using Alcibiades' shoulder to lever myself up to see. "'Soon I will have—'"

"Murderer!" someone nearer to the stage yelled. His words were slurred, as though he'd been drinking.

I saw our row-companion's eyes go wide with shock, though all around the theatre there was a buzz of approval.

The actor playing the Emperor did not falter, but rather held so still that I found myself a captive of his presence, unable to look away. There was no trace of remorse on his face. Indeed, there was no trace of anything at all. Rather, his expression was blank, devoid of any recognizably human emotion. It was like a palace mask, and yet unlike it, since the lines painted on his face made him look more demon than man.

Was that how the people of Xi'an viewed their new Emperor? It was a troubling thought.

"See if you ever track down your brother!" called another member of the audience, one less muzzy with drink.

Alcibiades sucked in his breath. Sitting as close as I was, I could feel it when he went tense, as though the play had suddenly turned all too real.

"What would his *father* have said? Turning against your own flesh and blood," a nearby woman muttered disapproval to her companion, shouting the last to the rest of the theatre.

"Perhaps he's gone mad, like his great-grandfather."

"Perhaps we need Prince Mamoru back here to overthrow him!"

"I can't hear *anything*," Alcibiades complained, looking upset.

It was then, with a tremendous crash, that the doors broke open.

Men in deep shades of imperial blue—robes just as fine as the costumes upon the stage—stormed in through the splintered wood and torn paper. They had helmets on, to shield their faces, and each man carried a sword. Not the wooden practice swords I'd grown accustomed to seeing, either. These were live blades, and they glimmered wickedly in the lamplight as the guards marched in.

One of them stepped up onto the stage, obscuring the actor completely.

"By decree of Our Lord, Emperor Iseul," he began.

Someone to our left booed loudly. They had clearly become carried away with themselves. The noise cut itself off suddenly, as though he or she had received an elbow to the stomach or a hand over the mouth.

"This play is over!" the guard shouted, driven to the edge of his patience. I felt Alcibiades beginning to stir next to me, and felt a familiar rush of excitement mixed with apprehension. Such interesting things always happened when I was with the general. It was a good thing I'd thought to bring my fan, which I unfurled to obscure my face.

"What's more," the guard went on, unsheathing his sword as his fellow soldiers strode up the aisles in organized lines. "The lot of you are under arrest, pending the apprehension of those *responsible* for this piece of filth."

A shout of dismay went up from the audience. Alcibiades surged to his feet, dragging me up with him.

There was a moment when I felt suspended in time, like an actor onstage myself. I saw the other patrons—our audience—as though frozen, anticipating the moves of the guards, our villains, dressed in blue.

The costumes were all wrong. "The heroes are supposed to be in blue," I told Alcibiades in an excited whisper.

There was a flurry of crimson movement onstage; and, as though it had all been a part of the script, the pretend-Emperor brought his wooden sword down hilt first on top of the guard's head. We in the audience had time for a roar of approval, putting all our praise for the play into one primal cry of appreciation.

Then the guards were on us.

Alcibiades pulled me forward, choosing to travel down toward the stage and against the flow of the crowd, which was surging back toward the far wall. I had no choice but to follow, since he was a dreadfully strong brute when he had a mind to be. And besides, I was no battle strategist.

"I shouldn't think it would look very good for two of Volstov's diplomats to land in jail," I remarked, cheerfully tripping a guard who'd grabbed a young lady by the arm. She smiled at me before she wheeled around into the crowd, disappearing from view.

"We're not going to," Alcibiades grunted, pausing a minute to look around.

I took that opportunity, brief and breathless as it was, to examine the room myself. There were many patrons who appeared to be running for the nearest exit, like ourselves, but to my shock I saw more than one who'd stayed to land a punch or two against the guards. Onstage, the pretend-Emperor's fellow actors had joined him, with the larger Benkei standing as a defensive wall against the surge of increasingly angry enforcers. I had looked up just in time to see the young prince-actor, delicate as a moonbeam, roundly kicking a guard in the shins, then dropping him down an open trapdoor.

I let out a whoop of approval. Alcibiades looked at me as if I were mad.

"Caught up in the moment," I explained.

"Uh-huh," Alcibiades said.

Then, quicker than I'd seen him move yet, he pulled me underneath the footbridge that traveled from the stage to the audience, connecting the two together in a brilliant stroke of theatrical innovation.

"We're going out the back way," he told me, bent almost double in the low space beneath the bridge. "You've got those knives with you, don't you?"

"How could I go anywhere without my fan?" I said, pleased that he'd come to know me so well.

"Use them," Alcibiades said, in a tone that made me think he must have been a very different person during the war, with so much fighting to keep him busy and less time to be sullen about every little thing.

The next thing I knew, we were moving again, under the overpass and back into the audience seating. Alcibiades lifted me under my arms—making no attempt to be careful about my clothes at all—and slung me up onto the bridge like a sack of common potatoes. He hauled himself up next and caught me at the shoulder, pulling me to my feet. All around us people were shouting. Some were rallying cries; others were threats of legal action. It was becoming impossible to sort one from the other.

I couldn't help but feel a mounting sense of excitement, since Alcibiades had us running *straight toward* the actors, so that we might actually see them up close.

A guard pulled himself up onto the bridge and Alcibiades dragged me back behind him. Very shortly I was going to get tired of being so manhandled, as it was behavior I would never allow under normal circumstances, but there was something crudely touching about the whole matter. Never mind that it made me feel quite like the prince in question, and Alcibiades my loyal retainer, sworn to protect me and guard me while nonetheless treating me like merchants' wares to be hauled about.

The guard said something that I was quite sure was rude, though his dialect was one I was unfamiliar with.

Alcibiades moved with the same baffling quickness he'd shown a moment ago, ducking close around the guard's sword to punch him square in the face.

I gave a hop of delight, and hurried forward to take his sword. It was *much* heavier than it looked, but I presented it quite proudly to Alcibiades all the same.

"What the hell did he say, anyway?" Alcibiades demanded, taking it.

"He said that your outfit is *very* dashing," I told him. "Do let's make our escape."

"After you," Alcibiades sighed, and booted me down through the trapdoor.

It was dark beneath the stage, but it was far from quiet. Above us was a cacophony of footfalls, the sounds of set pieces crashing in the chaos. All those pretty things—utterly ruined. What was worse, though, was what might happen to the poor author of the play. He'd certainly landed himself in hot water, and all for the sake of pursuing his art.

Alcibiades landed with a heavy thud, almost on top of me, though I managed to step out of the way just in time. "Be careful where you're landing," I chided him.

"What do you know about these theatres, anyway?" Alcibiades asked, charging in front of me. "Any more trick doors, or do we have to improvise?"

"This is how the Emperor came onstage," I reasoned. "So there must be some way to get backstage—aha!" A wood panel just at my fingertips swung outward, and light shafted in quick and warm into the darkness. We were in a sort of waiting box beneath the stage, and there was our way out. That is, unless the guards had already filed backstage themselves.

There were clothes everywhere, and prop swords; a few masks set upon low tables, and more face paint than I'd ever seen on the most vain old baroness's bedside table. There was the red, and there was the blue, and there was the white.

"Do you think the prince got away?" I asked Alcibiades, catching his eyes for a brief moment.

Alcibiades snorted. "Which one?"

He grasped my wrist and tugged me toward what appeared to be a side exit. And it was just in time, as well, for as we slipped past the door

I heard a crash behind us, and the shattering of glass. The backstage mirror overturned as the guards poured into the room.

Alcibiades pulled me into the dark alley. We were behind the theatre. We could still hear the shouts from within, as well as those that poured out onto the streets. Lights were flickering on all down the length of the theatre district, lanterns peeking out of every window. People were yelling at one another, answered peremptorily by the abrupt orders of the guards. All of that was undercut by the unsteady rhythm of armor against armor and heavy bootfalls.

"If they catch us, we're sunk," Alcibiades told me.

"I suppose we'd better run," I replied.

"Pity you're not wearing those shoes with the platforms," Alcibiades said dryly. "You're going to get the hem of that thing all muddy."

"Not if you carry me the rest of the way," I suggested impishly, before I pushed myself off an alley wall and started off toward a back alley—one of the dark streets I'd been cautioned by Lord Temur himself not to travel.

Luckily, they were almost eerily empty; everyone had either locked up tight to avoid whatever was happening or had rushed off to join the fray. There weren't even any poor young women plying their single trade; I could imagine them all, pressed against their windows, watching the lights flicker on and off and straining to catch even one word amidst the chaos of voices.

"Why is it," Alcibiades said, shaking his head; he still hadn't abandoned the sword I'd stolen for him, and showed no signs of being about to do so, either, "that when I'm with you, shit like this always happens?"

"Oh, my dear," I replied, stepping out into the main street to find it, too, empty and abandoned, "I was about to ask you the very same question!"

CHAPTER TEN

KOUJE

The actors were preparing for that evening's show when I drew Mamoru aside, gently, by the elbow.

"Oh," he said, his face faltering. "I had hoped we might stay for the show. It's a version of *The Thousand Cherry Trees,* about the banished prince, you know. I hear he's very dashing—though he's nothing in comparison to his loyal retainer who, I believe, is the coveted star role. You should have heard them all arguing over who would get to play him."

"It's exactly why we can't stay," I replied.

The last thing we needed, in a border town, when tensions were so high—when we'd had such trouble getting across in the first place—was to be caught up in that particular performance.

My lord never knew the trouble there had been one summer, at least ten years back, when all the plays were about dragons and their riders. The theatre district had nearly been shut down because of it. While the capital was another matter entirely from the countryside, it never served a man to tempt fate when she had been so kind to him already.

Just thinking of the crowded streets of the city in comparison to the quiet houses of the countryside, cluttered together for only a brief moment along the road, was enough to make a man homesick. Mamoru himself was unused to unpaved streets and thin mattresses—to what it meant to live in the country.

Honganje prefecture was even smaller than that, a fishing village old as time itself, barely cutting its own survival into the face of the mountains looming over it. The salt and the sand got into everything, as did the stench of fish.

He'd never be able to live there. It would have been better to stay on with the caravan at that rate.

"They're not going in the right direction, anyway," Mamoru agreed. "And it would be somewhat vainglorious to watch a play that's about—"

I hushed him, momentarily, a finger to my lips, as I heard footsteps passing us. It was Goro, looking for his script; or Ryu, looking for his plectrum; or Aiko, searching out a missing piece for someone's costume, a wig, or a mask. All those details were becoming second nature. If only they had been going in the right direction. But we had no place among them, and I could no more afford to raise my lord's hopes than I could afford to raise my own. That was most dangerous of all.

"As much as I've been looking forward to the show," Mamoru amended, toying with his sleeve. It was a habit I'd only seen in him when he was a little boy. The court, his father, Iseul, and even I, had long since trained him out of it.

It suited him there. At least we were capable of relearning what we'd been forced to forget.

"As have I," I agreed. "I've lifted enough boxes to enjoy the fruits of my labor."

"I'll go when you deem it best," Mamoru said. "It seems so rude not to thank them—not to let them know we're in their debt."

"Hey, Goro!" Aiko called from somewhere within the makeshift playhouse—the inn we'd be staying at that evening, if we were staying at all. "If you've gone off with that mask again, I'm going to skin you alive and feed you to the mountain demons!"

"They'll be busy enough with the preparations for the play that they won't have a chance to notice we're gone," Mamoru said, not allowing himself to sound as wistful as we both were. "Do you remember the poem about—what was it—floating weeds? I always found it so mournful when I was little. Perhaps this is why."

"It won't be that way forever," I counseled, though I knew absolutely nothing when it came to poetry.

"No," Mamoru agreed. "Soon enough we'll be weeds with roots. I wonder what sort of plant a weed becomes when it is watered by the sea?"

"Excellent for your constitution," I promised. "You'll never have a winter's fever again."

Mamoru rested his cheek against the side of the inn. We were lucky it was summer and there was little danger of my lord catching fever. He didn't have his brother's constitution; he never had. It was as though the first son had taken everything he would need to become Emperor, leaving nothing in turn for the second. Now that I understood our new Emperor a little better, it would have scarcely surprised me to discover that was his plan all along.

"I do still wonder if this might not all be an accident," Mamoru said. "As much as I once would have welcomed the chance to run away with you, Kouje, I fear the days for such rebellion have long since passed."

"You're not as old as all that," I reasoned.

When was the last time we had spoken so freely with one another? My lord had been certainly no older than a boy of five, so I at twelve would still have been too young to realize the impropriety of my informal ways.

"I did think of it often enough," Mamoru admitted. "That we might never have to go to war, as my brother did; that you and I could live, with your sister, in some small fishing village, and that I would never have to dress myself as a girl again. At least, I'd thought those days were over." He laughed warmly.

"I would never have allowed it," I said. "I'm sorry."

"You would have been right to stop me," Mamoru replied. "I may be well versed in this part, but any other and I would fall miserably short."

I moved to shield him—from what was less certain. He seemed so small, and his cheeks were flushed with the heat of memory. It was the same look he got in his eyes when he did have a fever: those long, terrible winters when there was no one but me to visit him, and the servants were all but certain we would lose him that time. "Unless they wished for you to play the prince," I said.

"Oh, no, Kouje," he said. "It would be most difficult to play that role. I'd have no distance at all from it; I'd assume too much."

"I'll get our things once the show begins," I promised. It was all I had to offer him; that, and a bed of grass for the night.

Think of how far you've come, Kouje, I cautioned myself, before the usual refrain. *And think of how far you have yet to go.* It was an old trick: Reward yourself before you warned yourself, and you would get far enough on your own two feet.

We passed from behind the inn to the front, where men and women were filing into the theatre, and Goro himself was shouting advertisements from a stone raised beside it. "The greatest adventure you've ever seen!" he yelped, in a voice that was much larger than he was. "You'll never know such daring and excitement!"

No one was paying any attention to us; especially not Goro, who was testing his luck every time he called my lord "princess." All that saved him was the fact that Mamoru seemed to enjoy it, and coming to blows with an aspiring playwright over an innocent nickname was too much even for me. Even where Mamoru was concerned.

"I've heard that the loyal retainer is able to leap from mountain to mountain in a single bound," Mamoru said, falling into step beside me, just in my shadow. He'd taken to doing that lately, and I'd taken to accepting it. Once, I'd walked behind him; walking at his side should have been anathema to me.

It was part of the roles we played. If a wife walked before her husband in the streets, there would be such a fuss that the Emperor himself would have come to see the novelty.

"A single bound?" I asked. "He must have very long legs."

"They also say he is so handsome that no one dares to look upon him," Mamoru added, somewhat slyly. "The women say that, at least."

"They talk far more of the prince's beauty," I said, though I felt my cheeks grow hot. He was teasing me, and I him, but we had not indulged in such behavior since we were children. It fit a bit stiffly—the same way an old glove might—but it fit nonetheless.

"They flatter him," Mamoru said.

"They flatter that poor retainer," I countered. "Who will never live up to such a standard. Jumping across mountains? If only he could."

The last statement burned more hotly in my throat than I'd

expected, and I was grateful it was so dark, so noisy, so crowded upon the street. The gossips were out in full force, along with the other eager theatregoers, travelers and merchants and locals alike, each hoping that some noble grace would touch them through the hand of the make-believe prince. Someone jostled against Mamoru's shoulder and I caught him, drawing him gently aside.

"There is one among these numbers who used to believe he *could* do all that, and more," Mamoru said, the hint of a smile ghosting over his lips. "A silly little boy with too much time for imagining things, though. You'd barely recognize him now."

"He has grown quite a bit," I agreed. "But his eyes are the same."

"At least someone recognizes him," Mamoru agreed.

We slipped into the inn through the side entrance, which faced another one of the small, simply made houses. In the main hall, one could hear the excited whispers of the audience as they were arriving, and it did seem strange that we should not be allowed to watch a performance in which—at least in the barest of ways—our own actions were represented.

Our things, minimal as they were, had been tossed in with the others' trunks and boxes; on the second floor, in a series of connected rooms, all small and clean and cast into utter chaos by the arrival of the merry band. I saw Mamoru cast a longing glance toward one of the beds, over which a series of brightly colored scarves had been scattered, and I knew what he would miss the most: rice in the mornings and not having to comb twigs from his hair.

"We could always take a pillow," I suggested, already knowing what his answer would be.

"That would be stealing," he replied. "Unless we could pay for it."

Which we couldn't.

I dug through the very garments I'd helped to unload—the only way I could pay for anything; with my hands and my shoulders, both of which were aching—and found the last vestiges of what belonged to us.

"They did say they could use the horse," Mamoru sighed. "Very fine, that creature. I do wonder . . ."

"We need him more right now than the diplomats," I soothed, though I bowed my head for a brief moment in apology.

"Well," came a third voice. "There you are. First sign of work and you run away: I see how it is."

"Aiko," Mamoru said, startling.

The question on both of our minds was whether or not she thought us common thieves—and how long she'd been standing there.

"We haven't taken anything," I began, holding up my hands.

"Of course you haven't," Aiko muttered. "Because you're two noble idiots. If you did take something, it would serve you better than it did us. A blanket, maybe, or some money—yes, money. You need that to live out there."

I cast an uncertain look to Mamoru, who seemed just as baffled as I was. "I don't think I follow," I tried again, inching closer to Mamoru. In case of what, I didn't know. It was first nature to me now, not second. I didn't trust the look in Aiko's eyes—as though she knew something we didn't.

"Cut the pretending," she said. "Neither of you is any good at it." My throat tightened around the pulse there, and I knew I'd been right to come between her and Mamoru.

"Aiko," Mamoru said. "I can assure you, we don't know what—"

"When I was little, the prince passed through my town," Aiko insisted. "I've seen him before. So've some of the others; it's just that I'm the only one who recognizes you."

Mamoru reached out to grip the back of my shirt and I let him, preparing myself—though for what, I couldn't be sure. It was possible Aiko had already notified the authorities, close as we were to the border crossing. It was possible they were already waiting for us just downstairs.

I would die there before I let them take Mamoru, I thought, and set my jaw.

"Don't look at me like that," Aiko snapped. "What are you even thinking? I'm telling you . . ." She trailed off for a moment, as though she'd only just realized the weight of her accusation. Whether or not she'd always known she was standing before a prince, speaking the words made them all the more real. With a stifled, uncomfortable sound, she dropped to her knees and held something up: a soft leather wallet, heavy with coins. "I'm telling you to take this," she finished, eyes cast to the floor. "That's what I'm telling you."

It took both of us too long to understand what it was she was saying; then, before I could do anything at all, Mamoru had stepped out from behind me to kneel on the hard floor of the inn. I found that I could not breathe, and the expression that came over Aiko's face indicated she felt much the same way as I did.

"Stand up," she said, a little too roughly. "We all want you to get away. But not like this."

"I don't understand," Mamoru said. I would have gone forward then and pulled him to his feet, but I was frozen where I was—as though I was a member of the audience, watching a play I could not join. That wasn't my cue; it wasn't even my scene.

"Why do you think idiots like Goro write these plays?" Aiko said, her brow furrowing. She was very beautiful in that moment—more beautiful than any of the court ladies, none of whom had such fine, clear eyes—torn as she was between laughter and complete disbelief. Most felt that way when faced with Mamoru in all his finery; and he was at his finest then, kneeling before a common stagehand. His brother would never have done such a thing.

That was why his people loved him. His kindness was unmistakable, and his concern for his people was one not shared by his brother. The Ke-Han people had made him into a hero simply because to them he *was* one. They saw Mamoru as I did. Mamoru himself seemed oblivious to such admiration, but that made him seem all the more worthy of it.

"I didn't think," Mamoru said, and cut off, shaking his head. "Because it's a good story?"

"Why not write it about the Emperor?" Aiko said. "Take the money. Don't be stubborn."

"Whose money is it?" Mamoru asked. "Is it yours?"

"Maybe," Aiko said. "Maybe not. We're making good coin off your story tonight. You deserve a cut. Take it and get out of here. All due respect," she added, glancing up to me. "Your..."

"Don't say it," I managed, my voice grinding out hoarsely. "He—it's difficult as it stands not to—"

"What my... What my *husband* means to say," Mamoru said, with far more delicacy than I could have managed, given the circumstances, "is that perhaps, especially given the material of the play, we shouldn't speak of things that may cause the gods to believe we've become carried away with our own luck."

Aiko nodded, and I could see the conflict warring in her face, the sharp downturn of her brow. I recognized that look from one I'd worn constantly—a mixture of pride and exasperation.

My lord, it seemed, brought such emotions out in people.

"Take the money," she said finally, laying the bag on the floor between her and Mamoru. "Please. Think of it as a gift."

It was very difficult for me to keep still, but I held my tongue. Something told me, perhaps my intuition, that it was Mamoru's decision to make, and that I would be doing him no favors by stepping in to influence him.

"You must allow your people," she said, raising her head, "to do something for you beyond putting on a play."

My lord shook his head, and spoke so quietly that for a moment I was sure only I could hear him. "I don't know what I've done to deserve such friends."

He truly didn't. Perhaps my lord did not yet understand how deeply his kindness had been felt during the war. While his father and brother had fought valiantly to crush our opponents, Mamoru had organized camps for the refugees of cities too close to the mountains. He was beloved as Iseul was not—respected not only for his actions on the battlefield but also his compassion off it—and our new Emperor's attack on his brother had merely brought that affection to the forefront.

He had even gone so far as to take the place of one of his men who had been wounded on the battlefield. He was a common soldier and nothing more, but to rest wounded without finding a man to take his place would have been a great blow to his honor. My lord Mamoru took up his mantle without hesitation—a fact I was later both displeased and awed to learn. The deception was not discovered until the next day, and it had since become a favorite tale of the playwrights.

The Ke-Han people were bound by tradition. But we were not so bound as to forget kindness, either.

"Plays are well enough," Aiko went on, either ignoring him or simply at a loss for what to say. "They inspire the people well enough, let them dream a little about life as it ought to be rather than how it is. But dreaming isn't enough sometimes."

She rose to her feet, having made up her mind about something, and pressed the money pouch into my hand. The look on her face promised ill if I refused it.

"You can't afford rice for your lady wife on dreams alone," she said, and I thought I caught the hint of a smile on her face. "Take it, or I'll start screaming that I've found the errant prince."

Finally, *finally,* my lord rose to his feet. He took my arm to steady himself, and the expression on his face was one of wonderment and gratitude.

There was a time when I would not have been able to keep myself from kneeling. Indeed, I could not even so much as imagine a time when I would have been the one man left standing in a roomful of those on their knees. My father would have died of shame at even the prospect. It seemed that my lord was not the only one who'd grown since leaving the palace. I turned my face toward Mamoru when I might instead have bowed, and offered the gift to him.

"My . . . *wife,*" I said carefully. "It is for you to decide."

Mamoru reached his hand out, fingers hesitating at the last moment. He looked first to me, then Aiko, as though on the brink of some terribly important decision. Then, without warning, he sprang forward, catching her up in a tight embrace. Aiko made a startled sound, then returned the gesture, an awed smile upon her lips.

We both knew, if my lord did not, what an honor it was. And yet it was also a gesture of pure friendship—without hierarchy interfering.

"No one's ever going to believe me," she said, looking wistful when they parted. It was a strange expression to see on her face, when I was all too used to her practicality. But then even particularly practical stagehands, it seemed, could not hold strong when it came to my lord.

"Thank you," said Mamoru sincerely.

For my part I bowed, much lower than was proper. When I lifted my head, Aiko was wiping at something on her face, though I hadn't seen any tears there moments ago.

"Come on," she said, marching over to one of the makeshift beds with a renewed purpose in her eyes. "Let me teach you nobles how to prepare for more than one night out in the woods."

There was nothing for us to do but to accept her help, it seemed. She outfitted me with one of the heavy canvas bags used for toting smaller props. It was sturdy, and would keep out water so long as I didn't do anything foolish like drop it in a river. *That* I was almost more grateful for than the money, since it would allow us to carry more food than we could fit into our mouths at one sitting.

"Good luck," Aiko said as we were leaving. "Everyone's watching the play, so if you leave through the back, no one will catch on."

"What about the things we've taken?" Mamoru asked, the smallest of frowns creeping across his brow. "Are you sure it's all right?"

Aiko knelt once more, formal as a courtier in her acrobat's clothing and the bright ribbon tying back her hair.

"We are your people, my lord," she murmured. "Even if the current climate would have you believe otherwise."

Overcome, I found that I could not have put it better myself.

"We must go while the play still holds their attention," I said, to remind myself as much as to remind Mamoru.

It was with no small amount of regret—as well as with two blankets, wrapped around a pillow for Mamoru taken at my insistence—that we left. As my lord and I crept around the far side of the inn, leading the Volstov diplomat's horse, we could hear the raucous tones of the audience that had gathered to watch Goro's play.

Mamoru hesitated a moment, so that I nearly walked into him before I noticed and stopped myself.

"I *do* wish we could at least stay through the first act," he said, turning his face up to smile at me in a way that I knew meant he was joking with me, but that he was also serious.

He might have been surprised to learn that he was not the only one who felt that way. That Aiko had surprised me as much as anyone, and that if I'd been about to trust anyone but myself with Mamoru's well-being, I might have up and asked her to come with us.

I put a hand on his shoulder, not quite able to shake the idea that perhaps it was not too late to learn a life of juggling and acrobatics. My lord had the sort of face that would draw crowds of hundreds, even thousands, and he liked the theatre well enough. He was a very excellent wife.

The horse snorted, as though he could hear my thoughts and knew as well as I did how ridiculous they were.

The sad facts of the matter were that I could never entrust our safety to such chance circumstances. In such a large group, the truth was bound to come out sometime, and even if we were fortunate enough to not be turned in, it would mean treason for every man and woman in the troupe should someone else discover us and notify the proper officials. We were damned either way, and while I knew that I might be able to bear the guilt of putting a friend in danger, my lord was not as thick-skinned as I. I would protect him. That was my pleasure, duty, and burden.

Exile was a lonely existence, and one I dearly wished to shield Mamoru from as long as I could. I'd spent a great deal of my life doing such things at the palace, after all. Perhaps I might manage it in other places just as easily.

"I'll tell you all about the play," I promised, shifting my newly weighted pack against my shoulder. "Though my memory is poor, and I may require some help in putting together the complete tale."

"Of course," Mamoru said, drawing close to my side as we'd grown accustomed to walking. The evening had a certain chill to it that made me doubly glad for the blankets we'd taken. Soon we would have to start riding to cover more ground, but I saw no reason to speed us along just yet.

"I am especially poor with endings," I confessed. "And this one in particular I cannot recall."

"How terrible," said Mamoru. "You were always very good with the endings of the stories you told me. I remember them all!"

"That is because you liked only happy endings," I told him. Above our heads, a bat took flight in crazed, looping circles. I hoped it was feasting on mosquitoes.

My lord shook his head. "Then I suppose this story too will have to have a happy ending. Otherwise, I won't permit its telling."

"But Goro will be *so* disappointed," I said, feigning horror. That made Mamoru laugh, and soon I found myself joining him, though in a quieter tone, still unable to shake my caution on the open road.

"Do you suppose..." Mamoru began, then seemed to lose himself in thought.

I myself became lost in trying to guess what he was asking. There were a great many possible directions for his question to take, each equally valid in its own right. Did I think there were more commoners sharing in Aiko's sentiment? Was it possible that we had become something like local folk heroes and not traitors at all? Or did I think our own story would have a happy ending, even if I had to craft one from air the way I had with my lord's old storybooks? It was difficult to say.

"I think," I said, choosing my words carefully, "that tonight we will be sleeping with blankets and a pillow, and that tomorrow we can buy rice for breakfast."

That surprised a smile from him, and he paused at last so that I might help him up onto the horse.

"I hope that no one misses that pillow," he said, covering a yawn with one hand.

I didn't speak my next thought, partly to let Mamoru sleep if that was his desire, and partly because I had a feeling he'd make us turn back immediately if he knew that the pillow Aiko had given us had been her own.

CHAPTER ELEVEN

ALCIBIADES

I was getting really sick of sitting on my ass for reasons that had nothing to do with diplomacy.

Not that diplomacy hadn't been bad enough. It was still pretty high on my list of invented Ke-Han tortures, right above having my fingernails pulled out one by one and right *below* sitting next to Caius Greylace at dinner while he cooed and cawed like a pigeon and raised all sorts of hell when I got food on his fancy sleeves.

Those sticks were impossible to eat with. That was that.

Still, I got to add a new kind of torture to my exciting list, and that was interrogation in a language I only half-understood.

No one had caught us coming out of the theatre. Caius had led us back through some kind of rat-warren maze of back alleys and side streets until we'd made it back to the palace, leading me to question how and why he knew the city this well and what all else was stuck up there in that crazy head of his.

But the palace was where we'd run into that letch, Lord Kencho, who'd probably been sneaking out to visit the pleasure district or whatever they had there in place of Our Lady of a Thousand Fans, and figured we'd blow the whistle on him if he didn't do it to us first.

And so we were, more or less, considered traitors—to a man we weren't even loyal to, either—when all we'd done was go out for a night of theatre.

"You did look *ever* so slightly suspicious, my dear," Caius said on our way back to our rooms, like all the questioning hadn't put him out at all.

Then again, his Talent had something to do with questioning, I thought, and maybe they hadn't managed to get a thing out of him. All I knew was that I felt real sorry for whatever poor bastard had got stuck with Caius Greylace in his quiet little interrogation room. Then I chuckled, very privately.

"Yeah, and you didn't?" I snorted, just to emphasize how stupid *that* was.

"*I* was not the one brandishing a sword and sweating like I'd just defeated the entire Ke-Han army at Dragon Bone Pass," Caius pointed out.

"Don't say things like that," I barked, secretly pleased at the image it conjured. "They've probably got eyes on us now. If they didn't before."

"You worry far too much," said Caius, and his eye flashed in a way that made me kind of happy I was on his side, and kind of *really* sorry for that poor bastard who'd been interrogating him. Poor son-of-a had no idea what he'd got into. Caius let out a little sigh, like all this had been mildly trying, and ran his fingers through his hair. "I'm in need of a nice hot bath. Would you come and collect me before the talks begin? I have a feeling things are going to be especially interesting today."

I wanted to tell him to hang the talks, and that I was going straight to bed after being kept up all night with that babble. Riot in the streets or *not*, there'd been no way for Emperor Almighty's guards to prove we'd been doing anything more inflammatory than walking the streets at night. The sword had been a little more difficult to explain—it being an imperial guard's sword, after all, but it was pretty amazing what kind of lying you could get by with just by playing dumb and not speaking the language. *Excuse me* and *I don't follow* were easy enough. Little Lord Greylace would've been proud of the way I'd lied, right through my teeth without blinking.

"Yeah," I said. "Just let me change my shirt."

Only Josette was waiting for me in my room.

"My dear!" Caius exclaimed, but I shut the door neatly before he could get anything else out. Hopefully I got him right on the nose.

"You," Josette said, "are causing *so* much trouble."

"It's Greylace," I replied. I didn't want to be rude, but how'd she got herself in, anyway? Besides which, I needed a new shirt, and I didn't like the way she was looking at me. Like I *had* done something wrong, and that wasn't the sort of situation in which I could feign ignorance. "He's trouble, that one."

"So are you," Josette said. "These are important diplomatic proceedings. I'm not sure if you're aware of it, but if things fall through here, we're in a great deal of trouble."

"Politicians," I muttered, busying myself with whatever was in the closet. In the time I'd been there, Caius Greylace had slowly been infiltrating my wardrobe. There were all kinds of silks I didn't recognize. I just wanted a shirt, damn it all, made of cotton, that I wouldn't feel bad tearing or dribbling on. Something that felt like home and a little bit like *me*, and if it made the others stare, I didn't mind one whit. "All this didn't matter in the field, you know."

"I wasn't aware we were in the field any longer," Josette replied neatly. "Unless of course you are intending to place us back there—but I myself would prefer a bit of peace."

"Peace," I said. I didn't know exactly what I meant by it, though. Peace was supposed to come hand in hand with quiet, but I certainly hadn't gotten any of that. Peace was supposed to be home: going back to the farm, maybe, and feeding the chickens, who never told you that what you were wearing was "all wrong." Instead, I'd somehow distinguished myself to th'Esar in a way that stuck me with a vacation across the mountains, and it was really starting to irritate me. There had to be more people than just me with a Talent no one knew about. I was getting really sick of being some kind of ace up th'Esar's sleeve.

"Yes," Josette replied. "Peace. Which we haven't brokered yet. If you're going to be angry, be angry with our ineffectiveness here, not with the ideal."

I supposed she was right.

"I've got to change," I said, at a loss.

"Fine by me," Josette replied. "I hear from Lord Temur that Lord Greylace was very interested yesterday in what performances there were down in the city. Would you know anything about that?"

"Theatre," I said. "Not my thing."

If she wasn't going to leave, I couldn't just keep standing there doing nothing, shirt in hand, like a dumb ox. If she wasn't going to leave, I was just going to have to change right here in front of her. She was a fine, strong woman. She could handle it.

I put my hand on the top button, almost a warning, to see what she would do.

"I'm trying to decide," Josette continued, as though she hadn't even noticed, "whether trouble follows you around—whether you are the most unlucky man I've ever met—or whether you are the one who causes it."

"I speak my mind," I countered, lamely. "I won't sugarcoat who I am for these fucking—"

"Temper," Josette interrupted. "I understand your position, Alcibiades; I truly do. You were an unfortunate choice for this mission, but that doesn't mean I will allow you to run amok, like a bull in a china shop, tearing everything down around you. What I can't decide," she added, softening, "is whether Caius is the one waving about the red flag. No pun on colors intended, I assure you."

"Ah," I said, feeling helpless. I wished Caius were there. He would have done all the talking, and they could have left me out of it. "Well."

"Not that I believe seeing a play is something to be condemned," Josette concluded. "I just wished you'd thought to invite me, that's all. Are you going to change, or are you just going to stand there staring at me?"

Diplomats, I told myself. Politicians. Talents. I'd rather have chickens any day, and I didn't care who looked twice at me about my preferences.

"Change," I said. "Right." Might as well actually use one of the standing screens—even if it did cut off right around my armpits, made for a smaller man than I, and one who liked floral patterns more. I stepped behind it and changed without looking at her—why was she still there, I wondered, and thought again that Caius would have known—and then I moved toward the connecting door between our rooms, mostly because I knew him and I knew he was standing there listening to everything we said, or everything she was saying, considering how the conversation had gone.

"Oh, hello there," Caius said, standing there like a little saint. He'd already managed to change into something completely different, of course, though I noticed with some grim amusement that his hair wasn't wet. He hadn't yet bathed. If anything could ruffle his fur, that would. "Are you having a lovely time?"

"You might as well come in, Greylace," Josette said, somewhat grudgingly, "since you two are such bosom buddies, and never go anywhere without each other. Far be it for me to separate you two."

"Hold on just a . . ." I began, but then Caius was in the room, and I knew I'd never get another word in edgewise again.

"You look lovely this morning, Josette," Caius said, before taking the only other seat there was. That left me to sit cross-legged on the bedding, which I *did,* but I sure as bastion wasn't *happy* about it. This way, both Josette and Caius towered over me, and I felt like a child who was being punished.

"And you do too, as always," Josette replied. "Now tell me what the blazes is going on."

"How do I know you won't go straight to Lord Temur and tell him everything I've told you?" Caius countered simply.

Josette looked like she wanted to throttle him, which I only halfway understood. Something was going on that I didn't quite grasp, but they were each accusing each other just on the surface of other things that hadn't been spoken yet. This was an entire level of diplomacy I hadn't been made for, but here I was anyway, watching everything go down. I wished I had my sword. I wished I knew how to kick them both out, and let them go at each other on their own time.

"Are you suggesting that I'm sleeping with the enemy?" Josette demanded, once she regained her composure. "Because I'll have you know, *Greylace,* that they aren't the enemy any longer."

"You two are very close," Caius said.

"Indeed," Josette replied. "Fostering good relations between sides is what I've been brought here to do—not brawl in the streets like a common thug."

"I did not brawl," Caius said.

"It's true," I agreed, though I didn't know who I was defending, or why. "He didn't. He's much too small for that." Caius looked deeply pleased, and I turned my eyes elsewhere, immediately regretting that I'd spoken up at all.

"You're both behaving like idiots," Josette said at length, "and I won't allow it. If no one else speaks to you—admonishes you for the way you've been comporting yourselves—that's fine. But I'm here to do my duty. If I wake up to the news that two of *our* number have been interrogated again, I'll interrogate you both myself!"

"How delightful," Caius said. "In that case, I think I should tell you that all our mail is being read without our consent—and, quite likely, altered."

"Oh yes," Josette said. "That I know. Why else do you think I have attempted to become so close to Lord Temur?"

"I had hoped," Caius replied. "You're such a logical sort. But then, think how romantic it would be—a lord of the Ke-Han and a magician from the Basquiat, thrown together by accident. Amidst the whirlwind of diplomacy and treason, they can only trust each other . . ."

"No thank you," Josette said, just as I expressed my disgust with a low grunt.

"Well, I would support it, if you *did* love him," Caius said, almost petulantly. "Nonetheless, I'm glad to see you've kept your head."

"Unlike some," Josette returned dryly. "What tipped you off to the letters?"

I listened to Caius's explanation of the situation with some measure of disbelief and a significant amount of confusion. Whatever'd just happened made no sense to me, but if they'd intended to talk about this all the while, why hadn't they come out and said something? Unless each one had some reason to distrust the other—which meant that Josette had come here because she hadn't trusted *me*.

"I'm not a traitor," I said, in the middle of Caius's monologue about Yana.

"I didn't think so," Josette said, grinning.

"Indeed," Caius added, "neither of us would ever suspect you capable of such double-dealings."

"Was that an insult?" I asked. "Because I for one don't think anyone should be proud of being smart enough to *betray*—"

"Yes, yes, that's all very well," Caius said, resting his hand upon my shoulder. "Do you suppose that your lord Temur knows of what's happening? I really will be crushed if he is not the man I believed he was."

Josette sighed, a heavy sigh, from deep in her chest. "*I* don't believe he knows. Not for the reasons you might be thinking, Greylace, so keep that to yourself, but . . . In my opinion, he's not aware of it."

"He's one of the seven warlords," I said, unsure. "If he doesn't know what's going on, then who would?"

"It might be an imperial order," Caius murmured, in a way that made me feel like maybe we'd come to the heart of the matter at last—what we'd been trying to say all along, and what we'd had to dance all around first, while Caius tested the waters. This was what little Lord Greylace had been planning on discussing from the very beginning, and Josette and I had somehow managed to stumble right into his trap like painted marionettes.

Well, I, for one, wasn't going to make things any easier for him than I already had. I didn't like what was going on, and I sure as hell wasn't going to pretend that I understood it, of all things.

"You mean he went right around the warlords?" I asked, lowering my voice too, just in case the guards got bored with their pacing and decided to linger next to my door a little, because odds were there was something exciting happening in here.

Well, that was what they got for sticking me in a room next to a madman. That'd teach them.

"I don't know that he would go that far, my dear," said Caius, looking at me with the same fondness a man reserved for particularly talented house pets. "I merely believe it possible that he made the decision without their knowledge, then presented it to them as a resolved matter—one which they would have no choice but to agree with lest they seem like traitors themselves."

Josette leaned forward, elbows braced against her knees. "What reason would he have to do something like that?"

She looked as though she was trying to work it out on her own, frowning and gazing off to one side the way she did when negotiations weren't going our way. I knew that look. Any minute, Josette would leap up and turn the tides for us. Or at least explain things for my benefit, which no one else had bothered to do.

"Maybe he got sick of listening to their yabbering on and on about nothing," I said pointedly. "Maybe he just wanted to get something done."

Caius looked almost disappointed. "*Do* use your head," he said imploringly. "I know you can."

"Unless, unless . . ." Josette was muttering to herself, toying with her too-long sleeves. She'd been dressing in the Ke-Han style of late, which suited her about as well as it suited Caius. Whether that was another mark of diplomacy that I'd somehow missed—dressing like the enemy to flatter them or whatever—I wasn't sure. What I *was* sure about was that no one, not even Caius Greylace, was going to get me into another one of those complicated dresses again. They were too damned hard to run in, and I didn't see any of the Ke-Han warlords dressing like *us*. We'd only won the damn war, but we weren't supposed to expect any flattery?

Josette suddenly sat up straight, as if she'd caught a nasty splinter somewhere unfortunate.

"*Unless* this isn't the first decision he's made without their approval," she hissed, looking at Caius with triumph like she'd solved a riddle I hadn't even known we were trying to solve.

"Hang on," I said, still trying to untangle the whole mess of what was going on. Why couldn't we just *tell* a person something instead of making him work it out like it was a fair question, which it wasn't? "Why do we even care if he's the one making the decisions? Isn't he the man *meant* to be making the decisions? Th'Esar doesn't have a court of nannying diplomats waiting around to slow down his every decision, and we do all right, don't we?"

"But is the current Emperor really the sort of man who seems like he ought to be making decisions all on his own?" Caius inquired slyly.

I thought about the Emperor's eyes when he'd come at me in the outdoor training grounds, and the look on his face when he'd slit the moon princess's throat.

"He's a madman," I said. "Utterly cracked, or cracking, if he's not quite there yet."

I didn't think that it would be a good idea to point out that I thought much the same thing about Caius. Particularly because I wasn't so sure that I did anymore, and I sure as hell couldn't explain the distinction between the two.

Maybe part of it was that Caius Greylace was on my side, and he seemed to like me well enough. And maybe part of it was knowing that Emperor Iseul hated me—all of us—maybe even more than I hated him, because the war had been on *his* soil, and it had been his city we shattered.

You couldn't expect any fairness in war, but that didn't mean you forgot all your grudges as soon as peace was dropped in your lap, either. I certainly hadn't, but then again, I wasn't supposed to be an emperor. The question—one I didn't know how to answer, because I'd never known the man *before*—was what had tipped the scales. His father's death, or his nation's defeat?

"Think of his brother, poor creature," said Caius, his voice taking on an odd quality, like it was coming from inside my head instead of outside of it. His lips were moving, though, and Josette was on the edge of her seat, so I could tell that she was listening, too. He was using something, though, some particular brand of his Talent. My head felt clearer, like I'd got a full night's sleep instead of a full night's interrogation. As Greylace dealt only in illusions, I was sure it'd wear off soon.

"You must remember how quickly things happened," Caius went on. "One evening he was enjoying dinner alongside us, and by morning he was a traitor! You know how difficult it's been for us to decide anything here, how etiquette demands a careful consideration of each option, weighing the positive and the negative out for endless hours. How, then, could a decision such as that be carried out so quickly *unless* it was made by one man, and a very powerful man, at that?"

Josette blinked, and opened her mouth as if to say something.

Caius shook his head, and dragged his little chair closer, indicating that she do the same.

"I have no reason to believe that the prince is innocent of such charges," he went on, looking almost regretful that he couldn't clear the little Ke-Han prince then and there, "but I have no reason to believe that he is guilty, either. And if he is not . . ."

"He's doing the same thing to us," Josette whispered, looking scared for the first time since I'd known her. "Isn't he? That's what you're trying to say. He's having our mail read . . . He suspects us of something."

"I am only saying that *if* the Emperor suspects something, then we are in danger," Caius said. "Just like the prince was; only he had no time to plan ahead, as we do. We know well enough that the Emperor moves speedily in the face of perceived threats, whether they are imagined or not."

I was starting to feel a little sick to my stomach, though whether that was because of conspiracy theories or just because I hadn't slept *or* eaten breakfast, I didn't know.

"I'll spend more time with Lord Temur," Josette said, firm and decisive like she thought she had to make up for sounding scared before.

Except I didn't like the sound of that plan one bit.

"Hold on just a minute," I said.

"That's excellent, my dear!" Caius proclaimed. "That's *just* what I was hoping for from you. I would do it myself, but you have a certain quality that I lack."

"Yeah, more like two—" I started, only I rethought things real quick when Josette shot me a look. "What I mean is," I said, changing tack while clearing my throat, "I don't like this plan."

"Really, Alcibiades," Josette said, but she looked a little less murderous, so I guessed she wasn't that mad at me after all.

"Well, it's just . . . the way I thought of it was," I said, trying my best not to be loud about it, "all those warlords are loyal to the Emperor. So maybe they *are* in on it, what with their obsession with loyalty, whatever that means in the Ke-Han Empire. And if we start sniffing around—and they're looking for betrayal around every corner, with more than just those mirrors of theirs—then the second you step out of bounds . . . I just don't like it."

We were all silent and grim for a long moment, trying to figure, or at least I was, what we even knew about the enemy, when a few days ago they were our so-called new allies and *friends.*

It was different from the battlefield, where colors signaled who each man was and where his loyalties lay. It was more like subterfuge, all the espionage I'd known took place but was never a part of, even if all the chances for promotion were there and everybody knew it. It was more like the way things got in the very thick of battle, at night, when you couldn't see what someone was wearing and you couldn't hear what he was screaming, either, and you just had to hope you were striking out at someone who was on the other side. You just couldn't think about it. You'd go mad, same as the Ke-Han Emperor.

"It's the only plan we've got," Josette said grimly.

We both knew she was right, Caius and I, and we sat there for a while longer, just to solidify our intentions. At least we had each other to trust—but after that, it was a free-for-all, a melee of instinct and uncertainty. It was what I'd thought I'd wanted all along—getting back to the dividing line, putting myself on one side and *them* on the other— but the terms were different now, and I was in Josette's camp. I'd never had anything against Lord Temur, at least not off the battlefield.

But for the moment, all our hopes hung on getting Lord Temur alone.

After that, we were relying on little Greylace, his one good eye afire with the promise of what might come next.

MAMORU

The second border crossing was closer than the first. It had been a little less than a week since we'd left Aiko and the troupe. Although the time seemed to pass for us very slowly as it passed without incident, when I looked back on the number of days that had elapsed, I felt quite surprised.

I knew the country from above like a bird, but the mountains and the plains had been as real as the words next to them, denoting each province distant and remote from my place in the lapis city. Kouje and I had campaigned once in the mountains, but even then we were no more than a few days' ride from the palace. I had traced the boundaries from childhood, and so I knew how close we were to the second checkpoint. After that, we would be in Honganje prefecture; Kouje's sister, and her fishing village, lay to the east.

It was a lucky thing that I had memorized my maps so well.

Imagine, Iseul had said, *that the mountains are the veins upon the back of your hand. The Cobalts are your knuckles. And so you see that all of Xi'an is within your grasp.*

I shivered, and looked to Kouje. Thankfully, he didn't notice.

We'd already been lucky; too lucky, I even thought, and the burden of that good fortune hung heavy in the air, like the tension before a summer rain shower. At any moment the clouds could break. I did not expect another Aiko to materialize out of trees and mountains beside us and to whisk us across the border as though Goro himself had contrived the device.

We were on our own for the next one. And I wasn't the only one to be troubled by it.

At least we were sleeping well, though each night I dreamed of Aiko, dressed as the second prince, posing on the stage with the blue makeup of the hero obscuring her face. Her pillow was enchanted, but the sleep itself was deep enough.

"We will come to the crossing by midday," Kouje said, the morning of the second day apart from the troupe. "I've no inspiration for it."

"I play the role of your wife well enough," I said, but Kouje shook his head.

"I don't feel safe," he replied. What he meant was, *I don't feel you are safe.*

"If only Goro had written that far." I laughed. "He would have thought of something."

The smoke from our fire dwindled; we were delaying setting out on purpose. With no solid plan and no inspiration, we were at a loss. And wasting time; I could see in the set of Kouje's jaw how anxious that made him.

I traced the veins on the back of my hand. Iseul would have killed me sooner if he'd ever guessed that I might have made it that far. Such a guise was impossible to imagine for someone of my birthright. My brother would have died for honor before he donned the robes I was wearing, but my brother had always known more pride than I. I'd envied him once, but I had come to see how pride had changed him.

All of Xi'an was, and ever would be, within his grasp. My fingers tightened involuntarily. Kouje began to clear up our camp, more meticulously slow than he ever had been. It was more to delay our proceedings—hoping for some grand inspiration, another stroke of luck—while the gods watched us, an impassive audience, rather than the active patrons of country theatre performed in a roadside inn. There were neither cheers nor curses to indicate we were playing our roles well or very poorly indeed.

I watched Kouje when his back was turned. He still held himself like a soldier, especially when we were alone. I myself was no less to blame for mistakes in comportment than he; it was no wonder Aiko had discovered us as quickly as she had. Among the others we'd been less immediately noticeable, but on our own it would be easy enough to discover I wasn't the woman I pretended to be.

Iseul—the Iseul I'd known from childhood—would have thrown back his head to laugh if he saw me then, both changed and unchanged, dressed as though I were about to sell travelers dumplings rather than lead my people, as my father's son.

Would Iseul even recognize me if I was caught?

How you've changed, little brother, he'd say. *How common you've become. I could barely tell the difference between you and your servant...*

"Kouje," I said, over the sound of him tramping through the brush, kicking branches aside.

He stilled, and glanced back toward me. "Please tell me you've just had an incredible idea," he said.

"Your servant," I explained. It wasn't clear yet, but it was my brother himself who'd inspired it. It was right; I *knew* it was. "They'll never suspect—if you are the lord, and I am the servant."

Kouje shook his head. As understanding dawned on him, I could see his disapproval; it went against everything that we were, and of course that was the point. No one would ever believe that a prince would lower himself so close to the ground as to play the servant. "No," he said. "I don't think I understand, Mamoru. There's got to be something else, if we just spend more time on it—"

"Your clothes now aren't all that wrong," I continued. He would have to overcome his misgivings; I would have to convince him to overcome them. "If you took the sash—my sash, from before—it would even look *right*. And you hold yourself better than a country lord; they'd believe you. And they'd never guess that anyone, *anyone,* would let the prince walk behind him, carrying our bags like a common servant. I could even lead the horse, and they would never even pause to look at me. If I were your servant, Kouje, they would not even *notice* I was there."

"No," Kouje insisted. "Mamoru, that is—You don't understand. It is too much."

His propriety would be both our undoing. I was up from my seat at once, and grasping him by the front of his shirt. "It is the only way, unless you wish to live here in the woods like two wild men. Perhaps, as Goro suggested, we might see the mountain spirits, and beg them for some supernatural power—then I could *fly* to your sister, and carry you with me! But should that fail, we will have done no more than to tarry here, wasting precious time, and angering those same gods who have given us all our chances thus far by squandering the same inspiration *they* have given us!"

"We would anger those gods if I led you along behind me like— Like chattel," Kouje said. His eyes were all dark anger. I recognized the darkness from nights in the mountains, when the dragons flew overhead; or when they tore through the wall, and the air rained fire down upon the capital, and all the animals of the menagerie were set free into the streets, and we could not find one another.

But this was not the same. This was pride—the same pride that had so changed my brother; the same pride that made Iseul believe all of Xi'an was written, like the future, upon the back of his hand.

"You are a prince," Kouje said.

"Not anymore."

Something went hard in Kouje's face, so that for a moment I truly thought that pride might be our undoing. Not some cruel, random act of fate, but something well within our bounds to control, and I was so angry I thought of striking him.

It would have been as ineffectual as a small bird trying to take its frustrations out on the tree that sheltered it.

"We *must* do this, Kouje," I said quietly, hand still twisting in the fabric of his shirt, more anxious then than angry. "Do you not see?"

"You do not understand what you ask me to do," Kouje answered, and I could hear the reluctance in his voice at having to deny me. He had always spoiled me, had always sought to give me what I desired, even when those desires had been headstrong and foolish.

Even when they'd been impossible.

If he'd been able to do it once, he should have been able to do it again. I pushed at that weakness, hating that I had to do it and hating the situation that made it necessary.

"Do this," I commanded, crushing all soft hints of begging from my voice. I raised my head to look at him, not as a friend, but as his lord. "It is not a request."

There had been a time once when I had wanted nothing more than to learn how to look at Kouje as a friend and not his lord. But it seemed I had to forget that once again in order to get us past this next border crossing.

"Do this for me," I added, trying to impress on him how important this was. "If you truly want my safety, then you will overcome that which holds you back and will remember your duty to me."

Kouje held still so long that I thought my words had woven some kind of forest magic and turned him to a statue. Then he lifted his hand, and put it over mine against his chest.

I felt a flutter of hope and tried not to let it show on my face.

"Will you?" I asked.

"I will do whatever you ask of me, my lord," he said finally, in a granite voice that was much like a statue's.

"It *is* for the best," I told him, and went to fetch our packs from the horse.

Kouje was silent all the while as I tied my sash around his waist, adjusting his shirt and pulling at the fall of his jacket to make it drape properly. There was nothing to be done about the shoes, of course, but country lords rarely saw fit to buy expensive shoes when they were just going to be mucking them up in the fields.

I stepped back to admire my handiwork, biting down on the inside of my cheek to keep myself from asking if he'd ever forgive me.

"That looks right," I said, faltering at the last. "You look very handsome! Just let me cover my hair, and . . . Well, it'll be a moment."

I turned away to fix my own clothing. We'd borrowed things from Aiko, leggings that might fit me, and which would prove less cumbersome than the robes I'd donned as Kouje's wife. In some ways I was still wearing women's clothing, but it could be made to look like a servant's with a few tugs here and a few adjustments there.

I was nearly done, and struggling with the wrap for my hair, when I felt Kouje's hand on my shoulder.

"Let me," he said, and I let go immediately, allowing his capable hands in place of my own.

I remembered how we had stood in the same positions once, though reversed. I had been the one to adjust Kouje's hair, all his fine braids gone as if they'd never been there to begin with.

Did the accomplishments mean anything, if what one had to show for them was gone? Was I still a prince if I lived in the forest with no one to see me but the birds?

"There," said Kouje, stepping away once he'd finished.

"Thank you," I murmured, not daring enough to raise my eyes. I couldn't bear it if Kouje were to decide that I'd done something unforgivable. Not after everything else.

"You look . . . very strange," he said at last. Something in his voice gave me the courage I'd been needing to look up.

There. It was very small, and rather forced, but Kouje was smiling.

I felt so relieved all at once that I couldn't help smiling back at him.

"You can pretend it's a play," I told him. "Such small things do not anger the gods. Plays only anger the mortal men who watch them."

Kouje shook his head quickly though I thought his smile looked a little less forced.

"It *will* be all right," I said, wishing just for a moment that I had my brother's force of will to put behind my words. Whatever else Iseul was, he was a man that people heeded.

Fortunately, where Kouje was concerned, I was that sort of man as well. I didn't know what I'd done to inspire such stubborn loyalty, one that extended far beyond the call of duty and what honor bound him to me and the palace. Kouje had acted against our code—the code of the Ke-Han—in order to save my life. When this was all over, I would have to ask him why.

"If you say so," said Kouje, thawing at last enough to put his hand on my shoulder. I could tell that he was beginning to regret his earlier reluctance, and that if I didn't move quickly, he'd be apologizing for *that* soon enough.

"I do," I said, ducking away to continue where we'd started packing up our belongings.

The clothing I'd changed into was much more freeing than what I'd grown accustomed to at the palace. I scarcely believed how simple it was to move around, and soon discovered that I would have to work a little at making sure my steps did not take me beyond Kouje when we walked together in the road. I had spent so many years clad first in women's clothing, then the cumbersome robes of the palace, that I had naturally learned to walk one way. It would not work with my legs suddenly so free.

"I feel odd," I confessed, coming to stand at Kouje's shoulder, just behind him as he had stood for me countless times before.

He lifted one of our large packs and slung it over one shoulder. "You'll get used to it."

I raised my eyebrows, gazing at the pack on his shoulder.

"Ah," he said, seeming to take my meaning. He eased our luggage off his back, then looked hesitant. "Maybe you should carry one of the smaller ones. I can put this on the horse."

"Kouje," I said, and stuck out my hand for the bag. The best way to make the illusion believable was to make it as real as possible. I knew that as an avid admirer of the theatre, though I'd never guessed it might help me in such a way on our journey.

"You're determined to kill me with this, I see," Kouje said, but there was something admiring in his voice. He handed our luggage over.

It *was* heavy. Fortunately I'd been expecting the weight, since I was certain if I'd buckled under it, Kouje would have insisted on its going with the horse, authenticity or no. I wouldn't be able to carry it on one shoulder, the way Kouje did, but so long as I held my back straight and kept my head down, it was certainly tolerable.

"You might as well ride the horse," I told Kouje, sharing a private, wry smile with him while I still could. "You'll look properly noble that way."

"Now you're just torturing me," Kouje said, but he swung into the stirrups and mounted our animal.

"It shouldn't be long to the checkpoint," I murmured, for myself as much as for him.

He gave a short nod and we started out.

It was much swifter traveling on the main road than on trails Kouje found—or sometimes made—for us, and it was not quite midday when we came to the place where the road widened. I could see a small crowd building where the traffic slowed to form an orderly line, and guards in black and dark blue were patrolling up and down to make sure no one got too impatient.

I felt the beginning of something sick and nervous in my stomach and took a deep breath to quash the feeling. I couldn't afford to be nervous. Nor could I risk looking to Kouje for comfort, when in my guise as a servant it would be considered the height of impropriety to lift my eyes to my lord. Instead I kept my eyes fixed on my sandals, where the dust danced and swirled with each misstep, and my mind on the road ahead.

"Wagons form a line to the right," one of the guards called as we passed by. "All those on foot to the left."

Another guard approached us and I was too apprehensive even to flinch.

"Might as well dismount here, my lord," he said to Kouje. "We're leading everyone through on foot."

"Very well," Kouje replied, and if he was nervous, I couldn't hear it in his tone.

He dismounted, and I scurried forward to take the reins from him.

The guard moved down the line to yell at a merchant whose chickens had got free of his wagon and were milling about in the road, clucking indignantly at all the fuss.

I breathed a quiet sigh of relief and tried to ignore the sense of mounting dread as the line crept forward. Kouje stood in front of me, silent and impassive as the border wall, but I drew what strength I could from his solemnity. Worrying about what *might* happen would only serve to make me look more suspicious, and I couldn't afford to do anything that might catch the attention of the guards.

I'd never spent so much time observing my feet before. It closed the world out, drawing everything that mattered to rest right there at my toes. There was a crowd there, and the line moved slowly under the sun.

At least, I thought wryly, I knew that there would be no holdup because the prince had been found. I scuffed my sandal against the dusty road and thought of what it meant to be a servant.

They were always small—smaller even than I was, though I'd never be an imposing man like Iseul or my father. Smallness was a state of mind, one which royalty were not encouraged to foster, but it was a different smallness from the mincing steps the women of the court took in order to better display their skirts and sleeves. They were small in the same way I'd realized, with a terrible shock on my thirteenth birthday, that even Kouje—Kouje, who'd always seemed so big—was small. Small by comparison, I thought, and hunched my shoulders around myself.

I reminded myself of sleeping on dirt, of catching my own rabbits to eat; I reminded myself of the way my brother treated the men and women of the house—as though they weren't even there.

I was concentrating so hard on what it meant to be small that I forgot, it would seem, what it meant to listen.

"I said, *move it along,*" one of the common guards repeated to me, kicking dust toward my feet. Beside me, Kouje stiffened, but I murmured the usual apologies in time-honored form before I scuffled in the right direction.

We were just at the door, where the wall opened up into a white-pebbled courtyard. There were the barracks where the border guards slept in rotation, the low walkways between humble buildings; and there, just beyond, were green fields with tall grasses, stirred by the wind. The low roofs were thatched, not shingled. Truly, we were in country provinces, as far from the capital as my imagination had taken me. We were in the commander of the Guard's territory: a man so unimportant that I'd never been required to learn his name. Country nobles and those from the capital rarely saw eye to eye, and had even less reason to. It wasn't as if we ever sat down to share our meals.

That was for the best. No man there would recognize me.

I knew the commander first by his shoes: fine, strong boots, not as muddy as the common guards' were, and he walked with a presence of bearing that revealed his status. I chanced a look no higher than his knees as he walked past us.

"Two," he said, addressing himself to Kouje, "is a very unlucky number these days."

"So I've heard," Kouje replied, adopting a country accent. Later, I would have to ask him whether or not it was from his own hometown, or something he'd conjured on the spot. "I've spent time enough already just trying to get back to my sister. She's just had a boy, you know."

"My congratulations on your honor," the commander said.

"My thanks on your congratulations," Kouje replied.

He was being careful, addressing the commander with the strictest courtesy available. It was a mystery to me how he'd slipped into the role so easily, until I realized that Kouje, being a better servant than I, had mastered both the art of being small as well as the art of listening. He was echoing everything he'd heard, every conversation that had taken place before him as though he were nothing more than a mirror. He'd learned from them, well enough to play at being a noble himself.

I had to prevent my face from showing surprise when I realized that Kouje was everything my brother feared most in his servants. He was too clever, almost, and I was glad he'd come with me before anyone in the capital had had reason to discover his intelligence.

I stared at the commander's boots instead, afraid to be caught observing anything higher. He moved back and forth between us like a hunting dog deciding upon its prey; but, at the very least, he hadn't yet addressed me at all. If he continued to glance over me—like my brother glanced over his servants—then we'd be safe.

"So you are headed to Honganje," the Commander went on, "in order to visit your sister's newborn son?"

"Traveling since the war ended," Kouje replied stiffly, clearing his throat.

"Not a ruffian, I hope," the commander said.

"Just can't seem to settle down, that's all," Kouje said.

"You traveled all this way alone?"

"I had some companions with me. Men I met in the war."

"And your companions?"

I could hear a smile creep into Kouje's voice. "Lost them to the bright lights of the capital, I'm sorry to say. Just couldn't drag them away from the pleasure quarters. But me? I couldn't settle down in a place like that, with all the women looking at me behind my back like I'm some kind of bear. I need more space than those rooms allow."

"Hm," the commander said. "You'll forgive me for all the questions, my lord. We must take as many precautions as we may."

"I understand your duty as well as I understand my own," Kouje replied.

The commander cleared his throat, and I saw him gesture with a willow branch toward two of the guards—whose feet were waiting, boots caked with dust, just behind him.

"Pardon our interference," the commander said. "It will only be a moment, but our duty demands that we search your belongings."

"I understand completely," Kouje replied.

But he couldn't, I thought desperately. My clothes were in there—the fine silk robes I'd worn the night Iseul meant to kill me. Those were no country lord's effects, nor were they a courtesan's parting gift. They were too fine for that. The moment the guards saw them we would be suspect. Had Kouje forgotten them, or had he simply seen no way to prevent the search without appearing yet more suspicious?

If only I could have seen his face. His eyes would have told me everything. But, without that, I knew I had to warn him.

We were close enough that I managed, with my free hand, to grab at his sleeve.

The guards, just at our horse, stood still.

"Your manservant is overly familiar," the commander said. "What a curious choice for a simple lord such as yourself." He advanced upon me, lifting the willow branch as command. "Show me your face, man," he ordered.

"No need," Kouje said, a terrifying steel in his voice. "He has shown such disrespect before, and I have always taken care of it."

"Perhaps not well enough," the commander said. "Show me your *face.*"

Kouje moved more quickly than I knew he could, as quickly as the fabled warriors of old lore. With a sharp cry—to anyone but me, it would have seemed a noise of rebuke, but all that I heard was pain—he'd grabbed the commander's willow branch in one hand.

And then he was beating me with it.

The first lash was too much of a shock to hurt. I registered no pain at all, but the second was fierce enough to send me to the ground. I fell, and the dust clouded up around me as Kouje brought the willow branch down upon me like a lash. Like, indeed, a master beating his servant.

I brought my arms up to shield my face, though I noticed too late that he was not aiming there, but for my forearms and shoulders—where, perhaps, I might not be too badly injured. Pebbles dug into my legs and I curled in around myself, wondering whether or not Kouje had taken leave of his senses entirely, if the madness of our escape had at last driven *him* mad.

Surely he had a reason.

The willow branch sliced into the rough cloth at my elbow and tore it. Blood had been drawn, and I was not the only one to know it.

"That should be sufficient," Kouje said, hoarse and breathless.

"You have been too cruel," the commander replied. There was some rebuke in his voice.

"Servants must learn their place," Kouje countered, and kicked at me. "Get up."

"Still . . ." the commander said, but trailed off. No man dared to tell another how to treat those under him. It was up to his discretion, and interference was an insult.

I stumbled to my feet, the bags I carried heavy, my mind swirling with the dust. Of course, I realized in a sudden burst of misery and relief, Kouje had distracted them from their purpose. They wouldn't think to look in our bags. What servant would ever beat his master so? What loyal subject would ever strike his prince?

We were of no more interest to them. We were irrelevant to their duty.

But Kouje, I knew, would never forgive himself.

The guards by our horses stepped away at a gesture from the commander, and I tried to feel grateful, not muzzy with pain and the gentle wet dripping of blood into my sleeve. I thought of rocks, and mountains, and the forbidding, solid posture of the men who played heroes in the theatre and I held my place. I didn't sway, or stumble. If I had done that, then surely everything would have been lost. As it stood, I was unsure and afraid of what was holding Kouje together.

I knew that it would be terrible when whatever he was clinging to crumbled at last.

"My blessings on your nephew," said the commander, which meant we could go. His voice was less cordial than it had been before, as though he'd decided that Kouje was not a man he'd like to know after all.

The injustice of it rose thick in my throat like the dust, so that I had to swallow around my unhappiness. I held silent, and dropped my gaze so that I could not even see the commander's boots.

"My thanks for your courtesy," Kouje said, and handed back the commander's willow branch.

If the gesture was a little too swift and abrupt, it could be taken as apology for the commander's displeasure. The bow that came next could be taken for the same, but I knew that it was only so that Kouje could take shelter in a brief moment of hiding his face.

I took the horse's reins once again, my movements perfunctory, as though I were a puppet putting on a show of humanity.

Kouje walked ahead of me. He did not look back even as we passed out of the courtyard and into Honganje prefecture.

CHAPTER TWELVE

KOUJE

It was quiet on the plains. To our left were the humble rice paddies of country farmers, and as the sun set it cast light across the murky water, so that it burned silver. To our right, in the far distance, were the Cobalt Mountains, over which the dragons flew during the war. Their peaks disappeared into the clouds, and if I tried to follow them, my eyes burned with the fading sunlight.

"I understand why you did it," Mamoru had explained, many hours ago, after I'd helped him to mount the horse. My hand had rested upon his forearm, where that very same hand had drawn blood. I had nothing to wrap the wound with.

Those were the last words he'd spoken. I'd offered none at all.

When we stopped for the night, and there was no more promise of putting that moment yet farther behind us—then I could answer for what I'd done, confront it, stand like the fabled warrior protecting his lord on the bridge with my weapon at the ready.

That story had been my father's favorite. It recounted the tale of the loyal retainer, the last barrier between his lord and their enemies, fighting off a garrison of men on his own while his lord prepared means for suicide high in the castle keep. They died together, my father said, and they were honor itself. But those men came from a time long before ours, a time when honor ran thicker than blood, and bound each man to another—a hierarchy, itself more violent than magic. It was a principle upon which our entire world was built and I had defamed it with one simple stroke, with a weapon as simple and as beautiful as a willow branch.

Put that in your play, Goro, I thought; but even that was too outlandish, and no audience would ever believe it. It had been, in short, the perfect ruse—so perfect that they had not bothered to check our bags, in which Mamoru's silk robe lay coiled like a snake to destroy the two of us.

Mamoru knew why I had done it.

If he knew that much, then he knew what it meant for both of us that I had raised my hand against him. We did not speak the next day, nor the day after that, but rode on toward our goal as though we were strangers. In some ways, we surely were. I could no longer think of us as a prince and his retainer, since I had surely destroyed those skins for us.

I slept poorly, when I slept at all, and the bandage on my lord's arm was a constant reminder of what ill I'd done alongside the good.

Never before; never again. I'd done it for him, hadn't I, and not for myself? The answer would never be sufficient. Another day passed us by like a dream, my lord trapped by my very silence.

It was another day before he spoke again. He was ever braver than I, in this respect.

"Kouje," Mamoru said, from somewhere far and high above me. He was riding the horse as I walked beside him, but the distance had grown with each step so insurmountable that it was a miracle I could even hear him.

I said nothing.

For a time after that he was quiet, and I was a coward and grateful for the quiet, until he spoke again, that time with more vigor. "We ought to stop soon. I hear the sound of a river."

The horse whinnied, a steadfast though foreign mount, and gazed at me as though he meant to condemn me, too. I'd driven them both too hard, but the smaller injustices withered when placed next to the only one that mattered.

"Come," I whispered to the horse, and led him toward the water to drink.

Mamoru dismounted without my help and fell to making camp. By then, the shadows were too deep to see his face and I sat against a log to consider what came next. I would take him to Honganje, then I would lock myself away like that lord in the keep. At dawn, I would do the honorable thing, with Mamoru safe and my service fulfilled.

My arm should rot away as we walked for what it had done.

I should wake in the morning to discover it had turned to snakes, writhing beside me.

The flesh should turn the color of ash and my fingers would be burned into the soil first, followed by the palm and the wrist, until nothing was left of the offending limb.

No apology was true enough, no action clear. I did not watch my lord as he readied himself and went to sleep, and I sat with my back against the log until I, too, drifted off, where dreams rose up to cover me with thorns.

I woke to the sound of my lord shouting.

At last, they'd caught us, I thought, despite all that we'd both sacrificed. I fumbled for something to use as a weapon, and cursed myself for thinking all was safe enough to rest. With a stick in hand—my new weapon, it seemed—and the bark rough against my palm, I raised my arm and prepared to attack the enemy.

But not even the sound of footfalls greeted me, and no shadows of soldiers moved across the moonlit darkness.

We were alone, and my lord was crying out in his sleep.

I dropped the branch and moved to his side. It had been many years since last Mamoru had experienced a nightmare. When he'd been a boy, I'd slipped into bed beside him and rocked him back to sleep, feeling his feverish brow and calling for the servants when he was peaceful at last. They brought him cold water and the usual medicines, teas, and powders, none of which seemed to make one whit of difference. We had no such assistance with us, but when I pressed my hand against his brow, I felt that it was fiercely hot.

"Mamoru," I whispered, all else forgotten. "Mamoru, wake up!"

He writhed—much like a snake himself—and struck out at my face. His nails caught against my skin and tore at it, and I was too stunned by the blow to say anything when his eyes opened, and fixed upon me in the night.

A fever, at this time of year?

Perhaps we had gone too far too quickly. Or, with his constitution, so many nights spent blanketed by the evening chill and the morning dew had at last taken its toll.

Or I had beaten him too hard, a guilty voice added, twisting its miserable fingers deep inside my belly, the blade of a knife carved solely for suicide.

Mamoru whimpered, his arm falling limp against my shoulder, and I felt something still within me. I had no time to be feeling guilty when my lord was in need of me.

"Mamoru," I said again, now that his eyes were open. I passed my hand in front of his face, and his eyes did not follow the movement. "Mamoru, *please.*"

He gasped, as though breathing had become difficult for him, and his hand clenched tight, grasping at my shirt against the advent of some unseen enemy.

"No," he moaned, low dread tainting his voice. "Don't... It isn't..."

In his illnesses as a child, the fever had sometimes given my lord deliriums, so that for a period of time he was entirely lost to me. There, he wandered in some land of his fevered brain's devising where I could not follow, and therefore could not protect him.

"I am here," I said, praying that it wasn't *me* his fever had conjured, someone meant to protect him now turned against him. "It's all right. You should have some... water."

There was a great river that stood between our destination and us. We would have to cross it in order to reach my sister's house, and I'd meant to tackle that obstacle when we came to it later, but now I thought that perhaps it would serve us best to try and reach it that night. Without the powders, teas, and medicines available at the palace, I was rather at a loss as to how to bring Mamoru's fever down. With his constitution, there was no telling what lasting damage might be done to his body if he remained so hot. He burned where I touched him, through the rough homespun cloth, torn here and there.

I dared to touch his arm, where the blood had dried against the fabric, as though by covering the wound I could heal it.

"Kouje," he gasped, and I felt my heart leap like a startled animal.

"My lord," I murmured, too close for anyone else, even the birds, to hear. "I think we should try to get to the river."

"The trees are moving," he moaned, gazing at me without seeing me.

"That's just the wind," I said, and took him in my arms to stand us both up.

My lord was terribly thin, though he hadn't once complained about the sparse meals we'd grown accustomed to on the road. Carrying him was like holding a bundle of sticks, already set to blazing with the illness in his blood. How long had it been since Mamoru had last been taken with fever? I couldn't remember. The physicians had all said he'd grown out of it—once he weathered his thirteenth winter, he'd long since outlived their predictions—and indeed he'd fought capably enough in the mountain campaigns without ever falling ill.

It was enough to make me wonder—as I had never allowed myself to before—whether or not my lord's illnesses had been entirely organic. If Iseul was capable of calling him traitor, who knew at what point he had begun to feel animosity for his brother?

I placed him on the horse, then mounted behind him so that I might catch him if he fell. The horse would never forgive me for not only depriving him of his rest, but also doubling his load, but I hoped the beast might manage to hold out a little longer. That it too might recognize its duty to Mamoru and push itself past its own natural limits, as I had tried to do.

Perhaps the horse would be more successful than I'd been.

Mamoru fell into a fitful sleep as we rode, muttering nonsense and clutching at whatever he could grasp with his small fingers, so that I found it hard to concentrate on the task at hand when I could not take my hands from the reins to comfort him. The sound of the horse's hooves against the ground echoed loudly beneath us, our only company. The entire scene was like one from a dream.

Of course, the terrible thing about that sort of fever was that even if I could have put all my attentions to comforting him, he would likely not recognize the effort. He might not even know me.

Better, then, to head for the river, where I might at least do some good by bringing down his fever in water that ran frigid from the mountains to the sea.

It was a warm night, at least. The comfort I derived from knowing that Mamoru would have certainly taken sick from sleeping outdoors in the winter was a meager one, because if it was *not* the weather, then what was it? I thought again of my suspicions, dark as a shadow over my heart. If Iseul had caused Mamoru's sickness in the past, then by now he was surely comfortable with the art of blood magic. I could not confirm what I thought against my lord's fevered state, however, and it was pointless to think of such things when I could not resolve them.

I felt the sharp pang of guilt again, of having harmed someone I'd sworn to protect. What I'd done had been as wrong as a fish taking flight, and as in all cases of nature's laws being flouted, there *would* be a price to pay.

I had only hoped to make that payment with my sworn life. I'd never guessed that the gods would choose to punish *Mamoru* for such a thing. He was as blameless as a new day, fresh with promise and none of the weight of yesterday's mistakes hanging over him. He did not deserve such unworthy servants, who were *not* so blameless as he.

I was so caught up in my own thoughts that I didn't notice it when we came to the river. It was only the sudden splash of water that caught my attention, as in the dark the horse hadn't seen it either. Mamoru chose that moment to cry out from the fever, and our horse shied in surprise and confusion. I tugged hard on the reins to keep him from bucking.

"Mamoru," I murmured, then, since there was no one to hear us, "my lord. We have reached the river."

He made a noise like an animal in pain, and turned his bright, glassy gaze up toward mine. "It's *hot*," he complained softly, "all over. I can't . . ." His head dipped, and fell against my shoulder. "Kouje?"

"It's fine," I told him, fighting to believe it myself. "Everything's going to be fine."

I helped him down from the horse, his body swaying like a doll's, limp and pale. He was still dressed like a servant.

"Easy now," I said, edging us both toward the riverbank.

It was a warm night, I reminded myself, and there was no time to think of myself. I waded in fully clothed, with Mamoru held close against my chest. He thrashed in my hold like a fish for a moment, and then went still again as the water washed over him, cold even in the summertime. The Suijin River was one of the larger ones in Xi'an, so wide that the far bank was nearly invisible in the dark, and so long that it crossed over the Cobalts and into Volstov before it once again met with the ocean. I wondered if they had another name for it there, across the mountains, and if the river god ever became confused at having more than one name for the same body of water.

"It's cold," Mamoru said.

"Yes," I replied.

"Don't let the fish eat my toes," he pleaded.

"I won't," I promised, and recalled that morning in the forest, when the catfish had so startled him. It seemed an unthinkable length of time when I looked back, though it had been no more than three weeks. Not such a great length of time, though it was long enough for our story to have caught the imaginations and satiric attention of the playwrights. It was as though my lord and I were no longer real people, living and breathing among them, but something lofty and far off, removed from the world and entered into legend.

Had the loyal retainer stood as tall as the mountains when he stood on the bridge to defend his lord against a dishonorable death? Had he truly been the figure worthy of legend that my father had talked about?

Or had he been like me: tired and watchful, always suspicious of a stranger, and even more so of a good turn of luck? Had he ever stood in a river alongside his lord, soaking wet, just praying that the fever might go down, that they might make it safely to their destination with no further complications, no more obstacles to block their path?

I wondered when he'd realized that they weren't going to reach their destination. Then I thought of Mamoru's stubbornness, and I wondered how the legendary retainer had managed to convince his lord to leave him there on the bridge in the first place.

Perhaps we weren't the stuff of legends after all.

"It hurts," Mamoru whispered, crumpling suddenly as though he'd been struck.

I moved once more to hold him up.

"It hurts *all over*," he said, looking up at me with pleading in his eyes. "I can't bear it. I *can't*. It's too much."

"The water will help," I said, willing the conviction into my voice. "It is uncomfortable because you are so warm, and the cold is such a shock, but it will help," I promised. "Trust me."

Mamoru swallowed, and made a noise of protest in his throat, but he didn't attempt to argue. I held him as I had when he'd been a child starved for attention, and myself not yet old enough to keep from allowing him his indulgences. I could feel him shivering despite the heat still in his body, and I felt the beginnings of fear flicker to life deep in my heart. We were still too far from my sister's house for him to be so ill. If I could coax the fever down, then that would be one thing, but if I could not . . .

The problem was that I couldn't shake my gut instinct—that this had something to do with Iseul. I did not want to believe that such a thing was possible, that it would be so simple for one brother to turn against the other in such a final way—using forbidden arts—but then, Iseul had already turned his heart and his hand against Mamoru. What else could I expect?

"You'll be all right," I told him.

I had no way to render what I offered, but I promised it nonetheless. It was part of my own stubbornness and pride—the very same flaws that had caused me to imagine I, of all men, could protect my prince outside the palace. These were the very same flaws that had inspired me to tell him: *Run.*

When we were both numb from the water, and long past the moment I'd grown accustomed to the sound of my teeth chattering, Mamoru stilled and his breathing evened. I pressed my wet cheek against his and listened, closely, for each rasp.

"I'm better," Mamoru whispered.

We'd see about that.

I took him up onto shore nonetheless and wrapped him in the silk. It would soon be ruined, soaked through and stained forever; no longer would it give us away to any man who knew his cloth.

The sun was beginning to rise as I set out, following the course of the river. I listened closely to each sound Mamoru made, but he slept soundly upon the horse, his cheeks only the barest pink. He was no longer as burning hot as he had been the night before, but I refused to let my guard down. Following the river only took us a few miles out of our way, and for now, it was the only cure I had should the fever return.

That night, it did.

It was as soon as the sun dipped beneath the mountain horizon that his teeth began to chatter. Almost immediately I could feel his skin begin to burn, as though some furnace had been ignited within his chest, pumping his blood molten hot through his limbs. In the fading light his cheeks were flushed red, but around his mouth the skin was deadly white.

I dismounted and pulled him after me, and once more we spent hours in the river as the water lashed around me and I held on tight.

He struggled to free himself—if he did, he would drown—as though I were the unlucky fisherman who fell in love with a mermaid and sought to keep her as his wife. He was slippery and strong enough that I had trouble keeping my hold firm, but I wrapped my fingers in his sleeves and stood strong against him.

"Let me free," he pleaded—begged—commanded. "I know how to swim, Kouje, I'll be all right."

"I cannot agree to that," I replied.

He abandoned begging. Speaking became too much for him. At long last, his arms and legs tired of beating and kicking and he stilled, only to shake now and then with a shiver or a sob.

"Please," he said, once, his voice rough with effort.

"I cannot," I said again.

After that, he saw it was no use, and whatever demon had taken hold of him relinquished. It was only me against the fever then, but that was the worse of the two enemies. I lost track of all time as I held him in the water, until at last I felt him go limp and knew he was sleeping.

Again, I wrapped him in the silk. This time, I waited upon the shores of the Suijin for the sun to rise before I mounted up and spurred the weary horse onward.

We were drawing ever closer to the mountains, and when we came to a shallow part of the river, we waded across the water to Honganje province itself. It was what we'd both been waiting for, but now I couldn't wake Mamoru to tell him we'd arrived. If I had, I'd have no assurance that he'd understand me—no assurance that the fever would not take that opportunity to strike again.

Once again, I followed the river. Once again, the fever returned as soon as the sun set.

During the day, it was not so difficult to hold the illness back, but once darkness fell upon us there was nothing I could do but wade into the river and wait.

Mamoru did not struggle so much this time as he had the last. It was easier to keep him from slipping away from me, yet that was no turn of good luck.

"You'll kill me in the water like this," Mamoru whispered, deceptive and cold, his eyes white-hot slits. He observed me from behind a face like a mask, and I knew it was the fever speaking. It assumed it knew my lord better than I did. It assumed it could outsmart us with its sly words. "You know how weak I am, Kouje. Do you think I can make it much longer?"

"We shall have to see," I said.

Mamoru let out a sharp cry, as though I'd pierced his stomach with a blade. It lingered on the air, over the sound of the rushing water, for a long moment; too long.

Then, from somewhere beyond the riverbank, I heard an answering shout.

It was no echo.

I cursed the moon, the sun, winter, and summer; I cursed my father and my mother, the very day I was born. I cursed until I had run out of curses, but all the while I was dragging Mamoru—who'd found new strength to kick and bite and claw and shout—out of the water and up onto the horse.

The horse reared and whinnied, one last act of defiance, before I jammed my boots into his flanks and he tore off alongside the river, slipping occasionally upon the wet pebbles that lined the bank.

I could only imagine the men following us, chasing the lone cry in the night. Bandits, or worse—state officials, soldiers, Iseul's men, closing in on us.

When was the last time I slept? I had no memory of it, nor indeed of what sleep felt like. In my altered, dizzied state, I imagined all those shadows that had been haunting us closing in on their prey at last, owls upon two field mice.

I covered Mamoru's mouth with one hand, muffling his cries, and steered the horse with the other. There was only one place along the plains that we could go where we wouldn't be revealed to the open sky when the sun rose: the mountains. And if my feelings were right, and Iseul had finally shown his hand in using blood magic once again, then there was only one direction we could head for help and sanctuary. I jerked the reins, perhaps too hard, and the horse tore off across the river, away from Honganje. Water flew up around us in an ice-cold spray, and Mamoru tried to bite at my palm.

"Hold tight, my lord," I said, knowing full well I spoke to someone who was no longer there.

I rode on.

If we could only reach the foothills before the sun began to rise. I had no way of telling whether the men who'd answered my lord's fevered call had been mounted on horseback, but if they were not, that would surely give us the head start we so desperately needed.

Mamoru pitched forward, his fingers twisted in the horse's mane as though he meant to bring us down, and I snaked an arm around his chest, pulling him back. He whimpered, then fought against my hold, while I did my damnedest to steer the horse one-handed toward the looming dark of the mountains ahead of us. It didn't work very well, and I was forced to let my hand fall.

"You're not making things very easy for me," I said, because my lord couldn't hear me.

"You're so *cruel*," he moaned.

I ignored that, as one ignored everything brought on by a fever, and dug my heels in harder. I do not think that I took the time or space to breathe until the ground turned rockier and began to slant upward.

It was then that I began to realize we were going to have to dismount in order to continue. There were footpaths in the Cobalts—secret winding ways that we'd used in the war against Volstov and her dragons. It wouldn't be safe to ride along them—especially not with my lord in such a state—but one might lead a horse along them efficiently enough.

I just didn't have any idea how I was going to coax Mamoru into walking. More than that, I didn't know how I was going to coax him into the sudden change of plans.

Best to confront those problems head-on instead of worrying about them, though. I urged our horse onward, looking for a familiar marking, etched into stone by a simple blade, that would tell me where one of the hidden paths started. They were much harder to spot in the moonlight. I took heart from the fact that Mamoru had not tried to leap from the horse since I'd grabbed hold of him, as though whatever had possessed him had been exorcised by my own sheer stubbornness.

I didn't flatter myself that I was capable of such things, of course. I was merely glad that whatever it had been seemed to have passed. The fever was opponent enough for me. I was just a man and no figure of legend.

Finally I recognized a marking, a symbol scratched into the rock for soldiers to follow. It would do well enough for my lord and me. I pulled

Mamoru from the horse when I myself dismounted, and held him in front of me like a bundle of reeds wrapped in silk.

"Walking," Mamoru sighed, as though it was an unimaginable burden.

"I'll help you," I promised, maneuvering around him to take the horse by the reins.

There was a moment, thankfully brief, when the world spun beneath my feet, and the bright blue of the rocks swirled together with the dark ground. Then, the horse tossed its head impatiently and broke my attention. I was freed from the vortex. I didn't think it was anything more serious than my own exhaustion, but it was yet another thing to watch for.

There were more causes for a fever than I could count. If I fell prey to illness because of my own exhaustion, then everything fell to the gods.

We traveled in relative silence, Mamoru struggling to put one foot in front of the other, while high above us over the mountains, the sun began to rise. He clutched at his robes with thin, pale fingers, as though the silk gave him comfort against the strain of walking. At least, I thought, we could be thankful that losing the cover of darkness would mean losing the worst of the fever for the day as well. It left him weak, though, and leaning heavily on me in order to keep one foot following the other. I pushed from my mind any thought of what might happen if I weakened too—such a turn of events was unacceptable; I refused it—and we pressed on.

The mountains were brightly colored even in the faint hazy light of dawn, blue as the very heart of the country. For one as devoted as I, it was difficult to see the land as a danger, potentially housing enemies at every turn. The fourteenth pass, the one we were using, was unoccupied these days because of its extreme proximity to the Volstov capital. Clearing it out had been one of the first agreed-upon provisions of the treaty, or so my lord had told me, in the weeks after the war had ended.

We moved deeper into the mountains, while memory blurred with my thoughts and the sound of each ragged breath—my own mingling with my lord's.

At the heat of midday we stopped to rest, and Mamoru slept so deeply I checked his breath with my palm in front of his mouth more than once to reassure myself. He was still breathing though more quietly.

Even the horse sensed our troubles, and he was restless in the sunlight. I soothed both beast and my lord with alternating hands, let Mamoru drink from a skin dangerously low on water, while the horse whinnied in chastisement. We were both beasts of burden—perhaps, at last, we'd come to appreciate one another. Even if the horse was himself a foreigner.

Just on the other side of the range was Volstov, a country less our enemy than our own Emperor was. It was dragon country no more. From our position, twinkling faintly in the far distance, were the jeweled rooftops of Lapis, like a little toy city, as easily scattered by a child's hand as it had been by the dragonfire.

I turned to show Mamoru, but his eyes were shut against the sunlight, and I thought the better of it. Instead, I whispered his name against his temple and gently led him on.

CHAPTER THIRTEEN

CAIUS

It had been nearly a week since Josette, Alcibiades, and I had shared our tête-à-tête in the general's room, and we had yet to find an opportunity in which to get Lord Temur by himself.

The man was simply impossible!

"Of course, we would have to pick one of the more popular lords." I sighed, murmuring my complaint to Alcibiades behind the fall of my sleeve. "He's much too sociable for a Ke-Han warlord."

"I thought that was what you liked about him," Alcibiades countered in a maddening fashion.

He reached over me to spear one of the fried dumplings that had somehow begun cropping up at our table. Alcibiades did well enough with his sticks, even if he *did* use them as if they were weapons instead of eating utensils. I couldn't help but think that his improved mood had a great deal to do with the fare, though that in turn was doubtless more to do with my helpful little suggestions to Lord Temur—all of them exquisitely tactful—than any hint the cooks might have taken from Alcibiades' plates of fish going back untouched.

Josette, on my left, took a sip of her tea, watching our quarry with an expression that I might have termed intimate concern were I feeling more romantic about the whole thing. Really, she almost made it *too* easy for me. She was much like Alcibiades in that fashion, poor thing. Some people just couldn't keep anything to themselves.

"Are we sure this is the proper way to go about things?" Josette asked.

"Oh, surely not proper," I said, unable to keep the smile from my lips, "but it will be simplest. And it's dreadfully efficient. I'm a bit out of practice since the war ended, and unlike Alcibiades, I haven't had *any* opportunity for fun."

"Fun," Alcibiades snorted. "I wouldn't call it *that,* exactly."

I was starting to take the impression that my companions were experiencing what amounted to a softening of the heart. It was not quite a *change* of heart, since Alcibiades at the very least could be counted on to stick to a decision once he'd made it, but I could still tell that the poor dears were having doubts. Even to men such as Alcibiades, hardened on the battlefield, my Talent was a questionable force. When asked directly, the most explanation that people could manage was that it didn't seem "quite fair," all things considered.

That was all right. It was an attitude I'd grown rather used to in my eighteen years of living at the palace, and subsequently in exile. I was an ally, but not trusted—a necessary weapon, whose means were considered underhanded and whose actions left a considerably sour taste in most people's mouths. The fact that I enjoyed my work seemed to be what distressed them the most, but I *was* good at it, and I made it a point always to enjoy the things I was good at.

So I was quite prepared to go through with our plan, even if it meant losing the friendships I'd cultivated there. I held no real illusions about the strength of such relationships, anyway, knowing full well that Josette only put up with me because my good general did, and that *Alcibiades* only put up with me because he was, bless him, an endearingly simple creature to baffle, and I thrust myself into his company more often than not.

That, and I considered us friends. He would simply have to forgive me my transgressions. And he would, given enough time.

Besides, it was terribly cumbersome living beholden to the whims and expectations of other people. I'd gone dreadfully overboard in my enthusiasm on first arriving within the Ke-Han capital, and it was time to prune back what had bloomed.

Everyone made their jokes about the instability on my mother's side of the family, but the truth was it made things *very* difficult when one came out of a spell of madness to find one's life all askew. It had happened once, just before my period of exile, but I was grateful for that one—it meant I had to recall very little of my first few weeks therein. I sometimes felt as though I spent at least half my time putting things to right again. It could be exhausting, but there were moments that made it quite worthwhile.

Getting the chance to exercise my powers was certainly one of those moments, and in the week that followed our decision, I confess that I trailed Lord Temur like a lynx, lithe and hungry.

It had been *so* long since my last prey.

As luck would have it, my opportunity came just as I was nearly ready to give up altogether and ask Alcibiades' aid in knocking Lord Temur over the head.

I was sitting at my vanity table, unhooking the clever wooden fastenings of the hair ornaments I'd borrowed from Josette without permission, when the door connecting mine to Alcibiades' slid open, and the general himself appeared.

If I hadn't already been sitting, I'd have fallen over with shock.

"My dear!" I said, rising at once and casting the little lacquered butterflies onto the desk. "If I'd known you were coming, I might have waited to undo myself. Come in, come in."

I rushed over to take him by the arm, lest he change his mind before entering and duck out again straightaway. To my continuing shock, he allowed himself not only to be pulled into the room proper, but pressed into a nearby chair as well.

"You've got a bug in your hair," he said, staring up at me.

"Oh!" I said foolishly, running a hand through my hair for the stray clasp. There it was, caught at the back. I fished it out, careful not to let it snag. "Well, fancy that. I completely missed it. Have you come to be helpful? Because there's a knot in this sash that I can never seem to quite—"

"Josette says we're doing it tomorrow," he blurted out, interrupting me in the middle of turning around.

"Are we?" I asked, whirling around again at once to face him. I hadn't meant to look so eager, but the fact remained that I had begun to think we'd never have an opportunity at all.

"You don't have to look like it's your birthday come early,"

Alcibiades grunted, but there was a small, hard smile on his face that I hadn't seen before.

"But you couldn't have planned it better if it *had* been my birthday," I told him earnestly, clasping my hands together.

"You're an odd bird," Alcibiades said, in a way that made me think that perhaps it was a compliment, coming from him.

"The very finest of peacocks, my dear," I said. "Now I'm afraid I'll have to ask you to leave, I've a great deal of preparation to do for tomorrow."

If I hadn't known better, I'd have thought the look on Alcibiades' face was almost disappointed.

"All right," he said, rising to his feet. "Just so long as we can get this over with."

"I do hope it doesn't bother you, my dear," I said, softening considerably. "As I know how traditional you like to be about things."

"If it were up to me," Alcibiades began, then cut off, shaking his head. "Doesn't matter, does it? Since it's not."

"That's the most sensible you've ever been," I replied, patting him on the shoulder.

It was only when I returned to the task at hand—the clips for my hair—that I noticed that my hands were shaking.

I was often asked what it meant to be a *velikaia* by the men and women who came to visit me during my "sojourns" in the countryside—all of them lonely, silly people desperate for gossip to get them through the country life. If it wasn't chasing down poor, helpless little foxes during hunts—I liked to rescue them and keep them in my own private menagerie—then it was sitting about wondering what was happening in the capital, that distant, glowing, glorious zenith of social importance.

Some asked only for news of the Esar and the Esarina; this margrave or that; the latest news from Thremedon, and who was wearing what, and who had married whom—the usual trifling bits and bats we all longed for. Myself, I must necessarily admit, included.

But some, the poor creatures, had no idea about real manners at all. After a time, everyone found some way, tactful or not, to ask the questions they were so desperate to have answered.

What did it mean to be a *velikaia*? Were all the rumors they'd heard—bastion-only-knew from whom—true?

I always answered the question about the rumors first, because that really was the more interesting. Yes, I had been involved with the incident of Margrave Aulame; but no, his pretty young wife did not kill herself because of it. Yes, I had begun to assist the Esar when I was only seven years old; but no, I had assuredly *not* played a part in the untimely death of the Arlemagne duchess who married the Esar's eldest son. Yes, I *had* played a significant role in information garnered during the war—but really, it wasn't all *that* grisly; just asking questions and receiving answers, more quickly than if I did not have my Talent.

And as for my Talent . . .

That was another matter entirely. They really ought to have asked Mme. Antoinette about that. But seeing as most country lords and ladies, desperate for some taste of the urban life, did not have the opportunity to ask Antoinette for themselves, it was up to me to provide the information.

What did it mean to be a *velikaia*? For me, the fascinating question always was, what did it mean *not* to be a *velikaia*? It was merely a chance happening, the well water that ran like pedigree through my blood. It was only that my family had sought, through various means, to keep that blood as pure and our Talents as keen as possible. It was good business sense more than it was madness—the madness that had developed over time, and of which I, perhaps, was a product.

All it required was a little blood spilled. I couldn't go about reading minds hither and yon; that would have been so very messy. Once blood was exchanged, however—and this was where rumors of torture, knives, scars, et cetera, came in—it was a different matter, and the mind was, to use a favorite phrase, as open as a book.

Or—I could add this to my repertoire—as linear as a hand scroll.

No doubt, Alcibiades had some terrible ritual all planned out in his mind since, for a man who displayed very little imagination, he was nevertheless prone to flights of fancy. I knew well enough what he might be envisioning. When it came time to speak with Lord Temur, he'd be at the ready, sword drawn, waiting for me to tell him to go out and kill a goat and bring its blood, along with the legs of thirteen frogs and the eyes of thirteen snakes, back to the ceremony room. But all we needed was something as simple as a needle, a pinprick at Lord Temur's finger, and I would know what I needed to know.

Country folk were always so superstitious. At least, in Thremedon, everyone worth talking to knew exactly what I was capable of. They also knew that the most frightening Talent was that which required no fanfare at all, that which slipped unnoticed to lie beside you at night and whispered *hello* from the other side of the pillow.

It wasn't mind reading. It was the art of pure compulsion—a charisma no man could refuse. Those under my influence always told me what I needed to know, and that was why I had always been so useful to the crown.

I barely even noticed the second knock on my door though I did turn at the sound of the door sliding open.

There was Alcibiades again, looking nervous and somewhat like a recalcitrant child. He might well have been about to admit to me that it was he who'd stolen the cookies, and he couldn't live with the guilt of it any longer. I softened as I looked at him.

"Yes, my dear?"

"It *really* doesn't bother you?" he said.

I blinked. "What doesn't bother me?"

Alcibiades gestured with one enormous hand as though he were trying to grasp the words from midair. "All this," he settled on finally. "All these tricks. It doesn't bother you to just *take* what you want from him?"

I smiled thinly. "Not at all," I replied.

That appeared to be both the wrong and the right answer, for Alcibiades was quiet and grim and gray as a bleak sunrise. Like a day in the country when all was set to rain for the next week, and not even the thrill of the hunt—a hunt I'd orchestrated to futility by rescuing all the foxes beforehand—could offer illumination in the darkness.

"We've all done terrible things for our country," I said, trying to keep the blow as gentle as possible and remaining cheerful as ever, so that he wouldn't worry. "You and I for Volstov; Lord Temur for the Ke-Han. Does it really make so much of a difference that you and he have done those things while looking your enemy in the eye, and I've conducted my business in the shadows?"

"I thought it did," Alcibiades said. "Let's just get this entire mess over and done with. How are you planning to . . . you know . . ."

"Corner him?" I asked, and Alcibiades nodded, not quite looking at me. I did hope this wouldn't affect our relationship. I did hope he could pull through his misgivings. Things would be so awful—so awfully boring—without him. "I plan on using this," I continued, and held up a particularly sharp hairpin.

"Sometimes..." Alcibiades muttered, but he didn't finish his sentence.

We met Josette and Temur in the gardens the next morning, at what was still left of the menagerie that had once been the greatest in the land.

"...so you see," Temur was explaining to Josette, "that when the one raid came that close to the palace, the glass was shattered, and there was chaos in the streets as the rarest white tigers, lions long caged, elephants tossed into a frenzy of fear for their young, and even peacocks desperate to escape the flames, ran out into the streets."

"I hear that the younger prince was caught in that terrible tragedy," Josette said, ever the perfect diplomat.

"Ah," Lord Temur replied, with a reticence I understood. Then, noticing me and my companion, he turned and bowed stiffly in greeting. "I see that we are blessed with company."

"You know him," Alcibiades grunted out. "Always has to be where the party is."

"I just love peacocks," I added, playing along. At least, that was what I thought I was doing. One could never tell when Alcibiades was being ingenious or merely surly.

"There are many here who, given the opportunity, would gladly donate a peacock to your cause," Lord Temur said. He was always so flattering—a real gentleman. It was a pity that I did have to use subterfuge on a man so honorable, but I was not as tangled in my morals as some. Much like those peacocks, I did not enjoy being kept in a cage when the fire was near. Much like those peacocks, I would have done anything within my ostentatious nature to escape with my life.

"Oh dear," I said, the hairpin spilling from my sleeve and clattering upon the blue-tiled walkway beneath me. "I seem to have dropped my—Oh, that is *most* kind of you, Lord Temur, you really shouldn't!"

It was the sharpest hairpin I could find, sharpened yet further. Personally, I was quite proud of my handiwork, and I was certain that even Lord Temur could have appreciated the time and effort I'd put into the piece. He leaned down deftly, with all the honor bound up tight as coils within him, to retrieve my bauble, and when he pricked his thumb, I didn't even see him flinch.

Ke-Han warriors were a fascinating study. I wished that I could spend the rest of my life among them—but then, Alcibiades would never have approved of that. All he wanted to do was go home to dear, sweet Yana. To each his own, no matter how banal.

"Oh my," I said, as the pin was returned to me. "You seem to have pricked yourself. I *do* feel awful about that." My fingers, small and white, slipped against his, which were long and dark and callused from a lifetime of the sword. The Ke-Han army was also comprised of skilled archers, madmen with the longbow, and Lord Temur was no peacock himself—not an ornamental piece, like so many at Thremedon or the surrounding countryside, but the real blade, meant for combat. "Come here, Josette," I continued, as Alcibiades loomed like a disapproving shadow just beside me, curious despite himself. "You must come help me with Lord Temur's wound!"

I did hope I wouldn't let anyone down.

"It is nothing, Lord Greylace," Lord Temur said, and I could tell that he was amused at the fuss I was making. Yes, I wished to agree, the diplomats from Volstov are so very particular when it comes to the little things, like an accidental scratch, or being kept prisoner. "You make a mountain out of a—what is your phrase?"

"Molehill," Alcibiades supplied softly.

Temur's blood, a mere drop, stained my fingertips. It was all the closeness I needed to begin, and when I caught his eyes, they stilled immediately. They were a very deep brown, and not black at all, as I first assumed.

Somewhere deep in the menagerie a bird cawed. Animals always knew more than men when something was not right.

"Lord Temur," I said softly. "I have a few simple questions to ask of you."

Temur blinked once, twice, three times, sensing danger himself, but every movement was as slow as if it had been first passed through a jar of honey. "Greylace," he said, slowly.

"Is that it?" I heard Alcibiades hiss to Josette, and then, "Ow," which meant she must have elbowed him to be quiet.

I admired Josette. If we'd been rooming next to one another, we might have been the best of friends already—but fate had put General Alcibiades and me together more than once, and it was fate I'd chosen to guide me in this endeavor.

"Our letters, Lord Temur," I said. "Who has been reading our letters?"

Temur was silent for a long time, fighting with himself and, of course, fighting with me. I didn't know what it felt like on the other side—I could only feel the tension in a conquered mind as the body struggled to keep tight reins on its wayward thoughts, as the lips tried to refuse the commands from the brain. But I knew that a man born and bred on straight-backed duty would be more difficult to crack.

But I had cracked many a Ke-Han lord before. The only difference was that I'd spoken to Lord Temur before the session began.

"Perhaps you would like to sit down," I suggested, and, on my signal, Josette and Alcibiades moved quickly forward to assist me, ushering Lord Temur to one of the spindly-wired benches that lined the tiled walkways. "There," I said, as I eased him down. "Isn't that much better?"

"Yes," said Lord Temur.

The answers always came more quickly when the question was innocuous. With some men, it was a simple matter of asking the easy questions until they became so used to the answering that they didn't realize your last question concerning the weather had *really* been concerning the defenses of the city wall. I wasn't depending on that technique for Lord Temur, since he'd already proven that he was more than proficient in our language, and a little more familiar with me personally than I'd have liked.

One matter on which Alcibiades and I might have agreed upon immediately was that all this business of diplomacy certainly had made our jobs more difficult.

"Now," I said, brightening. "This is much friendlier, isn't it? I do hate to be a bore and go on repeating myself, but since you refrained from answering me the first time, I'm afraid I must ask again. Who has been reading our letters?"

Lord Temur swallowed, and wet his lips with his tongue.

With a touch of regret—I had hoped, however foolishly, to get through this without applying too much force—I leaned forward, filling his field of vision so that there was only my face to focus on.

Behind me, I could hear Alcibiades give a sigh, though whether it was out of impatience or disgust, I couldn't tell. I couldn't afford the distraction of trying to parse his unexpectedly layered mannerisms at the moment, though. I had a duty there. Not to the Esar, but to *myself*—and to Alcibiades as well, whether he knew it or not—and surely that was the most important sort of duty a man could ask for.

"Lord Temur," I whispered.

He murmured something in the Ke-Han tongue.

"What did he say?" Alcibiades asked. "Ow!"

"Be quiet," Josette muttered. "Let Greylace *work.*"

I pursed my lips, regretting that I hadn't been given the opportunity to learn more of the colloquial Ke-Han language. I'd picked out the word the lords used whenever the demon of their Emperor was floating about, and I knew the most academic form, the old dialect used for plays, but no more common tongue.

"The Emperor?" I asked gently, like leading foxes from the hunt. "Is it his command?"

Lord Temur's jaw clenched, and I sighed a little, myself. If he was going to make things difficult, then I supposed there was no way around it. I twitched the fabric of my sleeve back above the elbow, and pressed cool fingers to his temple.

His pupils dilated sharply like an unexpected eclipse, and for a moment I thought I might have gone too far too quickly. There was no point in worrying about what had been done, though, and *certainly* no point in mentioning it to the others. Best to concentrate on the matter at hand until we'd got what we needed out of him.

The rest I would deal with later. If there was anything left to deal with, of course.

"The Emperor is having our mail read," I said, taking a new tack with this unforeseen change in winds. "Does he suspect us of something?"

"This . . . is treason," Lord Temur managed, his lips stiff around the foreign words. "For all of you, and . . . myself, as well."

"That does not answer my question," I said shortly, feeling the beginnings of impatience growing within me. I did so want this to go as smoothly as possible, but it had been *so* long since I'd been given a chance to exercise my Talent, and Lord Temur's stubbornness was simply begging for a taste of true pressure.

I could have broken him so easily.

Instead, I took a deep breath, running my tongue along my teeth to gather my thoughts.

Lord Temur shifted on the bench, as though he wished to escape, but found he could not quite wriggle out from under my gaze.

"Yes," he said softly, eyes fixed on mine. There was a seed of fear in his expression, though somehow I didn't presume that *I* was the cause of it. "The Emperor..."

He stopped himself, nostrils flared with the effort it took to keep his mouth closed.

"Please," I said, pressing my fingers against his temple to keep them from twitching. "Don't make this difficult for yourself."

He moved with a swiftness I hadn't been expecting—since so many of my guests in the Esar's dungeons had been chained, and therefore rendered harmless—grabbing me by the front of my robes and hauling me close.

Behind me, I heard Alcibiades cry out, and the unmistakable sound of a dagger being unsheathed; since the rules still prohibited swords, Alcibiades had taken to hiding one of *my* smaller weapons in his belt. If I'd had the time to think on it, I'd have been flattered. But Lord Temur made no further move to harm me, and I could hear his breathing, shallow and fixed in my ear.

"It's all right, my dear," I said, waving my noble protector off. I'd meant to say more, but that was when Lord Temur began to speak.

"The Emperor sees enemies around every corner," he rasped, "and ghosts in his teacup. He has not yet managed to catch sight or word of his brother the prince, and that exacerbates his condition."

"He *has* become excessively paranoid," I agreed quietly. People always felt so much better when they were offered agreement, even and especially if they happened to be betraying their lords and countries.

"He has taken certain measures to ensure his victory over Prince Mamoru, though the council of warlords was set against using it unless matters changed so drastically that it became a necessary course of action. There are those among our number who believe that the Emperor, caught up in his imagined world of treachery, will go ahead with this plan without our agreement. It would not be the first time he has done such a thing since assuming his honored father's responsibility. After the Emperor died..."

Josette gasped softly and put a hand against my shoulder, to steady either myself or her. I wasn't sure, and couldn't afford to pay enough attention to the distraction in order to tell.

I'd asked about our mail being read, and instead I had uncovered something dark and rotten at the center of the Ke-Han court. I felt like an adventurer who'd stumbled upon an ancient treasure. My fingers twitched again with the urge to break Lord Temur and draw out all the information I desired as quickly as I wanted.

Something held me back, as stubbornly as Alcibiades himself might have, had he known what I was thinking.

I had to phrase my next question very carefully.

"What is the plan?"

Close as I was I could feel Lord Temur shudder—in horror, or the effort it had taken to resist me this long.

"It is a forbidden magic," he whispered. "The Old Way. Blood magic, outlawed as too cruel since before the war with your Volstov."

I felt a shiver of delight pass over me. I'd read accounts of Ke-Han blood magic, but they were all ancient, and terribly outdated, with hysterical illustrations of what fate befell the men foolish enough to allow their spilled blood to pass into the hands of their enemies.

"One only needs a drop," Lord Temur went on. "The smallest amount is enough to bring a grown man down."

"The Emperor's necklace," Alcibiades said suddenly, and I felt at once admiring and annoyed that I hadn't been the one to get it—like the cogwheels of a dragon sliding into place upon completion, when she was ready at last to take flight.

All of a sudden I was being jostled aside, and Alcibiades crouched in front of the bench where Lord Temur sat.

"That's it, isn't it? He's got the prince's blood in that freaky-looking necklace of his, and he's going to use it to do something. Something bad."

Lord Temur's eyes seemed to lose some of their glassiness as he looked at Alcibiades.

"Yes. If he hasn't already."

Alcibiades' next question was better than my own. "Does he have our blood?"

Temur fell silent; darkness flickered across his eyes, and I knew how they must be burning now, desperate just to blink. "The warlords are the most dutiful," he whispered. These weren't his own words, but a speech he'd memorized long ago. "Seven of them there are, and honored most beside the Emperor. Each gives his blood at the first; each gives his life at the last."

"What does that mean?" Alcibiades hissed. He was going to break my concentration, and Lord Temur's, and there would be no slipping through the cracks again. "I don't want poetry, I want answers!"

"Duty," Lord Temur said, then he collapsed.

KOUJE

It was sometime past the heat of midday, while the sun cast jagged shadows all throughout the pass, that I heard the crunch of gravel from behind us.

The passes had long since been cleared, one through twenty-seven. I assumed it was an animal of some sort, a mountain lynx, or perhaps one of the big rams the people living in the borderlands hunted for food. But what I heard next was *speaking*, though—real words from real voices in my own native tongue. It was a man, a low, muttered complaint that made my blood freeze in my veins and my heart stop short with the shock of it. I had enough presence of mind to wrench our horse sideways by its reins, pulling at Mamoru by the sleeve, and dragging them both off the pathway into the sanctuary of the rocks.

"Kouje," Mamoru whispered, his voice hoarse from the ravages of his illness. He straightened up, taking his weight from my shoulder to lean against one of the smooth blue boulders while I led the horse off farther still so that he wouldn't be spotted from the road. "I heard— Was that you speaking? It seemed so far away . . ."

"I don't know," I said under my breath, answering his unspoken question. "There shouldn't be anyone around here."

The gravel crunched again, and that time I saw the boot responsible, crouched as I was beneath an overhang of rock. Mamoru ducked lower behind the rock as I tried desperately to see and not be seen. The man was clad in a soldier's uniform, cloth dyed cobalt blue. Dressed that way, he was nearly invisible against the backdrop of the mountains.

He rubbed his palms together and crossed his arms, staring out at nothing.

I couldn't see his face, which might have been for the best. He might well have been one of my fellow soldiers—a comrade in arms.

"Might as well have sent us to the ass-end of the world," he grumbled, and I heard a short laugh from somewhere behind him.

My heart skittered sideways with sudden panic. How many of them were there?

"Better than them up at the eighth pass," said his companion. "Not even a hint of a *hope* of action there. Least we're going to be useful."

"If there's ever any use for us."

"Don't be ridiculous. A man can see the entire capital from here. *Thremedon*. Like being an eagle, watching a mouse. We'll be useful, and that's enough insolence from the likes of you."

The soldier's companion passed into view. He was an unshaven, sharp-looking man, with a long scar that traveled raw and ugly from the corner of his eye back past his hairline. His hair was braided like a general's and parted like a hero's.

Next to me, I felt Mamoru go still as the stone he leaned on.

"That's General Yisun," he gasped in a voice like a ghost's. "He served under Iseul for the duration of the war. But he's . . . He went back to live with his family."

I held my finger up to my lips, and Mamoru quieted, though he still tormented the ragged hem of his sleeve.

I cast about for anything I might use as a weapon, should it come to that. A large rock. More large rocks. I didn't think that any kind of rock would be much help against the man who had allegedly trained the eldest prince in place of his father. I'd heard of him, of course, but my own service had kept me with Mamoru and not among Iseul's retinue of servants and soldiers. I'd only seen him in passing, but I knew enough of his reputation to feel the bile rise in my throat.

I put my hand on Mamoru's shoulder, signaling that we had best move farther off the path and attempt to keep going. I couldn't imagine what one of our most formidable generals was doing holed up in the mountains with an unknown number of soldiers at his disposal.

They weren't the only group stationed, either, if what he'd said about the eighth pass was to be believed.

I paused in the middle of rising to my feet, rooted in place with half curiosity, half dread. I didn't want to know what was going on. As far as I was concerned, Iseul had stopped being predictable the night he'd declared Mamoru a traitor. To try and understand the motives of such a man was pointless, and time was a resource I couldn't afford to waste. Not now, when Iseul's devilry boiled in my lord's veins. And yet I found that I couldn't move. I had to know.

What madness had Mamoru's brother wrought in the time since we'd fled the palace?

Had the war begun again, in our absence?

"There'll be a use for us, all right," General Yisun repeated, lighting a long-stemmed pipe and puffing easily, as though he really *were* home with his family. "Can't answer for the poor bastards elsewhere, but *we're* set to move straight into Thremedon, soon as the Emperor's given us the signal. Shame his attention's been diverted by that whelp for so long, but that'll soon be over."

"I don't care what else is going on, so long as we get moving soon," said the soldier. "It's too hot during the day and too cold during the night in these damned mountains."

"Mind your manners before a superior officer," said General Yisun, and he flicked his ashes into the wind. "I won't tell you that again."

The soldier coughed.

I straightened up slowly, ever so slowly, and gently pulled at Mamoru's shoulder. He nodded, seemingly unable to tear his gaze away from the soldiers down in the pass, so that I had to tug at him again before he would move, stepping as softly as any servant might have.

He had picked up such an eclectic mixture of skills during our time on the run. I felt an odd flush of pride in my chest at his accomplishments, too myriad to denote with simple braids.

"I don't understand," he said to me, once we'd rejoined the horse, ducking and weaving through the complex of rocky outcroppings and hideaways. His voice was still shadowed with caution and the effects of the fever.

"There are soldiers in the mountains again," I said, not that it was an answer. I didn't understand what it meant. I didn't see how we *could* understand, without seeing firsthand in the capital what Iseul was planning. My own concerns were more immediate: traveling as far as we could before the fever set in again and curing the fever once and for all.

I did my best to ignore the nagging voice in my head that wondered what General Yisun had meant by *that'll be over soon*. Did he have some information regarding Iseul's pursuit of us that I did not? All I could know was that he must have been in close contact with the Emperor. As much as I hesitated to speculate, I was beginning to fear my lord's fever in the same way I feared his brother the Emperor. I hated the power he wielded over my lord and how we'd been blinded to it for so long.

I had to know for certain.

"Stay where you are," I whispered, holding my hand up to Mamoru as I would have to a skittish horse. "I'm going back."

"Why," Mamoru said. "Wait—Kouje—"

I couldn't listen to him. I had to learn more—for there might come a time when knowledge of Iseul's next move would be our only salvation. And if there was more that Iseul had up his bright sleeve, I would have to be the shield between that knowledge and Mamoru.

The soldier and the general were still talking when I returned, hidden behind the rock and the lichen, my palms pressed against the rough surface, hoping against all hope that I remained hidden.

"...so that's his trick," the soldier was saying, before he whistled softly. "To his own brother?"

"Traitor to the country," General Yisun replied. His voice was dry, in a way that indicated he didn't believe *that* story for a moment but had no trouble agreeing to it. "There's no punishment too harsh for those."

"Blood magic," the soldier said. I could feel the terror in his voice, even when he tried to swallow it down. "Have you really seen it?"

"Our Emperor wears the vial around his neck," General Yisun said. "It's just blood, Ichikawa. Now get back to work."

The sounds of their footsteps faded in the opposite direction. I leaned against the rock to glean strength from the mountain itself before I returned to my lord's side.

My worst fears had been confirmed. There was nothing to do but move forward.

"Kouje," said Mamoru, brightening the moment he saw me. He tucked a stray length of hair behind his ear with fretful fingers. "What is it?"

"I do not know what your brother intends," I told him. I had no reason to burden him in his state with information, but I had only the horse to speak to—and my lord was far cleverer than I. For the time that he was still cogent, still himself, I needed to consult with him. I needed his permission for what I sought to do next. "And I admit that I am . . . afraid of what he will do."

Mamoru was quiet, though his fingers continued to twitch; he bit at his nails, a habit he'd never had, as though he barely noticed what he was doing. "Do you think the fighting's started again?" he asked at last. "Do you think the talks have failed because Iseul's been so distracted with trying to find me?"

"I don't know," I answered honestly, though it was just like my lord to blame himself for starting a war when he was as far removed from the capital as a field mouse himself. "I admit that I cannot think of any other reason—any *good* reason—for some of our best soldiers to be stationed in the Cobalts unless they are planning some sort of . . . attack." I drew a deep breath. "Mamoru—you and Volstov share a common enemy."

Mamoru watched me with fevered eyes. His voice was dry. "What did you hear?"

"Your brother will kill you unless I find some magic to stop him," I said. "There are magicians just beyond this mountain range. But I do not know what I can barter for your safety."

There they were: all my worries, spread before him. I could no more shield him from the truth than I could think of a solution myself, and so we must counsel with one another for inspiration.

"I am a prince," Mamoru said. "Which means I must think of my people before myself. Our focus should not be on what we might barter for *my* safety, but rather, how we might still preserve the peace negotiated first by my father before his death. Iseul has dishonored his memory by betraying that—betraying the wishes of our father—and stationing these men in the mountains as if to start another war on the heels of the first! If Iseul will not think of our people, then it must fall to me." His cheeks flushed again, though this time, I feared, it was due to a different kind of fever altogether.

I was shocked. Since our flight from the palace I had only ever thought of what my lord had lost in terms of station and a proper home. It had never occurred to me what the *people* had come so close to losing—a leader who cared enough to think of them before himself.

He was like a rare gem, my lord Mamoru, and I knew then—as I had most assuredly known before—that I would follow him to my very death if that was what he wished.

I did not speak of any of that.

"We will barter our knowledge of the enemies in the pass for my . . ." Mamoru swallowed thickly, as though it pained him. ". . . life, I suppose."

"And you think they will believe us? Or even understand us?"

Mamoru blinked. "Every man, no matter his mother tongue, understands the truth," he said, as though this should have been evident. Then he added, "Besides, I'll make them believe us."

I stared at my lord, his arm healing from where I'd struck him and his hair wild with the previous night's ride to the mountains. His lips were chapped, and his face was dirty. I'd never seen a more perfect heir, his clothing torn and stained with mud.

He looked every inch the prince.

I was going to carry him into the belly of the dragon in order to save him.

"There is another way," I told him. "Come."

There *was* another branch to the fourteenth pass. One that had been tunneled deep into the earth long ago, to keep it safe from dragonfire, and most who had worked on it had been killed in the dragon's final assault on the city. Not even many among the Ke-Han army had known about its construction since it had happened so late in the war that our forces had been mostly scattered all over. It had been omitted from the treaty for that very reason—I'd only remembered it just then, and I'd spent the better part of my adult life fighting beside my prince in the war around those very mountains. It was unlikely the diplomats at court had even heard of its existence; certainly, Iseul would not have been the one to alert them to it.

But General Yisun, who had spent so much time in these mountains many jested he'd become its guardian deity, had every reason to know of its existence. I had no real way of knowing the way was safe. What was worse, I had no better options left to me.

I hated to take my lord into uncertain territory, a place where I might not be able to protect him, but it seemed that we had little choice in the matter.

In the stories that my father told me of the old magic, a bond forged by fever would allow Iseul to know what Mamoru knew and see what he saw.

We would simply have to outride him.

CHAPTER FOURTEEN

ALCIBIADES

Lord Temur was no longer asleep in my bed.

In point of fact, he was awake in my bed, and staring at me like I'd taken leave of my senses, which, all things considered, I probably had.

We were at an impasse, like two opposite forces on either side of the same bridge, and neither side willing to give an inch of ground, and each with death firm in his jaw and hard in his eyes. We were enemies now, and we always had been, and, what was worse, *both* of us had done something that went against our codes of honor as men and as soldiers, and being Ke-Han or Volstovic had neither hide nor hair to do with it.

We might have hated each other, but, what was worse was that we hated what we'd done to each other, and we hated that we each *knew* what we'd done.

It wasn't honorable behavior.

We were no longer honorable men.

That wasn't the kind of thing that bothered Caius, of course, who'd told Josette and me—after we'd dragged Temur back through the hallways, limp as a sack of uncooked dumplings—that he had a headache and needed to lie down for a bit, so could I please look after the helpful lord until he awoke?

"I'll spot your shift," Josette said. "But right now I have to talk to Fiacre."

"Right," I said.

"And I think I'll be better at explaining things to him than you will be," she added.

"Right," I agreed.

And that's what left me on guard duty, sitting at Lord Temur's bedside like some kind of lovesick admirer, instead of a man who'd just violated everything sacred and true about the peace between our two countries, and indeed peace itself. The only thing keeping me from going mad from shame was knowing that he and his Emperor were no better than we'd been—but that still didn't justify what I'd done. Or what I'd helped Caius do. Or anything. *Everything.*

"Lord Greylace is indeed quite talented," Temur said. "I have never had the opportunity to see one of your—what is it? Ah yes, *velikaia*—I have never had the opportunity to see one of your *velikaia* in action. I thought I might never have the opportunity, given the peace, but I am glad that at least I have been favored in one of my more anomalous requests."

I didn't even know what "anomalous" meant—it sounded filthy, if I was being honest—and it was a word in my own damned language. I grunted, just to show him I meant business and wasn't into idle chatter with just anyone, mind.

"You are lucky to have him as a friend," Temur continued, his eyes fluttering shut. "It is not in a Ke-Han warrior's nature to complain, but my head feels like a broken egg."

Or a shattered dome, I thought. Not my finest moment, I'd be the first to admit. "He's not my friend," I protested, out of habit.

"Is that so?" Temur replied. "Hm."

Things were real quiet and real awkward for a long time after that, and I wished that Josette was around because she knew how to talk to these people, and to people in general, and I just didn't. Even having Caius would have been preferable, because he would have started talking about the cuisine or the jacket Lord Temur was wearing while we broke into his thoughts like common thieves, and everything would at least have felt a little more normal.

Which nothing was.

Things were—to put it simply—*bad.* The situation couldn't be fixed, and it was clear to us all by now that the Emperor had been planning on it all along. We'd just stepped right into his neat little trap and he'd been waiting all that time, laughing to himself, to spring it. There was no way to contact anyone outside of the capital, which meant we were prisoners of a war we'd thought, up until a few hours ago, had actually ended when we crushed the bastards.

Except he hadn't seen it that way. Apparently being beaten didn't have the same definition to him.

Lying bastard. I cursed the day Iseul was born, and it must have showed a little in the expression (more like a grimace) I was making, because suddenly Temur was talking like *he* was the mind reader and not "my friend."

"Do not think that because an emperor behaves one way he influences the behavior of all his people," Temur said. "I, too, thought that peace was possible."

I snorted. "I'm not allowed to say anything," I said finally. "Josette'll kill me, for one. Whatever I talk about'll just make things worse."

"It is not as though things can get much worse at the moment," Temur replied, "considering you have taken me prisoner as a counteraction for being taken prisoner, yourself."

"Well, I don't want to see if they *can* get worse," I replied. Because, chances were and with how everything had been going, they could. And they were going to. And I didn't want to be behind it all any more than I already was.

If that was even possible. I wasn't sure anymore, especially considering the company I'd been keeping lately. It was one of the things I'd have written Yana about if it'd been Yana I was writing to and not some poor bastard Ke-Han scribe stuck writing responses to our letters.

"There are not *many* crimes in the Ke-Han Empire worse than holding a warlord captive," Lord Temur said, turning his words over carefully. That wasn't anything new. "You could attempt to assassinate the Emperor himself, of course, but as you no doubt remember, the punishment for that is considerably more dire."

"Your laws don't bind us," I told him, trying to make it sound like I knew what I was talking about and not like I was making it all up as I went along. "What I mean is ... Well, you know. We're not the same. You can't just stick us in the ground and call us lilies when we're really petunias."

Lord Temur raised his eyebrows. "Petunias? I don't believe I've seen that particular specimen in our gardens."

"Country flower," I said, crossing my arms and staring down at the floor. My boots still had mud on them from our adventure at the theatre. If Josette came in, she was going to rip me a new one for talking when I'd as good as promised not to. But I was starting to think that maybe our fine captive lord was right, that there wasn't much worse we could do than kidnapping one of the seven warlords.

Fighting the war had been a lot damned easier when everything had been out in the open. I wasn't made for all that subterfuge.

"A country flower," Lord Temur repeated. There was a funny look in his eyes when he opened them, almost like he was sharing a joke with me. "Much like I am. Wouldn't you say so, General Alcibiades?"

"Suppose so," I muttered, wondering just when he'd gone and cultivated a sense of humor. Probably planned it just to throw me off for that moment. I knew enough now not to assume anything about the Ke-Han as a whole, but most of them were *definitely* tricky enough to try a tactic like that.

The thing was, I'd never thought Lord Temur was one of the tricky ones. And even if I'd been wrong and he had been, after the number Caius'd done on him, I'd have been surprised if he could scheme his way out of bed, let alone getting past me. I didn't entirely like the look of him, pale as the folding screen in my room and tired as if he'd spent the whole night out drinking, which was an image that nearly set me to laughing.

"Am I to be kept here, then?" Lord Temur asked caustically. His eyes flicked from one wall to the other, scanning the room. "You will doubtless have many uncomfortable nights ahead of you if that's to be the case."

"I'll be just fine," I said, because I sure as hell wasn't about to admit that I didn't know what we were going to do with him. "Not like your beds are all that comfortable to begin with."

Josette would know what to do, I told myself. Fiacre too, if Josette could get him to calm down long enough to come and see the situation for himself. I was a mite worried about our leader in diplomatic proceedings, since he did a little *too* much bowing and scraping for my tastes, but Fiacre wasn't half-bad when you got right down to it.

And we were definitely down to it.

"Say . . ." I said, not really sure where I was going to go from there, or even what I was doing besides preventing Temur from asking more questions I didn't have the answers to.

There was a soft cough from the adjoining door and the familiar dull sound of wood sliding against wood, and without warning—which was how he liked it best—Caius Greylace arrived with impeccable timing so I didn't have to say a thing. I was grateful for the little peacock, feathers and all.

He was wearing white, a color he hated, but with a bright red beneath it like fresh blood on snow. Probably making a statement. When wasn't he? Trouble was, I couldn't tell whether he was trying to be patriotic or just plain creepy. Maybe he thought they were one and the same.

"Oh, you're awake!" Caius said, as if Lord Temur were a guest he'd invited for dinner and not a man he'd just spent the better part of the day torturing with visions and mind tricks and bastion-only-knew what else.

"Been awake for a while now," I said, feeling uncomfortable again in the face of all this pretending that everything was normal. Everything wasn't normal. Fiacre was going to string all of us up by our privates before we could get a word in edgeways—but, knowing Greylace, the little nut would probably enjoy it.

"That's very good," Caius said, slinking over to stand on the other side of my bed like a viper waiting to strike. "Perhaps then he can tell us what's happened to our esteemed head of proceedings."

"Fiacre?" I asked, confused again and liking it about as much as I always did. "Isn't he with Josette?"

Caius shook his head, not looking away from Lord Temur, though I had to admit the warlord looked about as baffled as I was by the new revelation.

"She's still looking," Caius explained. "She wanted to come in and ask Lord Temur himself whether he had any thoughts, but the poor dear has a temper much the same as yours, Alcibiades, and I felt it best—well, I may have persuaded her just a touch, just the *slightest* touch—that it would be the best for everyone involved if I was the one to do the questioning."

"Wait," I said, "hold it there. You did *what* to Josette?"

"Please try and focus on the larger picture, my dear," Caius said, clasping his hands like he was some kind of saint and I was the trouble-maker.

Lord Temur closed his eyes again and moved to sit up. I stood the moment he shifted, one hand against my sword just in case he did something stupid. He didn't seem like the type to make a move—too much prudence and all—but you never knew what a man was capable of after he'd been tortured. I saw Caius's hand creep into the fall of one of his long sleeves, too, so I knew that he'd been thinking the same thing I had.

It turned out we were both wrong. Either Lord Temur was confident in his expectation of rescue, or he wasn't the sort of warlord who carried around poisoned arrowheads or daggers, or anything else that clumsy.

"This is news to me, as well," he said. "You say that your head of proceedings, Fiacre...He is nowhere to be found?"

"Not in his rooms, nor the meeting rooms," Caius said. He hadn't taken his hand out of his sleeve, even though I'd sat back down. "He wasn't seen going into the city, and he wasn't seen at breakfast. I happen to know that breakfast is his favorite meal, even without traditional Volstov fare, so I find it all quite unsettling news."

I started to get a really bad feeling as Caius went on, listing all the places that Fiacre should have been but wasn't.

"Have you looked in the gardens?" Lord Temur asked. "He holds great affection for our fireflies, and can often be found there in the early evening."

"Well, you've just been making friends with *everyone*, haven't you?" I exploded, even though I wasn't the one conducting the investigation, and I probably should've waited for Caius to say it was my turn, or whatever. I was done doing things this way. I'd tried being diplomatic, and that hadn't worked, and now what? It was all just some crazed Emperor's ruse to get us here, *spy* on us, then trap us here indefinitely. I could feel the bars of the cage sliding into place and I hated it.

The whole thing was ridiculous.

"This is ridiculous," I said, because I had to say something as Caius and Lord Temur both were staring at me. "This whole time, *he's* probably been watching us and reporting back to the Emperor with bastion knows what. How we like our tea and how many fried dumplings I bought at that stand and how many steps it took to get from the theatre district to the artists' alley. Did you tell him about all those prints we looked at, Lord Temur? The ones that called him out for the brother-hunting madman he is? Or did you tell him about the play, and how his brother what's-his-name is some kind of *folk hero* now that he's gone and declared him a traitor? How about how many people booed when *his* player got up onstage? Does he know it's common opinion that he's about as good as a raving, conniving lunatic who—"

"Alcibiades," Caius said.

I shut up. So much for not talking. I was so angry I could feel my face turning red like a lobster in boiling water.

Lord Temur folded his hands against the blanket like it was a table, and we were having another one of those diplomatic meetings, just the three of us this time. The only thing different I could see was that there was a ring of white flesh around Lord Temur's mouth that made him look like he'd caught fever or a plague. Somewhere in his soul, tradition meant that he should kill me for what I'd just said about his Emperor; and, somewhere in his soul, he also knew I was right.

That shut me up good and proper.

"I was..." Temur began. "Rather I am, still, quite curious about Volstovic customs and culture." He spoke slowly but firmly with his head held up. The Ke-Han had seventeen different ways to bow, but apparently none of those applied to torturers and kidnappers. "My interest led me to speak first with Lord Greylace and Margrave Josette, both of whom seemed to harbor a corresponding curiosity about our own traditions and habits. It was through their association that I also came to meet you, General Alcibiades, and, though I can hardly expect you to believe me under the circumstances, no machinations more complicated than that."

His face darkened for a moment, and he looked at me.

"Of course, my lord Emperor is exceedingly clever at using a situation to his advantage if you will take my meaning."

Caius made a noise like a hiss and sat down on my bed to look Lord Temur in the eyes.

"So while we were enjoying your very fine company, you were informing him of everything we said. Something like that?"

"It was my duty," Lord Temur said. It was simple as that for him.

Maybe to the Ke-Han it was, and that was what I didn't like about them. I respected th'Esar, but when he mucked it up it was our duty as citizens to make sure he knew it, not serve him to the brink of madness and beyond.

I'd have spat on the ground if we hadn't been inside. As things stood, I had to settle for snorting.

"Why tell us now?" Caius asked. "Of your own free will, even! I did a fine job on you, certainly, but there isn't any . . . lingering control."

A silence followed, during which I started thinking of all the things that might have been happening to Fiacre if Iseul the Stark Raving Mad was responsible for his being nowhere to be found. None of them were good things. All of them were shades darker than bad.

"You must understand," Lord Temur said quietly, "that there are those of us who feel that matters have been taken quite out of hand. In understanding that, however, you must also know that our customs bid us do nothing but follow blindly, even in the face of such a leader as our Emperor."

"That's batty," I said, disappointed because maybe I'd sort of almost got my head around *not* minding Lord Temur, only it turned out he was as crazy as the rest of them.

He shrugged.

"Those are our ways," he said. "They may seem strange or unfathomable to you, but they remain very important to us."

"But surely even someone as set in tradition as yourself, Lord Temur, must see that the Emperor has gone too far," said Caius, spinning it a lot more delicately than I'd have done given the chance.

"Why do you think I'm allowing you to keep me here?" Lord Temur asked, giving us a look like maybe we were a little slow. "It is hardly an ideal place for confinement. Why, I might have escaped at least half a dozen times over now if I were not here by my own consent."

"Now wait just a minute," I said, and then stopped confusing the matter because it actually made sense.

Caius smiled—a thin little reptilian smile that made him look mad as the Emperor himself. Somehow I didn't mind it as much on him.

"Well," he said, like we'd all been having tea together, "I suppose this makes us comrades of a sort. How thrilling."

"Yeah," I said. "I'm really thrilled."

"I am concerned for your Margrave Josette," Lord Temur said after a moment, when everyone'd been thinking about all the people *other* than us they'd have preferred as comrades at that moment in time. "If she asks too many questions about your leader, and if it *is* the Emperor who is behind his disappearance..."

"Fuck," I said, standing up immediately.

Caius followed me with his lone eye cold and strange, catching me for a moment and holding me in place. As little as two weeks ago, he would've definitely taken something like that as sure proof of some kind of love affair—and if not that, then at least something to drive Josette crazy babbling about. But it was like we'd unleashed some kind of beast in him with his Talent, like the snake that had got into our Well and poisoned everything in the night. He was different.

It was eerie.

"I'll keep a weather eye on our guest," Caius said, smiling thinly. "You go and play the hero. Drag her back kicking and screaming if you have to, which I suspect you might. And do try not to attract any attention if you can, though I know that's your specialty."

I nodded, though I still wasn't entirely sure how I felt about leaving Lord Temur in the custody of Caius like that.

"Do not worry about my well-being," Lord Temur said.

I snorted again. "Don't worry," I assured him. "I won't."

The hallways of the Ke-Han palace were as serpentine as ever, and the mirrors reminded me like always that no matter what we did, we were being watched. Those were the same halls Fiacre had been walking hours ago for all we knew, feeling safe and cocky as any blue-blooded diplomat had to in order to put on a good show of it. I was a soldier and, for once, that made me feel less like a fox in the henhouse and more like I was in my element. Though if the Emperor really had gone mad, I wasn't skilled enough with a sword to best him one-on-one—barring divine intervention or, more likely, a sizable portion of foul play.

Things were grim, simple as that. We didn't need signs like a Ke-Han warlord up and changing sides on us to tell me *how* grim, either. I didn't take to being held captive—though who did? It was tighter than the Basquiat in the narrow halls with no windows, and Fiacre's room was quiet from within.

The guard in front of his door watched me coolly with eyes trained beyond emotion. None of that'd ever sat well with me because I had no talent for it, but I cleared my throat and tried, anyway, to be polite.

"Did a woman come by here?" I asked. "The Margrave Josette?" I gestured vaguely as to her proportions—about this high, this wide, hair this long—and the guard pointed soundlessly down another hall.

"The menagerie," he said, and bowed as low as if I'd been a visiting emperor.

It all felt so unclean. That was the trouble. Caius sitting on Lord Temur, mirrors winking at me from the corners, and that guard watching me all the way until I turned the corner.

Just walk slowly, Alcibiades, I told myself. *Everything's fine. Everything's all right. You just want to look at the striped cats. Who doesn't like a good striped cat? No harm in visiting the zoo now and then, seeing the native wildlife.*

And a little bit of sunlight would do me a spot of good, too.

I don't know what I'd been expecting when, at last, the palace opened up into its private gardens. Maybe I was preparing to burst in and rescue Josette from the hands of ten, maybe twenty, expressionless Ke-Han guards, dragging her off to wherever it was Fiacre was being kept. I didn't realize how I'd steeled myself for combat until I turned a corner past some giant white-blossomed tree to find her watching the tigers. There wasn't even a single assassin lying in wait for her—though that didn't mean I was going to give Greylace his dagger back anytime soon.

"Have you come to rescue me?" Josette asked, giving me a look over her shoulder that signified, as always, she wasn't exactly impressed.

I cleared my throat. "Fiacre's missing," I said, coming close enough to her to whisper.

"It would seem so," Josette said. "But don't worry. It's not as though I'd kick up some kind of idiot fuss trying to find him."

"Greylace says I should drag you back kicking and screaming, if I have to."

Josette laughed. "I'll save my kicking and screaming for a few other choice inhabitants of this palace," she replied.

"Well," I said. All my nerves were on fire—waiting for a storm that was about to come, with the clouds too far off in the distance to gauge the precise timing the deluge would erupt. "Would you do me the honor of escorting me back to my quarters?"

"Why, General," Josette said. "I never suspected you of having any manners." She heaved a deep sigh then, her face tightening as she watched the tigers, too sleepy in the heat to even pace back and forth. I could sense a little of what she was thinking, at least in the barest out-line of a metaphor, because bastion damn me if those cats didn't re-mind me just a little of myself. There was even a baby one, all white; no use saying which *that* one was.

Right. No use thinking about it.

We walked back through the quiet hallways together, and as we walked, I felt like we were heading deeper and deeper into the belly of a winding beast—one great big snake made out of formality and sliding doors and cypress wood and mirrors. The deeper we got, the less of a chance there was we'd have any way of slicing our way out again.

I was half-expecting Lord Temur and Caius Greylace to be gone by the time we returned to my chambers, whisked away by the guards like they were just cleaning the place up. Josette and Caius and I had been cockeyed to the point of being blind, so caught up in the problem with the letters that we hadn't reported our findings higher up along the diplomatic chain. And now, we were separated from the rest of the group, the age-old and generally effective tactic of divide and conquer.

What I wasn't expecting was to find Caius serving Lord Temur tea from the hearth in the center of the room, the two of them drinking from the delicate cups and savoring the taste.

"I've made enough for you and Josette," Caius said brightly as we entered. "I know that Josette prefers her tea strong, so I've let it steep. Alcibiades, would you be a dear and put a wedge in the doorframe? You never know who will stop by, and it's best always to be prepared."

I hesitated for long enough to see Lord Temur's face—he was watching Josette, and, as far as I could tell from Ke-Han expressions, he was even more glad to see her in one piece than I'd been.

And that, no doubt, was because he'd known the kind of shape she might've been found in better than I did.

I did as Caius told me, using two extra wedges for good measure, before I took the cup of tea, because it was something to hold on to. Josette made herself comfortable on the floor, then we all must have re-alized how crazy we all looked, since after that all four of us—Lord Temur included—were laughing.

"Soldiers get like this in the trench," I said, once we'd sobered some.

"How fascinating," Caius said. "What of our fellow soldiers?"

Josette drank deeply from her glass before she spoke. "I've been sent to this room and that all day," she explained, "on someone or another's directions. First I was told Fiacre was in a meeting with the Emperor—but they must have known that explanation wouldn't hold water for long, since the rest of us would've been there for that kind of an event, now wouldn't we? Then I was told he was out in the gardens—which he wasn't—but a nice young woman in the gardens told me he'd gone back to his room, except he wasn't there either. As you can see, I've been given something of a runaround. Your help really should be better informed, Lord Temur."

Lord Temur said nothing, but bowed his head and sipped his tea. After all he'd been through, I didn't blame him for feeling ashamed. I felt it, too, instead of letting myself feel other things in which fear was heavily involved.

And once you let fear in, panic settled over you, so we were lucky, at least, that all four of us had different kinds of level heads.

"So it would seem that our companions have been taken captive," Caius said, after a long pause, like he was saying, "I do so love that flower arrangement" or "The tea is a tad too strong."

"It would seem that *we've* been taken captive," I added.

"Just in a different manner of speaking," Josette agreed.

"Well, we are lucky at least in one respect," Caius said, blithe as you please, "since we have an asset that our companions were unfortunately lacking."

All three of us—Caius, Josette, and I—turned to look at Lord Temur, who was holding the teacup in his hand like it was alive and he was afraid of hurting it. He'd drained it, and turned it over on his palm, so that it formed a pale blue dome in his hand. Something like wry defeat passed across his face.

"What do you plan to do?" he asked at last.

"We cannot hope to bring assistance to our companions unless we have gotten word out to the Esar of our predicament," Caius said.

"But I'm not leaving anyone here," I countered sharply.

"Nor can I leave," Temur said. "That far, I cannot go."

Josette smiled. "Then, General Alcibiades, Lord Temur," she explained, quick as you like, and her blue eyes hard and pretty as jewelry, "you will cause the distraction that gives us cover to escape."

"I figured as much," I said.

MAMORU

I woke in an alien world of clean white sheets and a pillow that was too soft—like resting upon something as untrustworthy as a cloud. It wasn't the bed I'd had at the palace, and it most certainly wasn't the ground I'd grown accustomed to sleeping on in recent weeks. My stomach clenched with a sudden rush of panic, followed by confusion. All around me, I heard voices whispering in a foreign language—one I'd taken great pains to learn, once, though it felt like another lifetime of lessons. A bright light streamed from an unknown source, making it impossible for me to see.

There was only one question to ask.

"Kouje?" I croaked, surprised to hear the quality of my voice, which was hoarse and raw, as though I'd been misusing it for some time. Had the fever done so much?

I heard someone issue a command, stern and brisk, but my head was still fuzzy and I couldn't understand it. The word for "summon" ...? Or maybe it had been "call". The fever had taken my clarity from me, even causing me to awaken with no memory of how we had come from one point to another. I remembered the mountains, and being unbearably cold. I remembered the night sky, and nothing so bright as the light focused upon me.

There had to be something I was missing.

I cast my mind back as far as I could remember. Kouje had spoken of going to Volstov, that there was where we would find the cure to the fever that raged in my blood at night. But Kouje hadn't answered my call, which meant he couldn't possibly be there beside me.

I held up my hands, the only thing familiar in the too-bright room, and passed them in front of my face, back and forth, until my fingers took shape and form, and I began to recognize the sight of my own palm. Then I reached over and pinched the skin on the back of one hand. It hurt, and I didn't wake up.

"Oh," I heard myself saying. "It isn't a dream."

"Hardly," said another voice. That one was speaking in my native tongue, though it stumbled over the softer consonants, and the familiar words were tinged with an unmistakable foreignness. "Unless you make a habit of dreaming yourself into medical supervision so that a crack team of strange magicians can eradicate your fever. Nasty business, so I'm told. Not really my specialty."

At least he knew the language well enough, though his tone was overly formal.

"Excuse us," said another voice. That one was female and more skilled with our language. "My companion was evidently not chosen for his manners, but rather for his familiarity with the Ke-Han language and customs. Neither of which, I'm sorry to say, he has displayed here."

"I was being *honest*," the man protested, in Volstovic.

As my eyes adjusted to the light, I could see that he had a beard, and was dressed in much the same fashion as the delegates from Volstov had been, if less ceremonial. His companion was a striking woman with dark skin and eyes; no Ke-Han woman had a gaze like that. She pinned me to the mattress with one glance, like a butterfly in a collector's display. I licked my lips to wet them before I spoke.

"My apologies," I said, trying to sound like a prince of the Ke-Han and not a mouse caught in the granary. "I am . . . in Volstov?"

"Thremedon, actually," said the man.

"If you are looking for your companion, I believe that he is sleeping downstairs," the woman added. "He was suffering from exhaustion, and even then we had to be quite persuasive with him in order to gain permission to take you here for observation."

"It certainly caused a scene," added the man. "I assume they hauled us in as translators to ward off the massacre, since the guards of the Basquiat barely speak *our* language, let alone yours, and that companion of yours is certainly something to be reckoned with when he's wielding a sword and shouting like the devil. Why, if we hadn't been able to tie him down—"

"Royston," the woman admonished.

The man blinked, then turned to me, bowing low in the Ke-Han fashion.

"I speak a great deal, Your Highness," he said. "Sometimes a great deal too bluntly. If an apology is in order, then you may rest assured that you have my sincerest one."

I shivered and tried to remember how a prince acted. It was more difficult than I'd hoped.

"Please don't," I said, before I could help myself. "It isn't necessary to be so formal. Not when you have already been so gracious as to take us in."

"Margrave Royston," said the man, gesturing toward himself, "and my lovely companion is the *velikaia* Antoinette."

The lady spread her skirts wide as a fan and bowed in her own, delicate way.

"Our magicians have been working through the night to discover the source of your ailment," she said. "We are keeping the symptoms at bay through... well, certainly unorthodox means, but... As of right now, we believe that we have it narrowed down, though we were hoping to speak with your retainer to perhaps glean some of the details."

"Kouje," I said, feeling a selfish desire to see him, even though it meant waking him. We'd come to a decision, however misty and distant it seemed now, and our friendship, not to mention my own duty, called for immediate action. "Yes. And after that, I—It is imperative that I speak with your Esar," I said.

Antoinette turned her gaze toward Royston though not before I caught the flicker of interest in her eyes.

"Surely your good health is of the utmost importance at the moment, Your Highness. I'm certain the wait to cure you will not be so long as all that."

General Yisun would not wait for my fever to recede. I was equally certain of that.

"I'm very grateful for your help," I said, "but it *is* urgent."

The translators shared another look.

"Well," said Royston. "Let's start by waking the poor bastard up."

I felt another stab of guilt as two men left the room at a command from Antoinette, going to rouse Kouje from wherever he'd been slumbering in this unknown place. What had Royston called it? *Basquiat.* I wasn't sure I could quite form my mouth around the word, but I felt certain I'd heard it before. No doubt it was someplace for which my people had another name—perhaps even a name far less favorable.

Not for the first time, I wished for something I'd had at the palace. It was my tutors, who'd known so much more about this foreign city than I could ever hope to learn. It seemed almost unfair that I was seeing it without them. They deserved the experience more than I did.

The room I was being held in was so unfamiliar that I had no way to translate it, either. A high ceiling, domed from within; decorations in inlaid stone that caught the light and scattered it, vibrant orange, across the floor; a high, polished door with a golden knob; ostentatious furniture, like a cabinet of some sort, also with inlaid knobs. No wonder I felt so blind there.

I drew my robes around me—at least those were familiar—and leaned back against the plump pillows. Perhaps it was difficult for me to remember the way of being a prince because I was in a strange bed, surrounded by people I'd never met and weakened by fever. When I grasped the fabric with my fingers they felt insubstantial, like water.

Somehow I knew that even all that would never have stopped Iseul from knowing how to be Emperor. It was in his blood like the fever was in mine, intractable and waiting for an opportunity to reassert itself.

"Mamoru," said a voice, breaking me from my reverie, and I found my gaze irresistibly drawn to the door—where Kouje was standing. He looked like a ghost come down from the mountains, all pale skin and purple shadows beneath his eyes. Surrounded by finery for the first time, it was evident *just* how tired he was, and how thin, like an imprint of a man instead of the real thing.

I wondered if I looked much the same. More than that, I wondered how Kouje had managed to get us into the city at all, considering the fact that we looked nothing at all like Ke-Han royalty. Even a palace retainer was better kept than we were.

Even fishermen were.

I drew in a deep breath to speak and realized I was smiling.

"Kouje," I said.

He came to stand by my bed, eyeing the men standing around us with a wary caution, as though they were something other than magicians or doctors or both. The man who talked too much—Royston—looked delicately away, though the others were not quite as polite as he. Now that I didn't have to squint, I could see that some of them were scribbling notes, while others were examining strange-looking instruments that shone silver in the bright light. It was fascinating, in a way, and completely different from our ways of medicine, not to mention our magicians, whose power had depended greatly on the great blue dome destroyed by the dragons' final assault on our capital.

I hadn't been homesick in all our time on the road. I'd missed things, certainly, but the danger had still been too close, and the need for vigilance so constant, that I had never allowed myself to sit down and simply miss *everything* before. Now I did. It was a sobering feeling.

"How are you?" Kouje asked, so quietly that I suspected he was wary of our translators as well.

"Better," I said, not bothering to lower my tone. "But it *is* morning, and they say that they haven't quite diagnosed it yet. I'm not sure what all this is." For the benefit of the others around us, I added, "We have no such instruments in the Ke-Han."

Kouje's gaze turned troubled, and he glanced away from me for a moment. Not for the first time, I felt the separation between us that had been caused by the fever. He knew things that I didn't, things I'd missed during my delirium and wouldn't ever have the chance to know.

If we'd still been in the forest, I'd have reached out to tug at his sleeve, drawing his attention to me that way. Yet we were in Volstov, and I could no longer act like a traveling actor, or even a fugitive. There was a protocol for refugees, especially those of royal blood, and I would not shame my ancestors by pretending to have forgotten it.

I sat up a little straighter, though the pillows helped me more than good breeding.

"Perhaps I should speak with them," Kouje said, as though wrestling with some invisible foe in his mind. "There are things that I could tell them—things you might not remember, my lord, since you were in the grips of it."

He had stumbled over not using my given name, so that I knew he'd remembered himself as well and was just as bound not to shame his family. It was almost funny, after how long it had taken me to convince him it was all right in the first place.

"Excuse me," Royston said, startling me. He bowed when we both turned to meet his gaze, and when he straightened up he kept his eyes on Kouje, as though *he* were someone to be wary of. Then again, I rather supposed he was. I hadn't been conscious for the scenes Kouje had caused—memories that he and Royston shared, and which echoed in the wary, intrigued amusement in Royston's eyes.

"We couldn't help overhearing," Antoinette added, resting a hand on Royston's arm. "We must insist that, if there is any information you've been keeping from us, now would certainly be the time to share it. It could mean the difference between a speedy recovery and, well . . . A speedy recovery is preferable, I believe. Especially since Your Highness expressed a desire to see the Esar as soon as possible."

Kouje turned to look at me, surprise mixed with something else in his face. He nodded slowly.

"I will speak with you," he said. "Perhaps while my lord prepares himself for his audience?"

There it was again, the feeling that somewhere along the way Kouje had learned something I hadn't, and he had no intentions of sharing it with me.

"My retainer knows more of the situation than I do, it would seem," I acquiesced. I'd trusted him for so long, and he had proven himself far better than my equal. Even if I was royalty, friendship and expediency demanded that I give him his autonomy.

"Then I shall escort you to the Esar," Royston said, "for he is very keen to meet you."

"And I will discuss things with your retainer," Antoinette added. "That is, if this delegation of actions is agreeable to you."

Kouje looked after me with a flash of panic in his eyes, then glanced to the open window, where sunlight streamed into the already bright room. He nodded to me, once.

"It is most agreeable," I said.

"I take it that haste will also be agreeable," Royston said, while he and Kouje helped me from the bed. I felt separated from my body still, though how much of that was the fever and how much of that was the Volstov magic, I was uncertain.

"Will you be able to stand?" Kouje asked.

"Will you?" I countered.

Beside me, Royston snorted, though not impolitely; I saw, too, that the *velikaia* Antoinette was stifling a smile. "Come," she said, gesturing to Kouje. "All will go faster this way."

"And as for us," Royston said, "with your permission, I will teach you as we walk how to address our Esar."

"Is he very far away?" I asked, accompanying Royston from the room. He held one arm out for me, and I wished we'd been alone, rather than accompanied by three of the men who'd been in the room when I awoke. They were not magicians, I decided just by looking at them, but guards. I was hardly dangerous in my condition, but I supposed they had no reason to believe this wasn't a ploy of some sort.

"Not to worry," Royston replied wryly. "It is much less difficult to address *our* leader than it is to address *yours*. No offense, of course; merely a statement of truth."

"I understand," I replied.

"In fact, you need only bow slightly to him to flatter his ego, and he will bow back, to flatter yours. But I doubt we'll waste much time on formalities. The real crux of the matter is that he wishes to speak with you. So much so, in fact, that he has come to the Basquiat in order to meet with you as quickly as possible. If we have the time later, then I will explain why that is such an interesting break with protocol. Isn't it a lucky thing that these faithful guards have no idea what I'm saying to you?"

"I have some information of interest to him," I said.

"Ah," Royston said. "I look forward to translating it."

I was led down one impressive hall into one even more imposing than the last. The walls were hung with draperies, the wood carved to the very last detail, and the ceilings high. All was open to the sunlight, which shone in through enormous windows of stained glass and turned my skin all different colors as we walked. It was like passing into another world entirely.

There was too much color and too much light to appreciate the beauty beneath it. It was enough for me that I was placing one foot in front of the other without leaning too heavily on my impromptu translator, whose skill with words would have been baffling to me even if I had been in top form. Nonetheless, he didn't look at me quite as though I were an enemy—which admittedly the three guards were—and I was grateful for that. When he spoke, it meant I did not have to.

"It's just a few more architectural wonders this way," Royston added, leading me into an antechamber, followed by another, followed at last by a third, each, bafflingly enough, smaller than the last, though all of them equally crammed with tables and chairs and vases full of flowers, with portraits of foreign men on every wall. In the last room, three more men were waiting for us. They were simply dressed, though only one was sitting, his hand resting upon a white cane.

Royston, alongside our guards, dropped to his knees.

"You might wish to bow, Lord Mamoru," Royston whispered, in the Ke-Han tongue.

It had been a long time since last I bowed, and I wondered dizzily if I would topple over in the midst of the formality. Still, as I lowered my head and bent stiffly at the waist, I heard the man in the chair rise and do the same.

So, I realized. This was the Esar.

He began to speak, and Royston translated for me. "His Majesty beseeches you most politely to take a seat, for you have traveled a long way to arrive in our humble capital," Royston said, with a touch of humor in his voice. "Please, do sit," he added, and these appeared to be his own words. "You look as though you will collapse before you manage to say anything at all."

I took a seat gratefully after the Esar had done the same, not sure where to place my hands. We were separated by a long, polished table of very dark wood, in which I could see my own reflection. The legs of the chair were too long, and my feet barely brushed the carpeted floor.

"Now," Royston continued, translating once more. "He is eager to hear what you have to say—and, he adds, is in awe to meet a member of the imperial family of the proud Ke-Han at last."

I almost smiled. We'd been enemies for four times my own lifetime, and now I was the man the Volstov Esar met. Hardly a terrifying sight. I should have sent Kouje in my place.

I lowered my head to thank him for the opportunity to speak. "Your Highness," I said, as Royston spoke heavy Volstovic syllables beside me, "it is my honor to meet you, and, under other circumstances, I would offer more appropriate formalities than time allows me. I hope one day you will forgive me and allow me to greet you as befits your status." The Esar lifted one hand, and smiled behind his beard—a gesture I recognized as well as Royston did. *Go on.* "I am a member of the imperial family, it is true, though I arrive here in this unorthodox manner. The events leading to my presence now are stranger than even a playwright might divine, but I hope you will believe my story, Your Highness, as I have no cause to lie to you."

And then, I told him of my brother's betrayal, of Kouje's loyalty, and of what we had found during our flight through the mountains.

It had often been said that no man could read the emotions upon the face of a Ke-Han warrior—which was integral to every man's training—but in that moment I saw, too, how difficult it was to read the expression on the face of the Esar of Volstov, whose clipped beard and blunt features revealed nothing, even when I told him of the troops garrisoned in the Cobalt range.

We both knew that I was betraying my brother. We could at least tell ourselves that he had made the first move in betraying us.

"Water," the Esar said when I had finished speaking; it was a simple enough word, and I could recognize it well. "Bring the prince water." One of his guard disappeared to comply with his request, and once again I found myself bowing to him in gratitude.

"Your Highness," Royston said, "the troops in the mountainside will be dispatched easily enough, if the element of surprise is on our side. It is our diplomatic envoy in the capital that worries me."

"They will have been taken hostage, of course," the Esar said simply. "It is our royal duty to save our people."

"Including the diplomats," Royston said, a simple enough statement, though it was not entirely as though he was agreeing with the Esar. It seemed more as though he was attempting to remind him of something.

"We must think of what the best course of action is for all of our people," the Esar said, and though it sounded as though they were speaking of the same thing, I knew somehow that they weren't.

The guard brought me my water, and I took it gratefully, careful not to drink too greedily. To be truthful, I was glad to have something to occupy me beyond the tension rising in the room, thick like the air before a thunderstorm. As little as I knew of diplomacy in Volstov, I could sense well enough that my translator was speaking beyond his place, and the Esar was not particularly keen on accepting his counsel.

Royston's easy air from our previous conversation had disappeared, and in its place was a countenance of pure steel. I had known many men with each of those attributes, but it was much rarer to find both within the same body. At any other time, I would have dearly wished for the opportunity to know him a bit better.

However, it was not the time for my own wishes. I had the Ke-Han people to think about, and as a member of the royal family it was my duty to honor the provisional treaty my father had negotiated. Surely the Esar felt the same way. As a ruler, how could he not?

"You're going to leave them there," Royston said, with a terrible look on his face.

"I have no other choice," said the Esar, in his own tongue. It was a simple enough phrase that even I could understand it.

"The magicians can take care of themselves," Royston translated as the Esar continued speaking. The undercurrent of anger in his voice was subtle, but unmistakable when compared to a Ke-Han warlord's neutral tones. "He hopes that if we move swiftly enough, the troops in the mountains may be dispatched without the Emperor's knowledge. It would be difficult to replicate such a feat in the capital, and he does not wish to disturb the peace that has doubtless taken root among the people in your country. He feels that sending troops through to the lapis city would only set off a panic that could set the diplomatic process back months, if not to the very beginning. As we all realize," he added, and this was him speaking once more, "to march upon the capital, no matter what the circumstances are, would be an act of war."

I understood, then, what had caused the change in atmosphere and what Royston was frowning about now, twisting one of his many rings over and over as though he wished it were the Esar's neck. They were going to leave the diplomats in the capital to fend for themselves.

The cup slipped from my fingers, spilling what water remained all over the tabletop.

"He'll kill them," I said urgently, as one of the guards moved to dry the wood and retrieve the cup. In my fervor, I had little concern for what in the Ke-Han court would have been a humiliating breach in protocol. "My brother takes no prisoners. No warlord does. If he discovers what's happened, he won't bother to keep them as hostages. They won't have a chance."

"I'm aware of that," Royston murmured in Ke-Han, so that I understood that while I spoke enough Volstovic to get by, the Esar did not mirror my knowledge. Royston then began to translate what I'd said, though I could tell by his gestures and the tone of his voice that he'd added in several of his own personal flourishes.

The Esar touched his clipped beard with his thumb, clearly thinking something over. He, too, wore rings—it appeared to be a common practice for men there, though it made me wonder whether the ornamentation might get in the way of their swords—and they glinted like jeweled eyes in the light of the reception room. When he spoke next his words came more slowly, though even I was not naive enough to mistake that care for hesitance. My head was beginning to swim with everything that was in it, the importance of it all under the strain of the fever. Instead of trying to understand the Esar's words this time, I watched Royston. After all, Volstovics were not trained to hide their emotions, and my plan was the next best way of evaluating what was being said and how I was to prepare myself for a response. My translator had stopped toying with the ring, and indeed his hands were held completely still. His expression was harder to read than it had been before, and he kept his face turned from mine this time.

When he spoke next, it was with a wry smile, as though he'd tasted something bad in his food.

"He says that he understands now the need for action. He understands that for diplomacy to work between our two countries, we will need two leaders of a like mind, able to forge a future together based on trust and mutual benefit. If everything you have told us is true—and he believes that it is, based upon our reconnaissance in the Cobalts—then our solution is a simple one. What better way to earn the trust of the people than to put their beloved prince at an army's head? If we are to send in troops to rescue our diplomats in the capital, then we must have a familiar face to allay the fears of the people about a renewed outbreak of hostilities. If they see that *you* are the guiding influence of this change, then they will not complain."

"What about Iseul?" I asked, forcing my voice to be strong and even as the Esar's was. "My brother. He will not—He would never allow such a thing. He'd die first."

"That, I believe, is the Esar's intent," Royston replied, not bothering to translate for the man he served.

I felt something well up within me, like a rush of wind from the shows the magicians had once put on to entertain the royal family. It filled my lungs to bursting and made my chest ache with the sharp suddenness of it. I pressed my hands flat against the table, still damp from when I had spilled my drink, and straightened my back. Many people had been brave in order to bring me here, people who'd owed me nothing at all but had risked everything nonetheless.

Kouje, I was sure, had nearly killed himself bringing me over the mountains.

I would not lose strength and shame them all for their efforts.

"You...Your Highness intends to replace my brother with me," I said, ignoring the fluttering of panic in my chest, like the sails of a ship picking up wind. I was not ready to become Emperor. Iseul had been right in that, if nothing else.

"Just so," said Royston, though his expression remained unreadable.

I wanted a few days to think it over. I wanted Kouje at my side, to tell me what the wisest course of action was so that I could follow it. I wanted to go back to bed and sleep until the seasons changed, to wake up in a fisherman's hut with little wooden boats and nets and hooks.

I had never met Kouje's sister. As Emperor, I never would.

"Time is of the essence," I said, ignoring the lapping of waves against the shore. "We must move as soon as I am able, as soon as you are able to gather enough men together. I do not know when my brother plans to attack, but we cannot risk an assumption of its being later rather than sooner."

"I agree," said Royston, and he began to speak again, translating what I'd said to the Esar while I kept my head high, my gaze level.

He nodded, with what I hoped was his approval, then said something quickly that I wasn't able to catch.

"The main roads will take you there in a week if we send other troops to deal with the threat in the mountains. We will speed your party back as swiftly as possible. He worries only about your condition," Royston translated. "I've reassured him that we're doing our best and reminded him that magicians, as he so helpfully put it, can look after themselves."

I smiled faintly.

"Thank you," I said.

"I'm not so certain I deserve that, but I'll accept it anyway," said Royston. "That charmingly subtle hint is our cue to leave, in any case."

He pushed his chair back to rise, and I followed his example, holding on to the table only slightly more than I might have preferred. If we'd been required to bow again, I might have toppled over completely, but fortunately the guards moved to open the doors before I could start calculating how rude it might have been to use one's translator as support while showing respect for a foreign leader—and new ally.

"I'll accompany you back to your room," Royston said, taking my arm beneath the elbow as though it were nothing. I found myself immensely grateful for the gesture, nonetheless. "He'll be wanting to make a speedy retreat, get home, and wash all the magician germs off him, that sort of thing."

"I'm sorry," I said, conscious once more of the guards traveling behind us. "I don't quite follow."

"You would have to be a student of Volstovic politics traveling back to his grandfather's time in order to follow," he explained. "Suffice it to say, that was a very rare occurrence, his coming here, topped only by *your* esteemed presence in our Basquiat, of course. In any case, I hope your retainer has given Antoinette sufficient information to work with. It wouldn't be very inspiring to have you toppling off your horse somewhere in the Ke-Han countryside, now would it? You need each other—luckily—so we must find a way to keep you in prime shape."

I wasn't sure whether to laugh or cry, and it must have shown on my face since he paused, looking abashed.

"That was insensitive," he said. "You must excuse me; royal audiences make me into something of a tactless brute."

"It astounds me that one has that privilege here in Themedon," I said, and meant it.

Royston shrugged. "To an extent," he said. "Now. Let us see to your friend."

CHAPTER FIFTEEN

CAIUS

What an *adventure* this is going to be, I thought as I followed Alcibiades through the secret corridor—a course of action I'd never been quite so lucky before in my life to take. Secret corridors, however, were apparently all the rage in the architecture of the Ke-Han palace, and we were lucky enough to have Lord Temur, who knew them all, as our guide.

I imagined Josette was cranky chiefly because she'd wanted to tear the palace down around our ears, but Lord Temur had pointed out how foolish that would be when it seemed that Fiacre had gone missing, along with Lieutenants Casimiro and Valery. It was a favorite strategy of the Emperor when dealing with powerful enemies, he'd explained. Instead of trying to overmatch them—a costly, tiresome endeavor—one just took hostage someone close to them. It was much less messy.

I almost admired his efficiency.

"You needn't look so happy about all this," Josette whispered to me. There would have been more, I suspected, except we were all trying to be quiet.

"It is quite possible that we are moving in the same direction as the young prince," Lord Temur cautioned us, holding up a hand before he switched directions, leading us down the narrowest staircase it had ever been my pleasure to be squeezed through. I couldn't even imagine how Alcibiades' shoulders fit, not to mention Josette's skirts. "These passageways were designed for servants, and so they are kept well hidden from the rest of the palace. Yet that does not mean we should engage in any loud outbursts."

"I'm just glad there are no bastion-damned mirrors every which way," Alcibiades muttered.

Aside from a grim expression and darkened eyes, Alcibiades had actually been surprisingly acquiescent about the sudden turn our lives had taken. Perhaps it was something to do with the sudden need for alacrity and caution—and my friend the general had risen most admirably to the occasion. His conduct was more like the soldier in him coming to the forefront. I felt safe and sound in the knowledge that he remained my ally, though the air of seriousness enshrouding him *did* force one to shiver.

"This will take you to the stables," Lord Temur said, stopping at a fork before us. Down the darkened hallway there were no lights; it would be all fumbling for purchase from here on out. "You will turn left three times, and right once. If you mistake the directions, I believe you will find yourself in the barracks, which I do not suggest."

"Hm," Josette snorted.

We were all on the edge of a blade.

"We will continue to the location where the rest of your colleagues are being held," Lord Temur went on, his voice hushed. I couldn't see his eyes, nor did I know him well enough to gauge how he felt about his plan. Betrayal in the Ke-Han was a different matter entirely from betrayal in Volstov. The latter was unforgivable, it was true; but the former was a fate worse than death, a curse to future lives, and unending retribution. It would not assuage Lord Temur that what he was doing was the right thing, for "right" meant nothing to his bloodline. What a ridiculous system—where history dictated a man's loyalties, and a family's pride meant more than an individual's moral honor. It would make for a fascinating study, and if I was not killed in the next twenty-four hours I hoped to have the chance to pursue that course of inquiry further. "That is," Lord Temur continued, "*if* they are still being held there. It is possible that the Emperor has become aware of my absence and considers it a threat—a breach in the security of his plans. If that is the case, then their location will surely have changed, and I will prove no more help to you."

"You've been help enough already," I said, hoping somehow to soothe him. I could sense the turmoil of his thoughts, open and susceptible as I was to them, with the unsteady rhythm of his quickening heartbeat.

At last, Alcibiades had turned to me, though he *kept* turning until he was looking at Josette. "Here," he said, and held out a knife—it seemed it might have been stolen from one of our suppers. "I know *that* one's armed. But just in case. It never hurts."

"Most kind," Josette replied, and then, with less acerbity, "and I thank you. It's the most practical gift a man has ever given me."

Was this all, I wondered, that the great General Alcibiades would offer me?

"You know," I told him thoughtfully, "we might be separated forever."

"None too soon," Alcibiades grunted.

"And this *is* our last chance to bid one another good-bye," I said. "I should think, after all the time we've spent together..."

"No need," Alcibiades cut me off. "You're more resilient than that. I'll see you when this is over with, bastion help me, and you'll be just as annoying then as you are now."

My heart full of gladness, I knew there was no more I could squeeze out of him. I was grateful enough, as well, for his attempt at kind words, and squeezed his forearm as I moved past him. After that, we were on our own: turn left three times, then right once. In that direction lay the stables, and horses; Josette and I would steal a mount each and ride off in separate directions. She would use her Talent—pulling lightning straight from the cloudless skies if need be—and I would use mine. Whatever means were necessary, it was our intention that one of us must get through to the capital, while Alcibiades and Temur attempted to distract the attention of the Emperor and his forces with a fancy to-do over by the prisoners.

It was foolhardy, inadequately thought out, too slow, and all around a probable waste of effort, but we had no other option. If our horses were winged beasts, then we might have stood a chance, but as it was, nothing short of pure miracle would have us to Thremedon and back again in time to rescue our compatriots. All that was left was vengeance in their names, and I intended to wreak it.

All the while, I would have to trust in Alcibiades' resourcefulness, for he was just as stubborn as I. That was why we were such excellent friends.

We had to keep our heads clear, and our goals sensible. It made no sense at all to assume there would be no casualties in a situation like this one, and I could tell Josette was thinking equally grim thoughts with equal practicality as we slipped through the darkened, quiet passageways like a whisper of a secret. The only difference between us was that it didn't sit as well with her as it did with me—but then, I was so used to sacrifice.

As I settled my hand upon the final door, I wondered if this *was* the way the little princeling had stolen out in the dead of night, absconding with Alcibiades' poor horse in the process. I, too, was playing an important role in Ke-Han history.

It wasn't often a man was given the chance to play such a role both at home and afar. I hoped that Alcibiades was given the chance to appreciate it.

The stables were quiet, save for the occasional whinny of a horse, or the rustle of Josette's skirts as she bunched them in her hands to avoid the hay, or the stamp of a restless stallion snorting as he scented us.

"Do you have any particular preference when it comes to a mount?" I asked Josette.

"Something that can carry all this," Josette muttered, gesturing to her skirts.

She chose a larger mount, and I something of a slim little filly; the latter seemed as though she would be exceptionally fast, and I had always wanted to ride a Ke-Han racing horse. The beast huffed as I scrambled onto her without a saddle.

"There are two ways out of the capital," I told Josette. "I shall take the inauspicious one, which lies to the northeast."

A lucky thing that the Ke-Han capital was laid out on a grid. The inauspicious direction was said to bring terrible luck to all those who traveled out of the gate, which led me to wonder why they had built a gate in that corner of the city in the first place. It troubled me very little to think of curses or jinxes at a time like this; and anyway, I was being kind, thinking of Josette's safety before my own.

"This isn't going to work at all," Josette said, though her hands remained steady, even as she steered her horse out of his stall. "Are you sure there's no way for you to use your Talent to get in contact with the city?"

"It isn't at all like calling lightning down from the sky," I sniffed. "For you, the sky is always listening. But the Esar, as you know, is a very busy man."

"Whatever that means," Josette replied. "Southwest exit it is. Try not to get yourself killed."

"My dear," I replied, "I wish the very same for you."

I did hope I was given the chance to see if these famed horses were as fast as legend would have it. The slim creature beneath me hardly seemed exceptional—but then, that was what most people said about *me*. We were both equally suited to our mounts, Josette's powerful and unforgiving, and mine small but unexpectedly fierce.

I was just about to remark on what it meant that Lord Temur had not bid her a proper good-bye when a clattering sound against the stones of the walkway caught my attention.

Ah, how I wished right then for the cramped, close darkness of the secret passageways. But no: There we were, in full daylight, exiting the stables together, quite conspicuous, without any direction to turn, much less hide; and there were guards rushing toward us, dozens of them at least. I didn't know whether they'd been lying in wait for us, or if it was simply their very good fortune to run across two of the three remaining diplomats on their way past the gates. I found that I didn't much care for the reason behind it, though, and set instead to coming up with something nasty for them. It would be difficult to get them all. But at least half I could manage with more general visions—mothers dying, fathers leaving, children screaming, the broadest fare possible— while Josette found some way to take care of the rest.

Beside me, the lady in question swore in a *very* unladylike fashion.

"I can't chance hitting them when they're this close. Not unless I want to take down half the palace along with us, as well. And there goes any chance for warning the Esar about the others."

My horse whinnied and tossed her head fretfully. Perhaps my conjuring a vision was bothering her. Animals were far more perceptive than people in that regard. They could smell the thing coming a mile away.

"Stop right there," said one of the guards, leveling his spear in a decidedly undiplomatic fashion. "No one's to pass through the gates, entering *or* exiting. Imperial orders."

Josette heaved a sigh. Out of the corner of my eye, I could see her reaching for the knife Alcibiades had given to her.

"Think you can handle those seven on the left?" she asked with a delightful sense of grim humor.

I had never attempted to use my visions on a group so large. Then again, there were so many people depending on us, and I wasn't about to be cheated out of my place in the history books just because a handful of foolish guards didn't know to fall back when there were magicians of the Basquiat standing before them.

"Dismount," said the same guard, presumably the man in charge, "and we'll escort you to safety."

Josette drew out her knife. I patted my horse's neck to soothe her before I unleashed what I'd cooked up. The last thing I needed was for the vision to affect her; she'd buck me, throw my concentration, probably kill me in the process, in which case there was no point to the ploy at all.

"If you refuse to come peacefully," the guard began.

I gathered bits and bats of fear around me like the tendrils of a cloud. They were vague images, flashes of loss and unhappy memory, generalized and therefore clumsy. The more specific I was the more effective I was. This was the equivalent of throwing a net into the waters and hoping the holes were just the right size to catch the fish I was looking for. One or two would be too little; they would slip right through. Those I would have to trust Josette to take care of—and I did trust her.

What did the Ke-Han fear most? Betrayal, loss of honor, *dragons*.

The vision was gathering strength, and I was pulled along with it. I could feel it growing less and less transparent; it was almost enough to toss before me like a barrier between myself and these strange men.

Just then, the earth began to shake beneath us. It rumbled ferociously, cracking down the center of the gate path like a great snake slithering through water. The stones themselves parted as though they were no more than liquid; the sounds they made were unlike anything I'd heard before from any earthquake or explosion.

It seemed as if our mutual friend General Alcibiades had been lingering where he ought not to have been. Why, the dear worried about us *far* more than he'd let on!

A geyser burst up from the hole and my horse reared, her eyes white-rimmed with panic. One of the guards screamed and disappeared beneath the ground, while the other men scrambled about, trying to hold formation for a few brief, useless moments before they scattered, desperate to escape the earth itself as rock and dirt jutted upward, tossing heavy paving stones about as though they were nothing more than pebbles, and destroying the carefully-thought-out Ke-Han architecture every which way.

"Go!" Josette called to me, over the howls of the guards and the thundering of the earth. Her horse seemed less upset by that turn of events than my own, though it was dancing restlessly.

"Honestly," I said, sharing a look with her before turning my own mount in the direction of the inauspicious gate. "He might have hit *us*!"

KOUJE

I still remembered the day my lord had come to tell me there were no more dragons. It was after the fires in the great dome had been doused, and after the tigers had all been gathered up from the capital and returned to their menagerie. It had been in the early days of the provisional treaty—which was, I'd discovered, when Lady Antoinette and her companion had learned our customs—before the negotiations had begun in earnest. Before the Emperor had taken his life for honor, leaving his eldest son a madman and his second son a fugitive.

I still remembered that day because I remembered the feeling it had given me. Many loyal servants who'd devoted their lifetimes to fighting in the war had felt greatly displaced after its ending.

For those of my generation, the war had been a fact of life since birth. Many had assumed it would end at our deaths, and not before that. So for a great number of people, perhaps even all of us, the end of the war had meant a feeling of confusion and dissatisfaction. No one knew his place in life without the war to give it structure. We were all like the tigers, turned loose in the city streets and found again a bare day later, hiding ourselves in familiar, small spaces. It was all that we knew—a way of life better suited to us than freedom.

My own place, however, had always been at Mamoru's side.

There had been no uncertainty in my heart at all over the absence of those metal beasts. In its place there was only a kind of peace, and perhaps a relief that came from having served one's purpose during a difficult time.

I'd never imagined I would find myself riding at Mamoru's side once again, between the standard-bearer and the scouts, with a legion of foreigners in red at our backs.

I hadn't been able to speak with Mamoru properly since we'd left Volstov, so I couldn't know how the new responsibility was weighing on him. The colors were all wrong, and the mountains should have been between us and the sunset, not the sunrise.

At the very least, there was color in Mamoru's cheeks again—and we both owed that to this foreign land and their foreign magicians— some the very same men and women who had created the dragons in the first place. They were all very clever. I could grant them that.

"Ke-Han blood magic," Lady Antoinette had repeated, her hands giving away what her face did not. "We have heard rumors, of course, but I never imagined such a thing might... It *is* forbidden, isn't it?"

"Yes," I'd nodded. Forbidden. A shameful act to take against one's enemies, let *alone* one's own kin. It was a part of our culture, in that the warlords still pledged a vial of their blood to the current Emperor, but that was more of a symbol, signifying the trust it took to give one's lord such power voluntarily. The understanding was that it would never be used, that it was a mark of their loyalty. To pervert even that was unimaginable. The gods would see to Iseul's punishment in the next life, if not in this one.

"We can fix it," Antoinette had said hesitantly, as though thinking aloud. "It would be best if we could get the object from your current Emperor, of course, but it certainly isn't necessary. Blood magic operates on the principle that even when lost, a part of you will still wish to return to the whole. The whole, in turn, recognizes that part as something of its own, and a kind of... resonance occurs between the two. All we have to do is change it so that Lord Mamoru's body no longer recognizes the blood as something lost. It would be *far* simpler if we could just cast off the things we lost like a lizard with its tail, but we, as a race, are so inconveniently built."

"This is something that can be accomplished, then," I'd said, careful not to misunderstand.

"Yes. Luckily our magic, as perhaps you might know, rests in the blood instead of drawing directly from the Well, as it did once," she'd explained. "That's how we know more about it. It's different from yours, which as far as I understand involves a great deal of bartering with spirits and the like."

"I wouldn't know about that," I'd said. "Our magic is based in the land, in borrowing its power. Any man can use such a thing if he trains his mind around it. The details of it—the secrets—are quite well kept by those men who possess them. Only a rare few are given that position. The waters are not channeled, but..."

"Perhaps we will be able to study your wild rivers one day," Antoinette had said. "One day, when all this is over."

"Thank you for helping him," I added, allowing the gratitude I felt to seep into the words.

"His own brother," Lady Antoinette had said, this time conveying *everything* with her face, in a way that would have been considered most shameful in the capital, my lord's home.

I found it fitting somehow, after everything we'd been through.

"So we can help him," the Margrave named Royston told me. "A magical medicine, I suppose. One we've perfected since..." His lips twitched, and again I was reminded of the differences between our two peoples. "Well, since you-know-what."

I neglected to tell them that the snake in the Well had, in part, been Iseul's idea—a magic based upon the same feverish principles that plagued my lord.

Their medicine was better than any potion fed to him when he was little; it was no simple tea. It had been created to counteract the effects of poisoning from afar—Ke-Han blood magic, the same that had been used in the war against them.

It was strange to think they should be helping us. I hoped the gods would forgive us in time.

"This shall stand between his blood and...well, his blood, I suppose," Margrave Royston explained to me. He seemed to have taken pity on me—no doubt because I looked like a dead thing, without sleep and without peace—and so placed a hand on my arm as we waited for Mamoru to wake. "We shall hope it lasts long enough to stop it at its source."

"As you have also done in the past," I said.

"Well, that," Royston agreed.

It was a miracle to see my lord so well so quickly, though his limbs were weak and his coloring still paler than it had been. Time was of the essence, nonetheless. The moment he was standing, he said he was ready, and I allowed the lie. I even helped him saddle his horse.

I watched him like a hawk for any signs of relapse, but there were magicians among our number, and Margrave Royston had assured me they would do all they could.

"The Esar is behind this endeavor," he said. "Take comfort from the knowledge that he needs you."

I did, however grim that comfort might have been.

On the first night there were fires burning in the mountains, though from where we made camp I couldn't tell who was winning. Instead of trying to judge what was impossible to judge, I went to find my lord, who had retreated to his own tent since the sun had set, and hadn't emerged once.

I knelt as I entered. Then, when Mamoru did not bid me rise, I raised my head cautiously.

He was sitting against the far canvas wall, limp and as if still in sleep, though he was sitting, his head unbowed. His hair was braided as it had once been for his victories in the long war, but his clothing was new and a strange foreign imprint on the rest of him, which was so familiar to me. They should have at least clad us in blue, though that moment would prove striking in a print. When the art was made of that day, as I knew it would be, the color would serve as quiet commentary, that which would remain unsaid between the other lords.

"My prince," I whispered.

"It smells like dragons," he said, opening his eyes. In the flickering light of the lamp he'd lit, I could not read his expression. "The smoke from the mountains. Are we doing the right thing?"

"My lord," I said, not rising from my place. "Iseul has tried to kill you. He has broken two of our oldest laws; he has harmed a brother and he has manipulated the blood. It is your place—no, it is your duty—to make right what he has broken. Think of what your father would want if he were here to offer his counsel."

Mamoru nodded slowly though he didn't seem convinced.

"They—the Esar, and his men, that is—intend for me to kill him."

"He is too dangerous to be kept a prisoner," I reasoned, hating myself for being the one to speak such things. Mamoru's arm, at least, was no longer bandaged from where I'd beaten him to save his life, and the bruises were beginning to fade. *Those* wounds, at least, healed quickly. There were others—some of them I bore—that would take more time than that.

Slowly I rose, crossing the distance between myself and my lord to kneel properly at his side.

"When you are Emperor, Mamoru, you may take your summers anywhere you like. Even in a small fishing village in Honganje should you so choose."

Mamoru turned to me, his eyes wide with surprise. "What?"

"You look as though you're headed to an execution instead of home," I said.

Mamoru laughed, more quietly than I'd grown used to. "I *am* headed to an execution," he said. "Though hopefully it is not my own."

"The offer remains," I said. "I told you I would take you to my sister's home in the mountains. We've come this far."

"Then I might meet her after all," Mamoru said, drawing his knees up to his chest and turning his gaze into the lamplight.

There was so much of the Emperor in him. Looking at him was sometimes like catching an accidental glimpse of the sun. Both made my nose sting and my eyes hurt.

"She'll likely kill me for bringing an imperial entourage into her house without forewarning," I added. "We'll have to write to her first, in any case."

"She sounds wonderful," Mamoru said. There was a smile tugging at the corners of his mouth.

"Of course she's wonderful," I said. "If you're willing to wake up earlier than the gods in the morning to a punishing day spent in a boat smaller than a hollowed gourd."

"I happen to think I'd make an excellent fisherman," Mamoru pointed out. "Fear of fish notwithstanding." The smell of smoke hung heavy in the air, and when he spoke next there was a hint of uncertainty in his voice. "Do you think we'll make it in time?"

"Yes," I said. "I don't believe that we would have come so far only to fail in the final hour."

He smiled bleakly. "I hope you're right. Think how disappointed Goro would be if we ruined his play."

"You must forgive me my overconfidence in this one small area," I said, leaning my shoulder against his. "Since we *have* dared to accomplish the impossible so far, I find it hard to imagine that we mightn't do it here as well."

"The only question, then, is whether we will arrive at the capital in time to save the diplomats," Mamoru said, and turned his face toward the far wall.

"Yes," I said. I didn't envy them their positions; nonetheless, I wished we were with them already.

CHAPTER SIXTEEN

ALCIBIADES

So. There I was, with my only ally, Lord Temur—someone who *hadn't* been an ally up until a very short time ago, and maybe it said something about the state of my mind that I trusted him as much as I did, but I did. And there we were, about to be causing a whole lot of trouble for everyone, including ourselves. If Greylace had been around, he would have said something like *"Any famous last words, Alcibiades my dear?"* Or *"I'm so very happy to be sharing this moment with such dashing figures. Oh my!"* It was much nicer to be with someone who appreciated the solemnity of a moment like that one: about to go against an emperor by breaking into a veritable holding cell while all his guards, who were a whole lot better equipped than you were, came rushing at you with only one charge.

Kill.

"You seem nervous," Lord Temur said in such a wry tone of voice that for a moment I didn't even believe it was him. Gallows humor, I guess they called it. Even the Ke-Han must've had a word for it, too.

"Just feeling practical," I said, trying not to smash my head against the ceiling as the walkways got smaller and smaller. I'd done it twice already, and the last thing we needed was to alert our enemies to our presence because I was hitting my head on things. Places like this just

weren't built for men like me. Little snakes like Caius Greylace were another story entirely.

"Your friend is very resourceful," Lord Temur replied. "I would not
worry about him. I think he can survive anything."

"We're not actually friends," I began to explain, trying to find some
patience within me. "In point of fact, I can't stand the little bastard."

"Hm," Lord Temur said. "Time for that later, I suppose, if all goes
well."

He turned to look at me, and I could see his eyes in the darkness,
black for the most part but with a flash of light. Sheer determination. I
felt it too, coming up to knot in my belly; the way I always felt right before a fight broke out. A real fight, a fight that mattered.

"It is an honor to fight beside you," Temur went on. They were like
the words to some kind of ritual or prayer, and I felt awkward not
knowing what my part in all this was, and even more awkward because
of all the horseshit that had already gone down. "You are a worthy enemy; this makes you a worthy ally."

"I don't take stock in any of that," I muttered. "Just so you know, I
think all this honor and duty and fealty isn't worth the ground a horse
pisses on."

"About as much as you do not consider the Lord Greylace your
friend, I would wager," Temur replied. "The door is only big enough for
one. Who shall go out first?"

"Pardon me," I said, with a little flourish that would've made Caius
happy, "but I think I will."

We could have done this better, maybe; more subtly, definitely. But
that wasn't the point. The point was keeping them from worrying too
much about the two who were missing. The point was distraction.

So I put my shoulder against the door, which was too little for me
anyway, said a hearty *fuck your mother* to the element of surprise, and
flung myself out into the mirrored hallway where, as Temur had explained, at least six men would be waiting for me.

They were quick. One lunged right at me before he'd even got over
looking surprised, sword raised to kill, and this was no wooden blade
made to look like the real thing. I was expecting it, of course. The
sneaky bastards always *had* been quick, right up until the end when
they'd gone and poisoned us all without our knowing it until it was too
late. Lucky for both of us—the country lord and me—it was too close

quarters for anyone to be using those murderous longbows that could punch through a *horse,* not to mention a man.

I braced my sword against the first guard, shouting bloody murder all the while because I was completely finished with sneaking around.

I heard Lord Temur directly behind me, and had a minute of feeling like we'd maybe done a terrible thing to him and his honor and whatever, getting him mixed up in our business like this. Then I couldn't think about it anymore because the fighting had started and there wasn't room for *any* thinking. I lunged forward while the poor bastard on the other end of my sword began defending himself in the cornered way that meant the fight was over before it had even really started. He knew it, and I knew it, but every man has the right to be stubborn.

I'd fought against Lord Temur in the training grounds. Shit, I'd even dueled with the bastion-damned Ke-Han Emperor himself, and both those fights had given me more than enough experience when it came to the Ke-Han style of man-to-man combat. The only thing the guard had over me was speed, which I was used to after the Emperor had turned out to be some kind of demon. The only thing you had to worry about when you were slower than the other guy was that when you hit him, you really had to *connect.*

Fortunately, connecting was kind of my specialty.

I hit him the next time he blocked high, throwing my weight in with the strike against his chest and sending him flying. In a neat kind of trick I couldn't have planned even if I'd tried, he stumbled back into the next man heading toward us, blue sleeves tied back and cold duty in his eyes. I felt something knock into me from behind and realized none too soon that it was Temur, fending off an advance from yet another guard no doubt drawn there by all my noise-making.

We were in for it now. It had been a long time since I'd fought with anyone back-to-back.

"At least we know we're in the right place," I grunted, slamming the hilt end of my sword into some poor bastard's face. It cracked in an ugly way that meant I'd probably got his nose, and I jerked my hand away quick before the blood started to spurt.

Temur gave a short laugh like maybe he thought I was crazy, or maybe he just enjoyed that stuff as much as I did and it was finally putting some humor into him. I almost wished I could've taken a break from my own fighting just to watch him and see if he looked any different now that we'd got some trouble started.

Unfortunately for both of us, the Ke-Han were stubborn if they were anything, and just then they seemed *particularly* stubborn about making sure I had no time for breathing, let alone sightseeing.

I blocked high with my sword, and punched another man in the gut. He doubled over with a groan; I helped him with my boot.

"Are you looking forward to becoming a hero, General Alcibiades?"

Of all the times to develop a sense of humor, I thought, wheeling around to catch another guard's sword with my own blade. I only just did, and the way my arm ached with the impact let me know I'd caught it wrong and at too awkward an angle. It couldn't be helped. The light there was dimmer than in other areas of the palace—because who wanted to waste lanterns on a bunch of prisoners and their guards, no doubt—and if Temur hadn't been at my back, I'd have been worried about striking out at him too. Besides, they had all those mirrors helping them out. For all I knew, they were predicting my every move.

"If we make it out of this alive," I told him, "I expect people to be rioting at plays about *us.*"

Temur laughed in his brisk, polite way, just to humor me, before I heard the thump of a body hitting the floor. We made a good team, me and the warlord, which was something I'd never have expected in a hundred years.

"I had no idea you were such a fan of the theatre," he said, and because I was listening and not paying attention, I didn't notice the guard I'd punched getting up.

He charged straight at me that time with a yell of his own, the movement so sharp and unexpected that I only just stepped to one side in time. Pain flared hot in my arm, followed by a warm wetness against my sleeve that meant I'd only just dodged being skewered on someone's sword like a fried dumpling.

Being grateful for small miracles meant that I had to be glad it was only my left arm. I shook it out and swung my sword up into a defensive position. By then I was mad.

"Hey," I said, getting Temur's attention while the guard circled us, and more poured in from behind sliding doors and secret compartments and bastion-only-knew where else. Six guards, my mother's left tit. The Emperor'd known we felt cornered, and he was throwing everything he had at us just to show us how futile it was to try to fight back. "You know where the prisoners are being kept, right?"

My only answer was the sharp screech of metal against metal and a shout that turned into a wet kind of gurgling.

"I beg your pardon," said Temur, "but there was a situation I may have resolved too hastily. I did not hear your question."

"Prisoners," I grunted, keeping my eye on the son of a bitch who'd wounded me.

"Ah," said Temur.

"I'm thinking you go and get them," I elaborated. "I'll hold 'em off here at Tiger Tail Pass or whichever one it was where we beat your sorry asses all the way back to the dome."

"I do not think that I recall that battle," Temur said. "I must not have been a part of the defense."

I huffed and stepped in quick to attack before that guard got a taste for stabbing me again. The room we were in was built more simply than the others, no furniture save for the benches lining the walls and three lanterns hanging from the ceiling. There was a corridor just past where Temur and I had made our stand, even worse-lit than the room. That was probably the way to the prisoners.

Would've been nice if the secret passageways had led us straight to where we needed to be. Would've been all kinds of *considerate* that the Ke-Han didn't believe in.

This time, the guard squaring off with me moved too slow and I grabbed his arm, wrenching it back so that he had to drop his sword.

"Good night," I said and clocked him in the head.

I shook my arm out again, which was a mistake, since instead of being numb it just hurt like crazy. There were more guards in the room, too, shouting and breaking formation and coming in through the walls like they were actors in that play Caius had taken me to see. Except there wasn't anything make-believe about those swords or the duty driving the men who wielded them.

There were more guards in the room than when we'd started, now I was sure of it. If there hadn't been bodies on the floor, unconscious or dead, I would've started to get *really* disheartened.

"Look," I said, taking a chance on talking to Temur over my shoulder, "this is a waste of time. They're just going to tire us out here until they can overwhelm us with sheer numbers, and then this whole thing will have been for nothing. You get it?"

"You should be the one to go on ahead since your men will trust you better," said Temur, calm as you please.

Bastard had a point, too, but I wasn't about to give in that easily.

"You're the one who knows the way, remember?" I told him, before I broke a man's jaw—and maybe my own knuckles, too, it felt like. "That's the whole reason we brought you in the first place, so don't go getting all *useless* on me now."

I kicked a guard back, and when he fell, he broke through the wooden-framed screens and tore through the paper wall.

"Get going," I said, "or I'll break your head too and you'll have to explain to Greylace and Josette what you were doing *sleeping* in the middle of a battle."

"I do not know that I like the idea of explaining to Margrave Josette that I left you to fend for yourself, either," Temur retorted. He was leaning against me a little more heavily than he had been when we'd started, and I didn't think it was because he was preparing for a nap.

"Who's by themselves?" I asked, insulted by the very idea. "I'm not cutting you loose, mind. I'm sending you to get the reinforcements! If you're not back in fifteen minutes, I'm bringing down the palace, and if you're not sure whether I'm exaggerating or not, well then, it's probably a good idea just to come back right away, isn't it?"

Temur hesitated, which was his fatal error as far as I was concerned. It meant he agreed with me.

"Okay," I said, lowering my voice, and wishing not for the first time that the walls were built of something slightly more substantial, that I could trust myself to lean against them. My arm was stinging something ferocious and dripping all down my sleeve. "Here's how it's going to go. I distract them while you take your chances and make a run for it, all right? Fiacre's not an idiot, so if you explain the situation to him, I'm sure—"

An arrow whizzed past the side of my head, nicked my ear, and embedded itself in the far wall. The courtyard just beyond the wall, where the fallen guard had torn a hole in the screen, was filling with soldiers, all of whom were wielding those *damned* longbows.

I stepped abruptly away from Temur, hoping the loss of support wouldn't leave him stumbling. I had a kind of plan, though it'd only just come to me a moment ago—about the time I'd realized that the chances of us both getting past had been ground right down to zero, and the chances of me holding off a palace army by myself were... Well, easier to say that if our endeavor had been a play, there wouldn't have been a dry eye in the house.

I wasn't any kind of sentimental myself though—unlike Greylace, I didn't have a collection of lace hankies for every occasion—and if this was truly where my play ended, so to speak, then I was sure as hell going to make it one hell of a finish.

It was the last thing I wanted to do, but it would sure as bastion prove useful. One might even call it *poetic*.

"As soon as their attention's on me, you go," I said, resigning myself quickly to not explaining the plan. Temur was a smart man. He'd figure it out for himself.

I heard a shout from behind me. Whether it was Temur or whatever man was unlucky enough to be fighting him, I didn't know, but I couldn't pay attention to that at the moment. Another arrow hit the wall next to my hand and I jerked it away. Things would have been so much easier if I could have just closed my damned eyes.

I was about to do something I hated, and it kind of took all my concentration to do it.

The thing no one tells you about having a Talent is that it's a giant pain in the ass. I kept mine good and hidden for as long as I'd been able to, so long that most who found out after they'd known me still didn't really think of me as a magician. It was why I'd up and refused the title of Margrave, back when they'd been handing them out like caramel apples after the war. *General*, I told them, *suits me just fine.* I didn't want anything to do with being a magician, but that damned plague hadn't taken into account who *wanted* a Talent—cultivated it in their bloodlines like a fine wine—and who didn't. And after the plague, I was pretty sure I was never going to use my Talent again, no matter how useful anyone called it. Mine was a nature-based thing, the same as Josette's, which meant we could use them pretty much anywhere and that it was real hard to stick any kind of limitations on us. Not for the first time I was really starting to wonder how they'd managed to wrap up *both* Fiacre and Marcy, both neat little powerhouses in their own right, and the others no slouches themselves though Ozanne was a healer, and Marius's Talent had something to do with light. Casi and

Val didn't have any Talents to speak of. All the same, I was thinking they'd better have had a good explanation ready for why two of Volstov's lieutenants could get snapped up that easy.

It just plain made us look bad.

Maybe the Ke-Han'd used an old trick and grabbed just one of our own to use as a hostage against the other five. I wasn't any kind of magical scholar—needed Greylace for that, or Marius, in a pinch—but I had a feeling it was easier to neutralize just one magician, then threaten to kill him if the others so much as blinked.

Which might have meant that I was about to do a real stupid thing right about now, but I figured we'd already kicked up so much fuss by this time that it couldn't worsen matters one way or another.

At least, I really hoped it couldn't.

There was an underground water vein beneath the palace. It bubbled up in places as a courtyard fountain, or an ornamental pond, but the bulk of it stayed beneath the earth, like a tailor-made distraction just waiting for me to use it. It fed the hot baths Caius liked so much, among other things, but it was going to be real useful to my purpose. Even the smallest of houses needed a well. Needless to say, a palace required a whole lot more than that.

If I'd had more practice with using my Talent, I might have known better how to shape it to my will. As things stood, I just knew where the water was—uncomfortable as it was to admit it, I could feel it—and I homed in on that like a marksman on his target. As deftly as pulling back the bowstring, I yanked on the vein of water as hard as I could with all I had in me, just to get it where I *wanted* it to be.

The room began to shake, sending gravel skittering across the floor from where the soldiers had tracked it in. One of the guards screamed as an arrow sprouted in his shoulder, and I turned around quickly to find Temur.

He had the beginnings of a black eye, and a cut on his leg was seeping blood through the cloth, but other than that he seemed in decent enough condition. Also, he was wielding one of those longbows. It suited him.

"That's your cue!" I shouted over the rumbling, briefly swaying off-balance. "You'll lose your chance in a minute, so you might as well go for it now!"

I really thought for a minute he was going to make some kind of speech, like the remembrances left by poets and playwrights for fallen heroes, except if he'd tried that, I would have hit him. Instead he hesitated, and so I lunged forward and *shoved* him ahead of me, which seemed to snap him out of the mood quickly enough.

Not a moment too soon, since I could hear the hiss of water spraying up between the floorboards. Soon, I knew, the ground would start to crack under the pressure. Who knew where else the repercussions would be felt? I only hoped that, by then, Caius and Josette were on their horses and far away from the stables.

"I will return with your men," Temur promised, as a geyser erupted outside and the archers howled in surprise and fear.

"Get *out* of here, fool!" I grunted, turning away to guard his escape.

If Temur didn't make it through, then we were both sunk. Literally.

The polished floor beneath my feet groaned and stretched against the pressure of the water, swelling upward and knocking guards off their feet in a way that would have been almost comical if I hadn't been fighting for my life. At least I'd be able to take the looks on their faces with me to the grave. Meanwhile, I reached out with my Talent again, wrenching the water upward this time with everything I had.

The room exploded. Splintered floorboards shot upward as if caught in an upside-down waterfall and all the lanterns went out, extinguishing even the dim light that had shone before. I could see the shadowy outlines of the guards as they got caught up in the rush, but more than that I could hear them shouting in their language, which I'd never bothered to learn, calling for backup, or help, or maybe even their own gods. They were the same gods, I supposed, who gave me my Talent in the first place. Pleading with them would do little good.

I backed up quickly, throwing myself against the wall without throwing myself *through* it and squinting after Temur to see whether he'd got down the hall in time. I couldn't tell.

In the end, it probably didn't really matter that much. Not that I was a pessimist or anything, but Temur and I had both come there with reasonable expectations of what we were going to get out of this little rescue mission, and staying intact definitely hadn't been one of them.

Water swirled hungrily around my feet and rained down over my head, soaking me through in a matter of minutes. I heard a loud crack in the distance that nearly stopped my heart before I realized what it must have been—the giant fountain in the gardens crumbling under the pressure. Good. I hoped it was Iseul's *favorite* giant fountain, and I hoped it was ruined forever.

The earth was still shaking with the aftershocks of the explosions. I readjusted my hold on my sword and squinted into the dark and the sheeting rain I'd called upon. Under such circumstances, it was diffi-cult to tell just who was your friend and who was the guy you were try-ing to kill, which worked out *great* for me, since everyone seemed to be either clawing for their lives or running through the broken-down doors, or standing about uncertainly, not sure who to strike out at. Then I heard a shout from the hall Temur had ducked down, loud enough to be heard over the roar of the water gushing in dark geysers all around me. I didn't know what it was, whether it meant we were winning or losing or if Fiacre had decided he *didn't* feel like trusting any man at that moment and who could blame him, but I pulled as hard as I could with everything I had—if there'd been *oceans* nearby I'd have included those too—and just let loose.

If I was going to die in a country I hated, surrounded by soldiers I'd spent my entire life fighting and six weeks kissing up to, then I sure as hell was going to take as much of that damned palace as I could down with me.

Maybe if I'd been better educated in the ways of Talents, I'd never have tried it, since there were all sorts of rules about what you could do without draining your own life force. But the way I saw it, if it came down to dying on my terms or theirs, then I knew which side I was sticking to.

The courtyard disappeared with a *boom* like dragons exploding overhead, and white sheets of furious water exploded upward in its place, swallowing the trees and any soldiers yet trying to escape. The building rocked with the force of it all, knocking me clean off my feet and sending me through the far wall—grateful at last that they were made out of a bare wooden frame and mostly flimsy paper.

The water swirled after me eagerly like a hungry pet looking to be fed as I fought to get up. I blinked the droplets out of my eyes and shook my head out like the dog Caius had named me when we'd first met. One of the guards with better eyesight had finally taken notice of me, and I threw myself to one side. Moving was harder than it'd been when we'd first started that little campaign. I managed to block the guard's sword when he swung, but only just. Even my good arm was getting tired from having to take all the weight of the sword by itself.

The only problem was that Josette was probably going to kill me if I died, or worse, if I let Temur die, whatever *that* was about.

I was just resigning myself to fighting about as dirty as I possibly could—biting, clawing, scratching, you name it—when all of a sudden the guard went stiff like he'd been turned to stone. A moment later he toppled over, flat on his face in the rising water.

"Is Marcelline all right?" Fiacre asked, sloshing out from behind the guard, where I guessed he'd been standing. "Are the others? They said if I used my Talent, it'd mean a quick end for them, but I thought . . . considering the situation . . ."

"Alcibiades!" Marcy sloshed through the water toward me, clutching at Marius's sleeve. The better to drag him across the battlefield, no doubt. "Have you seen the others? I'd have torn this place down around us, only they said they'd *kill* the other delegates!"

She caught sight of Fiacre and stopped short.

"Ke-Han ingenuity," I said. "No doubt everyone got that story, and they were betting on us being good and attached to our fellow delegates."

"Yes, well I've no doubt that had you been in the same situation, you'd have upended the palace at once," Marius said, just as Casimiro appeared like a shadow, with Valery behind him.

"Hello," said Val. "Is this your rescue? Rather wet, don't you think?"

"It's the best I could do under the circumstances," I said.

"Well, you know what they say," Fiacre replied, clearly itching to take out his aggression on some of the soldiers. "You can't choose your Talent."

So that I wouldn't have time to think about Fiacre and the way he—and all men like him, for that matter—rubbed my fur in the wrong direction, I paused to take stock of our numbers. Fiacre, obviously, was in tiptop shape, although I noticed there was a nasty cut on his face; probably from the debris flying in all directions a moment ago. The others were all right, though shaken, and I didn't blame them. Marius was with Marcelline, and Wildgrave Ozanne was beside Lieutenants Casimiro and Valery. As sorry a ragtag group as I'd ever seen, but at least most of us had Talents. If ever there was a time to wish Margrave

Royston was on your side—and *at* your side—it was right about then. Even if you did have to hope he wouldn't blow you sky-high along with the enemy.

But no Royston, so Fiacre, the Wildgrave, Marcelline, and I would have to make do.

They called our glorious diplomatic leader "Fiacre the Spider" because of his particular skills, paralysis like a web around his enemies. I'd seen the Wildgrave, if he had time to practice his arts, bring a man back from the brink of death; the question here was only whether or not he'd have the time before we were all brought down under the Emperor's superior numbers. And Marcelline—thank bastion for darling Marcy. *She* could bend metal to her will, and, considering the number of swords we'd have to go up against, I probably could have proposed to her on the spot, with Lord Temur the officiating officer at our wedding. That is, if he agreed to play the part.

Lord Temur, though, looked like he had other plans in mind for the evening. All the expression his face had been lacking ever since the first day I'd met him was out in full force. In fact, one might even have said he was grinning like a maniac and grimacing through the rest. I didn't blame him. How many of the men he'd killed were friends, brothers in arms, soldiers he'd known since he was a little boy? Armies worked on the same principles the world around, and bastion if I was sure I couldn't've done what he had.

"Here's the plan, then," I said, done with taking stock.

"Forgive me." A cool voice, hard as metal that Marcy *couldn't* bend, came from behind me. "But it would seem you have made a mess of my palace."

Temur's shoulders stiffened, and I could feel all the short hairs on the back of my neck jump to attention. I knew that voice just as well as Temur did, and the look on Fiacre's face as he stared over my shoulder would have told me everything if I hadn't already managed to piece it together for myself.

I shifted my weight from one leg to the other, then, because there was no avoiding what came next, I turned around. Best to get it out of the way as quick as possible—that left less time for anticipating things.

There he was: Emperor Iseul, in all his glory. His eyes were glowing mad and that necklace around his neck, creepy as ever, caught the barest hint of the light, flashing red. There *was* blood in it, or I was a jackrabbit's grandpa. The whole rest of him was impeccable, though, like the image out of a nightmare. He was cool, calm, poised, without a single hair out of place. In other words, he hadn't just been fighting off dozens of damn soldiers the way I'd been, and he'd probably been preparing himself for this inevitability all along. He was ready to fight me; he was *eager*. It wasn't like the playing ground was even. But fuck it, because I had a plan.

"Leave the others out of it," I said, holding up my empty hand. I was between the rest and him. "I've used all my magic up, Your Highness, but we've got a fight to finish."

"Ah," the Emperor said. "An interesting brand of duty, I must admit."

"Fighting you's the only reward I want," I said, "for saving your life."

Everyone was real quiet after that, and I was satisfied even if the Emperor didn't let on that I definitely had him there.

"Very well," he said at length, and, with a flick of both arms that startled everyone around us, began to tie back his long sleeves.

We had an audience—just like last time, only more. There were the people on my side, the bare handful of them, and all of the bastards rooting for him—an assortment of guards and warlords whom I did and didn't recognize, men caught up in the various blasts and those who'd only just joined us.

"I give you my word that none on my side will interfere," I added, while he readied himself. "So long as you make the same promise, and we . . ." I cast my eyes about me for a place suitably distant from the rest of the room—a place far away enough for me to take only the two of us out and leave the rest to their own devices.

All these heroics were making my head hurt.

I wouldn't have turned down a little Ke-Han wine, either.

"Agreed," the Emperor said. "I too have wished to come to the conclusion of our . . . practice." He smiled at me like he was commenting on what I was wearing. I spat blood out between my teeth. That creepy vial around his neck glinted red.

"You cannot do this," Lord Temur said, stepping forward. "It is my place—"

"I have no reason to fight a dead man," Iseul said curtly. "It is for General Alcibiades to name the place."

"The courtyard," I said, and jerked my head in its direction. Water was everywhere, pooling between broken rocks and fallen beams, bits of paper floating in the pools like flower petals. It was the perfect site for me to get my ass handed to me, but I wasn't going to let it go that far.

Emperor Iseul lifted his hand, and the red-faced Jiro stepped forward to offer his sword.

"You cannot do this," Lord Temur repeated.

I looked him in the eye. "You're right," I said. "About Greylace, I mean. Tell him to make sure Yana lives in high style for me." When Temur's expression registered confusion, I laughed. "He'll know what I mean."

"Enough," Iseul said, striding past me and into the courtyard. "You have stated your objectives, General Alcibiades. You wish to kill an Emperor. In my court, men die for such treason."

"And many other things," I added, limping after him.

I didn't even plan to draw my sword. The second we were clear of the others, I would burst the final waterway beneath us; we'd go shooting up toward the sky like waterborne stars, and at least I could die for some purpose, which, considering my place as a general, was my *duty* in life, anyway.

The Emperor, though, was always just a hair too quick for me. His sword was already drawn, and the second I'd stepped away from the others he was on me, the blade whistling through the air and coming up against mine. The impact ran through me, all the way to my toes. I swore I could feel it rock through the ground—or maybe that was another aftershock.

I didn't have the time I needed to concentrate. He was on me, blow after blow, ceaseless and determined. Maybe he'd sensed, in his own mad way, what my plan had been. He had a keen nose for sniffing out danger. Whatever his motivations were, he was going to kill me. My arm ached so bad that my teeth were rattling in my jaw. It wasn't a matter of whether or not he'd slice me in two—it was only a matter of when.

Good thing I'd made provisions for Yana, I thought, and brought my sword up just a hair too slow. I could see the blade of his sword as it arced downward toward my nose.

I always knew a Ke-Han would kill me. Bastion, I should consider myself lucky that it'd taken them this long.

I stood my ground and braced myself for death.

It didn't come.

Instead, Emperor Iseul was frozen in time before me. For the first time, I saw an expression of surprise on his face—pure bafflement, I'd even say—like he'd just seen a ghost. At first, I didn't know what to make of it—whether or not I should look behind me; if the answer would even be there.

Then Iseul fell.

It took longer than it should have for me to piece things together: the arrow in Iseul's back—a fine arrow indeed, from one of those damned longbows. The figures in the distance, all wearing red. The shouting behind me, suddenly coming in loud and clear over the blood rushing at my temples. And the second prince, whom I recognized despite how long it'd been, clearer than all the rest, across from me on the opposite end of the courtyard.

"The punishment," Mamoru said, his face twisted in the dark, "for treason is death."

CHAPTER SEVENTEEN

MAMORU

On the seventh and final day of mourning, Kouje came to my chambers to tell me that my brother was dead.

It was always an ambiguous period, that week one spent in isolation, contemplating the death that was to come.

I'd survived two in my lifetime. I hoped never to have to live through another.

They'd given me the vial he'd worn around his neck, almost like jewelry, a living red stone that changed with every tiny movement. I'd debated on keeping it, for a time. However strange it might have seemed to anyone else, it would have served as a reminder as well as some kind of memento from my brother—but in the end Kouje had convinced me to have it destroyed.

It was too dangerous to have such a thing about. It never ought to have been created in the first place.

The stroke of the longbow had not killed Iseul—not even I presumed myself able to kill a man as fierce and strong as my brother; only the gods could do that. I merely wounded him badly enough to stop him in his tracks before he was able to murder any of the Volstovic delegates. To do such a thing under the banner of diplomacy was unimaginable, the act of someone whose reason had left him entirely. I was not so lucky. I knew what reason told me, that my brother was too dangerous to live with madness coursing through his blood as the fever had through mine.

But I had not been able to kill him. Iseul was my brother, and more than that, he was Emperor over us all. I would not put him down like a mad dog in the streets. He deserved the chance to take his own life, as every man did; he deserved to accept honor in death as he had not in life.

I met with him only once; after that, his last command was that I cease to visit him, and duty bound me to obey. Our last conversation was short and shed no illumination upon the man he'd been and the man he'd become.

"You aimed poorly," he said. Sitting in his cell, with bars between us, and Volstovic guards standing beside Ke-Han soldiers, his back was just as proud as it had always been—as proud as I imagined our father was, even at the last moment.

"I'm not the marksman you are," I replied.

My brother the Emperor turned his head away from me. "Father would never accept your excuses," he said. "When you are Emperor, and these red-coated fools infest our people and change the land, at least try to become a little more ruthless. When you miss your mark, you shame even your enemy. Dismissed."

That was the last I saw of him, and so I tried to remember him as he was when he was a boy: less beaten; imposing without imparting terror; on his way toward becoming a man.

It had been one week since the attack on the palace. Ever since we'd shut Iseul away in one of the holding chambers that had miraculously remained standing despite the assaults on our architecture by General Alcibiades—the diplomat whose horse we'd stolen—I'd been counting the days, knowing that my brother would do the same as our father before him. There were whispers from some who had come to believe that Iseul had engineered the death of the Emperor before him; I knew that was not so. There were many things my brother was capable of—I'd experienced a plenitude of them firsthand—but the murder of our father was not one of them.

We were both bound by the same tradition, one that wrapped itself around a ceremonial knife with a handle of carved jade.

Seated in my chambers, which had been my father's first and Iseul's second, my fingers traced the shape of one of the jade ornaments my brother had worn in his hair as Emperor.

"My aim with the bow is not as good as it once was," I told Kouje as he knelt.

I felt like a stranger in my new robes—black to denote mourning, blue to denote the land, and small designs of gold to denote my new station. After all my time outdoors, they felt stiff and nearly stifling. They would take some getting used to, along with everything else.

At least it was only the two of us in the room. Soon, after the sun had set on the seventh day, I would have to begin the long process of appointing new servants for my entourage, not to mention tallying up casualties among the palace guards and the troops my brother had hidden in the mountains, some of whom had starved to death chasing mountain cats while they waited for new provisions.

The Esar had sent a report to the capital shortly after we'd arrived, stating that the matter of the Cobalts had been settled and General Yisun was dead.

Such a turn of events was for the better if not the best, as there were certain men who would never be turned to my side, and the general who'd trained my brother had been one of them. Nonetheless, I was weary to lose so many of the great men of my past, now that they had no place in our present, much less the Ke-Han's future.

Kouje did not lift his head, his hair braided back like a warrior's once more. I wondered if his scalp ached the way mine did under the strictness of the style. His clothing was crisp and black; not a single hair was out of place, nor was there even the hint of mud and dust to stain the hem of his robes. It was a return to the Kouje I'd known all my life, and yet seeing him that way seemed strange.

"Provisions have been made for the delegates from Volstov to return to their homes," he said, "though as I understand it, a great many will be remaining behind not only in order to complete their original mandate of hammering out a permanent treaty but also to keep watch over our new council of warlords."

I nodded, feeling the sharp ends of the hair ornament between my finger and thumb. It had been my idea to assign a Volstovic diplomat to each of the seven warlords, since it seemed too dangerous to set them loose and too severe to have them all die alongside Iseul.

Perhaps it was naive of me, but I did not want the first days of my rule to be tainted with yet more death.

"We'll have to bring masons in for the palace walls," Kouje continued, "not to mention the palace itself."

I smiled at the humor in his voice and lifted my head at last as he did the same.

"These men from Volstov," I said, in the tone of someone sharing a private joke with a friend. "They do not know how to get a thing done without tearing the landscape apart first."

Kouje chuckled, then pressed his lips tightly together as though trying to stem the tide of laughter. Our time in exile together had fostered many bad habits between us. Most of them could be shared only in privacy.

"You should put that in your speech," he said. "That is, if they can convince you to make one. If anyone will be able to hear you over the cheering. You know they've been holding a festival in your honor since we came back? You can hear the drums at night. Well, perhaps *you* can't, but they are quite loud down at my end of the palace."

"They are not observing the period of mourning?" I asked.

"I believe their period of mourning ended the day you came back, my lord," Kouje answered.

I nodded, unsure of how I felt about that. Would they still hold plays in my honor? Or, now that my fate had been decided, was it more likely their attention would turn to something else entirely?

It was time for my attention to turn as well. An emperor did not have the same freedom as a fugitive to think about the theatre—although one day I would find Aiko and Goro, and at the very least donate a new traveling cart to their troupe.

"As I understand it, there is some special entertainment arranged for the farewell reception," Kouje went on.

"Is it time already?" I wondered. The light in my chambers was provided chiefly by lanterns, so it was difficult to tell the time of day. It was the best design for those prone to fevers in winter, Kouje assured me.

"I believe so, my lord."

I stood, and the weight of the fabric was heavy against my shoulders. That weight too would take some getting used to, but it would serve as a reminder until then; it would teach me how, as an emperor, I was meant to walk.

The farewell reception had been arranged to honor the men and women from Volstov whom my brother had taken captive—another gesture to try to mend what Iseul had so nearly broken. My brother had been proud, perhaps too proud to work in tandem with anyone who had defeated him. I finally saw that, though thinking about it was pointless since it made me hopelessly angry with a person from whom I could no longer seek any answers.

Kouje rose only once I'd reached him, and fell behind so that his steps would not take him alongside me.

"I hardly feel regal at all with you towering over me so," I whispered, hoping that I might cheer myself simply by acting cheerful.

Kouje paused as though I'd surprised him, and I wished that I might look back, just to catch a glimpse of his face. He was far too good a servant, though, and even if I'd looked, I knew I wouldn't be able to see him.

"I might always walk on my knees, my lord," Kouje said, catching me off guard so that I had to clench my jaw to keep from laughing at the thought.

Instead, I raised my head and sniffed. "From now on, I think that I will employ only very *short* servants in the palace."

"My lord might wish to wait until he has an actual palace to employ from," Kouje murmured, "and not a very fine heap of rubble."

I shook my head in despair, even as I felt relief like a warm wind against my face. In a time when everything had changed so drastically, so that even familiar buildings did not go unchanged, there were some things that remained the same.

One window in the hall was open, the lattice shade lifted to let in the sun. Down below the palace, sloping toward the rest of the city, I caught sight of the magician's blue dome. From that height, it seemed no more than a child's broken teacup overturned and, however momentarily, forgotten.

CAIUS

For once, Alcibiades and I were in complete agreement. It was high time we crossed the mountains and returned to Volstov—for I was going to come down with a bad case of the vapors, like my poor great-aunt Eurydice, if any more excitement was caused by us or to us in at *least* the next month.

We'd lived through the death of two Ke-Han Emperors in our short time in the lapis city, and it was time to remove ourselves from the premises before we fostered any further bad luck. I liked the new Emperor; he had a sweet little face, almost like a rabbit's, and I wanted him to do well. Therefore, for everyone's sake, I intended to return home, and have a nice cup of tea before I sought out my next adventure.

"You mean you actually *want* to go home?" Alcibiades asked me, without his usual vim and vigor. He was so tired, poor dear, after his little display, and I'd made sure to keep him resting despite his own wishes. The moment he'd come around after fainting—one couldn't blame him for that, either, after destroying nearly an entire palace before taking on the Ke-Han Emperor—and learned which way the wind was blowing, it had been his intention to hop the next carriage back to the Volstov countryside. I'd spent all my energy and persuasiveness convincing him to give it a little more time, and once he'd realized just how little leeway his body intended to afford him, he finally agreed.

It didn't mean he'd been very pleasant about it. But that was merely his *way.*

"I thought you loved it in this place," Alcibiades went on, grimacing.

I patted him on the shoulder. "A change of scenery *is* necessary now and then. And I wouldn't trade our time here for the world! It *has* been exceptional. But someone must see you home safe and sound, and I don't think anyone else is quite as fond of you as I am."

"Hmph," Alcibiades grunted, looking away, and I couldn't tell whether or not he was pleased—or, rather, I couldn't tell just how pleased he was.

Let him be shy. He had saved all our lives.

I busied myself instead with all the details: the carriage, the cushions, the blankets in case the evenings grew chill; I made provisions for my peacocks, the ones my admirers had given me, to send them to my country estate for the time being. Perhaps I would donate them to the Volstov zoo—which meant of course I would also have to see my way toward snagging a white tiger. And, if I was lucky, too, one of those darling red pandas I adored so much.

"Cultural exchange, hm, Greylace?" Josette said as she watched me instructing the men carrying the cages about.

"I'm merely stealing a few animals," I pointed out, "and *not* a warlord."

"I was assigned to him," Josette replied tersely. "The Esar's orders."

I had to pause for a moment to shout at some fool who was being careless with the white peacock's glorious tail. When I returned, I couldn't help but add, "It's very lucky of you, then, that he wishes to return to Volstov."

"Cultural exchange," Josette muttered. "That's all."

All that was left was to have an audience with the Emperor.

"Not on your life," Alcibiades told me. "I've had about enough Ke-Han Emperors for one lifetime, thank you very much."

"It's only *polite*," I pleaded, trying, however futilely, to fix his tie. Would he never learn how to do it up? "We simply cannot leave without exchanging a few pleasantries. For diplomacy's sake, Alcibiades—"

"Then stop talking about it and get it *over* with!" Alcibiades snarled.

He was excited too, poor darling, only he didn't know how to admit it. Just think of all the stories we could tell when we returned, triumphantly, to court! No one there would have seen the new Emperor face-to-face. And Alcibiades would have to carry a stick with him at all times to fend off the gossips.

When we entered the council room, the Emperor was sitting a long way away from us, across the narrow room, on a raised dais. Beside him stood his loyal friend, a man whom I admired not the least for the way he held himself. His warrior braids were drawn back off his face; when next to him, the Emperor looked less like a rabbit and more like a bear cub protected by his fearsome mother. If only I could have commissioned a portrait artist to capture that moment—but there was no time.

"It is my honor to meet with you," the Emperor said.

"Oh, *no*," I told him, bowing low. "The honor is all ours. Isn't that so, Alcibiades?"

"Yeah," Alcibiades managed, clearing his throat. "Right. Thank you."

It was hardly the beautiful speech I'd imagined—next time, I'd have to prepare one for him beforehand so he wouldn't spoil the moment—

but the prince seemed happy enough with the informality, and who could blame him? Even I, who reveled in the lush formality of it all, was ready to depart for a breath of fresh air. If I were the young Emperor, I thought privately, I would have preferred to stay in the mountains.

At *least* until my shoes got dirty.

I'd mentioned to Alcibiades that I had one last bit of business to accomplish, quite small but terribly important, and because of curiosity or boredom or both, he'd agreed to accompany me.

Of course, I'd always known I'd get him to see reason in the end. One just had to have the proper constitution for cultivating a friendship, and I very fortunately numbered myself among those lucky few.

"It's just this way, my dear," I told him, taking his arm as we turned down a mirrored corner. There were a great many things I would not miss about our sojourn in the Ke-Han palace, but I couldn't help but think I'd picked up one or two terribly clever ideas while there. I would have to see about getting mirrors installed in my own estate. If nothing else, they would keep me remarkably well coiffed at all times.

"I hope you're leaving us enough time to pack," Alcibiades said. "Not that *I* need as much time as some. Knowing you, you've probably got more clothes leaving than you did coming here."

I waved my hand to dismiss the idea, then reached out to open the door that led down into the stables.

"It just seems that way because the fabrics are so voluminous," I pointed out. "I'll be the first to wear such fashions in Thremedon. I predict they'll become a trend soon enough."

"Yeah," said Alcibiades, scuffing some hay aside with his boot. "Sure. I can't believe you're going back to all . . . to all *that*."

"Whatever do you mean?" I asked.

Alcibiades blinked down at me. "You're going back to Thremedon, I take it," he said. "City of pleasures and vices alike. Well, not me. I'm not even stopping there. I'm going straight to the farm, and I guess that's where *we'll* be saying good-bye."

I guided him through the bank of stalls that housed the mounts for the Ke-Han nobility. There was one at the end that held a horse much larger than normal, more like a farmer's draft horse than one meant for a diplomat.

"Oh, my dear," I said, releasing his arm as we drew up to the stall, "you have it all wrong. Do you think I would ever give up the opportunity to meet the famous Yana Berger?"

Alcibiades went still at my side. I glanced up at him, quite delighted with myself, only to find his expression changed. He looked quite serious all of a sudden.

I opened my mouth to apologize—or perhaps to express my shock at finally having provoked some emotion out of the general at last.

"It's *Petunia*," he said before I could speak, and the next thing I knew he was hefting himself up over the stable wall to put himself into the stall with his horse.

I sighed and plucked a stray piece of straw from my sleeve. I was going to have to have a whole new wardrobe made up for the countryside.

ABOUT THE AUTHORS

JAIDA JONES is a graduate of Barnard College, where she wrote her thesis on monsters in Japanese literature and film. A poet and native New Yorker, she had her first collection of poetry, *Cinquefoil,* published by New Babel Books in 2006. She also writes the Shoebox Project—a Harry Potter fan website with over 5,000 subscribed members.

DANIELLE BENNETT is an ex–Starbucks barista from Victoria, British Columbia, where she studied English literature at Camosun College. She has finally seen her first firefly in New York City. *Havemercy* was her first publication.